USBORNE BIG MACHII

DIGGERS AND CRANES

Caroline Young

Designed by Steve Page

Illustrated by Chris Lyon and Teri Gower

Additional illustrations by Nick Hawker
Cover design by Tom Lalonde

Consultant: D. Wheeler (Senior Plant Engineer, George Wimpey Ltd.)

Contents

Bulldozers

Bulldozers clear the ground ready for building. They push earth, stones and tree stumps out of their way with a huge metal blade. This is called dozing.

Crawler tracks

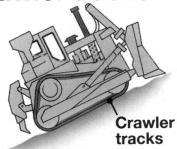

Crawler tracks

Crawler tracks help the heavy bulldozer climb up steep banks.

They can go over bumps more smoothly than wheels, too.

They help stop the bulldozer sinking into soft, muddy ground.

This is where the driver sits. It is called a cab.

The cab has a frame of metal bars. They protect the driver if the bulldozer rolls over.

In hot countries, the cab has no glass in its windows. This keeps the driver cool.

Fire extinguisher

This bulldozer has a powerful engine. It can push things much heavier than itself.

This tool is called a ripper. It drags behind the bulldozer breaking up hard, stony ground.

Metal crawler tracks cover the bulldozer's wheels.

This metal arm is called a tilt ram. It pushes the bulldozer's blade up. This helps it pile up earth.

2

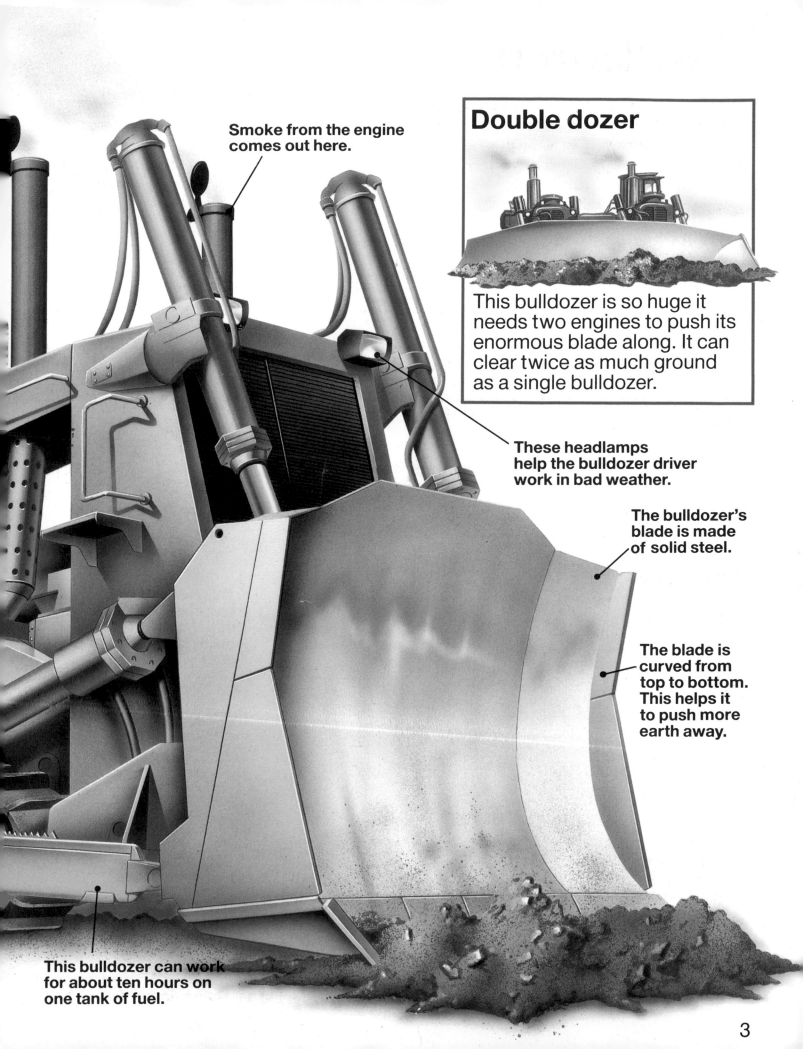

Smoke from the engine comes out here.

Double dozer

This bulldozer is so huge it needs two engines to push its enormous blade along. It can clear twice as much ground as a single bulldozer.

These headlamps help the bulldozer driver work in bad weather.

The bulldozer's blade is made of solid steel.

The blade is curved from top to bottom. This helps it to push more earth away.

This bulldozer can work for about ten hours on one tank of fuel.

3

Backhoe excavator

Digging machines are called excavators. There are lots of different sorts. Excavators can do other jobs, too. You can see some at work at the bottom of this page.

This digger is a backhoe excavator. It digs into the ground with a metal bucket called a backhoe.

These are rams. They slide in and out of their metal case. This makes the excavator's arm move.

This bucket can dig up more than 500 spadefuls of earth at a time.

This is the boom. The driver can make it shorter or longer for each digging job.

This is the dipper arm. It dips in and out of the ground as the excavator digs.

These metal teeth cut through the earth easily.

This mini-excavator is so small it could fit into the backhoe excavator's bucket. It does small digging jobs.

Other excavators

These excavators have tools that do many different jobs.

This excavator can carry earth in a loader bucket.

Claws help this excavator pick up pipes or logs.

This excavator's metal grab picks things up easily.

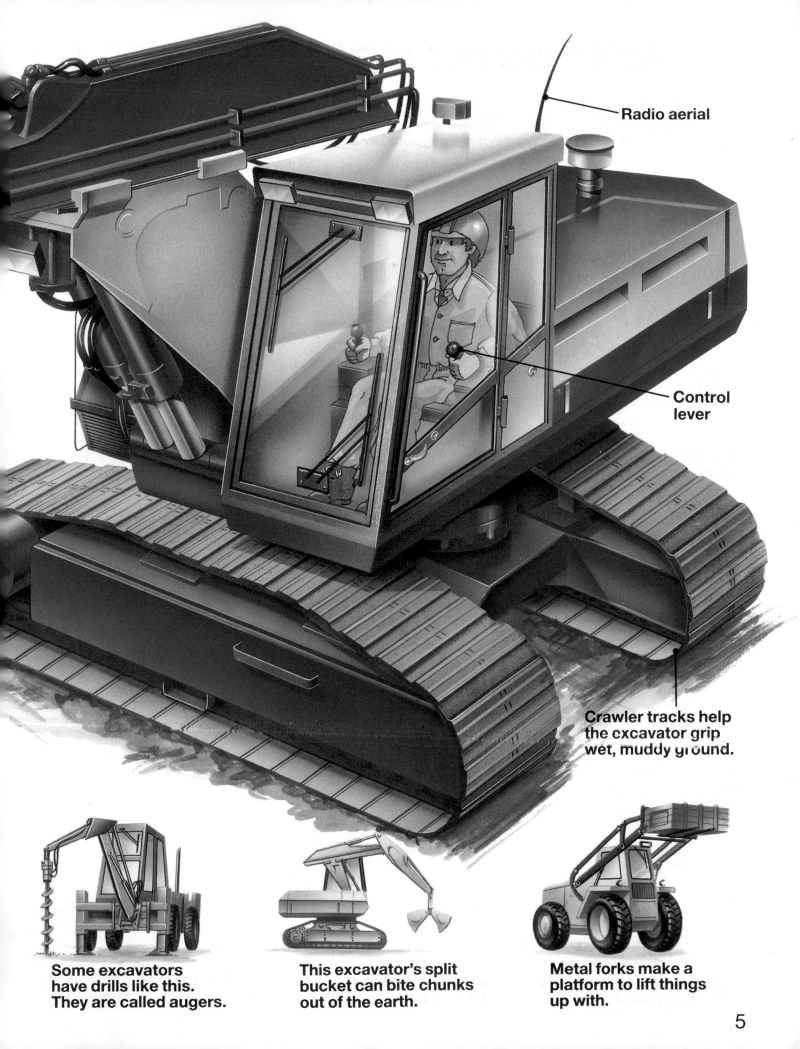

Radio aerial

Control lever

Crawler tracks help the excavator grip wet, muddy ground.

Some excavators have drills like this. They are called augers.

This excavator's split bucket can bite chunks out of the earth.

Metal forks make a platform to lift things up with.

5

Backhoe loader

This excavator can do many digging jobs. It can dig pits and trenches with a backhoe or scoop up earth in a bucket called a loader. It is called a backhoe loader.

The cab has glass all the way round. The driver has a good view as he controls the machine.

Up and down

Backhoe

The backhoe can stretch up as high as an upstairs window to dig.

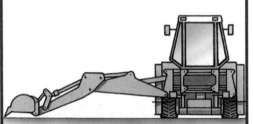

It can swivel around and dig at the side of the excavator, like this.

It can also reach down like this to scoop up earth and dig a trench.

The driver can turn his seat to face the loader or the backhoe.

Headlight

This bucket is called the backhoe.

The driver uses these two levers to control the backhoe.

6

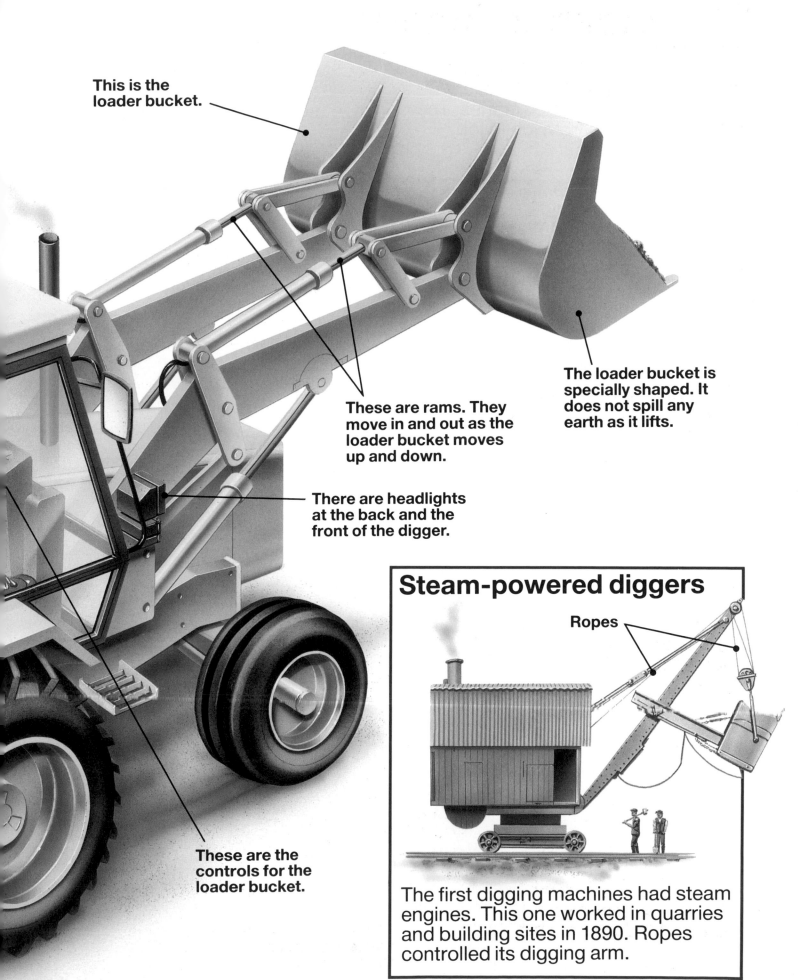

This is the loader bucket.

These are rams. They move in and out as the loader bucket moves up and down.

The loader bucket is specially shaped. It does not spill any earth as it lifts.

There are headlights at the back and the front of the digger.

These are the controls for the loader bucket.

Steam-powered diggers

Ropes

The first digging machines had steam engines. This one worked in quarries and building sites in 1890. Ropes controlled its digging arm.

7

Moving cranes

These cranes move around on wheels or crawler tracks. They are called truck cranes and crawler cranes. They can move quickly from job to job.

Ready to lift

Boom

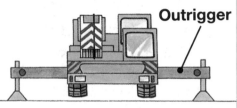

The truck crane arrives at the building site with its boom folded up.

Outrigger

Metal legs called outriggers lift the crane off the ground.

The boom slowly lifts up and slides out ready to lift a load.

Truck crane

Truck cranes are built on the back of a truck.

The arm a crane lifts with is called a jib or a boom.

This boom has four parts. They fold away inside each other like this when the crane is not lifting.

When it slides out, this boom can stretch up to the top of a six floor building.

A truck crane has two cabs. One is for driving the truck. The other is to control the crane.

Crane cab

The crane's engine is under here.

This is an outrigger. It supports the crane while it is lifting.

Outriggers slide away underneath the truck crane when it is not lifting.

The crane's wheels are not touching the ground.

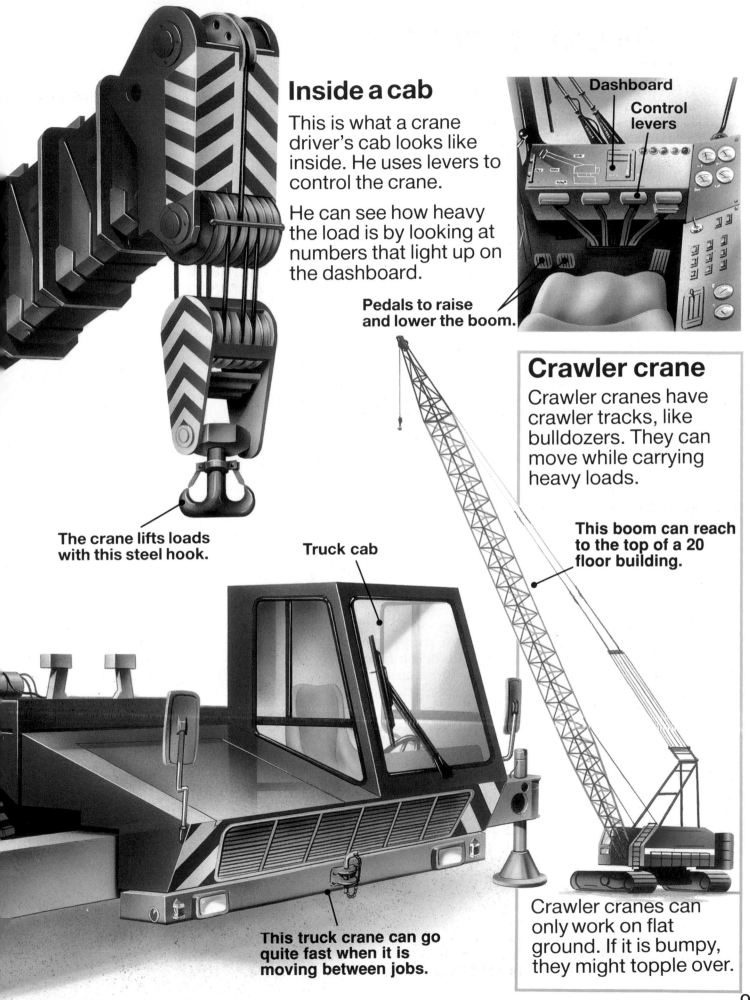

Inside a cab

This is what a crane driver's cab looks like inside. He uses levers to control the crane.

He can see how heavy the load is by looking at numbers that light up on the dashboard.

Pedals to raise and lower the boom.

Dashboard

Control levers

The crane lifts loads with this steel hook.

Truck cab

Crawler crane

Crawler cranes have crawler tracks, like bulldozers. They can move while carrying heavy loads.

This boom can reach to the top of a 20 floor building.

This truck crane can go quite fast when it is moving between jobs.

Crawler cranes can only work on flat ground. If it is bumpy, they might topple over.

9

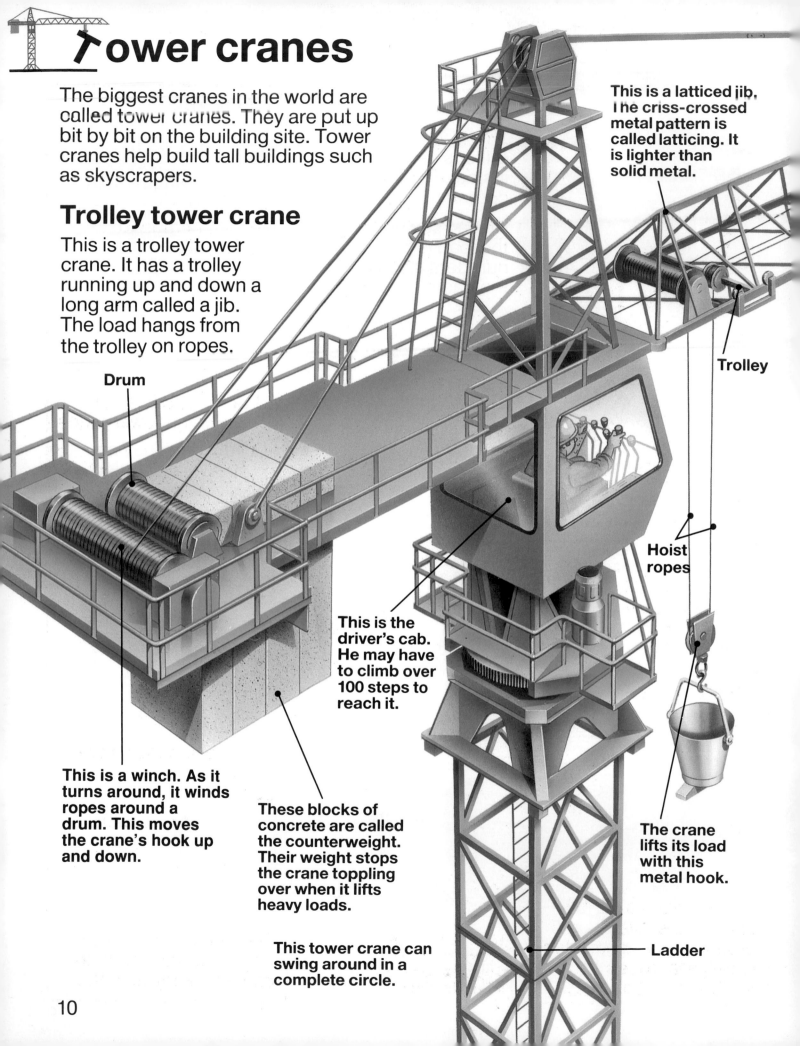

Tower cranes

The biggest cranes in the world are called tower cranes. They are put up bit by bit on the building site. Tower cranes help build tall buildings such as skyscrapers.

Trolley tower crane

This is a trolley tower crane. It has a trolley running up and down a long arm called a jib. The load hangs from the trolley on ropes.

This is a latticed jib. The criss-crossed metal pattern is called latticing. It is lighter than solid metal.

Trolley

Drum

Hoist ropes

This is the driver's cab. He may have to climb over 100 steps to reach it.

This is a winch. As it turns around, it winds ropes around a drum. This moves the crane's hook up and down.

These blocks of concrete are called the counterweight. Their weight stops the crane toppling over when it lifts heavy loads.

The crane lifts its load with this metal hook.

This tower crane can swing around in a complete circle.

Ladder

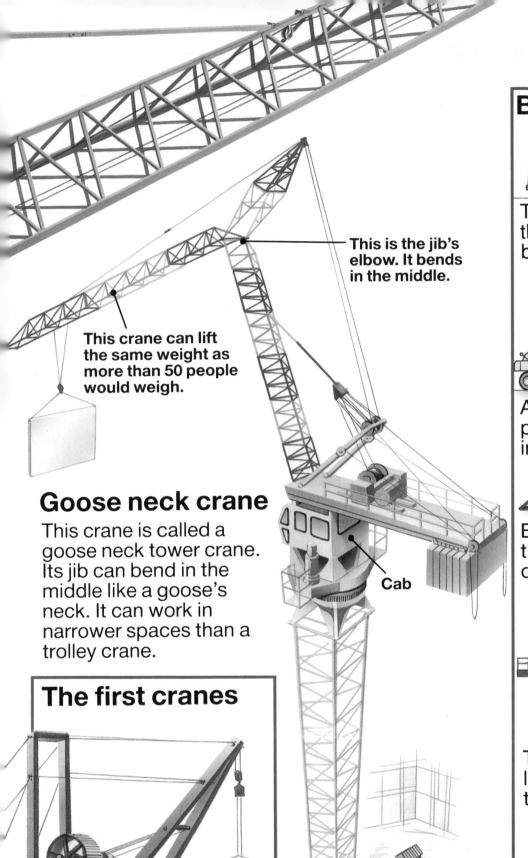

This is the jib's elbow. It bends in the middle.

This crane can lift the same weight as more than 50 people would weigh.

Cab

Goose neck crane

This crane is called a goose neck tower crane. Its jib can bend in the middle like a goose's neck. It can work in narrower spaces than a trolley crane.

The first cranes

The Romans built the first cranes. Slaves ran around inside a wooden wheel with ropes tied to it. This lifted things up.

The crane rests on heavy metal rails. Concrete blocks hold it in place.

Bit by bit

Trucks bring the parts of the tower crane to the building site.

A truck crane lifts the pieces of the tower crane into place.

Builders bolt the bits of the crane's jib together on the ground.

Jib

Cab

The cab and the jib are lifted into place by the truck crane.

Counterweight

The truck crane lifts the counterweight. Now the crane is ready to work.

Building roads 1

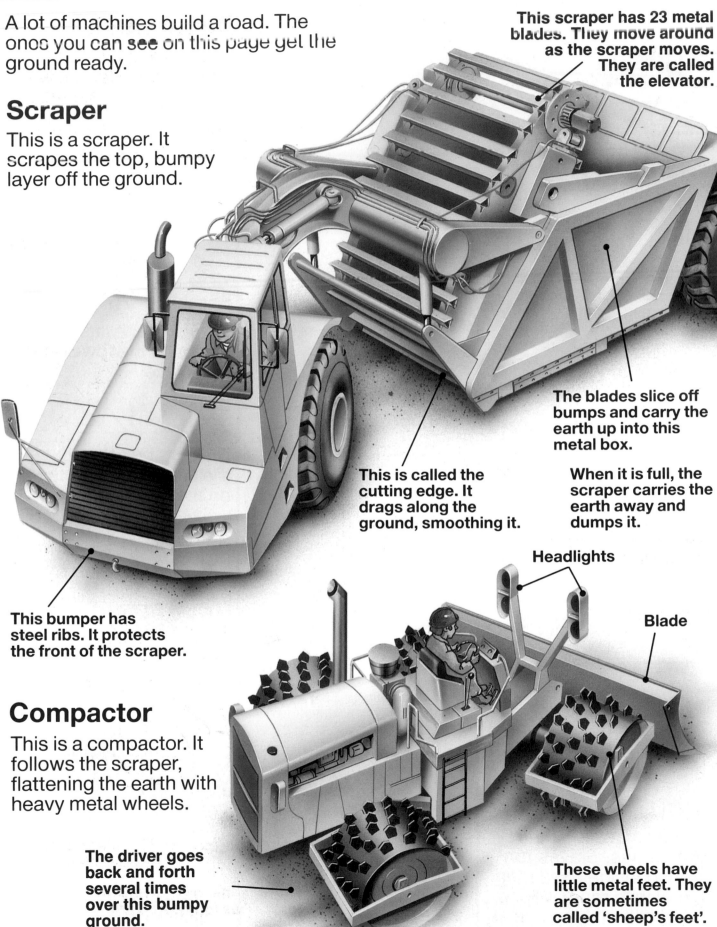

A lot of machines build a road. The ones you can see on this page get the ground ready.

Scraper

This is a scraper. It scrapes the top, bumpy layer off the ground.

This scraper has 23 metal blades. They move around as the scraper moves. They are called the elevator.

The blades slice off bumps and carry the earth up into this metal box.

This is called the cutting edge. It drags along the ground, smoothing it.

When it is full, the scraper carries the earth away and dumps it.

This bumper has steel ribs. It protects the front of the scraper.

Headlights

Blade

Compactor

This is a compactor. It follows the scraper, flattening the earth with heavy metal wheels.

The driver goes back and forth several times over this bumpy ground.

These wheels have little metal feet. They are sometimes called 'sheep's feet'.

12

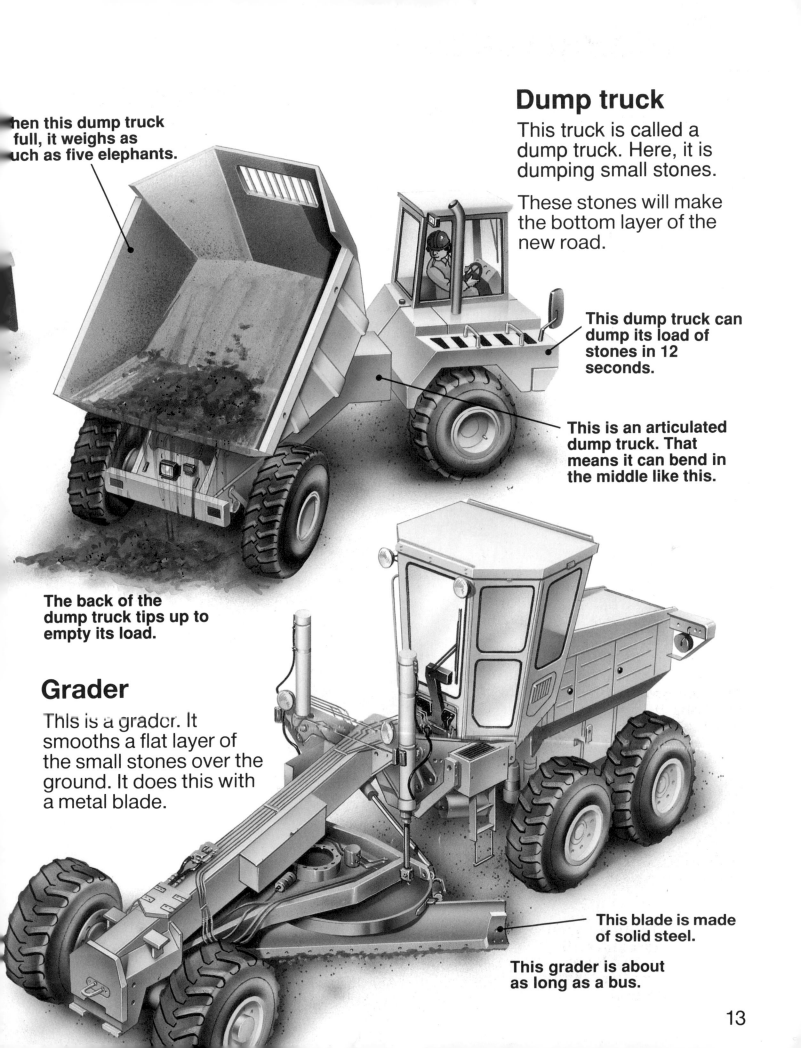

hen this dump truck **full, it weighs as** **uch as five elephants.**

Dump truck

This truck is called a dump truck. Here, it is dumping small stones.

These stones will make the bottom layer of the new road.

This dump truck can dump its load of stones in 12 seconds.

This is an articulated dump truck. That means it can bend in the middle like this.

The back of the dump truck tips up to empty its load.

Grader

This is a grader. It smooths a flat layer of the small stones over the ground. It does this with a metal blade.

This blade is made of solid steel.

This grader is about as long as a bus.

13

Building roads 2

A paver lays a mixture of hot tar and small stones on the road. A roller makes sure the road is flat.

Roller

This roller drives slowly behind the paver. It flattens the tar and stones with its heavy metal rollers.

It will go over the road several times to make it ready for cars and trucks to drive on it.

Steam rollers

The first rollers were called steam rollers. They had engines powered by steam. This steam roller was built in about 1847. It went very slowly.

This roller weighs about as much as 18 cars.

This builder is checking that the edge of the new road is neat.

There are small water sprinklers above each roller. They keep them clean and cool.

These wheels are hollow. They can be filled with water or sand. This makes the roller even heavier.

Paver

A mixture of hot tar and small stones is called asphalt. A paver spreads a layer of warm asphalt over the road. It sets hard as it cools.

Filling up

A truck tips asphalt into a box called a hopper. It is at the front of the paver.

The asphalt goes through the paver and comes out of the back as it moves.

The truck can fill the paver with asphalt while it works.

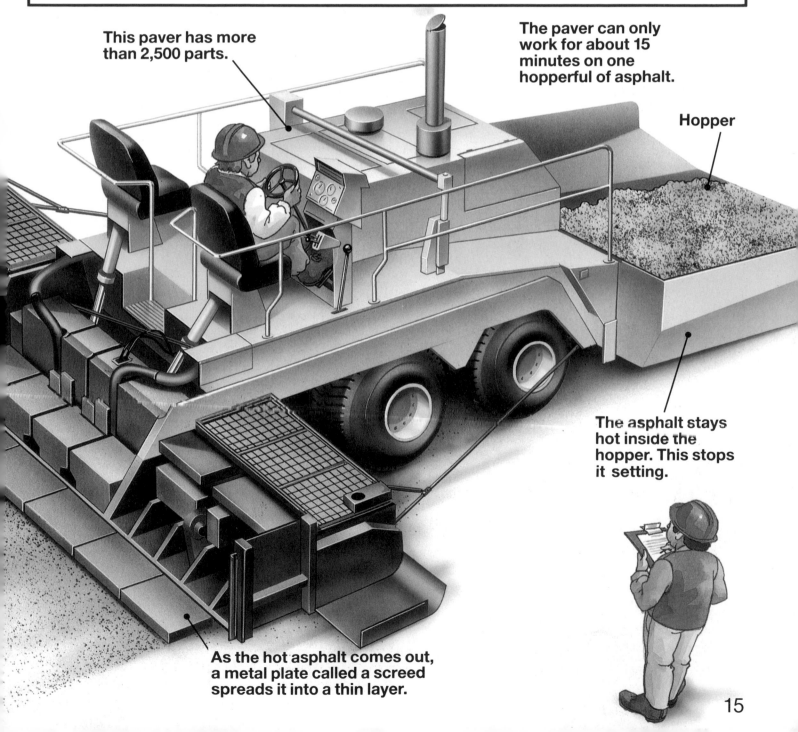

This paver has more than 2,500 parts.

The paver can only work for about 15 minutes on one hopperful of asphalt.

Hopper

The asphalt stays hot inside the hopper. This stops it setting.

As the hot asphalt comes out, a metal plate called a screed spreads it into a thin layer.

At the docks

Lots of different cranes work at the docks. Some are specially built to lift loads on and off ships. Others move cargo from place to place.

Container cranes

Many cargoes come in metal boxes, or containers. Cranes called container cranes can pick them up.

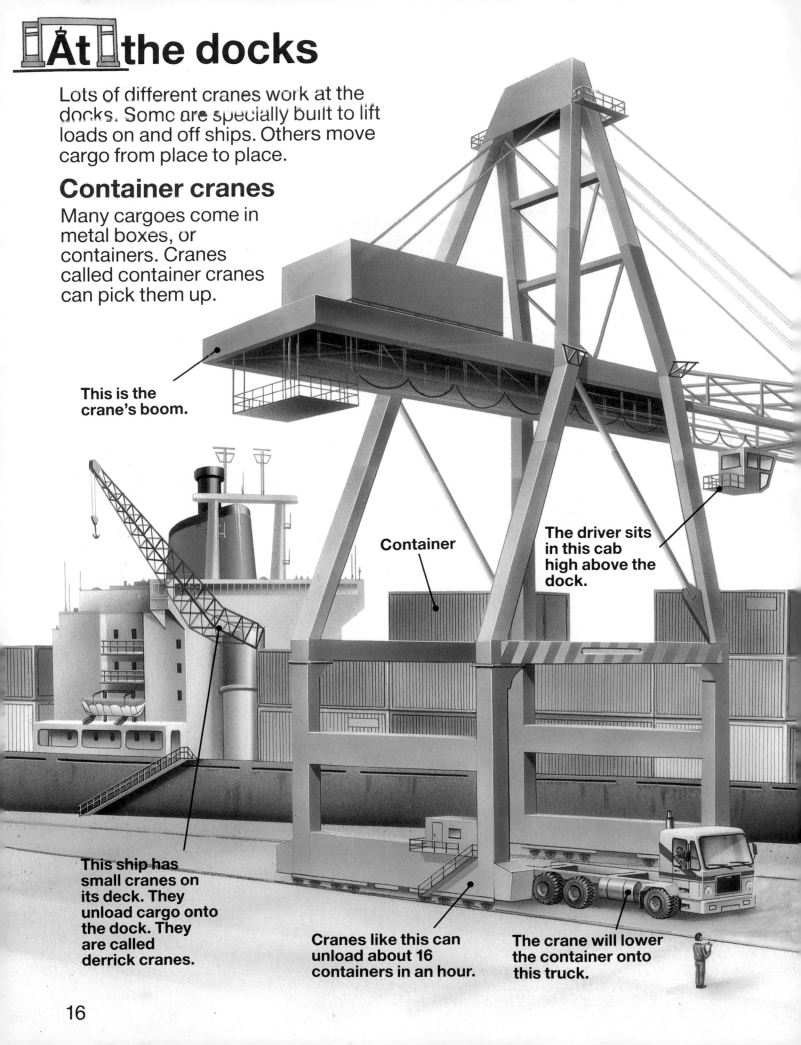

This is the crane's boom.

The driver sits in this cab high above the dock.

Container

This ship has small cranes on its deck. They unload cargo onto the dock. They are called derrick cranes.

Cranes like this can unload about 16 containers in an hour.

The crane will lower the container onto this truck.

Carrying containers

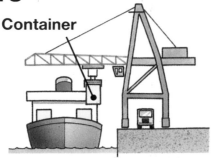

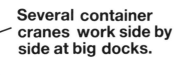

Boom

Trolley

Container

The crane's boom is above the ship. Ropes and clamps hang down from a trolley.

The clamps grab the edges of the container. The driver pulls a lever and ropes lift it up.

The trolley slides back along the boom. The ropes slowly lower the container onto a truck.

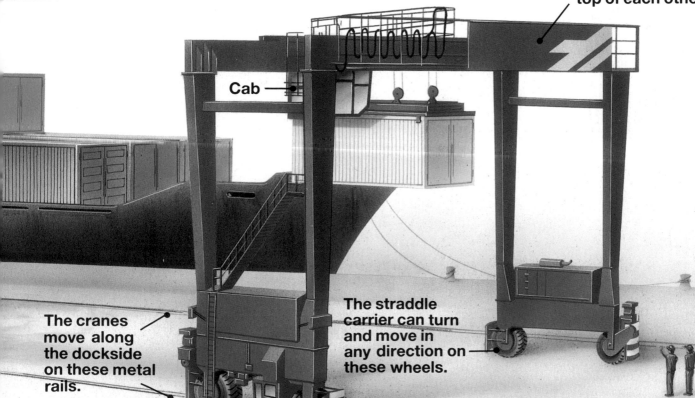

Several container cranes work side by side at big docks.

Each of these containers is taller than two people standing on each others' shoulders.

Straddle Carrier

This crane is called a straddle carrier. It picks up containers and drives them away to stack them up.

This crane can stack four containers on top of each other.

Cab

The cranes move along the dockside on these metal rails.

The straddle carrier can turn and move in any direction on these wheels.

17

Building machines

Tall buildings are very heavy. The ground must be strong to hold them up. These machines are drilling holes in the ground and filling them with concrete and steel rods. This will strengthen the ground.

Underground legs

— Auger

First a crane drills a hole in the ground with a tool called an auger. It is fixed to the crane's jib.

Then a mobile crane lowers long steel rods down into each hole. They make steel 'legs'.

Concrete comes out here.

A concrete pump fills the holes with concrete. Now the ground is strong enough to build on.

Concrete mixer

The hollow drum on the back of a concrete mixer can turn around. It has metal blades inside it to mix concrete.

The drum turns around about eight times a minute to mix concrete.

The chalk, stones and sand to make concrete are poured in here.

Water to make concrete is in this tank.

The builder controls the mixer's drum with levers.

Concrete pours out of this metal tube.

18

Mini-mixer

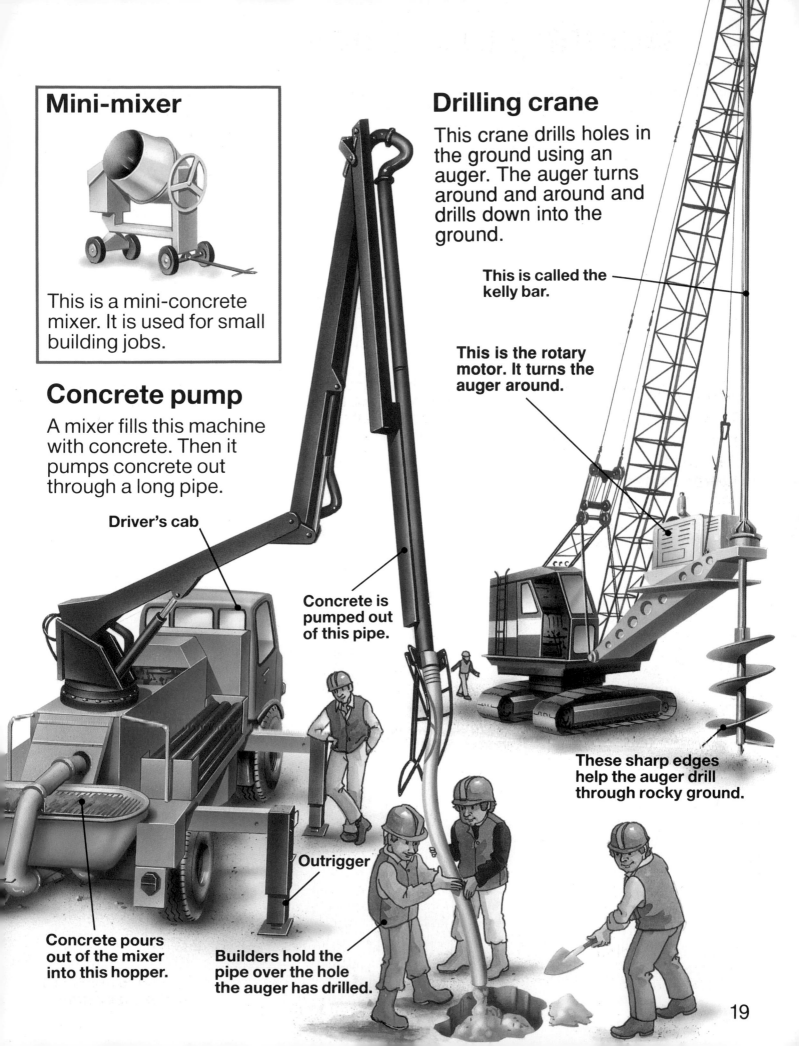

This is a mini-concrete mixer. It is used for small building jobs.

Concrete pump

A mixer fills this machine with concrete. Then it pumps concrete out through a long pipe.

Driver's cab

Concrete pours out of the mixer into this hopper.

Outrigger

Builders hold the pipe over the hole the auger has drilled.

Drilling crane

This crane drills holes in the ground using an auger. The auger turns around and around and drills down into the ground.

This is called the kelly bar.

This is the rotary motor. It turns the auger around.

Concrete is pumped out of this pipe.

These sharp edges help the auger drill through rocky ground.

19

Mining machines

Here are some of the diggers that work in mines. They dig up valuable things like coal, copper and gold. Some work underground and others dig on the earth's surface.

Bucket wheel excavator

Sometimes, coal is buried only just under the ground. This huge machine digs it up. It is called a bucket wheel excavator.

These wires lower the wheel until it is touching the ground.

Boom

The wheel turns around and around.

Buckets scrape up the coal as the wheel turns.

This sharp edge bites into the ground.

This excavator has 18 buckets. Each one can hold enough to fill a car with coal.

The wheel can scrape up about 40,000 bucketsful of coal in one day.

When all the coal is gone, people sometimes cover the mine with earth and plant grass again.

The driver sits in this cab to control the huge machine.

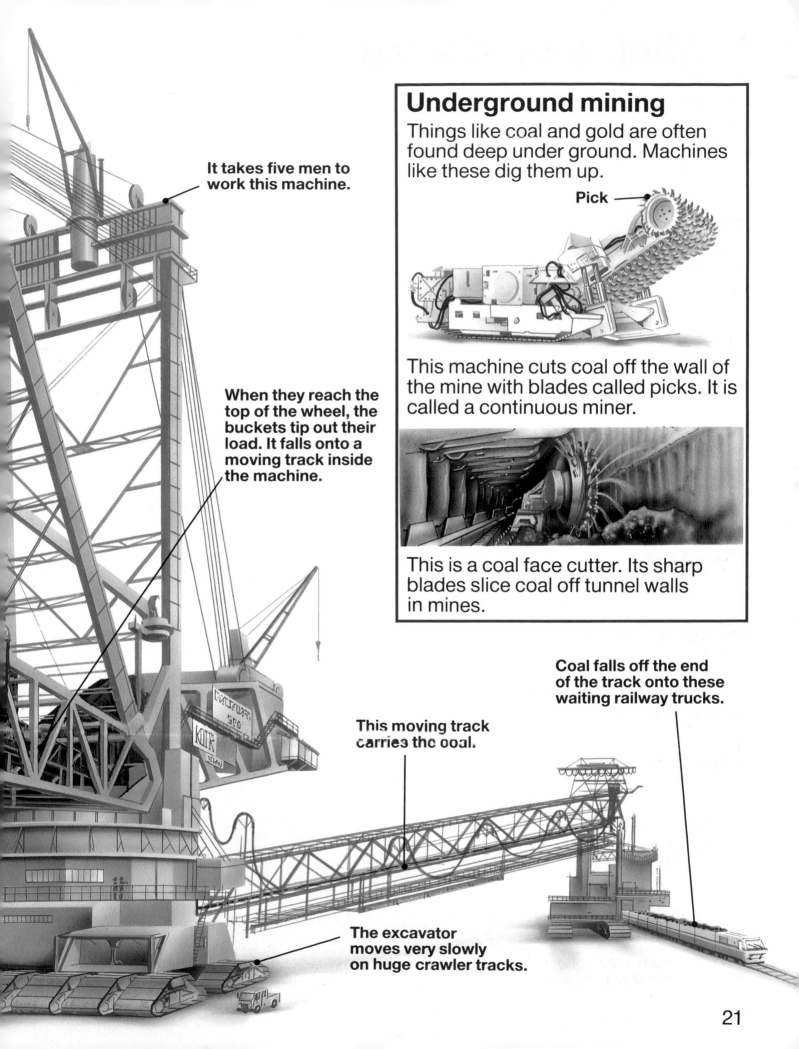

It takes five men to work this machine.

When they reach the top of the wheel, the buckets tip out their load. It falls onto a moving track inside the machine.

Underground mining

Things like coal and gold are often found deep under ground. Machines like these dig them up.

Pick

This machine cuts coal off the wall of the mine with blades called picks. It is called a continuous miner.

This is a coal face cutter. Its sharp blades slice coal off tunnel walls in mines.

Coal falls off the end of the track onto these waiting railway trucks.

This moving track carries the coal.

The excavator moves very slowly on huge crawler tracks.

Diggers and drills

People dig up stones and rock in quarries to use for building. They use these powerful machines.

Dragline excavator

This machine is called a dragline excavator. It can dig up much more than any other excavator in its huge steel bucket.

Boom

Dragging the bucket

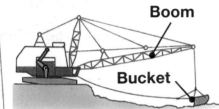

Boom

Bucket

The excavator has a bucket on the end of its boom. It lowers it onto the ground in front of it.

Dragline

Wires called draglines drag the bucket towards the excavator. It fills up with earth and rock.

When the bucket is full, the excavator empties it. Then the draglines let the bucket go again.

This bucket is big enough for a car to park inside it.

Dragline

Face shovel

A wall of solid rock is called a rock face. This machine digs into it. It is called a face shovel.

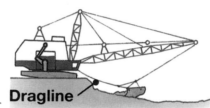

The two halves of the shovel split apart. The rock falls into a dump truck.

Crawler tracks hold the face shovel steady as it digs.

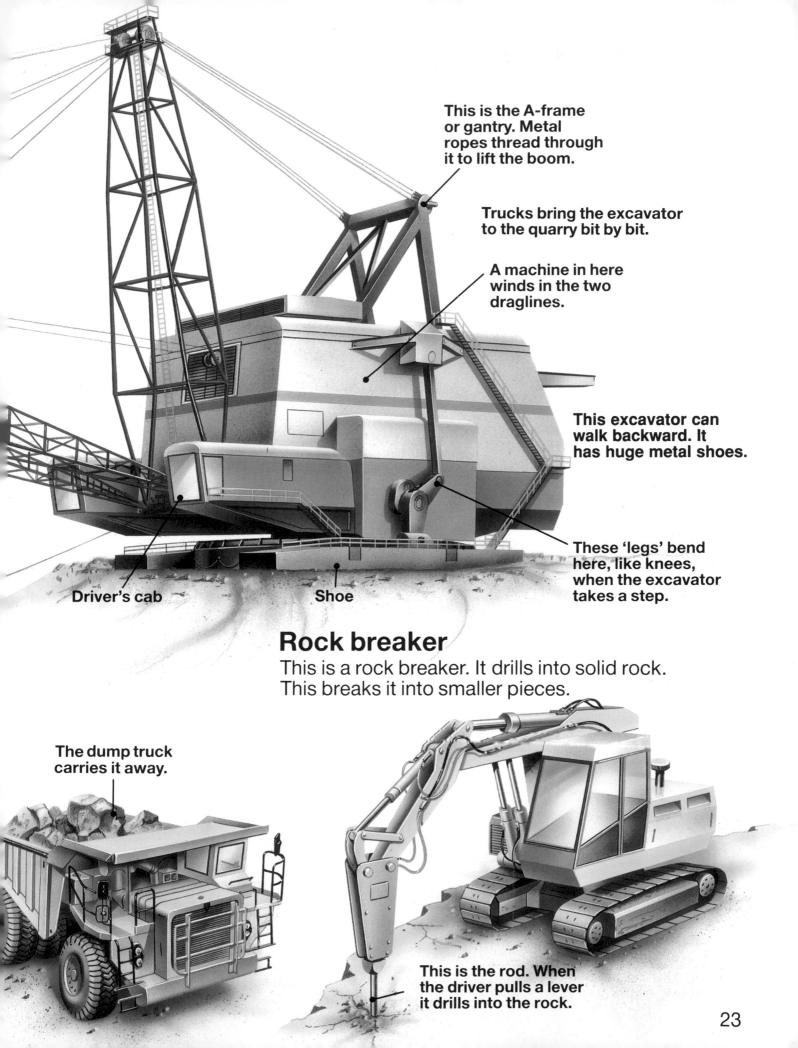

This is the A-frame or gantry. Metal ropes thread through it to lift the boom.

Trucks bring the excavator to the quarry bit by bit.

A machine in here winds in the two draglines.

This excavator can walk backward. It has huge metal shoes.

These 'legs' bend here, like knees, when the excavator takes a step.

Driver's cab

Shoe

Rock breaker

This is a rock breaker. It drills into solid rock. This breaks it into smaller pieces.

The dump truck carries it away.

This is the rod. When the driver pulls a lever it drills into the rock.

23

Floating diggers and cranes

The machines you can see here work out at sea, or on rivers. They are built on top of a boat.

Giant crane

This is a giant floating crane. It works at sea, sailing from job to job. About 350 men live and work on it.

There is a cinema, restaurant and a hospital on board the crane.

Two huge cranes and a smaller crawler crane work on the giant crane.

These are the crane's booms. They are so strong, they can lift whole ships.

The deck of this crane is as long as three swimming pools put end to end.

This is a helipad. Helicopters land on and take off from it.

This hook is about twice as tall as a person.

The crane has two huge propellers under the deck. They push it slowly through the water.

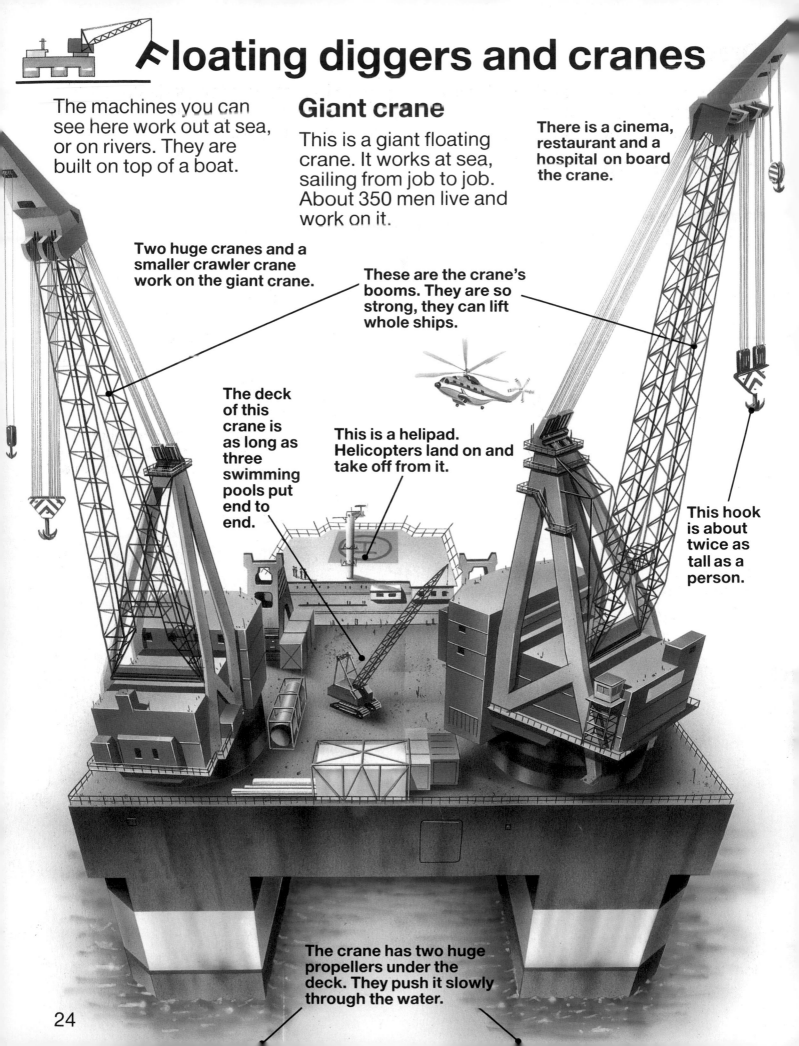

Dredgers

Dredgers dig up mud and sand from the bottom of seas and rivers. This one is called a bucket dredger. It digs up mud in a chain of buckets called a ladder. They go around and around like a moving staircase.

How a dredger works

If mud builds up on the sea bed or a river bed, ships can get stuck on it.

The dredger scoops the mud from the bottom and dumps it on barges.

The barges carry it out to sea. They dump it where the water is deep.

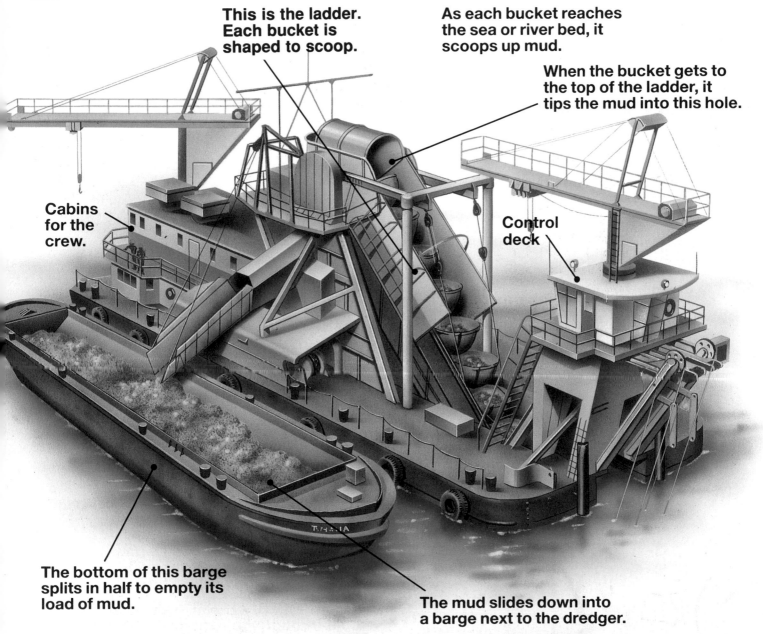

This is the ladder. Each bucket is shaped to scoop.

As each bucket reaches the sea or river bed, it scoops up mud.

When the bucket gets to the top of the ladder, it tips the mud into this hole.

Cabins for the crew.

Control deck

The bottom of this barge splits in half to empty its load of mud.

The mud slides down into a barge next to the dredger.

Tunnel diggers

Tunnelling machines have to be able to dig through earth, mud and even solid rock. The biggest tunnelling machines in the world are called TBMs. This stands for Tunnel Boring Machine.

Early tunnels

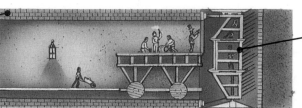

Builders covered the inside of the tunnel with bricks behind the machine.

This metal cage protected the men from falling earth.

This is one of the first tunnelling machines. It dug tunnels for underground trains in London over 170 years ago. Builders dug through earth with spades at the front as the machine moved forward.

A TBM

Tunnel Boring Machines like this one dug the Channel Tunnel under the sea between England and France. Here you can see what part of a TBM looks like inside.

The TBM grips the inside of the tunnel with four metal plates like these. They are called gripper shoes.

This is a segment erector. It covers the inside of the tunnel with concrete segments .

Cutterhead

The dug-out earth from the cutterhead is carried out on this moving belt.

The TBM has 20 rams like this. They push it forward as it digs.

This is the cutterhead. It spins around and cuts through the earth with sharp blades.

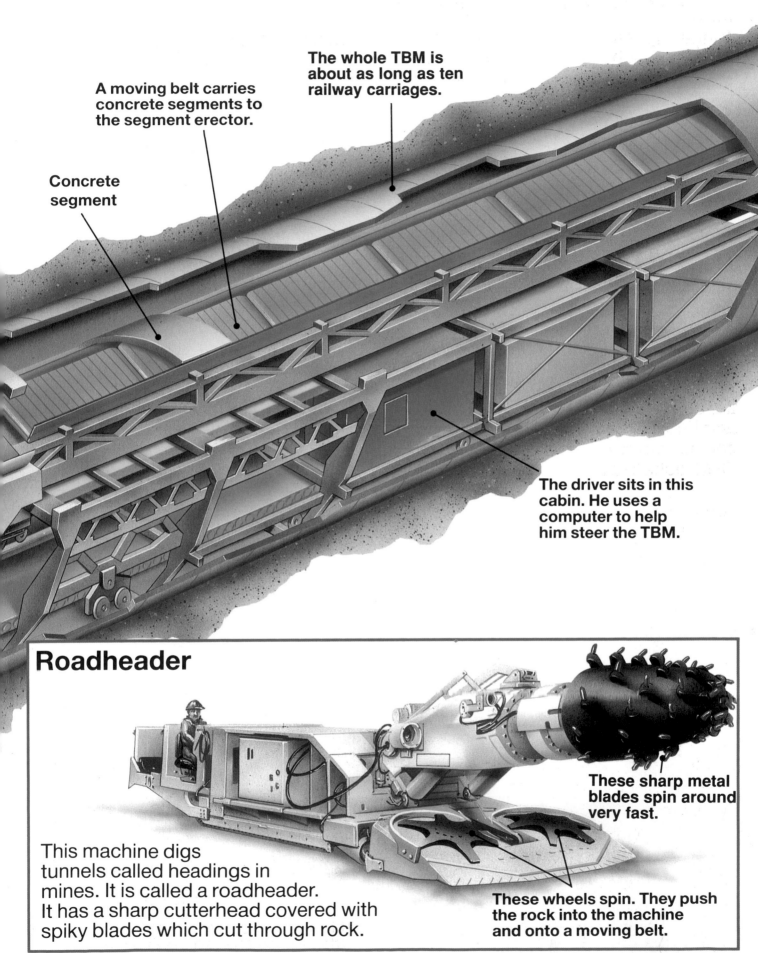

A moving belt carries concrete segments to the segment erector.

Concrete segment

The whole TBM is about as long as ten railway carriages.

The driver sits in this cabin. He uses a computer to help him steer the TBM.

Roadheader

This machine digs tunnels called headings in mines. It is called a roadheader. It has a sharp cutterhead covered with spiky blades which cut through rock.

These sharp metal blades spin around very fast.

These wheels spin. They push the rock into the machine and onto a moving belt.

Machine facts 1

On the next four pages are some facts about many of the machines in this book. They are medium-sized examples of each machine.

Bulldozer

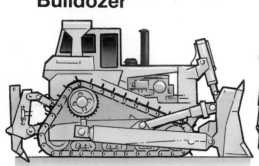

Height: 3.5 m/11.5 ft
Length: 6.3 m/21 ft
Fastest speed: 10.5 kph/
6.3 mph

Backhoe excavator

Boom

Height: 4 m/13 ft
Length: 3.5 m/11.5 ft
Length of boom: 2.4 m/
8.5 ft

Backhoe loader

Height: 3 m/10 ft
Length: 6.18 m/20.5 ft
Deepest dig: 4.3 m/14 ft

Excavator with claws

Claws

Height: 3 m/10 ft
Length: 6.2 m/25.5 ft
Number of claws: 2

Excavator with grab

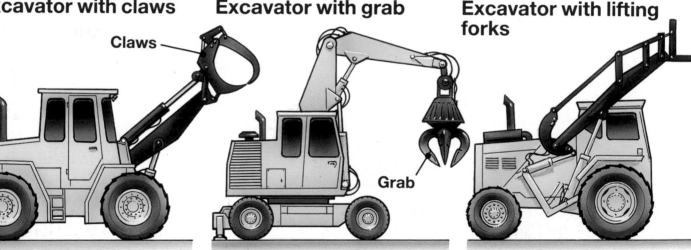

Grab

Height: 3.2 m/10.5 ft
Length: 4.6 m/15 ft
Number of fingers: 5

Excavator with lifting forks

Height: 3 m/10 ft
Length: 6.2 m/20.5 ft
Highest stretch: 3.5 m/
11.5 ft

Loader excavator

Height: 3.5 m/11.5 ft
Length: 7.3 m/24 ft
Bucket load: 10,360 kg/
22,839 lbs

Scraper

Blade

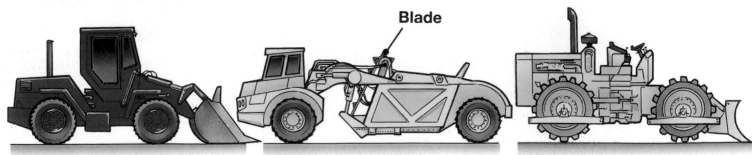

Height: 3.3 m/11 ft
Length: 10 m/30 ft
Number of blades: 23

Compactor

Height: 3.5 m/11.5 ft
Length: 6.8 m/22.5 ft
Weight: 20 tonnes/
19.6 tons

Grader

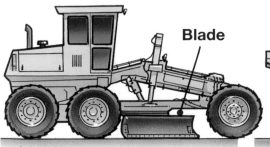

Height: 3.3 m/11 ft
Length: 7 m/23 ft
Length of blade: 4.2 m/
15 ft

Articulated dump truck

Height: 2.8 m/9 ft
Length: 6.5 m/21.5 ft
Biggest load: 12 tonnes/
11.8 tons

Heavy load dump truck

Height: 4 m/13 ft
Length: 9 m/30 ft
Biggest load: 55 tonnes/
54 tons

Roller

Height: 3 m/10 ft
Length: 5.2 m/18 ft
Biggest load: 10 tonnes/
9.8 tons

Paver

Height: 3 m/10 ft
Length: 5.9 m/19.5 ft
Fastest speed: 15 kph/
9.3 mph

Concrete mixer

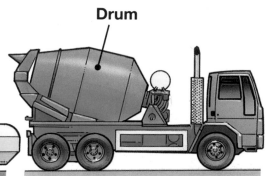

Drum

Height: 3.5 m/11.5 ft
Length: 5.9 m/19.5 ft
Drum speed: 12 turns per
minute

Concrete pump

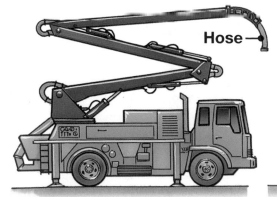

Hose

Height: 3 m/10 ft
Length: 8 m/26.5 ft
Full length of hose: 23 m/
76 ft

Rock breaker

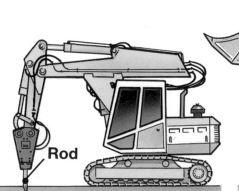

Rod

Height: 3.4 m/11 ft
Length of tracks: 3 m/10 ft
Length of rod: 0.6 m/2 ft

Power shovel

Height: 4.5 m/15 ft
Length: 6.3 m/21 ft
Highest stretch: 10 m/33 ft

Machine facts 2

Dragline excavator

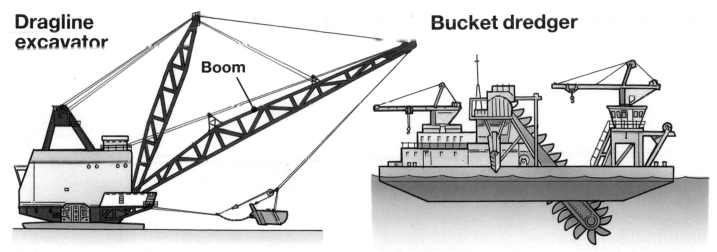

Boom

Height: 50 m/165 ft
Boom length: 79 m/261 ft
Crew: 2 people

Bucket dredger

Height: 23 m/76 ft
Length: 58 m/192 ft
Deepest dig: 25 m/83 ft

TBM (Tunnel Boring Machine)

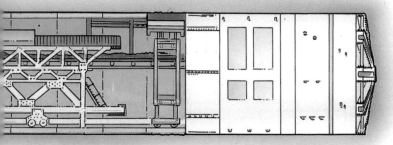

Height: 8.36 m/27.5 ft
Length: 220 m/726 ft
Digging speed: 6 m per
hour/20 ft per hour

Roadheader

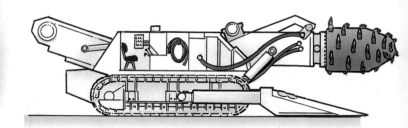

Height: 10 m/33 ft
Length: 9 m/30 ft
Weight: 42 tonnes/
41.3 tons

Continuous miner

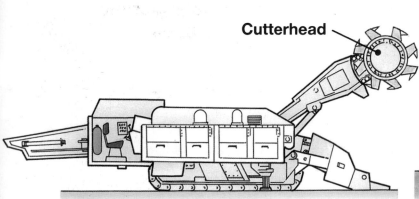

Cutterhead

Height: 1.5 m/5 ft
Length: 10.6 m/35 ft
Speed of cutterhead: 50
turns per minute

Bucket wheel excavator

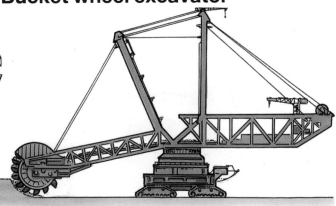

Number of buckets: 10
Deepest dig: 50 m/165 ft
Crew: 2 people

AN INTRODUCTION TO
SOCIAL
POLICY

Edited by
PETER DWYER
and **SANDRA SHAW**

Los Angeles | London | New Delhi
Singapore | Washington DC

Los Angeles | London | New Delhi
Singapore | Washington DC

SAGE Publications Ltd
1 Oliver's Yard
55 City Road
London EC1Y 1SP

SAGE Publications Inc.
2455 Teller Road
Thousand Oaks, California 91320

SAGE Publications India Pvt Ltd
B 1/I 1 Mohan Cooperative Industrial Area
Mathura Road
New Delhi 110 044

SAGE Publications Asia-Pacific Pte Ltd
3 Church Street
#10-04 Samsung Hub
Singapore 049483

Editor: Alice Oven
Assistant editor: Emma Milman
Production editor: Katie Forsythe
Copyeditor: Sharon Cawood
Proofreader: Audrey Scriven
Indexer: Adam Pozner
Marketing manager: Tamara Navaratnam
Cover design: Naomi Robinson
Typeset by: C&M Digitals (P) Ltd, Chennai, India
Printed by MPG Printgroup, UK

Library of Congress Control Number: 2012950317

British Library Cataloguing in Publication data

A catalogue record for this book is available from
the British Library

ISBN 978-1-4462-0758-1
ISBN 978-1-4462-0759-8 (pbk)

MIX
Paper from
responsible sources
FSC
www.fsc.org   FSC® C018575

This book is dedicated to the memory of Dr Helen Prosser. Helen was going
to write a chapter for the book before her unexpected death at a tragically young age.
A warm and much respected colleague at the University of Salford, we miss her very much.

Contents

About the Editors and Contributors

Dr Anya Ahmed is a Senior Lecturer in Social Policy at the University of Salford. She teaches and researches issues around social exclusion, retirement migration, gender, different forms of community and social housing. She has led a range of externally funded projects on hard to reach groups and specializes in qualitative data generation and analysis. She has a number of academic publications (journal articles and book chapters) and has written a number of reports for local government and voluntary sector organizations. She is currently writing a book on British retirement migration to the Costa Blanca in Spain and is leading a research project on the Somali community and social exclusion in London.

Dr Margaret Coffey is Programme Leader for the MSc in Public Health at the University of Salford, and a Senior Lecturer in Public Health. Margaret teaches research methods and evidenced-based public health on the MSc Public Health Programme, and her research interests focus on stress in the workplace, with an emphasis on the organizational, rather than individual, factors which impact on health and wellbeing in the workplace. In addition to this, Margaret is interested in evaluating behaviour change interventions in respect of lifestyle and the social determinants of health and health inequalities.

Dr Paul Copeland is Lecturer of Public Policy at Queen Mary, University of London. His research focuses on the political constellations surrounding EU social policy and the effectiveness of current governance tools within Social Europe. His work is strongly interdisciplinary and attempts to analyse the process of European integration surrounding Social Europe by engaging with the approaches and methods found within the broader school of the Social Sciences and Law. His most recent research analysed the EU's Lisbon Strategy and is entitled *The EU's Lisbon Strategy: Evaluating Success, Understanding Failure* (co-edited with Dimitris Papadimitriou). He is also currently writing up his research monograph: *EU Enlargement, the Clash of Capitalisms, and the European Social Dimension* (Manchester University Press).

Lindsey Dugdill is a Professor of Public Health at the University of Salford. Lindsey teaches evidence-based public health on the MSc Public Health Programme, and her specialist research areas are workplace health and physical activity. Lindsey is known internationally for her work in these fields and has worked directly (and published) with the World Health Organization on workplace health evaluation. In addition she has published over 100 peer-reviewed journal articles and commissioned reports and has been a member of several national expert groups such as the Department of Health Obesity Task Force (2005).

Peter Dwyer is Professor of Social Policy at the University of Salford. His research and teaching focuses on two main areas. First, a critical engagement with the notion of social citizenship, especially in relation to welfare rights and responsibilities and social inclusion/exclusion. Second, the impact of international migration on welfare states and migrants' rights. To date he has published four books and a variety of journal papers, chapters and reports on these themes and allied debates. His work has been funded by a range of organizations and he is currently leading a large ESRC collaborative project on welfare conditionality and conducting European Commission-funded research on Roma in nine EU member States.

Rita Haworth is a Senior Lecturer in social policy at the University of Salford. Her research and teaching focuses on two main areas. First, a critical engagement with the concept of user engagement in decision-making processes within health and social care settings. Second, an analysis of policy implementation and outcomes in relation to gender inequalities in the labour market. To date she has had published a number of papers in the above areas. Rita has received funding for a number of projects and is currently bidding for NHS funds to review and compare the impact of newly established adult mental health teams on service user groups.

Dr John Hudson is Senior Lecturer in Social Policy at the University of York where he is also currently Head of Social Policy. His research and teaching centre on two key topics: comparative analysis of welfare states and the politics of social policy making. He is author of *Understanding the Policy Process* (with Stuart Lowe) and *The Short Guide to Social Policy* (with Stefan Kühner and Stuart Lowe). He currently leads an ESRC-funded project examining the links between culture and welfare states.

Karen Kinghorn is Lecturer in Social Policy at the University of Salford. Karen was granted lifetime membership of the Millennium Awards Fellowship in 2001 for services to the community for projects in health and education. She completed her BSc first class honours in Social Policy (2005) at the University of Salford. Her subsequent employment was in the mental health sector working with carers. Her areas of interest include disability, care in the community, carers, and older people.

Dr Sandra Shaw is a Senior Lecturer in Social Policy at the University of Salford. Sandra's current teaching and research interests encompass children, young people and families; gender; and, comparative and global welfare. Recent publications include: *Parents, Children, Young People and the State* published by the Open University Press and McGraw Hill Education in 2010. A chapter entitled 'Gender: Continuity and Change; Gender and Welfare' was published in November 2012. She has undertaken a number research projects in health and social care, and authored other publications.

Mel Walker has extensive teaching and lecturing experience having worked in adult, further and higher education for nearly thirty years. In 2009 he was awarded a Teaching Excellence Award by the University of Salford for his 'outstanding contribution to teaching and the student learning experience'. He has a particular interest in teaching the social dimensions of health and illness; 'race' and ethnicity; social exclusion; and in the development of students' study skills and learning strategies.

List of Acronyms

ASB   Anti-social Behaviour
ASBO   Anti-social Behaviour Order
CCA   Camp for Climate Action
CSJ   Commission on Social Justice
CTC   Childcare Tax Credit
DWP   Department for Work and Pensions
EC   European Commission
ECJ   European Court of Justice
EM   Environmental (or Ecological) Modernism
EMOs   Environmental Movement Organizations
EMU   European Monetary Union
ESM   European Social Model
EU   European Union
GDP   Gross Domestic Product
GHG   Greenhouse gases
GNP   Gross National Product
IGOs   International governmental organizations
IHR   International Health Regulations
IMF   International Monetary Fund
IPCC   Intergovernmental Panel on Climate Change
IVF   In vitro fertilization
MNC   Multinational Corporation
MSP   Member of the Scottish Parliament
NEET   Not in Education, Employment or Training
NGO   Non-governmental Organizations
NHS   National Health Service
NMW   National Minimum Wage
OECD   Organization for Economic Cooperation and Development
OMC   Open Method of Coordination
RCVP   Riots Communities and Victims Panel
SEA   Single European Act

SEM	Single European Market
SEU	Social Exclusion Unit
UC	Universal Credit
UK	United Kingdom
UN	United Nations
WB	World Bank
WFTC	Working Families Tax Credit
WHO	World Health Organization

Editors' Introduction

Introduction

This book aims to introduce students to the study of social policy by offering an accessible consideration of certain key concepts, themes and contemporary issues and debates. It has been written for students who are studying social policy and welfare in the early years of their undergraduate studies, either as a major part of a single or joint hours social policy degree, or as a single module in related disciplines such as sociology, social work, politics or nursing and social care. More widely we also believe that the book will provide concise and user friendly introductions to key welfare debates for all students undertaking foundation degrees and access courses. It is an impossible task for a book such as this to cover the diversity of subject matter that contemporary social policy encompasses. For example, a critical discussion of the historical development of welfare states in particular nations is both a valuable and valid endeavour. Although certain chapters in this book do offer outlines of particular areas of policy development since World War II, wider historical debates about welfare are not a primary feature of this book. Rather than enter into a detailed chronological/historical discussion of particular policies each chapter attempts to highlight and summarize key debates and issues relevant to the topic under discussion. That said, students' comprehension of new policies needs to be grounded in an understanding of the context in which they emerged.

These are certainly interesting times for students of social policy. The onset of the global financial crisis in 2008/9 and the continuing issues facing economies in the Eurozone are already having a significant impact on welfare states around the world. Economic imperatives often dominate welfare policy decisions and provide a backdrop in which unprecedented cuts in public expenditure and the retrenchment of welfare dominate. It is highly probable that for the foreseeable future publicly funded social welfare services are likely to diminish with the responsibility for meeting needs increasingly being transferred from the state to individuals. At the time of writing the full impact of the new 'age of austerity' upon the lives of citizens has not yet been realized; nonetheless, it is already becoming apparent that as more and more people are likely have to turn to collective social provisions to meet basic needs, welfare states will offer less.

In terms of structure this book is divided into three main parts. Part 1 offers discussions around some of the key concepts that are central to understanding current policy and welfare debates. In Part 2 the authors consider policy issues in relation to individuals at key stages of the life course.

Discussions in parts 1 and 2 of the book draw largely, but not exclusively, on policy examples and developments in relation to UK social policy. The focus shifts in Part 3 to consider comparative and supranational policy issues. In the UK, New Labour's extended 13-year period of office ended in May 2010 with the unexpected emergence of the Conservative/Liberal Democrat Coalition government. Many of the chapters in this book, particularly those in parts 1 and 2 (see below), ground their discussions in the approach and legacy of the New Labour administrations alongside a consideration of the new Coalition government's policies; policies which appear to be shaped by a much stated need to reduce the ongoing public deficit and, arguably, antipathy towards big government and extensive publicly funded welfare provisions

In his opening chapter to Part 1 Hudson unpicks what he refers to as the key 'slippery concepts' at the heart of social policy. In offering discussions and definitions of 'welfare' and the 'welfare state' he reminds readers of the need to interrogate terms which are routinely used by politicians, policymakers, students and the general public. Having defined these often taken-for-granted terms he then draws on the work of Titmuss (1958) and subsequent scholars to discuss the social division of welfare and alert students to the need to consider the full range of redistributive welfare transfers in which states routinely deliver welfare. This allows for a fuller appreciation of welfare dependency beyond the myopic preoccupations of those who routinely speak of a welfare dependent 'underclass'. He then provides a brief discussion of the importance of the particular mix of welfare provisions that pertain in different national welfare states and introduces the idea of diverse welfare regimes. Hudson finishes by introducing the concept of well-being, an idea that is increasingly popular in some policy circles and one that is more fully discussed in Chapter 5.

Dwyer discusses the contentious issue of social justice in Chapter 2. In doing so he discusses differing views about the validity of social justice. He argues that social justice is about answering questions concerned with 'fair' ways of allocating and redistributing the resources and opportunities available within society and offers a critical discussion of three well known approaches to social justice as outlined by Nozick, Rawls and Sen, each of whom offer different and competing visions. Moving on from these essentially philosophical debates the chapter concludes with a consideration of the ways in which recent UK governments have conceptualized social justice. Dwyer argues that the Coalition government now offers an individualized and constrained notion of social justice that is primarily concerned with solving the problems of a disadvantaged minority.

In the first of his two contributions to the book, Walker focuses on the concept of social exclusion in Chapter 3. This chapter outlines the origins of the idea of social exclusion and the ways in which it became a prominent theme in UK social policy during New Labour's years in office. The chapter then goes on to make two main points. First, how social exclusion may offer more rounded explanatory insights into understanding disadvantage than the related concept of poverty by considering the experiences of people with mental health issues. Second, the malleability of the concept and how (utilizing the work of Levitas, 2005) differing discourses of social exclusion emphasize diverse understandings about the causes of and solutions to social problems. In Chapter 4, Walker moves on to explore issues of difference and diversity and outlines the importance of the role of social construction in understanding welfare policy implementation and developments. Although he considers how the construction of difference can impact across a range of dimensions, i.e. class, gender, age and sexuality, his main focus is on how racialized constructions have informed policy over time to discriminate against and disadvantage members of minority ethnic communities. Chapter 5 rounds off Part 1 of the book. Here Coffey and Dugdill initially highlight how differing definitions of health and wellbeing, and who does the defining, can have important implications for both individuals and providers of healthcare. Discussions then move on to consider the determinants of health, how such factors are distributed, and the impact of health inequalities and their consequences. Drawing on recent literature concerned with health and paid employment the authors then explore policy approaches aimed at improving health and wellbeing in the workplace.

Part 2 of the book offers four chapters on welfare and policy in relation to the life course. In Chapter 6 Shaw looks at children and families and provides a discussion of the 'traditional' family while simultaneously outlining the extent to which families and ways of partnering and parenting children have undergone significant change in recent decades. A consideration of New Labour's pledge to end child poverty and the ways in which poverty negatively impacts on the lives of children who experience it then follows. Next the definition and measurement of child poverty are highlighted and a critical consideration of the policies favoured by New Labour and the current Coalition government in attempting to eradicate it is outlined. Shaw concludes the chapter by arguing that recent changes in the benefit system announced by the Coalition government are likely to lead to increased hardship for many families, and the continuation of child poverty in the UK for the foreseeable future. In Chapter 7 she moves on to look at welfare policy and young people. She argues that negative perceptions of 'youth' are apparent in many policy areas and illustrates this view with particular discussions of the issues faced by those young people who are 'Not in Education Training or Employment' (often labelled as NEETs), and how young people are routinely subject to anti-social behaviour policy. Emphasizing that young people are not an homogeneous group, she also details how anti-social behaviour policies are most likely to be applied to youths whose lives are already blighted by poverty and social exclusion.

Chapters 8 and 9 consider aspects of policy that routinely relate to those at the other end of the life course i.e. older people. However, it needs to be remembered that policies related to death and end of life unfortunately have relevance for all of us regardless of our age in cases of terminal illness. In Chapter 8 Haworth starts by noting that there has been a significant rise in the number of people living into old age in developed nations since the 19th century. Allied to this, she points out that there has been a positive shift in thinking, away from the depiction of old age as a time of 'natural' dependency and ill health toward a more positive vision of active ageing, as many people live longer and healthier lives. More negatively, she also notes the simultaneous emergence of a view among many policymakers that ageing populations constitute a threat to economies across the western world due to the increasing amounts of money that will be needed to provide welfare services for older people in the future. Against this backdrop she offers an outline of key UK policy developments in three areas, namely housing, health and social care and pensions. In Chapter 9 Kinghorn reviews debates and recent policy initiatives in respect of death and the end of life. In addressing an aspect of the life course that is often missing from introductory texts, she presents discussions on a range of important issues such as palliative care, the hospice movement and the highly contentious issue of assisted suicide and the right to die. She then reviews the *End of Life Care Strategy* introduced by New Labour in 2008 and briefly outlines the Coalition government's early deliberations in this often emotive area of policy.

Comparative and supranational dimensions form the subject matter for Part 3 of the book. Kinghorn opens this section (Chapter 10) with a look at devolution in the UK and the implications that this has for welfare policy. She begins by outlining the makeup, roles and powers of the devolved governments in Scotland, Wales and Northern Ireland and their relationships with the UK government. Key questions about these still developing relationships are explored through a discussion of two issues. First, the ways in which funding is allocated to the devolved administrations. Second, the so-called 'West Lothian Question' whereby MPs in the UK Parliament elected to represent constituencies in Scotland, Wales and Northern Ireland retain the ability to vote on policy issues that solely impact on people who live in England – a debate that has become more contentious with the onset of UK devolution from the late 1990s. Devolution can also have an effect on welfare policy and the chapter finishes with a discussion of the differing approaches to the provision of care in the community that have emerged in England, Scotland and Northern Ireland.

Chapter 11 is on comparative social policy and opens with a discussion of comparative study. It outlines how welfare regimes can be described and categorized, setting out the work of Gøsta-Esping-Andersen as a key author in this area. Critiques of his work are then explored. These include a consideration of the basis for his analysis; whether or not countries were classified appropriately; how Mediterranean countries were excluded; and the need to expand the analysis to include new and emerging welfare regimes such as those in South East Asia. A significant critique of Esping-Andersen's work is that based on gender, and this is also explored. The chapter concludes by reflecting on the value of the regimes approach in accounting for welfare systems, and how this continues to develop and adapt.

In Chapter 12 Copeland turns to supranational policy debates and reflects on the European Union's role vis-à-vis social policy. Following a concise historical overview of the establishment and expansion of the EU, and having outlined its main institutions, he traces key points in the development of EU social policy. Noting continuing differences between the welfare states of various Member States and that the European integration process has predominantly been concerned with market integration, Copeland views the emergence of a more substantive EU social policy as unlikely. He believes that any further expansion of the EU's competency in welfare matters will depend on the enthusiasm of the governments of Member States to drive such change forward and that any such eagerness is only ever likely to emerge when centre-left political parties are in power in the majority of nations across Europe.

Globalization has been recognized as an increasingly important dimension of welfare debates. In Chapter 13, Shaw starts by discussing the process of globalization, moving on to look at the development of global social policy. The plurality and complexity of global governance are considered, and global health policy provides an interesting illustration of developments in global social policy.

The role of key organizations is also outlined, including the World Health Organization (WHO), the World Bank (WB), multi-national organizations (MNCs), and non-governmental organizations (NGOs) such as the Bill and Melinda Gates Foundation. A discussion of the global health agenda on infectious diseases including HIV/AIDS follows. The chapter concludes by looking at the broader health agenda, the Millennium Development Goals (MDGs), and the impact of environmental changes on health.

The book concludes with a final chapter that explores social policy and environmental issues. Here Ahmed discusses the inherently global issue of climate change and the challenges it poses for the 'traditional' concerns of social policy. She then highlights and discusses a number of landmark 'green' policy documents that have shaped international debates over the last three decades. Ahmed concludes by noting that while social policy and environmental policy share common ground, in that they are both often focused on setting out and achieving some notion of social justice, welfare policies which remain embedded in capitalist systems and linked to the necessity for economic growth will have to be rethought if a sustainable future is to be achieved for all and climate change tackled successfully.

As noted earlier in this introduction, our aim in putting this book together has been to provide students with accessible ways in to particular key social policy debates and issues. All the chapters have been written by academics who are experienced and active teachers on welfare and policy matters. We hope that both students and teachers of social policy will find the book, or the discrete chapters within it, useful as they endeavour to make sense of social policy and its impacts on the lives of us all.

Peter Dwyer and Sandra Shaw
September 2012

PART 1

Key Concepts

1

Welfare

John Hudson

Overview

- The notion of 'welfare' features prominently in the social policy literature but the term belies simple definition.
- The 'welfare state' is at the heart of the social policy debate but both scholars and politicians disagree on what should fall within its boundaries and what it means for a country to be or to possess a 'welfare state'.
- An exploration of the 'social divisions of welfare' makes it clear that state-supported welfare takes many forms beyond the provision of core social services.
- The welfare state is not a neutral player: it stratifies societies and can reinforce social divisions.
- Welfare is not delivered solely by the state: a mixed economy of provision is evident in all societies.
- Broad-based notions such as 'well-being' or even 'happiness' have become increasingly fashionable alternatives to 'welfare' in recent years.

Introduction

For any student of social policy, 'welfare' is a term that will be invoked on a regular basis, for studying the welfare state is at the heart of the subject. Moreover, unlike some of the other concepts explored in this book, it is also a term that features very prominently in policy debates too: the phrase 'welfare reform', for instance, has long been a staple element of political discourse in the UK and beyond.

Yet, despite its common usage – perhaps, even, because of it – the term is a slippery one that belies simple definition. Indeed, scholars and policy makers alike are prone to using the term somewhat unthinkingly, holding a general idea of what they mean by it but without a specific definition in mind. Partly this is because the term 'welfare' will always have a normative political dimension that makes it difficult to derive a commonly accepted meaning. This is true even for the everyday meaning of the word 'welfare', which is rooted in the fusion of the verb 'fare' with the adverb 'well': what does it mean for someone to fare well? What needs to be in place to ensure someone's welfare is protected? How can we be sure if someone's welfare is under threat? And does the word mean something altogether different if, say, we talk of the welfare of children, the welfare of families or even the welfare of animals, as people so commonly do? The answers to these questions will always remain, in part at least, political ones, reflecting different values, ideologies and world views.

However, the picture is further muddied by the fact that the term 'welfare' is regularly fused with other words and so can have subtly distinct meanings in specific contexts. So, for example, phrases such as 'welfare state', 'welfare service', 'welfare regime' and 'social welfare' all hint at different notions of welfare. Added to this, the meanings of these phrases are not permanently fixed and nor are they consistently deployed. So, for example, the meaning of the term 'welfare state' might change over time as governments expand or contract the range of services commonly provided to citizens. Similarly, while some scholars or policy makers might favour a very narrow definition of the term 'welfare state', others might argue that our understanding is enhanced by a much broader conception.

For those new to the subject of social policy, it may be frustrating to find that the term 'welfare' is used in such loose and overlapping ways. Certainly, it seems likely to be a source of confusion for some, for many authors use the phrase inconsistently or without precision and clarity. Worse still for our purposes here, many authors simply take the phrase for granted: there are numerous textbooks with 'welfare' in the title that begin with an introductory chapter that outline the author's understanding of the key elements of the book title but omit any definition of the term 'welfare'. Much of the time, the phrase is used merely to signal that the author's concern is with issues of pertinence to social policy rather than to policy and politics more generally. So, for instance, in *Understanding the Policy Process: Analysing Welfare Policy and Practice* Stuart Lowe and I use the term 'welfare' to flag that the book is concerned with how social policies such as health care or social security are shaped by the policy process and we ignore issues outside of this sphere such as those relating to defence policy or foreign policy (see Hudson and Lowe, 2009).

However, it is also fair to say that the term is often used in a rather general sense because scholars wish to avoid engaging with what can be rather complex definitional issues each time they flag 'welfare', broadly conceived, as the being the focus of their attention. As we will show in this chapter, these issues go right to the heart of the purpose of social policy in both theory and practice, so rehearsing them each time the phrase 'welfare' is invoked would be exhausting. Yet, as with so many first principle-type debates, periodic reflection on the issues is essential, for they act as both a guide for the subject as a whole and raise fundamental questions about the purpose of social policy.

The welfare state

The most common usage of the term 'welfare' in the social policy literature comes through the notion of the 'welfare state', the examination of which is at the heart of the subject. Indeed, as Hill (2000: 8) notes, 'The study of social policy, as it has developed in Britain, has been concerned to examine the extent to which the welfare state meets people's needs'.

Yet, in keeping with the tenor of the discussion so far, it may come as little surprise to readers that there is confusion over the origins of the term. McGregor (1961: 34) suggested it was 'a phrase first coined by some unknown [newspaper] sub-editor in 1945' but others have claimed the term can be traced back to 1941 when the then Archbishop of York, William Temple, used the term as a contrast to the 'warfare state' being pursued by Hitler in Nazi Germany (see Timmins, 1995: 6; Lunt, 2008: 415; *Oxford English Dictionary*, 2012). The timing of the first utterances is no accident: the Beveridge Report, published in 1942, outlined a radical and popular plan for addressing major social ills in the UK and it is commonly suggested that the raft of Beveridge-inspired social reforms implemented by the 1945–51 post-War Labour government marked the moment that the UK became a 'welfare state' (Alcock, 2008: 6; Fraser, 2009: 2). Yet, as Timmins (1995: 6–7) notes, the phrase 'welfare state' was hardly in common usage at that point, with the Prime Minister of the day, Clement Attlee, only adopting the phrase for the 1950 General Election, and *The Oxford English Dictionary* including its first entry for the phrase as late as 1955.

This confusion over the origins of the term 'welfare state' is accompanied by disagreement over its meaning. Indeed, in his classic exploration of welfare capitalism, Esping-Andersen (1990: 18) noted with some exasperation that 'the welfare state itself has generally received scant conceptual attention'. Bryson (1992: 36) suggests that the term 'is used when a nation has at least a minimum level of institutionalized provisions for meeting the basic economic and social requirements of its citizens'. Mishra (1984: ix) has suggested that even at the most basic level the term has a double meaning, including 'both the idea of state responsibility for welfare as well as the set of institutions and practices through which the idea is given effect'. More prosaically, Titmuss (1956: 38) distinguished between the 'performance' and the 'promise' of the welfare state.

Spicker (1995: 274) echoes the above in offering up one definition of the welfare state as 'the delivery of social services by the state [and] the strategy of developing inter-related services to deal with a wide range of social problems'. But, ambiguity exists in terms of which services might be deemed the 'social services' that fall under the purview of the welfare state. In the UK at least, it is not uncommon for scholars to draw the boundaries of the welfare state around services dealing with the five giant social evils identified by Beveridge: what we would describe in modern-day language as social security/income protection, health care, education, employment and housing (e.g. Timmins, 1995; Hudson et al., 2008), perhaps with the addition of social care too (e.g. Hill, 2000; Hill and Irving, 2009). Others, however, would draw the boundaries of the welfare state much more broadly, including areas such as transport policy, the environment, food policy and access to the internet (see Bochel, 2009), while some go even further and suggest that a 'new social policy' should include issues around leisure, consumption and sport (Cahill, 1994). It is perhaps fair to say that the majority view favours a more traditional approach. Spicker (1995: 5) even suggests that those who argue for a broad approach 'are really interested in a different subject area'. Yet even accepting the narrow definition of the welfare state brings definitional problems because the range of services that might fall under a deceptively simple heading such as 'health care' or 'education' is vast: should, for instance, an effective health service include access to gyms, cosmetic surgery or healthy-eating classes (Hudson et al., 2008)?

Ambiguity exists not only in terms of which services comprise the welfare state, but also in the extent and quality of the services required. Spicker (1995: 82) argues that there is an inherent ambiguity in the term because it is used 'both as a form of description and as a normative argument', and notes that there is an idealism or even mythology around the notion of the 'welfare state', which for some might also be defined as 'an ideal in which services are provided comprehensively and at the best level possible' (Spicker, 1995: 274). Therborn (1983, cited in Castles, 2004: 31) believes we should reserve the label for states in which the majority of routine policy activities are devoted to the promotion of welfare, rather than for the achievement of other goals such as defence or economic growth: in other words, much as we might distinguish someone who plays football from those who are football players, states that provide welfare services may not meet the definition of what constitutes a welfare state. Indeed, it is for this reason that some challenge the idea that the British welfare state emerged following the post-War Beveridge inspired reforms as it 'begs questions about […] why these reforms should be seen as achieving it' (Alcock, 2008: 6). Similarly, Timmins (1995: 7) worries that such a conception 'suffers the drawback of being static, as though "the welfare state" were a perfect work, handed down in tablets of stone in 1945'. As he notes, 'Beveridge hated the phrase and refused to use it, disliking its "Santa Claus" and "brave new world" connotations' (Timmins, 1995: 7).

Social divisions of welfare

These debates about what the welfare state is or should be make clear that the complexity of defining the 'welfare state' is more than a scholarly problem for it necessarily engages with normative political issues. One of the earliest scholars of welfare, Richard Titmuss, was hugely sensitive to such issues, not least because once the term 'welfare state' entered popular usage in the 1950s it was often invoked in a pejorative fashion as hostile commentators lined up to attack what they viewed to be the negative impacts of the growth of the welfare state. Indeed, way back in the mid-1950s Titmuss (1956: 37) warned of the 'tyranny of stereotypes' in popular debate that built on flawed conceptions of need, the welfare state and social services. He offered an analysis of the 'social divisions of welfare' to challenge these misconceptions, arguing that debate about the welfare state dealt purely with 'social welfare' – the provision of the core social services – while two other forms of state-sponsored welfare of greater benefit to higher earners – fiscal welfare and occupational welfare – remained largely unexamined.

Titmuss used fiscal welfare as shorthand for the range of tax breaks and allowances the state grants to individuals and households. These have varied in nature and significance over time but his central point that these allowances represent a form of social service remains as valid today as it was then. In fact, they have become increasingly prominent tools of social policy reform in recent years (Hudson et al., 2008). However, as they are less visible than (say) social security benefit payments or health service expenditures, they can be stubbornly difficult to measure and so often represent something of a 'hidden' benefit. Indeed, this was in large part the point Titmuss was making: fiscal welfare often favours those with larger incomes and so represents a hidden way in which their welfare is promoted by the state. As a case in point, at the time of writing this chapter, the UK government revealed the results of a Treasury analysis that showed that some of the richest people in the country were using tax allowances for charitable donations to bring their personal income tax rate to less than half the rate paid by the average citizen which, in some cases, allowed multi-millionaires to pay no income tax whatsoever (Winnett et al., 2012).

The notion of occupational welfare refers to the additional benefits that many employers provide their workers – often, as Titmuss noted, at some considerable expense to the Exchequer – in the form of items such as occupational pensions, company health care and sick pay schemes, education and training grants, company cars, and subsidized meals and rail tickets. Titmuss (1956: 52) suggested at the time that these benefits disproportionately favoured higher earners and, in effect, operated as 'concealed multipliers of occupational success'. Much the same is true today, particularly for those employed in the higher echelons of international corporations at the heart of the global economy where generous private health, education and housing allowances are commonplace as are 'equalization adjustments' that compensate for tax and social insurance contributions (Hudson, 2012).

Questions around the social division of welfare raise fundamental issues about who benefits from welfare provision. In drawing attention to these issues, Titmuss aimed to unpick narrow and simplistic stereotypes of the welfare state as being of benefit only to one group in society. In line with the Fabian thinking that imbued much of the early social policy literature, Titmuss's analysis was primarily (though not exclusively) concerned therefore with an analysis of class. However, later work, particularly from the 1980s onwards, offered a more nuanced analysis embedded in 'new critical approaches to welfare' (Williams, 1989: 39). This work called for a deeper analysis of the interrelations between welfare and gender and welfare and 'race' in particular, but also welfare and disability, age and sexuality too, all of which had been neglected in the welfare state literature. This, in turn, meant that many of the assumptions embedded within the welfare state about, for instance, the role of women in society had been inadequately explored or challenged in mainstream debates.

As Williams (1989: 161–2) has pointed out, while the Beveridge-inspired reforms of the 1940s

> were significant developments for the welfare of the working class [...] national and male chauvinism were built into the structure of these provisions. Woman's dependent status and her role as mother were reinforced by the developments, and the nationalist and imperialist sentiment of many of the policies created a ready framework for the unchallenged development of institutionalized racism.

In short, from the outset the UK welfare state prioritized the welfare of some groups over that of others, making it essential that we ask the question of 'whose welfare?' the welfare state promotes. Though there is greater awareness today of the ways in which the welfare state interacts with social divisions, no one could seriously claim that questions about the distribution of welfare no longer need to be asked. Instead, the social policy literature is replete with studies that demonstrate the opposite (two examples of useful, recently published textbooks relevant here are Craig et al., 2012, and Roulstone and Prideaux, 2012).

The 'whose welfare?' question flows into related issues around liberty and control for it is often the case that protecting or promoting the welfare of one person or group of people requires limits to be placed on the freedom of others. At the simplest level, we can observe that the taxing of an individual's income to pay for services for others restricts the liberty of the taxed individual with respect to how they spend their income, but more complex examples can be found in areas such as criminal justice, anti-social behaviour laws and social work where a core focus of policy is to protect the welfare of some by regulating the behaviour of others.

Welfare regimes and the welfare mix

As the above implies, the welfare state cannot be simply viewed as a neutral instrument that benevolently guards the welfare of citizens for it does not operate in a social vacuum. Instead, discussion of the social divisions of welfare makes clear that the analysis of welfare needs to be located in a broader discussion of the ways in which it interacts with other elements within society. As Esping-Andersen (1990: 23) argues: 'The welfare state is not just a mechanism that intervenes in, and possibly corrects, the structure of inequality; it is, in its own right, a system of stratification. It is an active force in the ordering of social relations'.

In his classic exploration of welfare capitalism, Esping-Andersen (1990) argued that this means we need to examine *welfare regimes* rather than merely examine the *welfare state* in isolation (see Chapter 12 for a further discussion). More specifically, he suggested that we should examine the roles played by the state, the market and the family in the provision of welfare (Esping-Andersen, 1990, 1999). In so doing, he suggested, we will find different models of welfare operating in different countries. Indeed, he argued there were, in broad terms, three types of welfare regime: a Liberal regime in which social rights were weak and there was little redistribution of income; a Social Democratic regime with strong social rights and high levels of income redistribution; and a Conservative/Corporatist regime with relatively strong social rights but modest income redistribution. Significantly, the roles of the state, market and family in the provision of welfare differ accordingly in each model of welfare (see Table 1.1) with, for instance, the state playing a minimal role in liberal regimes and individual citizens expected instead to make their own private welfare provision through the market where possible.

A crucial point to stress here is that while the balance between the roles the state, market and family play in welfare provision varies between societies, in all it is the case that each plays a role. Social policy theorists have used terms such as *welfare pluralism* (Johnson, 1987) or the *mixed economy of welfare* (Powell, 2007) to capture the idea that welfare is provided not just by the state but also by private companies, voluntary organizations and families and communities. While it has always been the case that welfare has been provided through a mixed economy of providers, the

TABLE 1.1 Esping-Andersen's welfare regimes summarized

	Liberal regime	Social Democratic regime	Conservative regime
Role of family in provision of welfare	Marginal	Marginal	Central
Role of market in provision of welfare	Central	Marginal	Marginal
Role of State in provision of welfare	Marginal	Central	Subsidiary
Strength of social rights	Minimal	Maximum	High (for breadwinner)
Key examples	USA	Sweden	Germany and Italy

Source: Esping-Andersen (1999)

subject of social policy has shown a stronger concern with issues around the welfare mix in recent years. In part, this is a reflection of current political trends, particularly in the UK where the main political parties have been keen to explore the roles that non-state actors might play in securing welfare. Indeed, Alcock (2008: 9) suggests that social policy analysis is now 'moving beyond state-based welfare, to focus not only upon public services but also upon partnerships between the state and other providers of welfare and well-being'.

From welfare to well-being

If the study (and pursuit) of welfare is not, therefore, simply concerned with the social services provided by the state, then we are taken back to our initial question: what does welfare mean in the context of social policy? Many scholars aiming to define 'welfare' on the basis of first principles have suggested that, ultimately, the term aims to capture a concern with the well-being of people. Indeed, Bryson (1992: 30) argues that 'at its most basic level, the word welfare merely means well-being', whilst Spicker (1995: 5) suggests that 'welfare can be taken in a wide sense, to mean "well-being"'. In recent years, perhaps in part because of the political baggage that has surrounded the term 'welfare', both scholars and policy makers have shown an increased interest in exploring 'societal well-being' as a closely related alternative to 'welfare'. Whether this is a helpful departure as regards to creating greater conceptual clarity is a moot point: as Allin (2007: 46) observes, 'the terms wellbeing, quality of life, happiness, life satisfaction and welfare are often used interchangeably'.

However, there has certainly been considerable progress in developing measures of societal well-being over the last decade or so (Allin, 2007). Indeed, one of the major international bodies responsible for gathering social and economic data – the OECD – has now made measuring well-being a central part of its activity (see OECD, 2011). There are many reasons why the notion of well-being has begun to command increased attention, but perhaps chief amongst these is that it focuses on outcomes (i.e. what has happened) rather than inputs (i.e. what is provided), and it demands a broad outlook that captures a wide array of outcomes relevant to well-being. As the OECD (2011: 18) note:

Defining well-being is challenging because it requires looking at many aspects of people's lives [...] most experts and ordinary people around the world would agree that it requires meeting various human needs, some of which are essential (e.g. being in good health), as well as the ability to pursue one's goals, to thrive and feel satisfied with their life.

A fundamental distinction can be drawn between measures of 'objective' and 'subjective' well-being, the former being based on material or social circumstances that can be externally verified (e.g. the level of a household's income) whereas the latter is based on self-assessment (e.g. an individual's personal assessment of how satisfied they are with their life). Most commentators agree that strong measures of well-being encompass both, and the OECD's Better Life Index (OECD, 2011: 25) includes data on the following components:

- income and wealth (e.g. household income)
- jobs and earnings (e.g. the employment rate)
- quality of housing (e.g. number of rooms per person)
- health status (e.g. life expectancy)
- work and life (e.g. time devoted to leisure)
- education and skills (e.g. educational attainment)
- social connections (e.g. the extent of social networks)
- civic engagement and governance (e.g. voter turn-out)
- environmental quality (e.g. air quality)
- personal security (e.g. murder rate)
- subjective well-being (e.g. life satisfaction).

Much of the increased interest in well-being has, arguably, come from outside the subject of social policy, particularly from Economics where an expanding number of analysts have begun to look beyond (growth in) national income as the main measure of social progress (Allin, 2007). However, each of the items included in the OECD Better Life Index is of direct relevance to social policy in a high-income democratic country such as the UK, and it has been suggested that social policy analysts have focused too heavily on issues around money (e.g. levels of income poverty) rather than focusing on broader conceptions of social well-being. Similarly, there has been a tendency to see welfare as being represented by welfare state inputs (e.g. the level of public spending) or outputs (e.g. the number of schools, hospitals, teachers, doctors), rather than focusing on the out-comes – improved welfare – that ought to be our core concern. A focus on well-being helps rectify this. Indeed, Dean (2006: 1) argues: 'My preference [...] is for the term "well-being" rather than "welfare" because well-being is about how well people *are*, not how well they *do* (which, strictly speaking, is what welfare means)'.

Though close connections between the notions of welfare and well-being mean the exploration of measures of well-being may help flesh out a practical understanding of welfare, we should note that not everyone agrees that the two terms can or should be seen as so closely related as to be near interchangeable. As Spicker (1995: 5) suggests, 'It is probably truer to say that social policy is concerned with people who lack well-being'. Indeed, there are those who remain sceptical about the well-being agenda which, in its most extreme form, asks us to focus on 'happiness' as the guiding goal of government policy (Layard, 2006). Though the notion of boosting happiness as the ultimate measure of social progress has a simple appeal, there is a risk that politicians might use such an approach as a smokescreen to deflect attention away from thorny and costly issues such as reducing poverty or income inequality.

Summary/Conclusions

- There are good reasons why 'welfare' is such a slippery concept. It means different things in different contexts and has a normative dimension that is impossible to escape.
- We can distinguish between the 'promise' and the 'practice' of the welfare state: the vision of a fair society that might be achieved and what is actually provided by government for citizens in terms of benefits and services.
- Deceptively simple and commonly used phrases such as 'the welfare state' are laden with normative assumptions about the desired scope, scale and structure of social services. Accordingly, questions such as 'What is the welfare state?' or 'Does the UK have a welfare state?' lack simple answers.
- Questions about the nature of 'welfare' cannot be value free and they demand we ask the question of 'whose welfare?'. The welfare state is not a neutral player, structuring society and with the potential to reinforce social divisions. Though social policies have boosted the welfare of many, this has often been at the expense of the welfare of others.
- Welfare is never simply about the 'welfare state'. We will typically find a mixed economy of welfare, with the state, market, families and local communities playing a role in the delivery of welfare.
- Welfare and well-being are sometimes used interchangeably and are closely related notions. A focus on the latter might help us to remain fixed on the outcomes we are seeking – the 'promise' of welfare – rather than on the money we spend or services we provide – the 'practice' of welfare.

Questions

1 How would you define the welfare state?
2 Pick an area of social policy you are familiar with: how far do you think current policies in this sphere reinforce social divisions and how far do you think they serve to ameliorate them?
3 With reference to a core area of social policy – such as health care, education or social security – what roles do you think the state, market, family, voluntary sector and local communities play in the delivery of welfare?
4 What indicators would you include in a measure of societal well-being?

Recommended reading

Alcock, P., Glennerster, H., Oakley, A. and Sinfield, A. (2001) *Welfare and Wellbeing. Richard Titmuss's Contribution to Social Policy*. Bristol: The Policy Press. Though written over 50 years ago, Titmuss's classic essay on the social divisions of welfare remains relevant today. It is reprinted here as Chapter 2 in Part 2.

Esping-Andersen, G. (1990) *The Three Worlds of Welfare Capitalism*. Cambridge: Polity. The first chapter of this classic text on welfare capitalism offers a rewarding and theoretically rich review of key definitional issues.

OECD (2011) *How's Life? Measuring Well-Being*. Paris: OECD. This is a contemporary analysis of well-being across the high-income countries of the world – and the challenges in measuring it.

Timmins, N. (1995) *The Five Giants: A Biography of the Welfare State*. London: Fontana Press. This is a good introduction to the history of the welfare state in the UK that also deals well with the idea of the welfare state.

Relevant website

The OECD's Better Life Index page offers an interactive approach to defining and measuring well-being in high income countries – www.oecdbetterlifeindex.org/

References

Alcock, P. (2008) 'The subject of social policy', in P. Alcock, M. May and K. Rowlingson (eds) *The Student's Companion to Social Policy* (3rd edn). Oxford: Blackwell.

Allin, P. (2007) 'Measuring societal wellbeing', *Economic & Labour Market Review*, 1(10): 46–52.

Bochel, C. (2009) 'Exploring the boundaries of social policy', in H. Bochel, C. Bochel, R. Page and R. Sykes (eds) *Social Policy: Themes, Issues and Debates* (2nd edn). Harlow: Pearson Longman.

Bryson, L. (1992) *Welfare and The State: Who Benefits?* Basingstoke: Macmillan.

Cahill, M. (1994) *The New Social Policy*. Oxford: Blackwell.

Castles, F. (2004) *The Future of the Welfare State: Crisis Myths and Crisis Realities*. Oxford: Oxford University Press.

Craig, G., Atkin, K., Chattoo, S. and Flynn, R. (eds) (2012) *Understanding 'Race' and Ethnicity*. Bristol: The Policy Press.

Dean, H. (2006) *Social Policy*. Cambridge: Polity.

Esping-Andersen, G. (1990) *The Three Worlds of Welfare Capitalism*. Cambridge: Polity.

Esping-Andersen, G. (1999) *The Social Foundations of Postindustrial Economies*. Oxford: Oxford University Press.

Fraser, D. (2009) *The Evolution of the British Welfare State: A History of Social Policy Since the Industrial Revolution* (4th edn). Basingstoke: Palgrave.

Hill, M. (2000) *Understanding Social Policy* (6th edn). Oxford: Blackwell.

Hill, M. and Irving, Z (2009) *Understanding Social Policy* (8th edn). Oxford: Blackwell.

Hudson, J. (2012) 'Welfare regimes and global cities: a missing link in the comparative analysis of welfare states?', *Journal of Social Policy*, 41(3): 455–473.

Hudson, J., Kühner, S. and Lowe, S. (2008) *The Short Guide to Social Policy*. Bristol: The Policy Press.

Hudson, J. and Lowe, S. (2009) *Understanding the Policy Process: Analysing Welfare Policy and Practice* (2nd edn). Bristol: The Policy Press.

Johnson, N. (1987) *The Welfare State in Transition: The Theory and Practice of Welfare Pluralism*. London: Harvester Wheatsheaf.

Layard, R. (2006) *Happiness: Lessons from a New Science*. London: Penguin.

Lunt, N. (2008) 'From welfare state to social development: winning the war of words in New Zealand', *Social Policy & Society*, 7: 405–418.

McGregor, O. (1961) 'Sociology and welfare', in P. Halmos (ed.) *Sociological Review Monograph No 4*. Keele: Keele University Press.

Mishra, R. (1984) *The Welfare State in Crisis: Social Thought and Social Change*. Hemel Hempstead: Harvester Wheatsheaf.

OECD (2011) *How's Life? Measuring Well-Being*. Paris: OECD.

Powell, M. (2007) *Understanding the Mixed Economy of Welfare*. Bristol: The Policy Press.

Roulstone, A. and Prideaux, S. (2012) *Understanding Disability Policy*. Bristol: The Policy Press.

Spicker, P. (1995) *Social Policy: Themes and Approaches*. Hemel Hempstead: Prentice Hall.

Therborn, G. (1983) *When, how and why does a welfare state become a welfare state?* Paper presented at ECPR Workshop, Freiburg.

Timmins, N. (1995) *The Five Giants: A Biography of the Welfare State*. London: Fontana Press

Titmuss, R. (1956) *The Social Divisions of Welfare: Some Reflections on the Search for Equity*. Liverpool: Liverpool University Press. [Page references to 1973 version published in R. Titmuss, *Essays on the Welfare State*, London: Unwin University Books.]

Williams, F. (1989) *Social Policy: A Critical Introduction*. Cambridge: Polity.

Winnett, R., Kirkup, J. and Hope, C. (2012) 'Wealthiest people abusing tax system with donations to charities that don't do charitable work', *Daily Telegraph*, 10 April, www.telegraph.co.uk/news/politics/georgeosborne/9195571/Wealthiest-people-abusing-tax-system-with-donations-to-charities-that-dont-do-charitable-work.html

2

Social Justice
Peter Dwyer

Overview

- Social justice is a much debated and contested concept.
- Diverse views about the validity of social justice and the most appropriate way to achieve it often reflect differing ideological positions about the the extent to which governments should interfere in market mechanisms to redistribute income and opportunities within a society.
- Social justice is about answering questions on 'fair' ways of allocating and redistributing the resources and opportunities available within society.
- It is therefore concerned with issues of equality and inequality, both between individual members of the same society and between different societies.
- Competing theoretical debates about social justice are utilized by governments to justify a wide range of policies.
- This chapter provides introductory overviews of three important competing theories of social justice alongside a discussion of how social justice has been interpreted by recent UK governments and policy makers.

Introduction

Everybody is in favour of social justice almost by definition. But what they mean by social justice, the priority they accord to it relative to other objectives, and the public policies they believe can follow from it, vary widely (Burchardt and Craig, 2008: 1).

The purpose of this chapter is to consider the idea of social justice and to shed some light on the questions raised by the above quotation. As a number of authors have noted, social justice is a much debated and contested concept within social policy (Burchardt and Craig, 2008; Lister, 2010; Taylor-Gooby, 2012). Discussions about whether or not social justice is an achievable and desirable goal for social policy, and the best ways to attain it, are indicative of wider philosophical and ideological debates about issues such as freedom, equality, citizenship, needs and rights and arguments about the fair (re)distribution of wealth and opportunities within society, topics which have long been central concerns for social policy (Macpherson, 2012). As Taylor-Gooby notes, social justice is very much about questions of 'who ought to get what' (2012: 29) and the most appropriate ways to ensure that the available resources within a society are held and distributed in a fair manner.

Before embarking on more philosophical and policy-focused discussions, a brief consideration of two hypothetical cases may be useful to illustrate the kinds of concepts and dilemmas that are routinely to the fore when considering the issue of social justice. In many nations, including the UK, national lottery competitions are an established part of day-to-day life. Opinions vary greatly about whether or not they are appropriate or desirable but most would agree that individuals should be free to choose to purchase a ticket if they wish and take their chance. The holder of the winning jackpot ticket then becomes wealthier than they ever imagined overnight. The vast majority of people would agree that the 'lucky winner' is entitled to their money, even though winning the money has little to do with whether or not they merit the money or are a 'deserving' recipient of such riches. No great effort was involved, merely chance. It would, however, be widely regarded as unjust to take the winnings away from them on the grounds that others have greater need or, indeed, based on moral judgements that other people would be more worthy recipients than the winner. Additionally, prizes in the UK lottery are tax free and there is no widespread campaign to seek to change such arrangements in the near future. Is such a situation justifiable?

At the highest level, professional footballers in England are often paid tens of thousands of pounds, and in certain cases well in excess of one hundred thousand pounds per week. Such a situation raises questions that are pertinent to discussions of social justice. Is it right to pay such vast sums (more money each week than the overwhelming majority of individuals in UK society will earn in a year) to a small number of young men merely because they are particularly talented at playing football? Likewise, why are there repeated and widespread calls to reduce the pay and bonuses of 'fat cat' bankers and executives while the level of remuneration paid to elite footballers largely escapes such criticism?

The football example is also useful to illustrate the ways in which an unequal distribution of rewards between individuals engaged in a collective endeavour may, in certain circumstances, be regarded as socially just. Two footballers play for the same top team. Footballer A is a gifted striker born with a 'natural' talent for the game. He does the bare minimum in training whenever possible but because of his proven talent at scoring goals he earns £100,000 per week. Comparatively, footballer B has more modest talents but all his career has worked hard to develop his skills through training and practising hard, while he only gets £30,000 a week. Is it fair that there is such a discrepancy between the wages of the two footballers? They are both in the same team, and the result is dependent on the collective efforts of all involved, so surely such inequality is unjust? Why reward the lazy one with more money, merely because of his greater talents? If we are interested in socially just outcomes, would it not be fairer to arrange things the other way round so the one who works harder is paid more because their efforts and attitude deserve greater recognition and recompense?

Initially, this chapter offers an introductory discussion of three different, influential philosophical approaches to social justice that attempt to make sense of and resolve such questions in very different ways. First, 'the justice of the market' approach to social justice, associated with the libertarian liberal New Right/thinking as championed by Nozick (1974), is outlined. Second, the egalitarian/social liberal ideas of Rawls (1971), an approach that is often linked to social democratic notions of social justice, is discussed. Third, the key elements of the so-called 'capabilities approach' to social justice developed by Sen (1992, 2010) are considered. The chapter then moves on to briefly outline the differing ways in which the most recent UK governments set out particular notions of social justice which reflect their policy preferences.

A view from the Right: Nozick and the justice of the market

For many on the political right (variously referred to as libertarian liberals, the libertarian Right, the New Right), the very idea of trying to define some form of social justice, beyond the outcomes that emerge from the functioning of a free market system, is seen as both damaging to society and fundamentally flawed. The notion of 'social justice' as a valid or valuable concept is dismissed. In outlining an essentially individualistic approach to justice, Nozick (1974, 1995) argues that a key responsibility for the state is to establish and maintain an economic framework that allows for the free exchange of goods and labour between people. The free market system provides opportunities for individuals to sell their labour, conclude contracts and buy and sell goods without interference. Provided that people do not cheat or violate another person's individual rights (e.g. by stealing), the distribution of goods that then ensues from an efficiently functioning market economy is to be regarded as fair. The criteria for judging whether or not the distribution of such 'holdings' (to use Nozick's preferred term) is just or not depends on how it came about, and individuals are entitled to the property and wealth that they have acquired in market-based transactions provided that what they hold was acquired fairly. Nozick therefore maintains that in a wholly just world, an entitlement theory based on three key 'historical' principles (historical because they are concerned with how people acquired their holdings) can ensure a fair distribution. These are that:

(1) A person who acquires a holding in accordance with the principle of justice in acquisition is entitled to that holding.

(2) A person who acquires a holding in accordance with the principle of justice in transfer from someone else entitled to that holding is entitled to the holding.

(3) No one is entitled to a holding except by (repeated) applications of 1 and 2.

> The complete principle of distributive justice would say simply that a distribution is just if everyone is entitled to the holdings they possess under the distribution. (Nozick, 1995: 138–139)

In outlining his theory of social justice, Nozick is endorsing the thinking of earlier theorists such as Adam Smith (1776) and Hayek (1944). All three hold the view that a freely functioning market economy (which is characterized as consisting of a multitude of diverse, non-coercive exchanges between self-interested individuals) is the most effective and just way of ensuring individual freedoms and collective social prosperity.

Nozick believes that beyond the random inequality generated by the market, it is impossible to reach a consensus about a fair distribution of wealth, and any attempt to reach one merely leads to false definitions. Any state action required to secure 'social justice', for example by taxing the population in order to pay for an extensive set of welfare provisions and benefits, merely interferes with the market, which is the key source of individual liberty. This may lead to a society in which great inequalities are possible, and indeed, likely. For Nozick, such inequalities are relatively unproblematic – after all, why should we expect equal outcomes for everyone in society when individual talents vary and some people are willing to work harder or take greater risks than others? In short, the past circumstances and actions of individuals combine to create 'just' differential entitlements.

Libertarian liberal notions of distributive justice, such as those laid out by Nozick, have important implications for social policy and the kind of welfare state that is possible. Such theorists believe that the correct function of government is to ensure that individual civil and political rights flourish in order for a thriving free market to operate. Beyond this, the state should not intervene and attempt to sustain an extensive welfare state in order to meet the needs of certain disadvantaged groups or to promote a particular ideal of a 'just' society. As an individual, you may choose to be charitable in order to reduce the poverty of others, but state welfare policies funded by tax revenues are considered coercive of individual freedom and an unjust form of the redistribution of holdings. As King (1987) notes, although there is a tentative and reluctant acceptance among libertarian right-wing thinkers that a small minority in society will need to have access to some form of collective welfare provision, these should, wherever possible, be market based. The scope of any government interventions into the field of welfare needs to be strictly limited and controlled if economic wealth and political freedoms are to flourish.

Rawls' principles for distributive justice beyond the market

Rawls (1971, 1995) moves beyond the previously discussed libertarian preoccupation with the redistributive justice of the market and sets out a theory of social justice which attempts to take into account the equality of claims of each individual in respect of basic needs and the means by which those needs will be met. In doing so, Rawls acknowledges the need for the state to recognize and deliver certain social rights. He rejects the idea that the market will distribute goods fairly, pointing to a random distribution of the talents and assets that help to define the end rewards under a market system. State intervention in the lives of individual citizens and the market, to ensure a redistribution of material resources so that all individuals can become free to pursue their own version of the good life, is, therefore, seen by Rawls as a legitimate and necessary step to ensure social justice.

Having established the case for redistributive interventions beyond the market alone, Rawls then asks the question: if the market cannot provide the foundational principles for a fair theory of distributive justice, how might we all be able to agree on the basic rules to underpin a theory of social justice that ensures both liberty (freedom) and a measure of equality? To resolve this dilemma, Rawls turns to what he calls a 'veil of ignorance' (Rawls, 1971: 136). In effect, Rawls invites us to choose the principles with which we would define a just distribution of goods in an imaginary situation prior to knowing our own individual standing – in relation to class, status, conception of good, etc. – in that society for which we were attempting to define the principles. He then goes on to argue that, in a situation where we were ignorant of our place within society, any rational person would arrive at two principles in order to define a just distribution of goods.

(1) Each person is to have an equal right to the most extensive total system of equal basic liberties compatible with a similar liberty for all.

(2) Social and economic inequalities are to be arranged so that they are both:

(a) to the greatest benefit of the least advantaged, consistent with the joint savings principle (the joint savings principle provides for a fair investment for future generations), and

(b) attached to offices and parties open to all under conditions of fair equality of opportunity (Rawls, 1971: 302).

Imagine for a moment that you are stood before a high gate that gives access to a closed society that you are about to become a member of, about which you know nothing nor your standing within it; you could be a princess or a pauper. Rawls is arguing that, because you do not know where you stand in that world, rationally you would accept his principles as they guarantee that everyone will enjoy basic freedoms, equality of opportunity and a society in which material inequalities are only allowed if such arrangements improve the circumstances of the worst off (see Piachuad, 2008; Wolff, 2008; Taylor-Gooby, 2012 for further discussion).

As an egalitarian liberal, Rawls (1971) sees it as right and proper (i.e. socially just) that societies should establish rules that allow for redistribution between individuals beyond the holdings acquired by individuals within market transactions. He clearly believes that state intervention in market mechanisms, organized according to the principles he outlines, is justified in order to promote social justice. This contrasts with the previously discussed libertarian Liberal approach to justice (e.g. Nozick, 1974) 'which legitimates the market order' (Taylor-Gooby, 2012: 29), and views attempts to define and apply social justice beyond justice of the market, such as those outlined by Rawls, as arbitrary nonsense that interferes with basic individual freedoms.

Sen's capabilities approach to social justice

The work of Sen (1992, 2010) proposes a shift from what he refers to as the 'transcendental institutionalism' that characterizes the approach of many thinkers including Nozick and Rawls, to a comparative approach to social justice. In doing so, he is attempting to build on and advance their work which focuses on 'the just institutional arrangements for a society' (Sen, 2010: KL 488) to consider the lives that individuals are actually able (or are not able) to live within a society. Sen argues that it is necessary to outline:

> a theory of justice that is not confined to the choice of institutions, nor to the identification of ideal social arrangements. The need for an accomplishment-based understanding of justice is linked to the argument that justice cannot be indifferent to the lives that people actually live. The importance of human lives, experiences and realizations cannot be supplanted by information about institutions that exist and the rules that operate. Institutions and rules are, of course, very important in influencing what happens, and they are part and parcel of the actual world as well, but the realized actuality goes well beyond the organizational picture, and includes the lives that people manage – or do not manage – to live. (Sen, 2010: KL 684–687)

> The question to ask in this context is whether the analysis of justice must be so confined to getting the basic institutions and general rules right. Should we not also have to examine what emerges in the society, including the kind of lives that people can actually lead, given the institutions and rules, but also other influences, including actual behaviour, that would inescapably affect human lives. (Sen, 2010: KL 552–558)

In his early work, Sen (1992) identified a need for theories of social justice to look beyond the income and resources people already own or may receive in welfare-based redistribution from the state to consider an individual's 'capability to function'. For Sen, a *functioning* is concerned with 'what a person can "do or be": achieve nourishment, health, a decent life span, self respect ... A *capability* is the freedom to achieve a functioning' (Wolff, 2008: 23). This notion of capabilities is central to Sen's approach to theorizing social justice. It is concerned with the extent to which people's differential freedom meets their needs and how each person is able to employ the various goods, services and resources available to them in 'the valuable activities that characterise our humanities' (Dean, 2010: 82). Sen, therefore, expands concerns for social justice beyond debates about the just redistribution of incomes and resources by arguing that a thoroughly just society is one in which all human beings are free to live as they would choose. Societies in which certain people are deprived of the agency or ability (i.e. lack the capability) to lead the kind of life they value cannot, therefore, be seen as socially just.

This approach to social justice is comparative in the sense that the capabilities of different individuals can be established by comparing the capacity of privileged and disadvantaged members of society to lead the life they would choose to lead (Dean, 2010; Macpherson, 2012; Taylor-Gooby, 2012). Although individuals may disagree when defining the kind of life they choose to lead and value, and conceptualizations of the good life will vary in different locations and times, societies in which some people lack the capacity to achieve the life they value are unjust because they are failing to provide such individuals with the substantive freedom to realize their goals as human beings. For example, what it is to be poor in one society may be substantively different from another, but poverty is unjust as it acts as a barrier or limit to what people can achieve or to who they can be.

Based on human rights principles, Sen's approach enables a diversity of needs to be recognized and asks that we consider the institutional and structural barriers that may exist in a society that deny some the ability to be free to lead the kind of lives they value. In many ways, he is calling for us all to be aware of the needs and concerns of others and to make possible a diversity of visions of the good life based on fair and impartial judgements that allow all human beings to flourish (Lister, 2010).

All three of the theorists (Nozick, Rawls, Sen) whose approaches to social justice have been outlined in this section have been criticized for a variety of reasons. The inherent individualism and assumption that a 'free market' will fairly redistribute resources, ideas that are central to Nozick's approach, have been challenged by those who argue that capitalist market systems perpetuate inequality and serve to meet the needs of the wealthy and privileged while simultaneously exploiting the working majority. Rawls' assertion, that under the conditions of the 'veil of ignorance', people would agree to a situation where inequalities would only be allowed if they improved the situation of the worst off in society, has also been criticized. Some people may choose to take a risk and endorse a highly unequal society on the limited chance that they may be one of the lucky privileged few. Under Rawls' rules, a high degree of inequality may also be justified by those skilful enough to argue that, for example, increasing the rewards of those at the top will ultimately improve the position of those at the bottom of society. Likewise, Sen's thinking has also attracted a number of critics, not least because he has declined to provide a list of what might be regarded as the essential common capabilities that are necessary for all human beings to thrive, and also because, arguably, the capabilities approach fails to address the problems inherent within capitalism (see Carpenter, 2009; Dean, 2009, 2010; Lister, 2010 for a fuller discussion).

Interpretations of social justice by recent UK governments

Having outlined three important theoretical contributions to debates about social justice, the next task is to move on to consider how contemporary notions of social justice have been constructed by recent UK governments. First, the Commission on Social Justice's report (CSJ, 1994) which set out New Labour's vision of social justice during their term in government (1997–2010) is considered. Second, an outline of the UK Coalition government's emergent thinking on social justice, as set out in *Social Justice: Transforming Lives* (HM Government, 2012), is then offered.

Established in 1992 by the late John Smith MP, the then leader of the Labour Party, in conjunction with a left-of-centre think tank – the Institute for Public Policy Research – the CSJ was an attempt to outline a new social democratic definition of social justice, one which went beyond the free market approach outlined by thinkers such as Nozick (1974) and favoured by the Thatcherite Conservative governments of 1979–1990. The CSJ (1993) saw their task as setting out a practical common-sense vision that the majority of the population could endorse and support if and when a Labour government returned to power. The Commission acknowledged the value of Rawls' (1971) theorizing but stated in an early discussion of their approach that many of the general public would find it hard to endorse his inherent egalitarianism and his 'veil of ignorance' approach for the redistribution of resources:

> Our task is to find compelling ways of making society more just. We shall be able to do so only if we think in ways that people can recognise and respect about such questions as how best to understand merit and need; how to see the effects of luck in different spheres of life. (CSJ, 1993, reproduced in Franklin, 1998: 40)

Ultimately, the CSJ came up with four key principles as central to their ideal of social justice:

1. The foundation of a free society is the equal worth of all citizens.

2. Everyone as a citizen is entitled, as a right of citizenship, to be able to meet their basic needs.

3. The right to self-respect and personal autonomy demands the widest possible spread of opportunities.

4. Not all inequalities are unjust, but unjust inequalities should be reduced and where possible eliminated. (CSJ, 1994: 17–18)

Throughout its report, the Commission emphasizes the need to ensure equality of opportunity. This is seen as radical and preferential to outmoded policies that try to achieve a measure of equality of outcome via the redistribution of income and wealth. A commitment to tackling unemployment is central to the realization of social justice as is the need to transform the welfare state so that it rewards individuals who actively strive to help themselves rather than providing generous benefits for inactive citizens who may choose to rely on welfare benefits to meet their needs. Some inequalities are also accepted as reasonable and legitimate. For example, the Commission recognized differential rewards for different activities within a market economy as just but discrimination on the grounds of sex or ethnicity would be unjust. Accordingly, for the CSJ social justice is about ensuring fair rewards and eliminating unfair discrimination within the overall context of a functioning market economy. This is not a radical Marxist conception of social justice nor should we expect it to be. The CSJ was clear that it rejected the old 'levellers' approach of the old Left, with its emphasis on a redistribution of income, as much as it rejected the 'deregulators' approach associated with the new Right. Instead it favoured what it called an 'investors' path to national renewal and social justice. In many ways therefore, the CSJ (1994) became a blueprint for many aspects of New Labour's 'Third Way' for social policy which signalled a shift away from the 'old' Labour Party's concern for policy to ensure a measure of equality of outcome towards an emphasis on equality of opportunity and fairness.

An interesting critical response to the CSJ's attempt to operationalize a practical theory of social justice was *The Citizens' Commission on the Future of Welfare* (Beresford and Turner, 1997). The authors point out that the CSJ failed to invite anyone with extensive experience of poverty or life on benefits at the sharp end of the welfare state to sit on its committee; similarly, there was little Trade Union representation. The Citizens' Commission was set up to try to begin to challenge the marginalization of poor people and give voice to welfare service users' concerns and opinions about social justice and the future of the welfare state.

Building on concerns outlined in the 'Broken Britain' thesis popularized by the centre-right think tank the Centre for Social Justice prior to the Coalition attaining power – which explicitly identifies an 'underclass' characterized by dysfunctional families, high levels of worklessness, benefit dependency and addiction (see, for example, Duncan Smith, 2007; Cameron, 2009) – the UK government has also recently outlined its strategy for social justice (HMG, 2012). A Social Justice Cabinet Committee has been established and tasked with:

> aspiring to deliver Social Justice through life change which goes much wider than increases in family income alone. Social justice must be about changing and improving lives, and the different ways this can be achieved. (Duncan Smith, 2012: 2)

The Coalition government's policy for achieving social justice is one of a triumvirate of strategies (the others focus on child poverty and social mobility), aimed at transforming the lives of the most marginalized members of society. In effect, they have redefined social justice as primarily being about breaking the cycle of multiple disadvantage faced by a minority of people in society. Six broad factors symptomatic of the multiple disadvantages that blight the life chances of this minority are identified: workless households; breakdown of the traditional family unit; low levels of educational attainment often accompanied by high levels of school exclusion; drug and alcohol dependency; debt; and involvement in crime and the criminal justice system. They aim to achieve their ends by emphasizing policy interventions that prioritize prevention while promising a 'second chance society' and support for those who face personal difficulties but who are committed to transforming their lives for the better. Five principles are identified as being central to overcoming these problems and promoting social justice:

1. A focus on **prevention and early intervention**

2. Where problems arise, concentrating interventions on **recovery and independence**, not maintenance

3. Promoting work for those who can as the most sustainable route out of poverty, while offering **unconditional support** to those who are severely disabled and cannot work

4. Recognizing that the most effective solutions will often be designed and delivered **at a local level**

5. Ensuring that interventions provide a **fair deal for the taxpayer** (HMG, 2012: 10, bold in original).

Focusing as it does on solving the problems of a disadvantaged minority, this is an essentially individualized and somewhat constrained notion of social justice compared to more expansive approaches which are concerned to ensure a more equitable redistribution of resources and opportunities across wider society. Nonetheless, it marks progress of sorts in relation to earlier Conservative Party policy; social justice is not a term that would have been openly used by previous Conservative administrations under Mrs Thatcher's leadership.

Summary/Conclusions

- Nozick, Rawls and Sen each offer different and competing visions of social justice.
- Nozick and Rawls are each concerned with outlining rules or principles to govern what they consider to be the fairest way of distributing income and opportunities with the minimal interference to individual freedom.
- Sen attempts to build on the ideas of Nozick and Rawls to outline a capabilities approach which moves beyond their debates about the just redistribution of incomes and resources to argue that social justice needs to encompass the issue of the extent to which all human beings are free to actually live the life they would choose and value.
- Legitimate inequalities are considered to be acceptable by many, if not all, proponents of social justice.
- The Labour Party (which subsequently evolved into New Labour under Blair's leadership following John Smith's untimely death) attempted to outline a Third Way vision of social justice that rejected both the competitive market-based approach to justice preferred by the Thatcher governments and the more overtly redistributive social democratic approach to social justice that preceded her administration.
- The extent to which the diminished version of social justice being outlined by the UK Coalition government will deliver substantive positive change for marginalized individuals facing multiple disadvantages, without an accompanying strategy for tackling broader inequalities within wider society, remains to be seen.

Questions

1 Which of the three theories of social justice outlined (i.e. Nozick's, Rawls' and Sen's) do you find most convincing? Outline the reasons for your choice.
2 List and discuss the key elements of Sen's capability approach to social justice.
3 How different is the UK Coalition government's idea of social justice compared to the approach favoured by the preceding New Labour administrations?
4 In outlining your own theory of social justice, would you favour protecting individual freedom or be more concerned to promote some kind of equality?

Recommended reading

Burchardt, T., Craig, G. and Gordon, D. (eds) (2008) *Social Justice and Public Policy: Seeking Fairness in Diverse Societies*. Bristol: The Policy Press. This edited collection is recommended for those who want to access more extensive discussions and debates about social justice.

Lister, R. (2010) *Understanding Theories and Concepts in Social Policy*. Bristol: The Policy Press. See Chapter 8.

Taylor-Gooby, P. (2012) 'Equality, rights and social justice', in P. Alcock, M. May and K. Rowlingson (eds) *The Student's Companion to Social Policy* (3rd edn). Oxford: Blackwell, pp. 26–32.

Relevant websites

Students interested in exploring how centre-left and centre-right leaning think tanks make use of the notion of social justice in respect of contemporary policy issues should look at the websites of the Institute for Public Policy Research – www.ippr.org/ – and the Centre for Social Justice – www. centreforsocialjustice.org.uk/.

For information on the Coalition government's approach to social justice, go to www.dwp.gov.uk/policy/social-justice/.

References

Beresford, P. and Turner, M. (1997) *It's Our Welfare: Report of the Citizens' Commission on the Future of the Welfare State*. London: National Institute for Social Work.

Burchardt, T. and Craig, G. (2008) 'Introduction' in T. Burchardt, G. Craig and D. Gordon (eds) (2008) *Social Justice and Public Policy: Seeking Fairness in Diverse Societies*. Bristol: The Policy Press.

Cameron, D. (2009) 'Putting Britain back on her feet', *Party leader's speech to the Conservative Party conference*, Manchester, 8 October. Available at: www.conservatives.com/News/Speeches/2009/10/David_Cameron_Putting_Britain_back_on_her_feet.aspx

Carpenter, M. (2009) 'The capabilities approach and critical social policy: lessons from the majority world?', *Critical Social Policy*, 29(3): 351–373.

CSJ (1993) *The Justice Gap: Discussion Paper No. 1*. London: The Commission on Social Justice, reproduced in J. Franklin (ed.) (1998) *Social Policy and Social Justice*, Cambridge: Polity Press, p. 3749.

CSJ (1994) *Social Justice: Strategies for National Renewal*. The Report of the Commission on Social Justice. London: Vintage.

Dean, H. (2009) 'Critiquing capabilities: the distractions of a beguiling concept', *Critical Social Policy*, 29(2): 261–278.

Dean, H. (2010) *Understanding Human Need*. Bristol: The Policy Press.

Duncan Smith, I. (2007) *Breakthrough Britain: Ending the Costs of Social Breakdown. Chairman's Overview*. London: The Centre for Social Justice.

Duncan Smith, I. (2012) 'Forward by the Secretary of State', in *Social Justice: Transforming Lives*, Cm 8314. Norwich: The Stationery Office, pp. 1–2.

Hayek, F. (1944) *The Road to Serfdom*. London: Routledge and Kegan Paul.

Her Majesty's Government (HMG) (2012) *Social Justice: Transforming Lives*, Cm 8314. Norwich: The Stationery Office.

Lister, R. (2010) *Understanding Theories and Concepts in Social Policy*. Bristol: The Policy Press.

Macpherson, S. (2012) 'Equalities and human rights', in P. Alcock, M. May and S. Wright (eds) *The Students' Companion to Social Policy* (4th edn). Chichester: Wiley-Blackwell, pp. 33–39.

Nozick, R. (1974) *Anarchy, State and Utopia*. New York: Basic Books.

Nozick, R. (1995) 'Distributive justice', in S. Avineri and A. de Shalit, A. (eds) *Communitarianism and Individualism*. Oxford: Oxford University Press.

Piachaud, D. (2008) 'Social justice and public policy: a social policy perspective', in T. Burchardt, G. Craig and D. Gordon (eds) *Social Justice and Public Policy: Seeking Fairness in Diverse Societies*. Bristol: The Policy Press, pp. 33–42.

Rawls, J. (1971) *A Theory of Justice*. London: Oxford University Press.

Rawls, J. (1995) 'Justice as fairness: political not metaphysical', in S. Avineri and A. de Shalit (eds) *Communitarianism and Individualism*. Oxford: Oxford University Press.

Sen, A. (1992) *Inequality Re-examined*. Oxford: Oxford University Press.

Sen, A. (2010) *The Idea of Justice* (Kindle Location 687). Penguin, UK. Kindle edition.

Smith, A. (1776) *An Enquiry into the Nature and Causes of the Wealth of Nations*. Edinburgh: Adam and Charles Black. (Reprinted 1828.)

Taylor-Gooby, P. (2012) 'Equality, rights and social justice', in P. Alcock, M. May and K. Rowlingson (eds) *The Student's Companion to Social Policy* (3rd edn). Oxford: Blackwell, pp. 26–32.

Wolff, J. (2008) 'Social justice and public policy: a view from political philosophy', in T. Burchardt, G. Craig and D. Gordon (eds) *Social Justice and Public Policy: Seeking Fairness in Diverse Societies*. Bristol: The Policy Press, pp. 17–32.

3

Social Exclusion
Mel Walker

Overview

- Compared to poverty, social exclusion is a relatively new concept for politicians and social scientists.
- Social exclusion is a contested and malleable concept which can be harnessed for different social and political purposes.
- Social exclusion assumed a significant role in New Labour's response to a range of social issues.
- The concept of social exclusion has greater explanatory power than that of poverty and its value becomes evident when exploring the experience of people with mental health problems.
- The use of different types of social exclusion discourses offers diverse understandings of the English riots of August 2011.

Defining social exclusion

Compared with established concepts such as poverty, class or social mobility, social exclusion has a relatively short history. The term itself was coined in the 1970s by French politician Rene Lenoir to describe that section of the French population that had been cut-off or marginalized from mainstream society and had slipped though the 'welfare net' (Pierson, 2010). By the 1980s, the concept had a prominent place in the European political agenda and today, the European

Social Charter guarantees all citizens of the European Union protection against poverty and social exclusion.

There are a multitude of definitions of social exclusion but no single official definition of the concept exists, and apart from the shared notions of marginalization and non-participation, particular definitions often emphasize different aspects of exclusion. The Social Exclusion Unit (1997: 1) described 'social exclusion' as:

> a shorthand label for what can happen when individuals or areas suffer from a combination of linked problems such as unemployment, poor skills, low incomes, poor housing, high crime environments, bad health and family breakdown.

The statement alerts us to the possibility that communities and not simply individuals can experience social exclusion. In addition, different forms of exclusion are cumulative and do not stand in isolation from each other. They are interlinked and mutually reinforcing; for example, poor health can impact on employability or family breakdown may impact on a child's educational performance and poor quality housing can undermine physical and mental health. Levitas et al. (2007) focus on this interconnectedness and the multidimensional nature of social exclusion. There is also an acknowledgement that exclusion is not just an individual experience but has wider implications related to the question of social cohesion.

> Social exclusion is a complex and multi-dimensional process. It involves the denial or lack of resources, rights, goods and services, and the inability to participate in the normal relationships and activities, available to the majority of people in society, whether in economic, social, cultural or political arenas. It affects both the quality of life of individuals and the equity and cohesion of society as a whole. (Levitas et al., 2007: 9)

Walker and Walker (1997: 8), drawing on T.H. Marshall's framework, identify social exclusion as the denial of citizenship. They recognize that exclusion is not simply an absolute state but that it has gradations:

> The dynamic process of being shut out, fully or partially, from any of the social, economic, political and cultural systems which determine the social integration of a person in society. Social exclusion may, therefore, be seen as the denial (or non-realization) of the civil, political and social rights of citizenship.

Social exclusion: a central theme for New Labour

From 1997, the idea of social exclusion played a significant role in New Labour's 'modernization' programme. Although the concept did not appear in its election campaign, it quickly emerged as a key element of its welfare reform project and was central to its social and political goals. Social exclusion would offer understanding into a range of deep-seated social problems and seemingly generate solutions to those problems. Concepts such as poverty and inequality were viewed as the language of the old Labour Party with social exclusion the preferred concept for New Labour. The Social Exclusion Unit with its co-coordinating role would be the vehicle to promote inclusion (Byrne, 2005). In his election victory speech of 2 May 1997, Prime Minister Tony Blair hoped for 'a Britain renewed … where we build a nation united. With common purpose, shared values, with no one shut out or excluded, no one told that they do not matter' (quoted in Marshall et al., 2008: 12). Likewise, Peter Mandelson (1997: 1), one of the architects of New Labour, three months into its first term of office, claimed that:

> the biggest challenge we face; the growing number of our fellow citizens who lack the means, material and otherwise, to participate in economic, social, cultural and political life in Britain today. This is about more than poverty and unemployment. It is about being cut off from what the rest of society regard as normal life. It is called social exclusion and what others call the 'underclass'.

Mandelson (1997) was adamant that the issue was not essentially one of redistribution. For New Labour, social exclusion represented a fundamentally different challenge, one distinct from the Labour Party's old enemy of poverty. Blair in a speech entitled Bringing Britain Together claimed that 'it is a very modern problem, and one that is more harmful to the individual, more damaging to self esteem, more corrosive for society as a whole, more likely to be passed down from generation to generation, than material poverty' (quoted in Jones, 2002: 13).

Throughout its period in power, New Labour's commitment to tackling social exclusion was variable, sometimes high on its agenda, sometimes seemingly having a low priority profile. In 2006, the concept underwent a revival. The Social Exclusion Unit was closed and its work transferred to a smaller Cabinet Office Task Force which would more effectively coordinate the government's attack on social exclusion (2006). Blairite Hilary Armstrong was appointed the first Cabinet Minister for Social Exclusion with a particular brief, in Whitehall speak, to tackle 'high risk' households. These were households in which exclusion seemed to be transmitted from generation to generation. The challenge was teenage mothers and 'dysfunctional families', whose problem was not essentially poverty but 'culture'. It was culture which locked them into a cycle of self-imposed exclusion. Early identification (even prenatal) and intervention was to be the key to breaking the cycle. Health visitors and child centre workers would have a pivotal role. For Armstrong (2006), the problem of social exclusion was residual and an issue for a relatively small number of 'deviant' households, left behind by a rising tide of affluence.

Despite initiatives such as Sure Start and the introduction of minimum wage legislation, there was little evidence of New Labour making significant progress towards a more inclusive society. Arguably, with the formation of a Coalition government in May 2010, social exclusion, along with tackling poverty, has been marginalized in the state's agenda. As Levitas (2012) has argued, the unprecedented spending cuts introduced by the Coalition can only intensify existing divisions and inequalities. In November 2010, the Social Exclusion Task Force was closed and its functions absorbed into the Office for Civil Society, which was charged with promoting the

Big Society and supporting the work of voluntary and community organizations in tackling social issues (Hurd, 2011).

Social exclusion: a more powerful concept than poverty?

How useful is the concept of 'social exclusion' and does it have greater explanatory power than 'poverty'? Similarly, does social exclusion offer us enhanced insights into the experiences of marginalized groups and communities? Many would argue that poverty is a narrower, more limited concept than social exclusion. Poverty focuses essentially on the distribution of material resources, on matters related to income, wealth and consumption. Social exclusion is a broader, more multi-dimensional notion which focuses on economic, political, cultural and social detachment (Walker and Walker, 1997). Room has argued that:

> the notion of poverty is primarily focused upon *distributional* issues: the lack of resources at the disposal of an individual or household. In contrast, notions such as social exclusion focus primarily on *relational* issues: in other words, inadequate social participation, lack of integration and lack of power. (1999: 169)

Poverty and social exclusion often go hand in hand. Poverty is frequently a significant element in social exclusion and can trigger social exclusion. However, the relationship is contingent rather than categorical; someone can be socially excluded without being poor. For example, there is no evidence that the experience of sexual minorities is essentially defined by poverty. Nevertheless, their lives continue to be defined by a social, cultural and political exclusion. They continue to be vulnerable to hate crimes and have their sexuality denied legitimacy. Likewise, not all people with a physical disability may be poor but will experience a degree of social exclusion, most obviously a lack of accessibility which impacts on their mobility and on social relations. Some elderly people may not be poor but in an ageist society they will experience a degree of social exclusion. There is, therefore, no simple or single relationship between poverty and social exclusion. The value of social exclusion lies in the fact that it offers explanatory insights beyond that of poverty.

Social exclusion and mental health

The Social Exclusion Unit report described people with mental health issues as 'one of the most excluded groups in society' (2004: 3). It is clear that the concept of poverty fails to capture and explain their experience, although poverty is often part of their lives.

> For some of us, an episode of mental distress will disrupt our lives so that we are pushed out of the society in which we were fully participating. For others, the early onset of distress will mean social exclusion throughout our adult lives, with no prospect of training for

a job or a future in meaningful employment. Loneliness and loss of self-worth lead us to believe we are useless, and so we live with this sense of hopelessness, or far too often chose to end our lives. Repeatedly when we become ill we lose our homes, we lose our jobs and we lose our sense of identity. (A mental health service user cited in SEU, 2004: 3)

The severity of the social exclusion experienced by people with a mental health problem is well documented – poor physical health, high levels of unemployment, social isolation, vulnerability to stigma and suspicion. The Social Exclusion Unit (2004) recognized that these deprivations are interconnected and may form a 'cycle of deprivation'. Some elements in this cycle are particularly significant. In terms of work, it has been said that there is greater discrimination against those with a record of mental illness than those with a criminal record (Mind, 1999). People with mental health problems have one of the lowest employment rates of all disabled groups. Unemployment can be an important driver of social exclusion (National Mental Health Development Unit, 2010) as it often has significant financial, social and psychological implications. Financially, unemployment means restricted power to consume in a society in which consumption is an important source of status. Exclusion from employment means a loss of, or reduced, social networks and psychologically, our sense of identity, our sense of self, is often defined by our occupation. As Secker (2009: 8) argues:

> In addition to the negative impact on confidence, self-esteem and mental health itself, unemployment can result in restricted income, fewer opportunities to meet other people or develop skills, and loss of a productive identity that, for many people, is central to a sense of belonging within society.

Through such studies, one begins to develop a sense of the intensity of social exclusion experienced by people with mental health problems. The concept of social exclusion alerts us to a dynamic and complex process; the ways in which different forms of deprivation do not exist independent of each other but interact and are mutually reinforcing. Poor mental health can be both a cause and consequence of social exclusion, and mental illness can cause or intensify social exclusion; similarly, social exclusion can deepen mental illness (Royal College of Psychiatrists Social Inclusion Scoping Group, 2009). While the concept of poverty will remain a vital tool for students of social policy, social exclusion expands the realm of our enquiries into issues of marginalization and disadvantage that may not be related to income and wealth.

Competing discourses of social exclusion: Levitas on MUD, RED and SID

As previously noted, there is no simple, single, accepted definition of social exclusion and the concept implies diverse things to different people with politicians of different political persuasions seeking to harness the concept for diverse ends. There are competing discourses of social exclusion which variably stress that the causes of social exclusion may be seen as being located at the level of the individual, the family, or locally, nationally or even globally. Rogers (1995: 53) notes that:

> Ideas are weapons and, like other weapons, their value lies in the use to which they are put. An 'exclusion' discourse is possible from many political perspectives. It can be a call for a radical restructuring of society, but it can also be a way of rendering major social problems innocuous by breaking them down.

It is this malleability which accounts for the popularity and wide currency of the concept. As Morgan et al. (2007: 482) suggest: 'It may be precisely this feature of social exclusion (its vagueness, with its multiple meanings and connotations) that makes it so useful in the world of politics'. How then can we make sense of this elasticity and the multitude of approaches to the concept?

Ruth Levitas (2005) has made an important contribution to our understanding and identifies three discourses of social exclusion. A discourse is a broad view of society or aspects. They are:

> sets of interrelated concepts (which) act together as a matrix through which we understand the social world. As this matrix structures our understanding, so it in turn governs the paths of action which appear to be open to us ... A discourse constitutes ways of acting in the world, as well as a description of it. It both opens up and closes down possibilities for action ourselves. If we can make it stick, it does this for others too. (Levitas, 2005: 3)

Social exclusion discourses are underpinned by different assumptions about the way in which society is structured and the distribution of power within it. They offer opposing accounts of the causes and extent of, and solutions to, social exclusion.

The first discourse identified by Levitas is a moral underclass discourse (MUD). Here, individuals and communities are excluded by their 'deviant' culture, an immorality characterized by lawlessness, welfare dependency and an inability to defer gratification. Often, poor parenting and the notion of the dysfunctional family is implicated. Deviant values and norms are passed from generation to generation. There is often a spatial dimension to this discourse, with an identified 'underclass' concentrated in deprived neighbourhoods, characterized by high levels of crime, poverty, unemployment and poor health, and low levels of educational attainment. This kind of analysis, notably associated with the work of American political scientist Charles Murray (1990), has attracted a powerful sociological and political critique. This is not the place to develop such a critique, although it is worth noting that cultures do not develop in a vacuum but can be understood as a response to a particular set of material conditions.

The MUD discourse was highly visible in the Coalition's and the media's response to the rioting experienced in a number of English cities in August 2011. Any analysis which implicated poverty or unemployment was generally dismissed as an excuse or justification for the disturbances. The rioters were essentially and variously seen as 'recreational', 'mindless', 'evil'. The problem was defined in terms of individual criminality, as a law and order issue. Home Secretary, Theresa May, quoted in *The Independent*, 8 August 2012, spoke of 'sheer criminality' when describing the riots.

Taking a classic functionalist approach, the riots were seen as due to a failure of key social institutions. Schooling was implicated but particular attention was given to the family and the growth of the 'dysfunctional' single-parent family. David Cameron, in a speech at a youth centre in his constituency, stated:

> Of course, we mustn't oversimplify ... this was about behaviour ... people showing indifference to right and wrong ... people with a twisted moral code ... people with a complete absence of self-restraint ... Let me start with families ... Families matter. I don't doubt that many of the rioters out last week have no father at home. Perhaps they come from one of the neighbourhoods where it's standard for children to have a mum and not a dad, where it's normal for young men to grow up without a male role model, looking to the streets for their father figures, filled with rage and anger. (*Conservative Party News*, 15 August 2011)

The application of a MUD-type discourse, such as the one used by the Prime Minister above, is ideologically driven and diverts attention away from social divisions such as 'race' and class, which are rendered insignificant in explaining and understanding the riots.

The second discourse identified by Levitas is the social integrationist discourse (SID). Here, social exclusion is viewed primarily as a consequence of exclusion from the paid labour market. SID was at the forefront of New Labour's attack on social exclusion where access to paid work was seen as the most effective way of overcoming social exclusion and the key to inclusion entry into the labour market. New Labour's preoccupation with SID was evident very early on in its term of office. For example, the Prime Minister was quick to stress that 'The best defence against social exclusion is having a job, and the best way to get a job is to have a good education, with the right training and experience' (Blair, cited in SEU, 1999: 6). A SID approach was also central to New Labour's New Deal and Welfare to Work programmes which were intended to encourage people into work. Under New Labour's conditional welfare state, welfare policy becomes a way of integrating people into the labour market. This strategy involved using a mixture of 'carrots' such as benefit incentives, and 'sticks', i.e. the threat of a reduction or withdrawal of benefits for those who failed to recognize their responsibilities to work (Dwyer, 2008).

There is a moral dimension to SID, as paid work is seen to offer more than simply income. The employed citizen is a 'responsible' citizen and exposure to the discipline of the workplace is viewed as important because it is said to give a structure to unemployed people's lives. This view has been echoed more recently in David Cameron's response to the riots of August 2011:

> Work is at the heart of a responsible society. So getting more of our young people into jobs, or up and running in their own businesses is a critical part of how we will strengthen responsibility in our society ... it's only by getting our young people into work that we can build an ownership society in which everyone feels they have a stake. (*Conservative Party News*, 15 August 2011)

The idea that work is the key to social inclusion has an attractive simplicity but Levitas herself is less than convinced. A social integrationist discourse seems to suggest that those in employment are equally 'included' but this ignores the hierarchical structure of the paid labour market and the fact that much work is poorly paid, insecure and casual and that many people who work hard remain in poverty despite their best efforts. It makes no reference to the status of the working poor – those who remain poor in spite of being in paid work. As Lister points out, 'inclusion in the labour market through marginal, low paid, insecure jobs under poor working conditions does not constitute genuine poverty-free social inclusion' (2004: 79). A SID can easily slip into a MUD, when politicians pathologize the unemployed by implying that they lack or have lost the desire for employment. Also, work within this discourse is very narrowly defined – it is paid work. Levitas argues that many of those excluded *are* employed. They are simply not in *paid* employment, rather they are engaged in informal, familial, 'caring' work. Such work, generally carried out by women, is often invisible, undervalued and unrecognized (Lister, 2004). More broadly, a SID lacks sociological rigour. It closes down analysis prematurely by failing to consider adequately the structural causes of unemployment.

In the third discourse identified by Levitas (2005), the redistributionist discourse (RED), social exclusion is viewed as a consequence of poverty and structural inequality. If SID was a defining idea of New Labour, then RED is associated with Old Labour and socialism. Here, poverty is not seen as a residual problem but as an inevitable product of capitalism. Social exclusion is therefore rooted in de-industrialization, global economic change and a rolling back of the welfare state. The other two discourses, i.e. MUD and SID, are seen as distractions or diversions which shift attention from the broader processes that cause social exclusion. New questions begin to emerge under RED, about power and the way it is exercised. If someone is excluded, then someone or something is doing the excluding. The focus is on the structural causes of that exclusion and not simply the operation of the labour market or the individual 'immorality' of the excluded. As Ruth Lister (2004: 96) points out, 'Behind the noun "exclusion" stands an active verb "exclude"', which implies the question "who or what is excluding?"'.

If the causes of social exclusion are seen as structural, then structural change is required to counter it, for example a programme of redistribution including a reform of the taxation system and an expansion of welfare benefits and public services: 'RED broadens out from its concern with poverty into a critique of inequality, and contrasts exclusion with a version of citizenship which calls for substantial redistribution of power and wealth' (Levitas, 2005: 7). RED offers a radically different perspective on the disturbances of August 2011, refuting any notion of 'pure criminality'. Riot is not simply a meaningless, abnormal phenomenon but is deeply rooted in British history and culture. Rioting can be understood as a form of political action – as a meaningful, if chaotic, protest by those who are socially excluded. Gary Younge (2005: 31) has argued that 'Like a strike, it is often the last and most desperate weapon available to those with least power. Rioting is a class act'. Evidence on the socio-economic background of those appearing before the courts for offences related to the riots suggested that they were disproportionately drawn from the most deprived social groups (Bell et al., 2011).

It is important to recognize Levitas's (2005) discourses as artificial constructs. They are ideal type accounts – grounded in reality but not capturing the diversity and complexity of that reality; nonetheless they have heuristic value and offer a framework to develop competing understandings of social exclusion. Thus it would be misleading to suggest, in a simple way, that MUD is a discourse of the New Right or SID of New Labour or RED of Old Labour; the reality of policy is more complex. For example, when examining the social policies of New Labour, there are traces of the influence of all three discourses – RED in minimal wage legislation and tax credits, SID in New Deal employment programmes, and MUD in Sure Start, its flagship programme aimed at 'breaking the cycle' by working to improve parenting and offer young children an enriched learning experience (Byrne, 2005).

Questioning the concept of social inclusion/exclusion

It is important to go beyond simple binary (i.e. consisting of only two parts) divisions in our understanding of social exclusion. For example, mental illness may be the defining experience of a person or group but it does not exist in isolation from other aspects of difference, and people with mental health issues are not an homogeneous group. The experiences of a person with mental illness may also be defined by their class, gender, ethnicity, etc. As Lewis (2009: 213) notes: 'Social inequalities of gender, class and 'race'/ethnicity, among others, can powerfully frame the specific forms of discrimination and exclusion that often characterise experiences of mental health services and access to rights'.

These divisions can intensify or soften an individual's experience of social exclusion and there is a need to avoid what Doyal (1995) has termed 'crude universalism'. Students of social policy need to be alert to such complexities. Mental illness can be an important driver of social exclusion but when this condition is associated with membership of an ethnic minority community, for example, that exclusion can be sharpened and even more debilitating.

It is also important to recognize that the opposite of 'social exclusion', i.e. 'social inclusion', is itself a problematic notion, and Spandler (2007: 3) has argued that 'the notion of social inclusion is difficult to critique because like other concepts in the government's "modernization" agenda (such as "choice", "user involvement" and "recovery"), it is presented as self-evidently desirable and unquestionable'. Social scientists do, of course, question the 'unquestionable' and the 'inclusion' imperative may be viewed as problematic because it is based on a number of dubious assumptions about equality and social justice; about the distribution of power and resources. It is an essentially uncritical, conservative and value-laden view. It assumes that there is nothing essentially 'wrong' with society. As Spandler (2007: 6), in exploring the issue of mental health, insists: 'One of the problems with the move to "promoting inclusion" is that inclusion in practice implicitly assumes that the quality of mainstream society is not only desirable but unproblematic and legitimate'.

Finally, social exclusion is not simply an issue for the socially excluded. It has a wider significance for issues of equality, citizenship, social stability and cohesion. Alcock (2006: 129) has argued that:

> social exclusion is not just a problem for those who are excluded, it is a problem for social structure and social solidarity generally. If significant numbers of people are excluded … then social order will likely become more polarized and unequal – and ultimately perhaps more unstable for all.

Furthermore, the existence of social exclusion has implications for the criminal justice system, the social security budget, the health services, social care, education and the economy at large. Social exclusion is likely therefore to remain an important issue for students of social policy and the concept itself, an invaluable, if contentious, tool.

Summary/Conclusions

- The concept of social exclusion offers insights and a level of understanding beyond that of 'poverty'.
- The issue of social exclusion, once at the forefront of New Labour's policy agenda, has now been relatively marginalized within the Coalition government.
- There is a lack of consensus around the concept of social exclusion and this ambivalence means that it can be harnessed for very different political purposes.
- A consideration of the multifaceted exclusion faced by people with a mental health problem illustrates the added value that social exclusion may offer in understanding inequality and disadvantage over poverty. Levitas's (2005) three competing discourses of social exclusion (MUD, RED and SID) illustrate the malleability of the concept of social exclusion and offer differing views on the causes of social issues and events, such as the rioting of August 2011 in the UK.

Questions

1 To what extent does the concept of social exclusion help our understanding of the rioting experienced in England in August 2011?
2 Discuss the claim that social exclusion seems to be a contested concept.
3 Explain the claim that the concept of social exclusion has greater explanatory value than that of 'poverty'.
4 Have the ideas developed in this chapter changed or challenged your views on poverty or social inequality?

Recommended reading

Levitas, R. (2005) *The Inclusive Society? Social Exclusion and New Labour* (2nd edn). Basingstoke: Palgrave Macmillan. This text combines a powerful critique of New Labour policies with a valuable discussion of social exclusion as a contested and problematic concept.

Lister, R. (2004) *Poverty*. Cambridge: Polity. Although as its title implies this book is primarily concerned with poverty, the text offers some excellent material on the closely related concept of social exclusion.

Payne, S. (2006) 'Mental health, poverty and social exclusion', in C. Pantazis, D. Gordon and R. Levitas (eds) *Poverty and Social Exclusion in Britain: The Millennium Survey*. Bristol: The Policy Press, pp. 285–311. This chapter explores the sometimes complex relationship between mental health and social exclusion.

Pierson, J. (2010) *Tackling Social Exclusion* (2nd edn). Abingdon: Routledge. Providing a valuable introduction to the concept of social exclusion, the book includes useful chapters on racism and social exclusion; on young people and social exclusion; and on socially excluded families.

Relevant websites

The Equality and Human Rights Commission – www.equalityhumanrights.com – is an invaluable source of material on social exclusion generated by age, disability, gender, 'race', religion, sexual orientation, etc.

Mind – www.mind.org.uk – campaigns for better mental health and the website offers a useful source for students with an interest in mental health and social exclusion.

References

Alcock, P. (2006) *Understanding Poverty* (3rd edn). Basingstoke: Palgrave Macmillan.

Armstrong, H. (2006) 'Social inclusion means tougher policies', *The Guardian*, 5 September, p. 5.

Bell, J., Taylor, M. and Newburn, T. (2011) 'Who were the rioters?', *The Guardian*, 5 December, p. 7.

Byrne, D. (2005) *Social Exclusion* (2nd edn). Maidenhead: Open University.

Cabinet Office (2006) *Reaching Out: An Action Plan on Social Exclusion*. London: HM Government.

Cameron, D. (2011) We are all in this together. Available at: www.conservatives.com/News/Speeches/2011/08/David Cameron_We_are_all_in_this_together.aspx (accessed 06/10/2011).

Doyal, L. (1995) *What Makes Women Sick: Gender and the Political Economy of Health*. London: Macmillan.

Dwyer, P. (2008) 'The conditional welfare state', in M. Powell (ed.) *Modernising the Welfare State: The Blair Legacy*. Bristol: The Policy Press, pp. 199–219.

Hurd, N. (2011) Open Letter, Minister for Civil Society, 11 October. London: Cabinet Office.

Jones, C. (2002) 'Poverty and social exclusion', in M. Davies (ed.) *Blackwell Companion to Social Work*. Oxford: Blackwell Publishing, pp. 7–18.

King, D. S. (1987) *The New Right: Politics, Markets and Citizenship*. Basingstoke: Macmillan.

Levitas, R. (2005) *The Inclusive Society? Social Exclusion and New Labour* (2nd edn). Basingstoke: Palgrave Macmillan.

Levitas, R. (2012) 'The Just's Umbrella: austerity and the Big Society in Coalition policy and beyond', *Critical Social Policy*, 32(3): 320–342.

Levitas, R., Pantazis, C., Fahmy, E., Gordon, D., Lloyd, E. and Patsios, D. (2007) *The Multi-Dimensional Analysis of Social Exclusion*. Bristol: Department of Sociology and School of Social Policy, University of Bristol.

Lewis, L. (2009) 'Introduction: mental health and human rights – social policy and sociological perspectives', *Social Policy and Society*, 8(2): 211–214.

Lister, R. (2004) *Poverty*. Cambridge: Polity.

Mandelson, P. (1997) *Labour's Next Steps: Tackling Social Exclusion*. London: Fabian Society.

Marshall, B., Duffy, B., Thompson, J., Castell, S. and Hall, S. (2008) *Blair's Britain: The Social and Cultural Legacy – Social and Cultural Trends in Britain 1997–2007 and What They Mean for the Future*. London: Ipsos MORI Social Research Institute.

Mind (1999) *Creating Accepting Communities – Report of the Mind Inquiry into Social Exclusion and Mental Health Problems*. London: Mind Publications.

Morgan, C., Burns, T., Fitzpatrick, R., Pinfold, V. and Priebe, F. (2007) 'Social exclusion and mental health: conceptual and methodological review', *British Journal of Psychiatry*, 191: 477–483.

Murray, C. (1990) *The Emerging British Underclass*. London: IEA Health and Welfare Unit.

National Mental Health Development Unit (2010) *Factfile 6: Stigma and Discrimination in Mental Health*. London: NMHDU.

Pierson, J. (2010) *Tackling Social Exclusion* (2nd edn). Abingdon: Routledge.

Rogers, G. (1995) 'What is special about a social exclusion approach?', in G. Rogers, C. Gore and J.B. Figueiredo (eds) *Social Exclusion: Rhetoric, Reality, Responses*. Geneva: International Institute for Labour Studies, United Nations Development Programme, pp. 43–55.

Room, G.J. (1999) 'Social exclusion, solidarity and the challenge of globalization', *International Journal of Social Welfare*, 8: 166–174.

Royal College of Psychiatrists Social Inclusion Scoping Group (2009) *Mental Health and Social Exclusion: Making Psychiatry and Mental Health Services Fit for the 21st Century*. London: Royal College of Psychiatrists.

Secker, J. (2009) 'Mental health, social exclusion and social inclusion', *Mental Health Review Journal*, 14(4): 4–11.

Social Exclusion Unit (1997) *Social Exclusion Unit: Purpose, Work Priorities and Working Methods*. London: HMSO.

Social Exclusion Unit (1999) *Bridging the Gap: New Opportunities for 16–18 Year Olds*. London: HMSO.

Social Exclusion Unit (2004) *Mental Health and Social Exclusion*. London: Office of the Deputy Prime Minister.

Spandler, H. (2007) 'From social exclusion to inclusion? A critique of the inclusion imperative in mental health', *Medical Sociology*, 2(2): 3–16.

Walker, A. and Walker, C. (eds) (1997) *Britain Divided: The Growth of Social Exclusion in the 1980s and 1990s*. London: Child Poverty Action Group.

Younge, G. (2005) 'Riots are a class act – and often they're the only alternative', *The Guardian*, 14 November, p. 31.

4

Difference and Diversity

Mel Walker

Overview

- From the 1970s, a new, more critical and sociologically informed strand of UK social policy emerged in reaction to the discipline established in the decades following the Second World War.
- The idea of social construction is an invaluable tool for social scientists.
- Social constructions of class, gender, race, disability, age and sexuality have informed the development of social policy and welfare practices.
- 'Race' remains an important issue for students of social policy.
- Constructions of 'race' have shaped the development of immigration policy and impacted on the experience of minority ethnic groups as providers and consumers of welfare.
- Social constructions are always unstable and contested and subject to challenge and transformation.

Introduction

This chapter starts from the premise that social policy is not necessarily or inevitably concerned with the promotion of social and economic well-being. It will suggest that in the 1970s the study of social policy underwent significant changes which resulted in the emergence of a more radical and more sociologically informed discipline. The chapter will explore the value of 'social construction' in understanding social policies and welfare practices. It will argue that social policies may differentiate and discriminate and may create, maintain or intensify social divisions and inequalities. Given the limitations of space, the particular focus here will be on 'race' and the ways in which racism has defined the experience of ethnic minority groups as migrants and as providers and consumers of health care.

The study of social policy transformed

In Britain, social policy as an academic discipline has a relatively short history. From its origins in the early part of the 20th century, the study of social policy was firmly located within a social democratic (see Chapter 2) Fabianist discourse of consensus and evolutionary change. It was reformist, seeking change within the system rather than a change of systems. The discipline was supportive of state intervention and of redistributive social policies, seeking a balance between freedom and equality. It maintained that the making of social policies should be informed by investigation and research as this would generate practical solutions to 'social problems'. However, by the 1970s, this approach was under challenge and beginning to break down and, arguably, the discipline of social policy was seen to be in crisis. It was seen by many as too narrow and leaving too many questions relating to difference and diversity unanswered or unasked (Williams, 1989). Critics argued that too often the established tradition failed to recognize the deeply political nature of social policy as an activity. It was seen to be overly descriptive, lacking a strong theoretical underpinning and marginalizing issues such as 'race', gender and sexuality with the potential to create and reinforce social and economic divisions and inequalities. Under attack, initially, from neo-Marxists and feminists and subsequently members of the anti-racism, disability and gay and lesbian movements, a new approach to the study of social policy began to emerge. This was to be a different kind of discipline, a more radical discipline, which recognized that the making of social policy is a deeply political activity and routinely an outcome of conflict rather than consensus. It was an approach that stressed that the making of social policy is not always a top-down process but often the outcome of pressure and struggle from below, from marginalized groups who have resisted dominant and debilitating constructions of themselves.

Proponents of this new critical social policy argued that the history of the welfare state could not be understood as a gradual and inevitable march of progress. They were much more ambivalent about its role and about the impact of State welfare interventions which were recognized as being potentially oppressive and not always benign. The provision of social security, for example, could be understood as a way of 'policing' the unemployed; as reflecting and reproducing women's economic dependence on men or as 'disabling' people with impairments. Crucially, an acknowledgement of wider social structures, such as capitalism or patriarchy, was now to be essential to the study of social policy. There was a recognition that social policy does not emerge in a vacuum and that its development and impact are often defined by the dominant ideas of the day – ideas that might be racist, sexist, disablist or heterosexist (Williams, 1989).

Social constructions and social policy

Within this more critical approach, there was a recognition that the development of social policy may be informed by a number of problematic social constructions. These constructions do not stand in isolation. They do not arise spontaneously nor are they sustained 'naturally'. They are linked to wider ideologies and as such can be seen to support different and competing interests. The notion of a social construction is a valuable tool for students of social policy but not always one that is easy to grasp. Social constructs are not *out there* waiting to be discovered, and they do not have an independent existence. For example, poverty as a concept, as something we can identify and measure, *is* a social construction. Social scientists, commentators and wider society create this category and determine what constitutes 'poverty'. It is an historically and culturally specific concept. If it is something which society creates, then its meaning and experience will vary from society to society and change over time. Our notion of poverty in the industrialized nations will be distinct from that of poorer nations such as Sudan or Bangladesh. It will not correspond to that of medieval England. As Nick Crossley maintains:

> To say, 'it's a social construct' ... means that we believe the phenomenon in question to be the product of a particular society or societies like it, rather than being something which is natural or inevitably hard-wired into our biological constitution and invariant. (2005: 296–7)

'Old age', for example, can be understood not simply as a biological category but also as a social construct. Growing older does, of course, involve physical change but it is the significance of these changes, the way they are understood, that is the concern of social scientists. In Britain we tend to construct old age in negative terms – as a time of deficiency, decline and burden (Timonen, 2008). This social construction is neither natural nor inevitable. Most importantly, it can have implications for social policy and welfare practices. Clarke and Saraga (1998: 2) have argued that:

> The construction of difference is a necessary starting-point for the study of social policy because how differences are constructed – the way they are made to mean something – is the basis from which decisions about social life flow. How we define or interpret a pattern of difference has profound consequences for how it is to be acted upon.

Ageist constructions can 'seep into' social policies and welfare practices to shape priorities and agendas. One can now begin to make sense of the claim that hospital services for older people are less well developed; of age-based rationing in health care; or that research into illnesses associated with ageing is less well funded (Bowling, 2007). The notion of ageist constructions can help us unpack inadequacies in the regulation and inspection of residential care for the elderly compared to that of younger adults (Commission for Social Care Inspection, 2009), or the relatively late arrival in Britain of laws against age discrimination.

Similarly, constructions of gender have had a powerful influence on the development of social policy. Historically, women were defined as 'the other', as dependent on men and as mentally and emotionally frail (Lister, 2003). Prior to 1882, on marriage, a woman's property by law was transferred to her husband (Gittens, 1993). Only in 1928 did British women achieve the right to vote on the same basis as men (Rowbotham, 1999). Before 1991, in England, a man could not be charged with the rape of his wife (Charles, 2000). These are policies which were underpinned by patriarchal notions about gender, gender roles and divisions. It is not only women who are the subject of distorted and debilitating gendered social constructions. Even today, traditional constructions of 'fatherhood' inform policies and practices on paternity leave and access to children following divorce – often to the detriment of men (Harris, 2007).

Feminists have maintained that health care policy and practices do not develop in a vacuum but are inevitably influenced by the powerful ideas of the day. Anne Witz (1992) has argued that medicine is an essentially 'male' institution. Until the 1876 Medical Act, women were refused entry into the medical profession and were excluded from medical school. They were deemed suitable to nurse but considered to be intellectually and physically incapable of practising medicine. Even today, the National Health Service (NHS) has a gender-stratified workforce. Although anti-discriminatory policies and equal opportunity policies are in place, men still dominate the heights of the medical profession. Women *are* represented in the ranks of general practitioners (GPs) but remain under-represented in the elite professional group of surgeons. The careers of women doctors continue to be hindered by 'the glass ceiling' and a hostile male culture (Connolly and Holdcroft, 2009).

Historically, medicine has reflected and reinforced the idea of men having the right to exercise control over women and their bodies. Surgeon Peter McEwan (1934: 575) writing in the *British Medical Journal*, insisted that 'Hysterectomy must not be resorted to without the intelligent consent of the patient, and, *if married, of her husband* (emphasis added) and the cooperation of her doctor'. Similarly, in the same publication, gynaecologist Michael Muldoon (1972: 84) confirmed the legality of female sterilization as a form of family planning given the informed consent of both the wife *and her husband*. Up to the 1960s, in Britain (and in many parts of the world today) a husband's consent was required before many hospitals would perform a hysterectomy (surgical removal of the womb). These policies and practices may seem extraordinary to us today but they mirrored and reinforced the dominant patriarchal ideas of the time. Similarly, the way we construct 'disability' will impact on educational and welfare policies related to impairment and define the experience of disabled people. Such constructions may not be grounded in reality and may be 'erroneous', however, as Hughes (1998: 80) points out:

> It is a well-established sociological adage that if people define situations as real, then they are real in their consequences. Thus if disability is defined and seen as a tragedy and/or a 'natural' and determining condition (as seems to have been the dominant categorization of disability in the UK in the twentieth century), then disabled people will be treated and responded to as if they are victims of a tragic accident or circumstance.

It was the rise of the social model of disability, championed by the disabled people's movement, which challenged such individualist accounts (Oliver, 2009).

It is important to recognize that social constructions can inform social policy, however the relationship between social constructions and social policy is more complex. It can be a two-way process, i.e. social constructions inform social policy *but also* social policy can shape dominant social constructions. For example, policies which educationally segregate children with a disability, reinforce a sense of 'difference'; not least in that able-bodied children are denied an opportunity to question the social construction of disability that they themselves have absorbed. Likewise, exclusionary immigration policies, while a response to a particular and negative construction of 'immigrants', implicitly serve to reinforce that construction. The concept of social construction is a very useful tool for social scientists and is an invaluable way of thinking about the development and implementation of social policy. However, social constructions are sometimes difficult to recognize *as social constructions* as they often appear to reflect 'common sense' statements – such as 'This is what women are like', 'This is what fathers should be', 'This is why black people are different from white people'. Initially, many social constructions appear to have a 'natural' quality that seem to reflect the social worlds in which we live. Where then does that leave us as social scientists, and what might it mean in terms of how we study and research social policy?

Social science demands a critical scepticism, that we think again about often taken-for-granted categories such as disability, 'race', gender, old age and sexuality. It is vital that we recognize that these categories are not 'natural' phenomena but social constructions. A critical approach to social policy requires us to put aside 'common sense', our preconceptions and prejudices and calls upon us to 'problematize' the taken for granted. This is an idea which is at the very heart of social science. Zigmund Bauman has argued that for social science to be an effective 'lens' through which to properly understand society, it must 'de-familiarize the familiar' (1990: 15). Similarly, Clarke and Cochrane insist that:

> in order to study society we must distance ourselves from what we already know. We need to become 'strangers' in a world that is familiar. The defining characteristic of a 'stranger' is that she or he does not know those things which we take for granted. Strangers require the 'obvious' to be explained to them. In doing social science, then, there is a need to stand back from what we already know or believe and be distanced from, or sceptical about, those things which 'everybody knows'. (1998: 10)

This requires a conscious effort, an 'openness' and a self-questioning by the student of social policy. Perhaps some of the most important questions we ask are questions we ask of ourselves – something that is not always a comfortable experience!

Finally, social constructions have a history, are fluid, are always subject to challenge, change and transformation, and are never entirely 'stable' but often overtly political and routinely contested. For example, people with impairments have sought to develop a social model of disability (Borsay, 2005) and challenge constructions of themselves as dependent, pitiable victims, as having 'problems' that lie ultimately within their own bodies. Similarly, gay and lesbian communities have challenged the medicalization and criminalization of homosexuality. Concannon (2008: 326) has argued that 'The *history* (emphasis added) of homosexuality is one in which lesbians, gay men, bisexuals and transgendered individuals … are viewed as abnormal and inferior; posing a threat to the stability of social order, family norms and political structures'. This is a view or construction reinforced by religion, medicine and the media, but one that perhaps has been challenged in certain contemporary societies that value and accept individual rights. It has also been undermined by the politicalization of sexuality which has contested the construction of homosexuality as 'sinful', 'criminal' or 'diseased'. The gay and lesbian movement, in the broadest sense, has been successful in re-constructing homosexuality as an authentic expression of sexuality. We continue to live in a society marked by heterosexism and homophobia, but in 2010 gay activist Peter Tatchell (2010: 30) was able to claim that in the UK/many western societies almost all homophobic laws had been repealed and sexual minorities have a visibility and acceptance unimagined in the 1960s.

Social construction, racism and social policy: understanding immigration policy

Why should the issue of 'race' be a concern to contemporary students of social policy? One view is that 'race' is arguably the most significant and contentious issue facing Britain and much of the world today (Winant, 2009), and this section argues that racism and racist constructions have been and remain an aspect of UK immigration policy.

Although the history of the human race is a history of migration, the post-Second World War period has been described as 'the age of migration' (Castles and Millar, 2009) as globally we are experiencing migration of an unprecedented scale and scope. According to Castles and Miller (2009: 7), 'international migration is part of a transnational revolution that is reshaping societies and politics around the globe'. More so than at any other time in history, people are crossing national boundaries to work, settle and rebuild their lives. In so doing, they transform the social and political landscape of the receiving and sending countries. In Britain, this transformation has social, economic and political implications and raises many questions regarding citizenship, integration and social cohesion (Castles and Millar, 2009). Issues such as the welfare of asylum seekers and refugees, the future of multiculturalism, the validity of faith schools, and how best to tackle racial discrimination have become central to the study of social policy.

Although as previously noted, we are said to live in 'the age of migration', the black and minority ethnic presence in Britain is not new but has a long and often hidden history. A royal proclamation issued by Elizabeth I in 1601, stated that she was:

> highly discontented to understand the great numbers of negars and Blackamoores which (as she is informed) are crept into this realm … who are fostered and relieved (i.e. fed) here to the great annoyance of her own liege people, that want the relief (i.e. food), which those people consume, as also for that the most of them are infidels, having no understanding of Christ or his Gospels [and] … that the said people should be with all speed avoided (i.e. banished) and discharged out of this Her Majesty's dominions. (Fryer, 1984: 12)

An understanding of history is a valuable resource for students of social policy but what can we make of this statement? What does it tell us? First, it reminds us that the black presence in Britain is not a recent occurrence. Second, that in Britain the 'problem of race' is not new. Third, the social construction of black people and migrants from minority ethnic communities as an economic and cultural 'problem' is deeply embedded in British history. This construction echoes down the centuries and is evident, not least, in current debates and perceptions of immigration. It is a construction which gives little acknowledgement of the economic contribution that 'immigrants' have made (Home Office, 2007).

This is not the place to elaborate on a complete history of UK immigration, however evidence suggests that much immigration legislation has been underpinned, explicitly or implicitly, by deeply racist ideas in which 'immigrants' are constructed as a problematic threat (Sales, 2007). Again, an historical perspective is informative. The 1905 Aliens Act was the first 'modern' immigration legislation, allowing 'foreigners' to be barred at the point of entry. The measure was aimed not at Jamaicans or Pakistanis but at East European Jews fleeing anti-Semitism and poverty. The Act was preceded by a series of moral panics – a fear of being 'swamped', of a threat to the British way of life and of increased competition for jobs and housing (Kershen, 2005). This is reminiscent of the example above from 1601 and much media coverage of 'immigration' today. History does not repeat itself precisely but 'problems' reoccur as do responses to those problems. An understanding of history can give a clearer perspective of the 'here and now' and illuminate the ways in which the 'problem' is reconstructed in different times and settings.

The 1962 Commonwealth Immigration Act for the first time controlled the entry of peoples from the Commonwealth into Britain (Solomos, 2003). This was the first of a series of prescriptive and exclusionary acts removing rights to British citizenship – acts which restricted the entry of black people while keeping the door open for white people. William Deedes, a minister without portfolio, was later to reveal the racist and discriminatory nature of the legislation:

> The Bill's real purpose was to restrict the influx of coloured immigrants. We were reluctant to say as much openly. So the restrictions were applied to coloured and white citizens in all Commonwealth countries – though everyone recognised that immigration from Canada, Australia and New Zealand formed no part of the problem. (cited in Solomos, 2003: 56)

This and subsequent exclusionary legislation was driven by a growing concern about uncontrolled immigration, a moral panic engineered by the tabloid press and politicians such as Enoch Powell in his 1968 'rivers of blood' speech (Solomos, 2003). They did not entirely speak to deaf ears but played upon real (if misdirected) grievances of the white working class about jobs, housing and public services. The hostility and suspicion were already there, fuelled by deeply entrenched stereotypes about black people rooted in slavery, the Empire and colonialism.

Ten years after Powell's intervention, Margaret Thatcher famously expressed concern that Britain was in danger of being 'swamped by people of a different culture' (cited in Solomos, 1993: 187). The use of the term 'swamped' is significant. To be swamped is not a desirable experience; one is swamped by something distasteful and unwelcome. A decade later, Ruth Lister (1998: 54) was to write: 'In Britain, the boundaries of exclusion have been tightened steadily in relation both to rights of entry and residence and to social citizenship rights. A succession of immigration and nationality laws have undermined the rights of black Commonwealth citizens and virtually closed off their lawful entry to Britain'.

The question of immigration remains at the top of the political agenda. The issue today is not primarily about migrants from India or Pakistan or Jamaica but from countries such as Somalia, Iraq and Ethiopia – asylum seekers and refugees – people forced to leave their homeland through war or the fear of persecution. In addition, since the expansion of the EU in 2004, the UK has also seen significant labour migration from Central and Eastern Europe (especially Poland).

As students of social policy, it is important to avoid simplistic and deterministic models for the development of social policy. There is no simple relationship between 'construction' and 'policy'. In terms of immigration policies, the negative 'construction' of immigrants represents only one understanding of the drivers of international migration. There are other forces at work, sometimes contradictory and pulling in the opposite direction – such as labour shortages in receiving countries, nation states' legal obligations under the United Nations Convention relating to the Status of Refugees, and rules governing the free movement of labour within the European Union. However, evidence suggests that a particular and negative construction of 'immigrants' has been a significant force in shaping British immigration and citizenship policies.

Racism, health and health care

Since its establishment in 1948, the National Health Service (NHS) has attracted particular support and is popularly seen as an institution that was governed by a caring and benevolent ethos (Torkington, 1991). For a long time, the NHS's position on 'race' was one of denial, however such a claim misrepresents the history of the service and the experience of black and minority ethnic people as providers and consumers of health care. As the 'new' critical discipline of social policy was to argue, the NHS does not exist in isolation; its policies and practices almost invariably reflect the society it serves. Today, the idea that the NHS is immune from racism no longer seems viable. The concept of racism is, of course, highly contentious and contested and usually defined in terms of a negative belief which justifies exclusionary and discriminatory practices. Thus, Miles (1982: 78–79) described racism as:

> an ideology which ascribes negatively evaluated characteristics in a deterministic manner … to a group which is additionally identified as being in some way biologically … distinct … The possession of these supposed characteristics may be used to justify the denial of the group equal access to material and other resources and/or political rights.

For many years, this formulation was orthodoxy. However, following the Macpherson Report (1999) into the police investigation of the murder of black teenager Stephen Lawrence, the concept of institutional racism began to increasingly inform debate, policy and practice in the UK. The Report defined institutional racism as:

> the collective failure of an organisation to provide an appropriate and professional service to people because of their colour, culture or ethnic origin. It can be seen or detected in processes, attitudes and behaviour which amount to discrimination through unwitting prejudice, ignorance, thoughtlessness and racist stereotyping which disadvantage minority ethnic people. (Macpherson Report, 1999: 321)

Here, racism is not viewed simply as individual prejudice but is inherent in the procedures and practices of an organization. The discrimination is not necessarily by intent – the emphasis is on outcome rather than intention, and it can occur through the absence of action. It is apparent, for example, in the history of medical and institutional neglect in Britain of sickle cell disease, a condition specific to people of West African descent (Dyson, 2005).

More than two decades ago, in her groundbreaking study, *Black Health: A Political Issue*, Torkington (1991) argued that the National Health Service does not operate within a vacuum and that health policies and practices always develop within a particular social and political context – one in which social class is significant, and in which racism and sexism continue as powerful ideas. Almost inevitably, these ideas are reflected and reproduced within the NHS – although not always necessarily in the same way or with the same intensity.

Individual racism and institutional racism are not mutually exclusive but mutually reinforcing. They have generated a racially stratified workforce in the social and health care services. Despite the NHS being the biggest employer of black people in Britain, Trevor Phillips, when Chair of the Commission for Racial Equality, famously pointed to the 'snowy peaks of the NHS – all white at the top' (quoted in Duffin and Parish, 2005: 22). The experience of Asian doctors has attracted particular attention. Over-represented numerically in the medical profession, needing to send more applications to secure a post and concentrated in the less prestigious specialisms such as psychiatry and the care of older people, Aneez Esmail (2007: 833) has argued that:

> while (Asian doctors) possessed the skills relevant to the British economy and the NHS, their status as pariahs determined their lived experience. Essentially, they occupy the lower-grade positions in the most unpopular specialities with a high propensity for long hours and shift work, from which promotion is restricted and pay and conditions are similarly affected.

A racially stratified labour force is not confined to the medical profession. The racism experienced by Asian doctors was paralleled by that of black Caribbean women actively recruited to nursing in the 1950s and 1960s to work in a fledgling NHS. They were directed into the lower-status State Enrolled rather than State Registered qualification (Baxter, 1988). They too were denied promotion and confined to the Cinderella services (Ramdin, 1999: 224). A more recent study commissioned by the Royal College of Nursing found that the work experience of black nurses and their relationships with patients, colleagues and management continue to be significantly defined by racism (Dhaliwa and McKay, 2009).

Individual and institutional racism has also shaped the way that the health problems of minority ethnic groups are understood, including the high rates of infant mortality within the British Pakistani community, the apparent 'epidemic' of schizophrenia among British Afro-Caribbeans, and the rediscovery of rickets in the British Asian community (Ahmad and Bradby, 2007). Much of the debate and some of the policies were premised on a particular and stereo-typical account of Asian culture which views diet, dress, cousin marriage, self-segregation and poor command of English as being at the root of minority ethnic communities' health problems. Here, 'ethnic culture' is seen as the obstacle to better health and cultural assimilation (i.e. that minority ethnic groups should take on the culture of the 'host population'), an appropriate answer to any issues. Darr (2005: 35) has argued:

> Locating the cause and solution to minority health issues within the cultural practices of those communities is well-documented. The ongoing approach serves to shift responsibility from policy-makers and service providers to individuals and communities; it continues to alienate minorities and hampers the process of devising responsive health services.

In fact, 'culture' has often been recruited to explain social inequalities. The poor educational performance of Afro Caribbean boys has been 'explained' in cultural terms and, similarly, the shorter life expectancy of working-class people as a whole. Social scientists tend to be cautious of explanations for social patterns which are couched exclusively in terms of 'culture'. Such accounts of culture are inclined to be static, simplistic and frequently neglect the complexity and dynamic and empowering qualities of cultures. By narrowly focusing on particular patterns of behaviour, they are diversionary accounts that shift attention from the role played by wider processes and structures. There is a danger of an overly static analysis, which emphasizes continuity to the neglect of change. Racism has shaped health policy and health care practices but this is increasingly counter-balanced by anti-racist and multicultural ideas – reflecting wider social and political changes in Britain. Health authorities are now required to introduce equal opportunity policies in employment. Asian doctors are increasingly represented in the hierarchy of the medical profession. There is a questioning of 'colour-blind' policies and a recognition of the need to provide a service which is responsive to a diverse and multicultural society. Nevertheless, social constructions of 'race', gender and other social divisions continue to inform health care policy and practice. This phenomenon remains a feature of social policy and welfare practices generally. The constructions are often less crude and less transparent than in the past and are more difficult to detect. The challenge for social scientists is to identify and expose the assumptions which underpin these constructions. The task is to 'deconstruct' the constructions, to understand how they arise and how they shape the development of policy and practice.

Summary/Conclusions

- A new more critical strand of social policy emerged in the UK from the 1970s onwards. The idea of social construction can be an indispensible tool in understanding social policy and its history.
- Social policies do not develop in a vacuum but are strongly influenced by social constructions of class, gender, 'race', sexuality, age and disability.
- Social constructions are 'fluid' and routinely contested.
- The social construction of 'race' and how it continues to structure the lives of black and minority ethnic communities remains a major issue for contemporary social policy.
- Racism has informed the development of immigration policy and has shaped the experience of minority ethnic groups as providers and recipients of state welfare.

Questions

1 Why has anti-discriminatory legislation had only a limited impact on the labour market position of minority ethnic groups?
2 What do you understand by the phrase 'the social construction of homosexuality'?
3 Giving examples, what do you understand by the claim that social constructions are routinely contested?
4 Have the ideas developed in this chapter changed or challenged your understanding of the development of social policy?

Recommended reading

Law, I. (2010) *Racism and Ethnicity: Global Debates, Dilemma, Directions*. Harlow: Pearson Educational. This is a wide-ranging introduction to concepts such as 'race' and 'ethnicity', and the text explores the experience and impact of racism globally.

Payne, G. (ed.) (2006) *Social Divisions* (2nd edn). Basingstoke: Palgrave Macmillan. This a useful and accessible introduction to the study of social divisions such as gender, sexuality, disability and age.

Saraga, E. (ed.) (1998) *Embodying the Social: Constructions of Difference*. London: Routledge. This is a valuable text which explores and develops many of the ideas introduced within this chapter.

Relevant website

The Equality and Human Rights Commission – www.equalityhumanrights.com – has a statutory responsibility to promote and monitor human rights and protect, enforce and promote equality on the grounds of 'race', gender, disability, age, sexuality, etc.

References

Ahmad, W.I.U. and Bradby, H. (2007) 'Locating ethnicity and health: exploring concepts and contexts', *Sociology of Health and Illness*, 29(6): 795–810.

Bauman, Z. (1990) *Thinking Sociologically*. Oxford: Basil Blackwell.

Baxter, C. (1988) *The Black Nurse: An Endangered Species – A case study for equal opportunities in nursing*. Cambridge: National Extension College.

Borsay, A. (2005) *Disability and Social Policy in Britain since 1750*. Basingstoke: Palgrave Macmillan.

Bowling, A. (2007) 'Honour your mother and father: ageism in medicine', *British Journal of General Practice*, 57(538): 347–348.

Castles, S. and Miller, M.J. (2009) *The Age of Migration: International Population Movements in the Modern World* (4th edn). Basingstoke: Palgrave Macmillan.

Charles, N. (2000) *Feminism, the State and Social Policy*. Basingstoke: Palgrave Macmillan.

Clarke, J. and Cochrane, A. (1998) 'The social construction of social problems', in E. Saraga (ed.) *Embodying the Social: Constructions of Difference*. London: Routledge, pp. 3–38.

Clarke, J. and Saraga, E. (1998) 'Introduction', in E. Saraga (ed.) *Embodying the Social: Constructions of Difference*. London: Routledge, pp. 1–2.

Commission for Social Care Inspection (2009) *The State of Social Care in England 2007/08*. London: CSCI.

Concannon, L. (2008) 'Citizenship, sexual identity and social exclusion', *International Journal of Sociology and Social Policy*, 28 (9/10): 326–39.

Connolly, S. and Holdcroft, A. (2009) *The Pay Gap for Women in Medicine and Academic Medicine*. London: British Medical Association.

Crossley, N. (2005) *Key Concepts in Critical Social Theory*. London: Sage.

Darr, A. (2005) 'Response – Cousin marriage is a social choice: it needn't be a problem', *The Guardian*, 2 December, p. 35.

Dhaliwa, S. and McKay, S. (2009) *The Work–Life Experience of Black Nurses in the UK*. London: Royal College of Nursing.

Duffin, C. and Parish, S. (2005) 'Freedom from racism', *Nursing Standard*, 20(4): 22–23.

Dyson, S. (2005) *Ethnicity and Screening for Sickle Cell/Thalassaemia*. Edinburgh: Elsevier.

Esmail, A. (2007) 'Asian doctors in the NHS: service and betrayal', *British Journal of General Practice*, 57(543): 827–834.

Fryer, P. (1984) *Staying Power: The History of Black People in Britain*. London: Pluto Press.

Gittens, D. (1993) *The Family in Question: Changing Households and Familiar Ideologies* (2nd edn). Basingstoke: Macmillan.

Harris, M. (2007) *Family Court Hell*. Brighton: Pen Press.

Home Office (2007) *The Economic and Fiscal Impact of Immigration: A Cross-Departmental Submission to the House of Lords Select Committee on Economic Affairs*. Norwich: Stationery Office.

Hughes, G. (1998) 'A suitable case for treatment? Constructions of disability', in E. Saraga (ed.) *Embodying the Social: Constructions of Difference*. London: Routledge, pp. 43–90.

Kershen, A. (2005) 'The 1905 Aliens Act', *History Today*, 55(3): 13–19.

Lister, R. (1998) 'New conceptions of citizenship', in N. Elllison and C. Pierson (eds*) Developments in British Social Policy*. Basingstoke: Macmillan, pp. 46–60.

Lister, R. (2003) *Citizenship: Feminist Perspectives* (2nd edn). Basingstoke: Palgrave Macmillan.

Macpherson, W. (1999) *The Stephen Lawrence Inquiry*. London: The Stationery Office.

McEwan, P. (1934) 'A study of hysterectomy based on the after-histories of 112 cases', *British Medical Journal*, 1(3821): 574–577.

Miles, R. (1982) *Racism and Migrant Labour*. London: Routledge and Kegan Paul.

Muldoon, M.J. (1972) 'Gynaecological illness after sterilization', *British Medical Journal*, 1(5792): 84–85.

Oliver, M. (2009) *Understanding Disability: From Theory to Practice* (2nd edn). Basingstoke: Palgrave Macmillan.

Ramdin, R. (1999) *Reimaging Britain: 500 Years of Black and Asian History*. London: Pluto Press.

Rose, H. (1981) 'Rereading Titmuss: the sexual division of welfare', *Journal of Social Policy*, 10(4): 477–501.

Rowbotham, S. (1999) *A Century of Women: The History of Women in Britain and the United States*. London: Penguin.

Sales, R. (2007) *Understanding Immigration and Refugee Policy: Contradictions and Continuities*. Bristol: Policy Press.

Saraga, E. (ed.) (1998) *Embodying the Social: Constructions of Difference*. London: Routledge.

Solomos, J. (1993) *Race and Racism in Britain* (2nd edn). Basingstoke: Macmillan.

Solomos, J. (2003) *Race and Racism in Britain* (3rd edn). Basingstoke: Palgrave Macmillan.

Tatchell, P. (2010) 'Beyond gay and straight', *The Guardian*, 3 July, p. 30.

Timonen, V. (2008) *Ageing Societies: A Comparative Introduction*. Maidenhead: Open University.

Torkington, N.P.K. (1991) *Black Health: A Political Issue*. London: Catholic Association for Racial Justice and Liverpool Institute of Higher Education.

Williams, F. (1989) *Social Policy: A Critical Introduction – Issues of Race, Gender and Class*. Cambridge: Polity.

Winant, H. (2009) *Race and Racism: Towards a Global Future*, in L. Back and J. Solomos (eds) *Theories of Race and Racism: A Reader*. Abingdon: Routledge, pp. 678–692.

Witz, A. (1992) *Professions and Patriarchy*. London: Routledge.

5

Health and Well-being

Margaret Coffey and Lindsey Dugdill

Overview

- Concepts of health and well-being differ, which has implications for the promotion of health and well-being.
- There has been a move away from narrow biomedical definitions of health, which focus on negative aspects of health, i.e. ill-health.
- Despite more 'holistic' definitions of health, performance indicators for measuring 'health' still predominantly focus on mortality and morbidity.
- Interest in well-being, both from an academic and a government/policy perspective, has grown significantly in recent times.
- Determinants of health and well-being are unequally distributed, giving rise to health inequities, which are considered to be unjust.
- The quality of work is a key determinant of health and well-being, which can be promoted through organizational policy and practice.

Introduction

This chapter will begin by considering concepts and definitions of health and well-being, who does the defining, and the impact of this. It will then consider the determinants of health and well-being, how these factors are distributed, and the consequences of this. Having considered these issues, the chapter will then focus on work, as a key determinant of health and well-being which has the potential to positively influence health and well-being for the working population.

Defining health and well-being

Historically, health has been defined from a medical perspective using deficit-based models which describe health as 'lacking illness or disease' (Blair et al., 2010). Biomedical definitions of health were commonly adopted during the 19th and 20th centuries, in western industrialized nations, during which time the predominant focus of public health was to control disease and infection. However, these definitions failed to recognize the complexity of the concept of health where states of both good and poor health could co-exist. It is now recognized that viewed from a holistic perspective, health can be experienced from a range of interrelated and interdependent dimensions, including physical, mental, emotional, social, spiritual (Ewles and Simnett, 1999).

In response to earlier critiques of the biomedical definition, the World Health Organization (1948) stated that health 'is a state of complete, physical, mental and social well-being and not merely the absence of disease or infirmity' (cited in Nutbeam, 1998: 351). This type of definition of health refocused a conceptual understanding of health away from the purely biomedical to a more holistic, all-encompassing view. Although the WHO was criticized for perhaps reflecting a view of health that was 'too utopian', it served to open up future debates regarding both 'how to' and 'who should' define health.

As academic understanding about the influence of social determinants on health developed (Black Report, 1980; Marmot, 2010), definitions of health began to encompass these broader social and environmental determinants and started to focus attention on the need for a supportive environment in order for people to realize health. In 1986, the Ottawa Charter for Health Promotion outlined five interrelated action areas for health promotion, including: (1) building healthy public policy, (2) creating supportive environments, (3) strengthening community action, (4) developing personal skills, and (5) reorienting health services. This understanding of health further developed into the concept of socio-ecological models of health where health behaviours and health outcomes were the result of the reciprocal relationship between individuals and their environments (Cohen et al., 2000; McLaren and Hawe, 2005; Rayner and Lang, 2012). 'Public health' was now being seen as an overarching concept encompassing political and social processes as well as biomedical intervention:

> Public health is a social and political concept aimed at the improving health, prolonging life and improving the quality of life among whole populations through health promotion, disease prevention and other forms of health intervention. (WHO, 1998)

From the mid-1980s onwards, evidence regarding inequalities in health was driving the concept of health towards one of being about social justice (see Chapter 2 for a discussion of differing principles and approaches to the definition of social justice). Marmot's *Strategic Review of Health Inequalities in England* (2010) stated that reducing health inequalities was a matter of fairness and social justice, and that the fair distribution of health, well-being and sustainability should be an important social goal. Further to this, he stated that there was a need to create fair employment and good work for all, which will be a focus for later stages of this chapter.

The need for policy-level intervention, to achieve social justice with respect to health, is required as people often had little individual control over the major determinants of their own health, as the following quote illustrates: 'Health is indivisible ... the domain of personal health over which the individual has direct control is very small when compared to the influence of culture, economy and environment' (Hafton Mahler – Director General of WHO, cited in Bunton et al., 1995: 21).

The need to focus on positive aspects of health (asset-based models of health; see Morgan and Ziglio, 2010) was reinforced when the concept of well-being was recognized as being integral to health and the terms 'health and well-being' began to be used in tandem (in the mid-2000s in the UK). For example, the UK New Labour government's *Commissioning Framework for Health and Well-being* (DH, 2007: 7) stated:

> We now need to keep the focus on people – not just people who are ill, but everybody. And we need to look further than just physical health problems, to promote well-being, which includes social care, work, housing and all the other elements that build a sustainable community.

The concept of well-being has existed since the mid-19th century but has always been contested (see the summary of definitions by Sumner, 1996). Definitions of well-being include the following:

> a positive physical, social and mental state; it is not just the absence of pain, discomfort and incapacity. It requires that basic needs are met, that individuals have a sense of purpose, that they feel able to achieve important personal goals and participate in society. It is enhanced by conditions that include supportive personal relationships, strong and inclusive communities, good health, financial and personal security, rewarding employment, and a healthy and attractive environment. (DEFRA, 2005)

And from Rath and Harter (2010):

> Wellbeing is about the combination of our love for what we do each day, the quality of our relationships, the security of our finances, the vibrancy of our physical health, and the pride we take in what we have contributed to our communities. (p. 4)

Asset-based models of health (see, for example, Morgan and Ziglio, 2010) focus on all the components present in an area or neighbourhood that can positively contribute to the health and well-being of the local community (sometimes referred to as social capital definitions which commonly emphasize the role of social networks, civil norms and social trust which lead to cooperation for mutual benefit). These assets might include: the community; parks and green spaces; social networks; leisure facilities; health services; and partnerships between different organizational sectors, such as business, social enterprises and voluntary organizations.

Despite these advances in the conceptual understanding of health and well-being, key government performance indicators for measuring health still tend to focus on mortality and morbidity, rather than looking at positive aspects of health as this sort of data has been routinely collected for many years – see, for example, population public health profiles. This may explain why health care spending globally largely remains focused on treatment, or secondary prevention, rather than on preventative services. For example, in the UK, Health England (2009) highlights that if pharmaceuticals are included, approximately 5 per cent of health expenditure is directed towards prevention. The need to refocus attention on well-being is now being addressed in some countries through the development of well-being indices (discussed below).

Lay and professional definitions of health and well-being

Lay definitions of health and well-being often differ in emphasis when compared with professional definitions. For instance, in a study in Australia, both young people and youth workers agreed that well-being was a multidimensional concept: however, youths were more likely to see the concept as relating to individual factors (e.g. relationships) rather than structural factors as emphasized by the youth workers (Bourke and Geldens, 2007). It is also recognized that the definitions of health and well-being given by providers of health care may influence the type of care they provide. For instance, good functioning, absence of disease, and having chronic disease under control are often prioritized within such definitions. The consequence of this could be that other aspects of health care such as supporting mental well-being may not be provided (Julliard et al., 2006).

Determinants of health and well-being

Health is shaped by the conditions in which people are born, grow, live, work and age. In turn, these conditions are shaped by how money, power and resources are distributed at global, national and local levels. In this respect, the evidence clearly shows that health follows a social gradient, i.e. better health occurs with increasing socio-economic position (see, for example, The Marmot Review: 'Fair Society – Healthy Lives' [Marmot, 2010] and The Acheson Report – 'The Independent Inquiry into Inequalities in Health' [Acheson, 1998]).

Such evidence has established the importance of social factors in determining health, as opposed to biological or genetic causes, which has led to 'increasing pressure in research, practice and policy-making environments to tackle these wider social determinants of health, through the implementation of appropriate interventions, and thereby reducing the gradient and health inequalities' (Bambra et al., 2010: 284). The main social determinants of health are categorized in Dahlgren and Whitehead's (2007) famous rainbow model, comprised of four layers. The over-arching outer layer includes general socioeconomic, cultural and environmental conditions, which influence/determine the next layer; living and working conditions. This layer subsequently impacts on social and community networks; which in turn influence individual lifestyle factors. All of these layers interact with predetermined factors, namely: age, gender, and familial genetic factors to influence the health status of a given population.

Over the past three decades, there has been considerable interest in academic research on the determinants of 'well-being', and there is now a substantial body of research that has been undertaken by economists, psychologists and other social scientists (The New Economics Foundation [NEF], 2012). This interest in well-being has more recently been taken up by policy makers at national level, evidenced by, for example, the formation of the Foresight Project on *Mental Capital and Wellbeing* (Foresight, 2008); more recently, the UK Prime Minister David Cameron announced that subjective well-being was going to be measured by the Office for National Statistics, to construct an index of national well-being – known as the 'Measuring National Well-being' programme (see www.ons.gov.uk/ons/guide-method/user-guidance/well-being/index.html) (NEF, 2012).

The main determinants of well-being are clearly established and have been found to include: income, health status, employment status and social relationships (see, for example, Fleche et al., 2011). In the UK, the domains for measuring national well-being have been identified following public consultation (Office for National Statistics, 2012) and are proposed (July 2012) to include: **individual well-being** (which includes four measures of life satisfaction)

- **our relationships** (which includes satisfaction with: your spouse/partner and your social life; and percentage who said they had someone they could really count on in a crisis)
- **health** (including life expectancy at birth; people not reporting a long-term limiting illness or disability; satisfaction with your health; the General Health Questionnaire [GHQ-12])
- **what we do** (including unemployment rates; satisfaction with your job and the amount of leisure time you have; and the percentage of people who volunteer)
- **where we live** (including crime rate per capita; measure of access to and quality of the local environment; and percentage of people who felt they belonged to their neighbourhood)
- **personal finance** (which includes the percentage of individuals in households below 60 per cent of the median income; household wealth; satisfaction with the income of your household; and percentage of people finding it quite or very difficult to get by financially)
- **education and skills** (human capital – the value of individuals' qualifications in the labour market; and percentage of the working age population with no qualifications)
- **the economy** (real household income per head)
- **governance – involvement in democracy and trust in how the country is run** (including: percentage of registered voters who voted; and percentage of those who have trust in national government)
- **the natural environment** (total greenhouse gas emissions; air pollutants; the extent of protected areas in the UK; and energy consumed within the UK from renewable sources).

We can see that the determinants of health and of well-being overlap and interact, for example 'what we do' and 'personal finance' (well-being indicators) overlap with 'living and working conditions' (social determinants of health indicators). This is why you often see 'health and well-being' being talked about or used simultaneously, such as in the recent development of 'Health and Well-being Boards' in the UK (see Department of Health, 2011). However, the most important thing to recognize at this point is the *crucial role* of social determinants to both health and well-being, and most importantly to *inequalities* in health and well-being (discussed below).

The determinants of health and well-being (e.g. income) are not equally distributed throughout any single national society or globally, and this unequal distribution results in health inequalities. Health inequalities are defined as 'differences, variations, and disparities in the health achievements of individuals and groups' (Kawachi et al., 2002: 645). Therefore, 'health inequality' is a descriptive term showing differences in health outcomes within a population (Kawachi et al., 2002). However, 'where systematic differences in health are judged to be avoidable by reasonable action globally and within society they are, quite simply, unjust. It is this that we label. It is this that we label health inequity' (WHO, 2008: 26). The Commission on Social Determinants of Health (WHO, 2008) asserted that putting these inequities right is a matter of social justice, and that 'social injustice is killing people on a grand scale' (2008: 26). In this respect, the Commission (2008) established three overarching priorities, in order to support countries to address those social factors which are leading to ill health and inequity:

1 Improve daily living conditions.
2 Tackle the inequitable distribution of power, money and resources.
3 Measure and understand the problem and assess the impact of action.

Looking at the scale and consequences of health inequities, within the European Union it is estimated that losses linked to health inequalities cost approximately 1.4 per cent of the Gross Domestic Product (WHO, 2012). In England, the Marmot Review (2010) highlighted that:

> people living in the poorest neighbourhoods, will, on average, die seven years earlier than people living in the richest neighbourhoods. Even more disturbingly, the average difference in disability free life expectancy is 17 years. (p. 16)

This means that people in poorer areas will spend more of their shorter life in disability. While there have been some improvements since the Marmot Review (2010) figures released to mark its second anniversary show that in most areas of England health inequalities have widened in the two years since the review (UCL, 2012).

> While overall life expectancy at birth in England increased by 0.3 years for both men and women between 2007–9 and 2009–10, inequalities in life expectancy between neighbourhoods increased by 0.1 years for men and showed no change for women. (p. 1)

Some of the key drivers of this widening in inequalities are a result of the current global recession, which has resulted in higher unemployment, a reduction in public spending and a shrinkage of welfare provision.

Workplace health and well-being

The definition of workplace well-being, put forward by the Chartered Institute of Personal Development (CIPD) (2007), is 'creating an environment to promote a state of contentment which allows an employee to flourish and achieve their full potential for the benefit of themselves and their organisation' (p. 4). Research indicates (see, for example, the Work Foundation's Report by Bevan [2010]) that there are benefits to organizations, both in operational and financial terms, of having a healthy workforce. Similarly, the evidence of the impact of well-being on workplace productivity is well established through *Working for a Healthier Tomorrow*, and the Boorman Review of NHS staff sickness absence, which was found to stand at 10.7 million working days per annum, with associated costs of £1.7 billion (Boorman Review, 2009). Additionally, the available evidence indicates that for every Euro invested in workplace health promotion a 2.5–4.8 Euro return is achieved due to reduced absenteeism costs (European Agency for Safety and Health at Work, 2010).

Work as a 'determinant' of health and well-being

> For people in employment, work is a key part of life. The environment we work in influences our health choices and can be a force for improving health – both for individuals and the communities they are part of. (Department of Health, 2004: 153)

Research indicates that good employment is better for your health than not having a job although the relationship between work and health is complex (Marmot, 2010; Naidoo and Wills, 2002). For example, Butterworth (2011) found that while unemployed individuals had poorer health than those who were employed, the mental health of those who were unemployed was comparable or superior to those in jobs of the poorest psychosocial quality (characterized by low job control, high job demands and complexity, job insecurity and perceived unfair pay).

Employment is important because it increases disposable income in the family, which influences a wide range of life chances, and personal self-worth and self-esteem. However, it must be recognized that the type and quality of one's occupation strongly influences attitudes and behavioural patterns (both positively and negatively) that are not directly work-related, for example: leisure time activity, family life, political activity and education (Kohn and Schooler, 1973, cited in Marmot and Wilkinson, 2003). Given the benefits of good employment, Marmot (2010) asserts that getting people into work is of critical importance for reducing health inequalities. Finally, given the amount of time spent at work (approximately 60 per cent of adult life), exposure to adverse or noxious job conditions (physical or psychosocial) carries a risk of ill health.

The changing context of work

There have been ongoing changes in the UK labour market, with considerable changes being seen in the past decade, particularly the later years, as a result of the economic recession. Key changes include de-industrialization; an increase in the relative importance of the service sector; the introduction of new technologies; and an increase in the percentage of older people. De-industrialization has resulted in fewer manufacturing jobs, a decline in trade unions and increased unemployment among manual workers. In the UK for men, between 2001 and 2007, the fastest declining jobs were: metal machining, fitting, instrument making (93,926); assemblers and routine operatives (64,688); process operatives (53,726); plant and machine operatives (53,650) and metal forming, welding and related (34,048) (Sissons, 2011). Similarly for women, there were also significant falls in employment in a number of manual process occupations, as well as areas where advances in IT technology have reduced the demand for labour, i.e. secretarial, finance and records administration occupations (Sissons, 2011). For women, there has been a big increase in 'personal services' employment, which includes both health care and childcare (Sissons, 2011). Globally, 'much of the rise in female employment has been in the service sector which accounted for 41% of female employment (compared to 37% of male) in 1999 and 47% (compared to just 40% of male) in 2008' (Kabeer, 2012: 15).

As noted in Chapter 8, there has been an increase in the percentage of older people in the population. Across Europe, people generally are healthier and live longer today than previously, while at the same time they have fewer children than they used to (European Commission, 2010). This is leading to an increase in the 'old age dependency ratio', with fewer young workers available to support the growing proportion of economically inactive people. As a result, there have been a number of policy reforms in the UK and across Europe, which have involved increasing the length of time that people spend at work before they can retire and draw their pensions (European Commission, 2010). For example, in the UK, the age at which first pension can be drawn is increasing from 65 to 67 between 2026 and 2028, and to 68 from 2044 (Directgov, 2011).

While this is a UK example, these trends of increasing pension ages, of inequalities in income and disability distribution are mirrored elsewhere in Europe. For example, data on Healthy Life Years (HLY) calculated by Eurostat (2009, cited in European Commission, 2012) show clear differences between Member States in life expectancy with no disability.

> The disability burden expressed in health-care expenditure (in kind and in cash) and pensions is a major proportion of national expenditure. Increasing age and life years spent in poor health mean greater medical needs, in particular with regard to pathologies such as degenerative vascular diseases, cancer, and Alzheimer's and other neurodegenerative diseases.

The sick elderly are a greater financial commitment than their healthy counterparts. If the retirement age is to be raised, people must be physically able to work and enjoy healthy life years. (European Commission, 2012: unpaginated)

With the percentage of the population aged 65 and over continuing to rise, the imperative to take action to improve the health of the working population, to support the increasingly ageing population, has never been greater. This means that the nature of work needs to be such that it supports people in remaining in good health. In this respect:

The worksite is one of the key channels for the delivery of interventions to reduce chronic diseases among adult populations. It provides easy and regular access to a relatively stable population and it encourages sustained peer support. (Moy et al., 2006: 301)

However, for this strategy to be effective, it is important that people remain healthy enough to continue working for longer. This has been shown however to be problematic, especially amongst those on lower incomes (Marmot, 2010; Office for National Statistics, 2012).

The changing context of work has resulted in increasing unemployment. As the economy has faltered, firms have continued to lay off staff, and unemployment peaked at almost 2.7 million at the end of 2011, which was the highest it had been for 17 years (Office for National Statistics, 2012). Globally, the International Labour Office (ILO) (2012) is asserting that after three years of crisis conditions in the global labour market, there is a backlog of global unemployment, at 200 million, which has increased by 27 million since the start of the crisis. Moreover, to avoid a further increase in unemployment over the next decade, more than 400 million jobs will be needed.

Unemployment is not equally distributed, with Sissons (2011) highlighting that the 'least skilled have suffered in the recession as people with more skills "bump-down" [regrading of skilled staff into lower grade levels] *in the labour market*' (p. 4). One of the worst affected groups in the UK, according to The Work Foundation, is young people who are NEET (not in employment, education or training) (Sissons and Jones, 2012). There are almost a million NEET young people, in England, which equates to more than one in every seven 16 to 25-year-olds. This is partly a reflection of the recession, however even before the recession, the number of NEETS was rising. Barriers for work for NEETS include: a lack of previous paid work experience; the nature of skills needed as a result of changes to the job market (highlighted above); health problems (including learning difficulties); drug and alcohol problems; and poor qualifications. While the recession has had some impact on the job market, Sissons and Jones (2012) highlight that even before the recession approximately 25 per cent of NEETs had no qualifications (see Chapter 7 for a further discussion of NEETS). This trend is mirrored globally, with young people nearly three times more likely than adults to be unemployed.

The rate of young unemployment rose globally from 11.7 percent in 2007 to 12.7 per cent in 2011, the advanced economies being particularly hard hit, where this rate jumped from 12.5 per cent to 17.9 per cent over this period. (ILO, 2012: 84)

Moreover, it is estimated that approximately 6.4 million young people have dropped out of the labour market, because they have given up hope of finding a job (ILO, 2012). For those young people in employment, increasingly these jobs are part-time and often temporary contracts, while in developing countries youth are disproportionally amongst the working poor (ILO, 2012).

Policy approaches to improving health and well-being at work

In order to create fair employment and good work for all, Marmot (2010) identified three key priorities:

1 Improve access to good jobs and reduce long-term unemployment across the social gradient.
2 Make it easier for people who are disadvantaged in the labour market to obtain and keep work.
3 Improve the quality of jobs across the social gradient.

Policy makers have recognized the importance of employment and of quality of work, and in this respect there has been a range of policy initiatives aimed at reducing unemployment in the UK over the past 15 years (Marmot, 2010). Both in the UK and within most Member States 'Active Labour Market Policies' (ALMPs) are key policy instruments to integrate the employed into work and combat employment and economic activity (Daguerre and Etherington, 2009; Marmot, 2010). ALMPS have become a major feature of international and domestic labour market policies and can be classified into different types: direct job creation; direct government wage subsidies to employers, or grants for entrepreneurial start-ups; and retraining and reintegration programmes (Marmot, 2010): 'The dominant philosophy is that claimants should not turn down employment offers since any job is preferable to economic inactivity or unemployment' (Daguerre and Etherington, 2009: 1). Examples of these policies in the UK include the New Deal Programmes, for example New Deal for Lone Parents (NDLP) (Marmot, 2010).

While the imperative to work is recognized, the barriers to work are often complex, and policy does not always align in order to get people into work, such as the need to care for dependants, given the shrinkage in welfare provision. However, the evidence suggests that ALMPs have had some success in getting people into jobs (Marmot, 2010), and in increasing income among recipients:

> though they have been most effective when combined with other fiscal and benefit measures to 'make work pay'. For example since the NDLP and complementary measures have been in place, lone parents in the UK have increasingly moved into employment and relative poverty among lone parent families has substantially declined. (Marmot, 2010: 111)

Card et al. (2010) conducted a meta-analysis of econometric evaluations of ALMPs implemented between 1995 and 2007, and found that 'job search assistance programmes' had favourable impacts; public sector employment programmes had less impact; and training programmes were associated with positive medium-term impacts. Marmot (2010) adds that the evidence suggests participating in ALMP training programmes can have a positive effect on psychological health and subjective well-being.

Daguerre and Etherington (2009) identify four key factors needed for these programmes to be effective:

- the need for activation programmes, e.g. NDLP, to provide personalized support and early intervention for those most in need
- adequate staff/client ratios
- particular effort and support for 'harder to help' customers to prevent drop-out
- subsidized work placements, together with on-the-job training, in order to achieve effective and sustainable employment outcomes.

Tailoring ALMPs to NEETs is particularly important, with Marmot (2010) highlighting that 'it is striking that the groups for whom no programme of assistance [ALMP] was available, young people aged 16 and 17, saw unemployment rise steadily' (p. 111). In this respect, policy recommendations for this group fall into one of two categories:

- **Prevention** – it is particularly important to intervene early to help young people to make effective transitions into the workplace, and offer intensive and early intervention support to stop young people becoming NEET in the first place.
- **Reintegration** – policies which can provide multiple chances for the NEET cohort to reintegrate into the workplace.

While getting people into work has been identified as a key strategy for reducing health inequalities, 'good jobs' are just as important for reducing health inequalities (Marmot, 2010). In this respect, the concept of the workplace as a 'setting for health' was first noted in the Ottawa Charter for Health Promotion (WHO, 1986), which asserted that the way society organizes work should create a healthy society. Marmot identifies 10 characteristics of 'good work', which have been found to protect and promote good health. Good work:

1 Is free of the core features of precariousness, such as a lack of stability and a high risk of job loss, a lack of safety measures (exposure to toxic substances, elevated risk of accidents) and the absence of minimal standards of employment protection.
2 Enables the working person to exert some control through participatory decision making on matters such as the place and timing of work and the tasks to be accomplished.
3 Places appropriately high demands on the working person, both in terms of quantity and quality, without overtaxing their resources and capabilities and without doing harm to their physical and mental health.
4 Provides fair employment in terms of earnings reflecting productivity and in terms of employers' commitment towards guaranteeing job security.

5 Offers opportunities for skill training, learning and promotion prospects within a life course perspective, sustaining health and work ability and stimulating the growth of an individual's capabilities.

6 Prevents social isolation and any form of discrimination and violence.

7 Enables workers to share relevant information within the organization, to participate in organizational decision making and collective bargaining, and guarantee procedural justice in case of conflict.

8 Aims at reconciling work and extra work/family demands in ways that reduce the cumulative burden of multiple social roles.

9 Attempts to reintegrate sick and disabled people into full employment wherever possible by mobilizing available means.

10 Contributes to workers' well-being by meeting the basic psychological needs of experiencing self-efficacy, self-esteem, a sense of belonging and meaningfulness.

Summary/Conclusions

- The concepts of health and well-being are contested and defined differently by diverse stakeholders, and consequently this influences strategic interventions for health improvement, such as treatment versus prevention approaches.
- A wide variety of largely uncontested social, cultural and economic factors influences the health status of populations which in turn may result in health inequalities.
- Health inequalities which are deemed to be 'unjust' in society are termed 'health inequities'.
- Work is a major determinant of health and well-being.
- The key characteristics of 'good work' include, for example, stability, job control, minimum standards of employment protection and fair employment, free from discrimination.
- Key policies which can make a difference are those which generate good quality employment, and those that target particular groups (e.g. NEETs and lone parents) and support their complex needs.

Questions

1 Consider the range of definitions of health and well-being; which do you think are most pertinent in today's society, and why?

2 Which determinant of health and well-being do you feel is most influential, and why?

3 What role does work play in improving health and well-being and in reducing health inequalities?

4 From the evidence base, what are the key characteristics of policies which are likely to be effective in maintaining a healthy workforce?

Recommended reading

Blair, M., Stewart-Brown, S., Waterston, T. and Crowther, R. (2010) *Child Public Health* (2nd edn). Oxford: Oxford University Press. Here, the authors discuss the concepts of health and well-being.

Marmot, M. (2010) *Fair Society: Healthy Lives – The Marmot Review*. Available at: www.instituteof healthequity.org/projects/fair-society-healthy-lives-the-marmot-review. This provides a good overview of the issues related to employment and good work; see particularly Chapter 4, 'Policy Objective C: Create Fair Employment and Good Work for All'.

Rayner, G. and Lang, T. (2012) *Ecological Public Health: Reshaping the Conditions of Good Health*. Abingdon: Earthscan/Routledge. Here, the authors provide a good overview of health and the interrelated factors that determine health and well-being outcomes.

Relevant websites

The International Labour Organization – www.ilo.org/global/lang-en/index.htm#a3 – works jointly to shape policies and programmes promoting decent work for all.

The World Health Organization has published a factfile on global health inequities – www.who.int/sdhconference/background/news/facts/en/index.html

For the World Health Organization's Social Determinants of Health, see www.who.int/social_determinants/en/

References

Acheson, D. (1998) *Independent Inquiry into Inequalities in Health (The Acheson Report)*. Available at: www.dh.gov.uk/en/Publicationsandstatistics/Publications/PublicationsPolicyAndGuidance/DH_4097582

Bambra, C., Gibson, M., Sowden, A., Wright, K., Whitehead, M. and Petticrew, M. (2010) 'Tackling the wider social determinants of health and health inequalities: evidence from systematic reviews', *Journal of Epidemiology & Community Health*, 64: 284–291.

Bevan, S. (2010) *The Business Case for Employee Health and Wellbeing: A Report Prepared for Investors in People*. The Work Foundation. Available at: www.investorsinpeople.co.uk/documents/research/the%20business%20case%20for%20employee%20health%20and%20wellbeing%20feb%202010.pdf

Black, D. (1980) *Inequalities in Health*. London: Penguin.

Blair, M., Stewart-Brown, S., Waterston, T. and Crowther, R. (2010) *Child Public Health* (2nd edn). Oxford: Oxford University Press.

Boorman, S. (2009) *NHS Health and Well-Being Review*. Available at: www.nhshealthandwellbeing. org/pdfs/NHS%20HWB%20Review%20Interim%20Report%20190809.pdf

Bourke, L. and Geldens, P. (2007) 'What does wellbeing mean? Perspectives of wellbeing among young people and youth workers in rural Victoria', *Youth Studies Australia*, 26(1): 41–49.

Bunton, R., Nettleton, S. and Burrows, R. (eds) (1995) *The Sociology of Health and Illness: Critical Analysis of Consumption, Lifestyle and Risk*. London: Routledge.

Butterworth, P. (2011) 'The psychosocial quality of work determines whether employment has benefits for mental health: results from a longitudinal national household panel survey', *Occupational Environmental Medicine*: 1–7.

Card, D., Kluve, J. and Weber, A. (2010) 'Active labour market policy evaluations: a meta-analysis', *The Economic Journal*, 120.

Chartered Institute of Personal Development (CIPD) (2007) *What's Happening with Wellbeing at Work?* Available at: www.cipd.co.uk/NR/rdonlyres/DCCE94D7-781A-485A-A702-6DAAB5EA7B27/0/whthapwbwrk.pdf

Cohen, D.A., Scribner, R.A. and Farley, T.A. (2000) 'A structural model of health behaviour: a pragmatic approach to explain and influence health behaviours at the population level', *Preventive Medicine*, 30: 146–154.

Daguerre, A. and Etherington, D. (2009) *Active Labour Market Policies in International Context: What Works Best? Lessons for the UK*. Department for Work and Pensions Working Paper No. 59. Available at: http://research.dwp.gov.uk/asd/asd5/WP59.pdf

Dalgren, G. and Whitehead, M. (2007) *European Strategies for Tackling Social Inequities in Health: Levelling Up, Part 2*. Copenhagen: WHO Regional Office for Europe.

DEFRA (2005) *Sustainable Development Strategy – 'Securing the Future'*. London: DEFRA.

Department of Health (DH) (2004) *Choosing Health: Making Healthy Choices Easier*. Available at: www.dh.gov.uk/en/Publicationsandstatistics/Publications/PublicationsPolicyAndGuidance/DH_4094550

Department of Health (DH) (2007) *Commissioning Framework for Health and Well-being*. London: DH.

Department of Health (DH) (2011) *Health and Wellbeing Boards*. Available at: www.dh.gov.uk/health/2011/10/health-and-wellbeing-boards/

Directgov (2011) *Changes to the Planned Increase in State Pension Age*. November. Available at: www.direct.gov.uk/en/Nl1/Newsroom/SpendingReview/DG_192159

European Agency for Safety and Health at Work (2010) *Workplace Health Promotion for Employers: Factsheet 93*. Available at: http://osha.europa.eu/en/publications/factsheets/93

European Commission (2010) *Joint Report on Pensions: Progress and Key Challenges in the Delivery of Adequate and Sustainable Pensions in Europe*. Available at: http://ec.europa.eu/economy_finance/publications/occasional_paper/2010/op71_en.htm

European Commission (2012) *Healthy Life Years (HLY): Data on HLY in the EU*. Available at: http://ec.europa.eu/health/indicators/healthy_life_years/hly_en.htm#fragment2

Ewles, L. and Simnett, I. (1999) *Promoting Health: A Practical Guide to Health Education*. Edinburgh: Harcourt.

Fleche, S., Smith, C. and Sorsa, P. (2011) 'Exploring Determinants of Subjective Wellbeing in OECD Countries: Evidence from the World Value Survey', OECD Economics Department Working Paper No. 921, OECD Publishing. Available at: http://dx.doi.org/10.1787/5kg0k6zlcm5k-en

Foresight (2008) *Mental Capital and Wellbeing: Making the Most of Ourselves in the 21st Century.* Available at: www.bis.gov.uk/assets/biscore/corporate/migratedD/ec_group/116-08-FO_b

Health England (2009) *Prevention and Preventative Spending.* Health England Report No. 2. Available at: www.healthengland.org/preventative_spending.htm

International Labour Organization (ILO) (2012) *Global Employment Trends 2012: Preventing a Deeper Jobs Crisis.* Available at: www.ilo.org/global/research/global-reports/global-employment-trends/WCMS_171571/lang--en/index.htm

Julliard, K., Klimenko, K. and Jacob, M.S. (2006) 'Definitions of health among healthcare providers', *Nursing Science Quarterly*, 19(3): 265–271.

Kabeer, N. (2012) *Women's Economic Empowerment and Inclusive Growth: Labour Markets and Enterprise Development.* SIG working paper 2012/1. Available at: www.idrc.ca/EN/Documents/NK-WEE-Concept-Paper.pdf

Kawachi, I., Subramanian, S.V. and Almeida-Filho, N. (2002) 'A glossary for health inequalities', *Journal of Epidemiology and Community Health*, 56: 647–652.

Marmot, M. and Wilkinson, R. (2003) *The Social Determinants of Health.* Oxford: Oxford University Press.

Marmot, M. (2010) *Fair Society: Healthy Lives – The Marmot Review.* Available at: www.instituteofhealthequity.org/projects/fair-society-healthy-lives-the-marmot-review

McLaren, L. and Hawe, P. (2005) 'Ecological perspectives in health research', *Journal of Epidemiology and Community Health*, 59: 6–14.

Morgan, M. and Ziglio, E. (2010) 'Revitalising the public health evidence base: an asset model', in *Health Assets in a Global Context: Theory, Methods, Action.* New York: Springer.

Moy, F., Sallam, A.A. and Wong, M. (2006) 'The results of a worksite health promotion programme in Kuala Lumpur, Malaysia', *Health Promotion International*, 21(4): 301–310.

Naidoo, J. and Wills, J. (2002) *Health Promotion: Foundations for Practice* (2nd edn). Edinburgh: Baillière Tindall in association with the RCN.

NEF (2012) *Well-being Evidence for Policy: A Review.* Available at: www.neweconomics.org/publications/well-being-evidence-for-policy-a-review

Nutbeam, D. (1998) 'Health Promotion Glossary', *Health Promotion International*, 13(4): 349–364.

Office for National Statistics (ONS) (2012) *Measuring National Well-being: Summary of Proposed Domains and Measures.* Available at: http://www.ons.gov.uk/ons/dcp171766_272242.pdf

Ottawa Charter (1986) www.who.int/hpr/NPH/docs/ottawa_charter_hp.pdf (accessed 08/01/08).

Rath, T. and Harter, J. (2010) *Wellbeing: The Five Essential Elements.* New York: GALLUP Press.

Rayner, G. and Lang, T. (2012) *Ecological Public Health: Reshaping the Conditions of Good Health.* Abingdon: Earthscan/Routledge.

Sissons, P. (2011) *The Hourglas and the Escalator: Labour Market Change and Mobility.* The Work Foundation. Available at: www.theworkfoundation.com/DownloadPublication/Report/292_hourglass_escalator120711%20(2)%20(3).pdf

Sissons, P. and Jones, K. (2012) *Lost in Transition? The Changing Labour Market and Young People Not in Employment Education or Training*. The Work Foundation. Available at: www.theworkfoundation.com/Reports/310/Lost-in-transition-The-changing-labour-market-and-young-people-not-in-employment-education-or-training

Sumner, L.W. (1996) *Welfare, Happiness, and Ethics*. Oxford: Oxford University Press.

UCL Institute of Health Equity (2012) *Health Inequalities Widen Within Most Areas of England*. Press release, 15 February. Available at: www.instituteofhealthequity.org/Content/FileManager/pdf/2-year-on-press-release-final.pdf

World Health Organization (WHO) (1986) *Ottawa Charter for Health Promotion*. Available at: www.who.int/healthpromotion/conferences/previous/ottawa/en/

World Health Organization (WHO) (1998) *Health Promotion Glossary*. Available at: www.who.int/hpr/NPH/docs/hp_glossary_en.pdf

World Health Organization (WHO) (2008) *Closing the Gap in a Generation: Health Equity through Action on the Social Determinants of Health*. Available at: http://whqlibdoc.who.int/publications/2008/9789241563703_eng.pdf

World Health Organization (WHO) (2012) *Fact File on Health Inequities*. Available at: www.who.int/sdhconference/background/news/facts/en/index.html.

PART 2

Policy and the Life Course

6

Families and Children
Sandra Shaw

Overview

- Changing trends in marriage, divorce and parenthood in the UK and other countries challenge traditional ideas about the family, but the concept of the 'ideal' family can still be powerful.
- For the New Labour governments, 1997–2010, a key policy was the aim to end child poverty, which is linked to concerns about the well-being of children.
- A central element of policy in this area was that work was seen as the solution to poverty and all parents were encouraged to do paid work.
- The Conservative/Liberal Democrat Coalition government elected in 2010 pledged support for the aim to end child poverty. Some of New Labour's policies have continued but an alternative approach to ending child poverty has been set out.
- Analysis suggests that child poverty has not been eliminated, and that it will be difficult for this to be achieved with the policies now in place, and in the current economic climate.

Introduction

Whatever form the family takes, we are all part of a family, whether children or adults. Not all of us will be parents or grandparents, but we may be siblings, or other relatives, and our families are important for our sense of identity and belonging, for support and care, or sometimes for the lack of these. The family is often seen as the 'building-block' of society, and where it fails, society is also seen to be failing. This chapter will focus on families with dependent children. There are links with Chapter 7, as in terms of policy, dependent children include those aged 18 years and under. Some factual information on families in the UK will be presented. A key area of policy that will be considered is the aim to end child poverty, which can be linked to broader concerns about children's health and well-being. Policies developed by the New Labour governments and the Conservative/ Liberal Democrat Coalition government will be presented, and progress towards eliminating child poverty assessed.

Why is the family important?

The family has been of central importance in welfare developments as it is where children are brought up, and children are often seen as 'the future' of the nation. In the 19th and early part of the 20th century, the ideal of the nuclear family, built around a heterosexual marriage, with a male breadwinner and female carer, was dominant (Lewis, 1998). The reality would have been different for many, as there have always been families with one parent only – whether as a result of death, the breakdown of relationships or the fact that parents had never married. However, ideas about the 'ideal' family and the most appropriate way to bring up children have been very powerful and have constituted a discourse or set of ideas about the 'right' way for children to be brought up. This discourse is still significant for many, despite the increasing numbers of lone-parent families in the latter part of the 20th century and early part of the 21st century, and the growth of other forms of families, for example same-sex couples having and looking after children (Wilson, 2007).

The heterosexual form of the family is often portrayed as 'natural' as it is linked to basic biological facts that in the past meant that men and women reproduced together. With the advent of reproductive technologies, it is possible for a woman to have a child without a male partner, or for same-sex couples to have a child, by using in vitro fertilization (IVF) or surrogacy. These possibilities and shifts in the formation of families reflect a rapidly changing society and this presents challenges for governments and for policy making. It can no longer be assumed that there will be two parents looking after children, and that one will be male and one female. This is not completely straightforward because there is still resistance to accepting social change – often on religious and moral grounds. This means that 'the family' and policies that affect the family are often highly contentious.

The changing shape of families

Official statistics measure different kinds of families. Child–parent relationships exist where children live with their families and this is the focus of this chapter, but it is also important to note that many non-resident parents have relationships with their children. In the UK, official statistics are available on the three main types of families with dependent children. These are

TABLE 6.1 Percentage of UK families* with dependent children

	2001	2010
Married couple family	65.4	60.4
Cohabiting couple family	10.9	14.0
Lone-parent family	23.6	25.5

Note: *Excludes a small number of civil partnership and same-sex cohabiting couples.
Source: Social Trends 41 (ONS, 2011)

married couple, cohabiting couple or lone-parent family. The proportions of children living in these different families have changed. Married couple families have decreased, while those in cohabiting couple families and lone-parent families have increased. The figures for 2001 and 2010 are set out above in Table 6.1, and show how family composition has altered.

In terms of the number of children, this means that in 2010, 8.4 million lived in a married couple family, 1.8 million in a cohabiting couple family and 3.1 million in a lone-parent family (the majority headed by a woman). There has been a decrease in the number of dependent children living in families, which is related to a decline in family size, so, for example, in 2010 over half of cohabiting and lone-parent families had a single dependent child, and most married couple families had two dependent children (ONS, 2011: 9). This can be related to trends, including deferred parenting (women having children later), and parents separating/divorcing when children are older. For example, by 2004, most children affected by divorce were 16 and over (ONS, 2011: 14).

While marriage is still the most prevalent form of partnership, there has been a decline in marriage rates in England and Wales, Scotland and Northern Ireland (ONS, 2011:10). While divorce rates have increased over the longer term, there was a decline in divorce rates from 2003 to 2009 which corresponds to the increase in cohabitation rates, and the decrease in marriage. Civil Partnerships could be formed from December 2005, though the exact dates vary for the different nations of the UK. These are partnerships for same-sex couples, with the same rights as civil marriages, but they are not religious ceremonies. From the end of that year until the end of 2009, 40,237 partnerships had been formed, with men more likely to be in a civil partnership than women. Up to 2009, figures show a continuing downward trend in civil partnerships in the UK for both men and women – Northern Ireland being the exception with a small increase in number (ONS, 2011: 12–13). Civil partnerships can be dissolved after 12 months, and civil partnership dissolutions have increased, with more female than male partnerships ending.

Live births outside of marriage rose from 65,700 in 1971 to 326,200 in 2009, meaning that 46.2 per cent of all births were outside of marriage, and live births outside of marriage have increased in all age groups since 2001 (ONS, 2011: 16). Over the same period, births within marriage decreased from 717,500 in 1971 to 380,100 in 2009. Statistics on birth provide us with some insight into overall trends and birth registrations provide additional information. By 2009, it had become more usual for births outside of marriage to be registered by parents living at the same address, with a figure of 65.7 per cent (ONS, 2011: 17). In addition, 20.9 per cent were registered by parents living at different addresses, with a smaller proportion of births being sole registered – 13.4 per cent; the latter figure remained 'fairly stable' between 2001 and 2009. The proportion of births outside of marriage was 50 per cent in Scotland in 2008, with a further increase in 2009, while the figure for Northern Ireland in 2009 was around 40 per cent. The increase in the number of births outside of marriage illustrates the fact that it is more usual and more acceptable to have births outside of marriage. At the same time, the figures on joint registration of birth, with the majority being co-resident, demonstrate that parenting is still likely to begin as a partnership.

The factual information presented here reflects overall changes in families across many other countries, though trends will vary between different countries and different regions (OECD, 2012). However, there is insufficient information about patterns in developing countries to be able to make clear comparisons. It is also more difficult to access statistical data on same-sex partnerships, including those with dependent children. With regard to industrialized nations, some broad trends can be identified. These include: a decrease in marriage; and, increases in divorce, lone-parenthood, co-habitation and births outside of marriage. In some countries, for example Iceland, Estonia and Mexico, over 50 per cent of births occur outside of marriage (OECD, 2012). On the other hand, rates of less than 10 per cent are recorded in Korea, Japan, Greece and Cyprus. These variations reflect differences in cultural practices, the influence of religion, and political and economic factors.

Another significant change has been the increase in the numbers of women, including mothers, in the paid labour market in the past 60 years. Families with dependent children are often dual-earner families, and the traditional version of the male breadwinner family has shifted. With regard to policies on poverty that are set out later in this chapter, supporting both parents into employment has been a central element of government policy, as work has been seen as the solution to poverty. Coupled with the drive to get parents working has been the expansion of the childcare system. Policies on gender and employment and on childcare have also been driven by EU objectives (Hantrais, 2007; Shaw, 2010).

Families and social policy

This increasing diversity in families has presented a challenge to policy makers, and writers have suggested ways of characterizing policy responses. Fox Harding (1996) writes of a continuum of approaches from authoritarian to liberal. The former position would promote policies that preserved and maintained the ideal of the male breadwinner/female carer (heterosexual) model of the family. A more liberal approach entails allowing people to make decisions about how they want to live their lives, and putting policies in place to support them, for example having benefits in place to support lone parents, or enabling civil partnerships. Or approaches can be identified as conservative, pragmatic or radical (Hatland, 2001). A radical approach accepts difference, and actively promotes equality. A more conservative approach would be one that again promotes the ideal family type and the male-breadwinner model. The pragmatic approach accepts that social changes are inevitable and policies need to adapt to meet changes. In democratic societies, governments tend to accept change and – despite criticism – diversity in family formation is recognized in social policies like that of the UK. However, the ideal of the nuclear family based on heterosexual marriage is still very potent and often presented as ideal, and conversely, other family forms, such as lone-parent families, are often criticized and seen as responsible for much that is wrong in society (Murray, 1990).

Family policies under New Labour 1997–2010

Polices affecting families can be explicit or implicit (Kamerman and Kahn, 1978), the former referring to policies that are targeted at families, and the latter recognizing the fact that wider areas of policy such as transport and the environment have an impact on families. During the years that New Labour was in power, there was a significant and explicit focus on families, children and young people. This included concerns about the welfare of children, and also about parents and parenting. This interest in families – seen as the basis of society – was evident in *Supporting Families* (Home Office, 1998) which set out a basic approach to families which can be seen to embody three basic principles:

> first, that the interests of children were paramount; second, that marriage was the 'surest foundation for raising children' and that therefore the government's aim was to strengthen marriage; and third, that state intervention in the family should be minimal, with the role of government being to support parents rather than substituting for them. (Clarke, 2007: 158)

The first point reflects the position set out in the Children Act 1989. The second point is interesting in the context of rapid social change, and indicates that New Labour's rhetorical approach to the family was initially more traditional than liberal. In reality, the policies that followed reflected a more pragmatic approach to the family. In the context of the raft of policies aimed at families and children, the final point seems some way from reality. There was increased interest in and involvement of the state in the lives of children and families. A policy agenda evolved that centred both on the health and well-being of children (and young people), and on the responsibilities of parents to bring up their children appropriately.

Parents and parenting

Discussion and debate around parents and parenting, and their role in bringing up children, have revolved around what it means to be a 'good' parent, or what is meant by parenting which is 'not good enough'. This again relates to what kind of family environment children need to be brought up in to thrive and do well as adults. It also includes considering the risks that children can be exposed to within the family where parents are incompetent, or just struggling. What this kind of debate implies is that there is some model of a 'reasonable' parent which is constructed by professionals, and all parents are judged against this (Garrett, 1999). The most obvious way in which this operates is where professionals, for example, social workers, work with families and have a responsibility to assess parents' capacity, and ensure the safe care of children and young people. Woodcock (2003) proposes that professionals operate with a particular model of parenting, and this is likely to reflect middle-class ideals about being a parent. Families seen as a problem are most likely to be under the surveillance of social workers and other professionals, and this includes families living in poverty and disadvantage and families seen as presenting a 'problem' for society. As mothers are still the primary carers for most children, including lone mothers, this can be seen as an 'engendered rhetoric of responsibility' (Standing, 1999: 481). Concentrating on the 'parenting capacity' of socially and economically marginalized families in society was an aspect of New Labour policies, alongside a desire to regulate and control the behaviour of parents (Sharland, 2006).

Another element of the New Labour approach to parenting was the prioritizing of the role of fathers in the lives of children. At times, mothers seem to become invisible (Lister, 2006) and subsumed under the category 'parent' (Shaw, 2010). The next part of the chapter will look in more detail at New Labour policies, starting with the aim to end child poverty.

New Labour 1997–2010 and child poverty

A major initiative under New Labour was the aim to abolish child poverty. This was announced in a speech by Tony Blair in 1999 (Shaw, 2010). The Conservative and Liberal Democrat parties, as well as the Scottish National Party (SNP) and Plaid Cymru (Wales), also supported the aim (Shaw, 2010), and the child poverty agenda continues to receive cross-party support. The matter of child poverty came to prominence due to the fact that the UK had higher rates of poverty than most other industrialized nations and the worst child poverty rate in the EU (DWP, 2008). Targets were set which included reducing child poverty by a quarter by 2004–05, halving it by 2010 and eliminating child poverty by 2020 (Shaw, 2010). The targets were significant as they meant that progress towards ending child poverty could be assessed. Initially, the aim was to abolish child poverty, though, over time, this was modified to improve the position of the UK in relation to other countries, and to lower it to between 5 and 10 per cent of children (Hirsch, 2006: 8).

Defining and measuring child poverty

There are different ways of defining poverty and measuring poverty. The two main definitions of poverty are: absolute poverty and relative poverty (Shaw, 2010). The former means lacking the basic necessities of life such as food, shelter and warmth. While it is often assumed that this kind of poverty only exists in the poorest countries in the world, some children living in poor households in the UK can also lack some of the basic necessities of life (Hirsch, 2006). Relative deprivation means being poor compared to other people within a particular country or society. Using this definition, people should have enough income to afford the basic necessities, and participate fully in society – to be like everyone else. Relative deprivation also has links with New Labour's agenda on social exclusion, which goes beyond income poverty, focusing on deprived areas, particular groups and issues such as crime, poor housing and unemployment (Shaw, 2010).

The way that poverty is measured has an impact on how many people are seen to be poor. For their child poverty agenda, the New Labour governments used three main ways to measure child poverty. These included: *absolute low income*; *relative low income*; and *material deprivation and low income combined*. Details on these are set out in Box 6.1 below.

Box 6.1 Child poverty – definition and measurement

- Absolute low income: this indicator measures whether the poorest families are seeing their income rise in real terms. The level is fixed as equal to the relative low-income threshold for the baseline year of 1998–9 expressed in today's prices.
- Relative low income: this measures whether the poorest families are keeping pace with the growth of incomes in the economy as a whole. This indicator measures the number of children living in households below 60 per cent of contemporary median equivalized household income.
- Material deprivation and low income combined: this indicator provides a wider measure of people's living standards. This indicator measures the number of children living in households that are both materially deprived and have an income below 70 per cent of contemporary median equivalized household income.

Source: HM Treasury et al. (2008), reproduced in Shaw (2010)

Child poverty was monitored against all three of these, with a target associated with the relative low income measure (DWP, 2003, cited in HM Treasury et al., 2008). This recognizes the fact that if a family's income is lower than that of other families, it results in negative outcomes for children (Shaw, 2010). Poverty can also be measured before or after housing costs are deducted from income. If the measure is before housing costs are taken out – which is what governments tend to do – there will be fewer families living in poverty, as it will appear as if households have more income.

The risk of growing up in poverty

Some children are at greater risk of living in poverty than others. An increased risk of poverty has been associated with living in a household where no one works; being from particular ethnic minority groups (for example, Pakistani and Bangladeshi) (Phung, 2008); living in a lone-parent household; coming from a family including a disabled person; and coming from a large family (Ridge, 2002; CPAG, 2004; Hirsch, 2006; HM Treasury, 2010). Other groups of children at risk include children of asylum seekers and gypsy and traveller children (Hirsch, 2006). Where there is one parent, earning sufficient income to support a family can be difficult (Hoggart and Vergeris, 2008), and having a disabled child can present extra costs to the family (Burchardt and Zaidi, 2008). While living in a workless household was seen as a key risk factor for child poverty by New Labour, it is now recognized that 'in-work' poverty is increasingly significant. This undermines the notion that paid employment is *the* solution to poverty – which was a central tenet of the New Labour approach, and continues to be important under the Coalition government.

New Labour policies on child poverty

To tackle child poverty, the New Labour governments introduced a range of policies (Churchill, 2011). These involved income-based policies, including the introduction of Working Families Tax Credit (WFTC) and Childcare Tax Credit (CTC) introduced in 1999 (Clarke, 2007), and increasing child benefit. The Child Trust Fund was set up in 2002 as a way of encouraging parents to save for their child's future (Shaw, 2012). However, their policies were broader than this, and recognized the importance of the early years of a child's life, and providing support to families. Setting up the Sure Start programme, establishing the Children's Fund in 2001, and providing a National Childcare Strategy were all examples of this wider approach (Hendrick, 2003). So too was the emphasis on early years, with free part-time early education places for all 3- and 4-year-olds of 12.5 hours a week (ONS, 2008: 30), and the growth of extended services based around schools and children's centres (Broadhead and Martin, 2009). Income-based approaches and these other programmes joined together to support an agenda of getting both parents in a two-parent family – and lone parents – into paid employment. Policies on childcare and getting women (particularly mothers) into employment also reflect objectives set out by the European Union (Shaw, 2012).

Sure Start was launched in 1999 initially targeting disadvantaged families (National Audit Office [NAO], 2006). It was a 10-year programme aimed at promoting the development of babies and children, and providing services aimed at meeting the needs of families and children (DfES, 2001). It was later expanded by the establishment of Sure Start Children's Centres (NAO, 2006). By November 2008, almost 3,000 centres had been established (Frost and Parton, 2009). Centres facilitate the concentration of a range of services in one place, including: childcare, early education, health, employment and support services for pre-school children and their families (Barker, 2009; NAO, 2006: 5). A later evaluation shows an improvement with regard to parenting practice and more optimism with regard to the service (Frost and Parton, 2009). Extending the reach of the centres to include all children can be seen as a positive development, but dilutes support targeted at the poorest and most vulnerable children in society.

Work as a solution to poverty

A central element of New Labour's approach was the belief that work was a solution to poverty. This was borne out by evidence showing that there was a greater risk of living in poverty for children growing up in 'workless' households (CPAG, 2004). Policies were adopted to ensure that both parents or the sole parent were in paid employment (HM Treasury, 2004). This was also associ-ated with the concept of citizenship, and of people putting something into society in order to get something back. Changes to the benefit system were grounded in the concept of conditional access to welfare (DWP, 2008; Dwyer, 2010), and the idea that people who *could* work *should* work. These ideas also reflected a concern to cut the costs of the welfare state by decreasing the number of those dependent on benefits, and as most lone parents were on benefits they were targeted as an impor-tant group to get into paid employment.

Every Child Matters

Associated with the aim to end child poverty, policies were developed reflecting a broader approach to safeguarding children's health and well-being (Broadhurst et al., 2009). Fundamental to this were the *Every Child Matters* publications (ECM) (DfES, 2003, 2004). These listed outcomes to be achieved by all children: being healthy; staying safe; enjoying and achieving; making a positive contribution; and economic well-being. The subsequent Children Act 2004 set out the 'legislative spine' for the reform of children's services (Shaw, 2010). Parents/carers have an important role to play in enabling children to achieve these outcomes, which are clearly related to the agenda to end child poverty, and *Every Parent Matters* (EPM) was aimed at *supporting, informing* and *empower-ing* parents (DfES, 2007: 2). However, if parents' main responsibility is the economic well-being of the family, this can create tensions around work–life balance and caring for children (Duncan and Edwards, 1999; Mahon, 2006; Perrons, 2006). Additional problems can be related to the availabil-ity of affordable, good quality childcare (Shaw, 2010).

Child poverty, health and well-being

Dealing with poverty is essential, because research indicates that poverty in childhood affects childhood development and carries adverse consequences throughout the life course (Bradshaw, 2003; Hirsch, 2006; Griggs and Walker, 2008). In a review of the literature, Griggs and Walker (2008) set out some of the health consequences for children who grow up in poverty. These include: an impact on maternal health and higher rates of infant mortality; nutritional problems in children from low-income households; an association with a range of illnesses; and poor dental health. Accidental deaths are also more prevalent in poor households (Underdown, 2007; Griggs and Walker, 2008). It can also affect the self-esteem and confidence of children and young people, and it has been noted that 'poverty breeds ill-health, ill-health maintains poverty' (Wagstaff, 2002: 97, cited in Griggs and Walker; 2008: 9). Poverty costs the individual child but also costs the state when looking at benefits and services designed to support disadvantaged families (Hirsh, 2006). The long-term costs of poverty include the loss of earnings potential for adults who have done less well academically because they have grown up in poverty or because of long-term health problems created by growing up in poverty. These include a loss in tax revenue, and the cost of benefit payments made to the unemployed or ill (Blanden et al., 2008).

Making progress on child poverty?

In April 2002, statistics showed that up to 2001, around 500,000 children had been lifted out of poverty – the target was one million. This was a significant achievement but the initial target had not been reached. Piachaud and Sutherland (2001) suggest that it was easier to help children and families just below the poverty line, than assist the poorest in society, and latter analysis indicated that it would be difficult to achieve the targets set out (Platt, 2005). Statistics for 2008 show the UK sitting around the OECD average for child poverty – approximately 13 per cent – despite the policies put in place to deal with it. Other countries, including the USA, had rates of over 20 per cent, with the lowest rates found in the Nordic countries (OECD, 2012). A culmination of policy in this area was the Child Poverty Act 2010. This enshrined the targets in legislation, making governments accountable for them. At the election in May 2010, the Labour government lost power, and a new Conservative/Liberal Democrat Coalition was established.

The Conservative/Liberal Democrat Coalition government – 2010 onwards

The Coalition government has attempted to reconcile the views of two political parties, though in some areas these may be drawing on similar political perspectives. With regard to the family, the Conservative Party was supportive of marriage in the run-up to the election, and the Liberal Party, as might be expected, did not advocate a particular form for the family. After the election, the former view has been modified, and David Cameron, the Prime Minister, has expressed support for gay marriage, though there are still more traditional views within the Conservative Party. A Childhood and Families Taskforce was established, though it appears to have been inactive (Churchill, 2012).

The State of the Nation report (HMG, 2010) stated that severe income poverty had increased over the previous decade, and that the distribution of poverty was uneven, with multiple disadvantage a significant problem. Pursuing the same agenda as New Labour, paid work was seen as 'the best and most sustainable route out of poverty' (2010: 27). A commitment was made to meet the 2010 child poverty targets, and to make Britain more 'family-friendly' (Churchill, 2012: 41). In April 2011, the Coalition published a four-year plan to reduce child poverty (HMG, 2010). This focused on the causes of childhood disadvantage, rather than focusing on income poverty. These were seen as: worklessness, educational failure, parenting and early child development deficiencies, family breakdown and health inequalities – all issues highlighted in the *Think Family* documents on disadvantaged families, published by the Social Exclusion Task Force (SETF, 2007, 2008) (see Shaw, 2010, for further details).

However, the most prominent issue has been dealing with the economic crisis, which has resulted in cuts in the public sector. The *Spending Review 2010* (HM Treasury, 2010) set out some of these cuts, though under the umbrella term of 'fairness' free access to early education and care for all disadvantaged 2-year-old children was announced, together with the establishment of a pupil premium for disadvantaged pupils. The Spending Review also set out plans for the introduction of Universal Credit (UC) and the white paper *Universal Credit: Welfare that Works* was presented to Parliament in November 2010 (Department for Work and Pensions, 2010). Child benefit was frozen between 2010 and 2013 and following the budget in 2012, changes were announced which meant that in future child benefit would effectively be 'means-tested'. These changes are due to come into effect in January 2013 (HM Revenue and Customs, 2012). This is a significant change as this once universal benefit has now become a targeted benefit. While the change may not impact on the poorest in society, it is likely to cause financial hardship to families already struggling in the economic recession.

Universal Credit will replace existing benefits, and is due to be phased in from October 2013 for new claimants (Bennett, 2012). Merging benefits and tax credits is seen as a way of simplifying the benefits system, and allowing people to work a few hours a week without being disadvantaged – a means of 'making work pay'. However, Bennett (2012) notes that simplification may not be that easy to achieve. Furthermore, as claims will be digital there may be problems with this approach related to dependence on the use of 'complex' computer systems and assumptions about claimants' 'digital literacy' (2012: 20). With regard to incentives to work, outcomes remain unclear. Concerns have also been expressed about the gender impact of UC 'because of its potential impact on women's financial autonomy' (2012: 20).

Ending child poverty?

A report on *Households Below Average Income*, published by the Department for Work and Pensions (DWP, 2012), indicates that child poverty was reduced between 1998/9 and 2010/11, with 1.1 million children lifted out of poverty before housing costs (BHC). This can be linked to policies aimed at increasing the number of lone parents in paid employment, and increases in benefits paid to families with children (CPAG, 2012). However, child poverty is projected to rise from 2012/13 with an additional 300,000 children expected to be living in poverty by 2015/16. It is predicted that this trend will continue with another 4.2 million children living in poverty by 2020 (Brewer et al., 2011). On the basis of these recent projections, it appears that the aim to end child poverty will not be realized. Associated with this pessimism about the future are the costs of growing up in poverty referred to earlier in this chapter, which accrue to the individual across their life course, with the potential of long-term disadvantage, and increased costs to society and the state.

Summary/Conclusions

- Families and children have been a central focus of government policy, as families are seen as the basis of society, and the locale where children are raised as citizens of the future.
- The New Labour governments' agenda focused on ending child poverty and ensuring the wider well-being of children, with work seen as the main solution to the problem of poverty.
- The Conservative/Liberal Democrat Coalition government supported the aim to end child poverty enshrined within the Child Poverty Act and also saw work as a solution to poverty.
- The interest in child poverty acknowledges the costs to the child, to the future adult, and to society and the state.
- The economic crisis at the end of the first decade in the 21st century has meant that Coalition government policy has been focused on reducing government spending, including spending in the public sector.

Questions

1 Why did the first New Labour government consider it desirable to end child poverty?
2 What were the key elements of the New Labour policy for reducing child poverty?
3 How do Coalition government policies impact on families and children?
4 Is it possible to envisage a future in the UK where no child lives in poverty?

Recommended reading

Hendrick, H. (2005) *Child Welfare and Social Policy: The Essential Reader*. Bristol: The Policy Press.
Lewis, J. (ed.) (2006) *Children, Changing Families and Welfare States*. Cheltenham: Edward Elgar.
Shaw, S. (2010) *Parents, Children, Young People and the State*. Maidenhead: Open University Press/ McGraw Hill Education.
Each of these texts will provide an introduction to key areas related to families and children.

Relevant websites

The Child Poverty Action Group (CPAG) – www.cpag.org.uk/ – is a campaigning organization that produces publications, press releases, campaigns and statistical information on child poverty.

The Joseph Rowntree Foundation – www.jrf.org.uk/ – is a useful site providing research reports, briefer findings and blogs on a range of issues connected to poverty.

Accessing government departments is useful for updates on statistics, and on policies. See, for example, the Department of Work and Pensions – www.dwp.gov – and HM Treasury – www.hmtreasury.gov.uk/

References

Barker, S. (2009) 'Sure Start Children's Centres and Every Child Matters', in *Making Sense of Every Child Matters: Multi-professional Practice Guidance*. Bristol: The Policy Press.

Bennett, F. (2012) 'Universal Credit: overview and gender implications', in M. Kilkey, G. Ramia and K. Farnsworth (eds) *Social Policy Review, 24*. Bristol: Policy Press.

Blanden, J., Hansen, K. and Machin, S. (2008) *The GDP Cost of the Lost Earning Potential of Adults who Grew Up in Poverty*. York: Joseph Rowntree Foundation.

Bradshaw, J. (2003) 'Child poverty and child health in international perspective', in C. Hallet and A. Prout (eds) *Hearing the Voices of Children: Social Policy for a New Century*. London: Routledge Falmer.

Brewer, M., Browne, J. and Joyce, R. (2011) *Child and Working Age Poverty from 2010 to 2020*. London: Institute for Fiscal Studies.

Broadhead, P. and Martin, D. (2009) 'Education and Every Child Matters' in R. Barker (ed.) *Making Sense of Every Child Matters: Multi-professional Practice Guidance*. Bristol: The Policy Press.

Broadhurst, K., Grover, C. and Jamieson, J. (2009) *Critical Perspectives on Safeguarding Children*. Chichester: Wiley Blackwell.

Burchardt, T. and Zaidi, A. (2008) 'Disabled children, poverty and extra costs', in J. Strelitz and R. Lister (eds) *Why Money Matters: Family Income, Poverty and Children's Lives*. London: Save the Children.

Child Poverty Action Group (CPAG) (2004) *Poverty: The Facts*. Available at: www/cpag.or.uk/ (accessed 12 January 2005).

Child Poverty Action Group (CPAG) (2012) *Child Poverty Facts and Figures*. Available at: www.cpag.org.uk/child-poverty-facts-and-figures (accessed 3 July 2012).

Churchill, H. (2011) *Parental Rights and Responsibilities: Analysing Social Policy and Lived Experiences*. Bristol: The Policy Press.

Churchill, H. (2012) 'Family support and the Coalition: retrenchment, refocusing and restructuring', in M. Kilkey, G. Ramia and K. Farnsworth (eds) *Social Policy Review, 24*. Bristol: Policy Press.

Clarke, K. (2007) 'New Labour: family policy and gender', in C. Annesley, F. Gains and K. Rummery (eds) *Women and New Labour: Engendering Politics and Policy?* Bristol: The Policy Press.

Department for Education and Skills (DfES) (2001) *Sure Start: A Guide for Fourth Wave Programmes*. Nottingham: DfES Publications.

Department for Education and Skills (DfES) (2003) *Every Child Matters*. London: The Stationery Office.

Department for Education and Skills (DfES) (2004) *Every Child Matters: Change for Children*. Available at: www.everychildmatters.gov.uk (accessed 30 August 2012).

Department for Education and Skills (DfES) (2007) *Every Parent Matters*. Available at: www.dcfs. gov.uk/everychildmatters/resources-andpractice/ (accessed 30 November 2008).

Department for Work and Pensions (DWP) (2008) *Raising Expectations and Increasing Support: Reforming the Welfare State*. Available at: www.dwp.gov.uk/welfareform/raisingexpectations/ (accessed 5 July 2012).

Department for Work and Pensions (DWP) (2010) *Universal Credit: Welfare that Works*. Available at: www.dwp.gov.uk/docs/universal-credit-full-document.pdf (accessed 11 November 2012).

Department for Work and Pensions (DWP) (2012) *Households Below Average Income: An Analysis of the Income Distribution 1994/95–2010/11*. Available at: http://research.dwp.gov.uk/asd/hbai/ hbai2011/pdf_files/full_hbai12.pdf (accessed 3 July 2012).

Department for Work and Pensions and Department for Education (2011) *A New Approach to Child Poverty: Tackling the Causes of Disadvantage and Transforming Families' Lives*. Cm 8061. London: The Stationery Office.

Duncan, S. and Edwards, R. (1999) *Lone Mothers, Paid Work and Gendered Moral Rationalities*. Basingstoke: Macmillan.

Dwyer, P. (2010) *Understanding Social Citizenship: Themes and Perspectives for Policy and Practice*. Bristol: The Policy Press.

Fox Harding, O. (1996) *Family, State and Social Policy*. London: Macmillan.

Frost, N. and Parton, N. (2009) *Understanding Children's Social Care Politics, Policy and Practice*. London: Sage.

Garrett, P.M. (1999) 'Mapping child-care social work in the final years of the twentieth century: a critical response to the "looking after children" system', *British Journal of Social Work*, 29: 27–47.

Griggs, J. and Walker, R. (2008) *The Costs of Child Poverty for Individuals and Society: A Literature Review*. York: Joseph Rowntree Foundation.

Hantrais, L. (2007) *Social Policy in the European Union* (3rd edn). Basingstoke: Palgrave Macmillan.

Hatland, A. (2001) 'Changing family patterns: a challenge to social security' in M. Kautto, J. Fritzell, B. Hvinden, J. Kvist and J. Uusitalo (eds) *Nordic Welfare States in the European Context*. London: Routledge.

Hendrick, H. (2003) *Child Welfare: Historical Dimensions, Contemporary Debate*. Bristol: The Policy Press

Hirsch, D. (2006) *What Will it Take to End Child Poverty? Firing on All Cylinders*. York: Joseph Rowntree Foundation.

HM Government (HMG) (2010) *State of the Nation Report: Poverty, Worklessness and Welfare Dependency in the UK*. Available at: http://webarchive.nationalarchives.gov.uk/+/www.cabi-netoffice.gov.uk/media/410872/web-poverty-report.pdf (accessed 4 July 2012).

HM Revenue and Customs (HMRC) (2012) *Child Benefit Income Tax Charge*. Available at: www. hmrc.gov.uk/budget2012/cb-income-tax.htm (accessed 4 July 2012).

HM Treasury (2004) *Prudence for a Purpose: A Britain of Stability and Strength*. Available at: www. hm-treasury-gov.uk/bud_bud04indes.htm (accessed 5 July 2012).

HM Treasury (2010) *Spending Review 2010.* Available at: http://cdn.hmtreasury.gov.uk/sr2010_completereport.pdf (accessed 4 July 2012).

HM Treasury (HM), DWP and DCSF (2008) *Ending Child Poverty: Everybody's Business.* Available at: www.hm-treasury.gov.uk/d/bud_08_childpoverty_1310.pdf (accessed 20 December 2008).

Hoggart, L. and Vergeris, S. (2008) 'Lone parents and the challenge to make work pay', in J. Strelitz and R. Lister (eds) *Why Money Matters: Family Income, Poverty and Children's Lives.* London: Save the Children.

Home Office (1998) *Supporting Families.* London: The Stationery Office.

Kamerman, S. and Kahn, S. (eds) (1978) *Family Policy: Government and Family in 14 Countries.* New York: Columbia University Press.

Lewis, G. (1998) (ed.) *Forming Nation, Framing Welfare.* London: Routledge.

Lister, R. (2006) 'Children (but not women) first: New Labour, child welfare and gender', *Critical Social Policy,* 26(2): 315–335.

Mahon, R. (2006) 'The OECD and the work/family reconciliation agenda: competing frames', in J. Lewis (ed.) *Children, Changing Families and Welfare States.* Cheltenham: Edward Elgar.

Murray, C. (1990) *The Emerging British Underclass.* London: Institute of Economic Affairs.

National Audit Office (NAO) (2006) *Sure Start Children's Centres.* London: The Stationery Office.

OECD (2012) *Family Database.* Available at: www.oecd.org/social/family/database (accessed 4 July 2012).

ONS (2011) *Social Trends 41 – Households and Families.* Available at: www.ons.gov.uk/ons/publications/rss.xml?edition=tcm:77-218733 (accessed 11 November, 2012).

Perrons, D. (2006) 'Squeezed between two agendas: work and childcare in the flexible UK', in J. Lewis (ed.) *Children, Changing Families and Welfare States.* Cheltenham: Edward Elgar.

Phung, Viet-Han (2008) 'Ethnicity and child poverty under New Labour: a research review', *Journal of Social Policy,* 30(1): 95–118.

Piachaud, D. and Sutherland, H. (2001) 'Child poverty in Britain and the New Labour government', *Journal of Social Policy,* 30(1): 95–118.

Platt, L. (2005) *Discovering Child Poverty: The Creation of a Policy Agenda from 1800 to the Present.* Bristol: Policy Press.

Ridge, T. (2002) *Childhood Poverty and Social Exclusion: From a Child's Perspective.* Bristol: The Policy Press.

Sharland, E. (2006) 'Young people, risk taking and risk making: some thoughts for social work', *British Journal of Social Work,* 36: 247–265.

Shaw, S. (2010) *Parents, Children, Young People and the State.* Maidenhead: Open University Press/McGraw Hill Education.

Social Exclusion Taskforce (SETF) (2007) *Reaching Out: Think Family – Analysis and Themes from the Families at Risk Review.* Cabinet Office. Available at: www.cabinetoffice.gov.uk/media/cabinetoffice/socialexclusion_task_force/assets/think_families/pdf (accessed 29 October 2008).

Social Exclusion Taskforce (SETF) (2008*) Think Family: Improving the Life Chances of Families at Risk* (accessed 29 October 2008).

Standing, K. (1999) 'Lone mothers and "parental" involvement: a contradiction in policy?', *Journal of Social Policy*, 23(3): 479–495.

Underdown, A. (2007) *Young Children's Health and Well-being*. Maidenhead: Open University Press.

Wilson, A.R. (2007) 'New Labour and "lesbian-and-gay-friendly" policy', in C. Annesley, F. Gains and K. Rummery (eds) *Women and New Labour Engendering Politics and Policy?* Bristol: The Policy Press.

Woodcock, J. (2003) 'The social work assessment of parenting: an exploration', *British Journal of Social Work*, 33(1): 87–106.

7

Young People
Sandra Shaw

Overview

- Youth is seen as a period of transition, where young people are 'becoming' adults.
- Negative perceptions of 'youth' often dominate the media, generating debate around the risk that young people present to others, and the risks they experience themselves.
- The concept of risk is related to rights and responsibilities, and these three concepts underpin contemporary debates around young people.
- Young people not in education, employment or training (NEETs) are at risk of long-term disadvantage and social exclusion.
- Anti-social behaviour, and young people's involvement in this, was a central concern for the New Labour governments.
- The riots that took place in the summer of 2011 in the UK brought to centre-stage the 'problem' of young people, and illustrated the way that some young people can become alienated and disengaged from society.

Introduction

There is not one clearly defined boundary between a child and a young person, or between the latter and being an adult, and social policies also confuse the matter by referring to different ages, or age groups, which is discussed below. This chapter explores two key areas relating to young people in the UK. The first is the number of young people in the country not in employment, education or training (NEETs), and the second is that of anti-social behaviour (ASB). These were both areas of concern for the New Labour governments of 1997–2010 and continue to be so for the Conservative/ Liberal Democrat Coalition government that was formed in May 2010. Throughout the chapter, the concept of risk is important as it underpins so much of the debate about young people, and has influenced the development of social policies aimed at young people (Sharland, 2006; Shaw, 2010). In addition, issues of young people's rights and responsibilities are important. The chapter concludes by presenting some information on the riots that took place in England in 2011, which brings together some of the material presented here.

Age, young people and social policies

When it comes to looking at areas of policy, definitions of 'young person' vary (Iacovou and Aassve, 2007). Key pieces of policy, for example the *United Nations Convention on the Rights of the Child* (UNCRC) (UN, 1989), refers to children up to 18 years of age, as does *Every Child Matters* (ECM) (DfES, 2003), published by the New Labour government. This means that the content in the previous chapter is also relevant to young people. Beyond 18, social policies still position people aged 18–24 as 'young people', rather than adults. Thus, young people under the age of 25 are not entitled to the same amount of benefit as those aged 25 and over, and the national minimum wage (NMW) is also lower for young people under 21. The age at which young people can legally do what adults do varies. Consensual sex at the age of 16 is legal, young people can (currently) drive a car at the age of 17, but not vote until they are 18. At the other end of the continuum of youth, it is not clear when a child becomes a young person. In England and Wales, a 'child' is seen as responsible for their actions within the criminal justice system at the age of 10 (and in Northern Ireland), though under-18s are tried and sentenced as juveniles. The age of criminal responsibility in Scotland was 8 but was raised to 12 in 2012. The age of criminal responsibility is much lower in the UK than in other countries, for example it is 15 in Scandinavian countries and 18 in Belgium and Luxembourg (Goldson and Muncie, 2006; Muncie, 2009). The concept of age is significant as it relates directly to social policies aimed at different aspects of young people's lives, and these policies have actual consequences. It is also important to note that 'youth' is quite a recent invention, and in other parts of the world, ideas about growing up and on childhood and youth (or adolescence) vary (Kehily, 2007; James and James, 2008).

Transitions

Within the literature on youth, young people are often defined in relation to adults. For example, young people are less responsible, dependent, vulnerable, ignorant, rebellious, and in the state of *becoming* an adult. Adults are supposed to have the opposite characteristics, of being responsible, strong, independent and knowledgeable (see, for example, Hopkins, 2010). These are oppositional categories, though in reality, many adults never become fully responsible, and not all young people are irresponsible, rebellious or ignorant. However, *making a transition* implies that there is some boundary that young people cross when they become adults. One problem with this kind of categorization is that it does not take account of gender differences or cultural differences, or allow for the inclusion of disabled young people. With regard to social policies, it has been suggested that the New Labour governments positioned children and young people as 'citizens of the future' – or as in the process of becoming adults (Lister, 2005), and a crucial aspect of being an adult citizen would be engaging in paid employment (Lewis, 2006).

Current policies are geared towards keeping young people in education or some form of training until they are 18. After that, some young people will go into Higher Education, which means a further period of time when they may not be fully independent, either in terms of their finances or their housing. With an extended period of time in education or training, or with a low income – either as an unemployed or employed young person – it will be difficult to find sustainable affordable housing, and have sufficient income to live independently (France, 2008; Shaw, 2010). It may actually be difficult to find a job, as can be seen from the discussion on young people not in education, training or employment (NEETs) in this chapter. The reality of contemporary society is that the transition from youth to adulthood has been extended, and can be contradictory and fragmented (Bradley and van Hoof, 2005; Furlong and Cartmel, 2007; Nayak and Kehily, 2008). Progress towards becoming an independent adult can be characterized by uncertainty and a constantly changing situation. Young people can be in and out of employment, and move in and out of the family home. There are also young people who are severely disabled, for whom the concept of becoming totally independent is difficult to achieve. These factors challenge the idea of the association of adulthood with complete independence. On the other hand, even when a young person over the age of 18 continues to live at home, there are still possibilities for establishing an independent identity and social network via the use of new technologies (Roche et al., 2004). The support of families remains important, whether a young person lives at home or has moved out, but this is not readily available to all young people, including care leavers, those from families where there is conflict, and where poverty and disadvantage mean that life can be difficult for the whole family. The process of moving on and moving out will be more successful for some than for others (Biehal, 2007).

Perceptions of young people

Representations of youth have often been negative (Cohen, 1972; Pearson, 1983; Kehily, 2007). Young women seem to be excluded by the term 'youth', which is primarily associated with negative male behaviours (Robb, 2007). The agenda on anti-social behaviour that developed under New Labour reflected anxieties about 'out of control' youth, and the need to regulate this section of the population, as well as making them take responsibility for their behaviour (Muncie, 2009). A contradiction here is that while young people have to be responsible, parents are also expected to take responsibility for under-18s. The concept of risk often underpins discussion and policy-making related to young people (Smith et al., 2007; Broadhurst et al., 2009). While they are often seen as a risk, there is also concern about the risks modern society presents for young people (Gladwin and Collins, 2008; Shaw, 2010). One of the major problems today for young people is finding employment. Not being involved in education, employment or training (NEET) puts young people in a position of disadvantage in society.

Not in education, employment or training (NEETs) and youth poverty

The number of young people not in education or employment (NEETs) has been seen as a problem for some time in the UK and other countries (Bradley and van Hoof, 2005). The term belies the differences that exist between young people, for example, on the basis of gender, race or disability. It can suggest that when a young person is employed, they no longer need support (Furlong and Cartmel, 2007). However, employment can be tenuous and even if employed, young people can be living in poverty (France, 2008; Mendola et al., 2009). The concern about youth poverty is an international one (Iacovou and Aassve, 2007). A gendered difference in pay can mean that young women earn less than young men (YMCA, 2007, cited in France, 2008), and there is a greater risk of poverty for young people in some minority ethnic groups (Platt, 2007, cited in France, 2008). (It is also important to remember that some young people will also be parents, and potentially bringing up their children in poverty.) New Labour governments focused on social exclusion, emphasizing the importance of education, training and employment as a means of preventing poor life outcomes. The *State of the Nation* report, published by the newly elected Conservative/Liberal Democrat Coalition government in 2010, also highlighted NEETs as a concern (HM Government, 2010: 29). At the time of writing, the figures are increasing, and the UK has a higher proportion of NEETs than most other OECD countries (HM Government, 2010). Recent information on NEETs is set out in Box 7.1 below.

Box 7.1   Young people in the labour market – 2012

In the three months to February 2012, there were 3.63 million 16–24-year-olds in employment, down 13,000 from the three months to November 2011.

There were 2.63 million economically inactive 16–24-year-olds (most in full-time education).

There were 1.03 million unemployed 16–24-year-olds, down 9,000 from the three months to November 2011.

The unemployment rate for 16–24-year-olds was 22.2 per cent in the three months to February 2012.

Source: ONS (2012)

If being economically independent is a key factor in being an adult, then the fact that there are increasing numbers of young people who are not in employment means that the possibility of full independence is further delayed. Current figures show that over one million 16–24-year-olds are unemployed, and this represents around 22 per cent of the population of young people (ONS, 2012). For New Labour governments, work was highlighted as the main solution to poverty, and the incoming Coalition government also saw worklessness as a major cause of poverty (Cabinet Office, 2010). However, work cannot provide a solution to youth poverty if young people's incomes are lower, or if they cannot find secure paid employment. A European study from the Joseph Rowntree Foundation found that:

> Employment protects young people from poverty. But in most countries the protective effect of employment is apparent only after the young person has held a job for at least a year. It is not getting a job that is important, but getting and keeping a job. (Iacovou and Aassve, 2007: 43)

The adverse consequences of poverty for young people follow on from those for children referred to in Chapter 6. This means that their earnings potential will be affected as adults, which, as noted, entails costs for the state, and their health is also likely to be affected, which means greater costs for the state. Some authors have suggested that youth unemployment is more sensitive to the economy, rising rapidly in recession and falling quickly in times of recovery (see Furlong and Cartmel, 2007: 37), which implies that this group in society is at greater risk of unemployment than older working-age adults. Given the scale of the problem, it is not surprising that governments have tried different policy approaches to provide a solution to the problem of young people's unemployment, some of which are described below. These usually involve training schemes or apprenticeships, which can be successful but are not without problems. Training needs to translate into long term jobs which are sustainable and pay enough to support young people (and, sometimes, their families).

Policies on youth unemployment

Under the New Labour governments (1997–2010) different strategies were developed to deal with young people's unemployment. The New Deal, launched in 1998, targeted those over 18, with a focus on tailoring support to individual needs (Furlong and Cartmel, 2007). The September Guarantee, introduced in 2000, guaranteed a place in education or training for all 16–17-year-olds. In addition, 35,000 additional apprenticeships were created, and money was invested in supporting 16–18-year-olds (Inside Government, 2010). These kinds of initiatives were also in place in other industrialized nations, and in 1997 the European Union agreed a set of common principles to assist young people who had been out of work for six months or more (Furlong and Cartmel, 2007).

A means-tested allowance – the Educational Maintenance Allowance (EMA) – was introduced in 1998, rolled out nationally in 2004, and paid to young people who stayed in education for a further two years after the age of 16. While the maximum payment of £30 seems a relatively small amount of money, it may have made a difference to students from poorer backgrounds. However, in 2010 the Coalition government announced that EMA would cease.

In May 2010, the Coalition government announced plans for the introduction of a National Citizenship Service, aimed at providing all 16-year-olds with an opportunity to develop skills and give them experience of the workplace. The government also proposed an extension of apprenticeship schemes. In 2011, details of The Youth Contract were announced by the Deputy Prime Minister Nick Clegg (DWP, 2011). This includes an extra 250,000 work experience places over the following three years, with incentives paid to employers to take on young people as apprentices. A £150 million programme was also announced to support 16–17-year-old NEETs and get them back into education, apprenticeships or a job with training (DWP, 2011; Cabinet Office, 2012). While the political rhetoric may differ, the policies developed by New Labour and by the Coalition government are similar. However, the creation of training schemes or apprenticeships has so far not solved the long-term problem of high levels of unemployment among young people, and the risk of being unemployed – with all that this implies – carries forward into adulthood.

Anti-social behaviour: New Labour policies

While youth justice was a focus for successive governments, after the election of the first New Labour government in 1997, the emphasis changed to dealing with anti-social behaviour (ASB), with a key element targeting the behaviour of young people. While the same legislation applies to youth justice and ASB, this chapter will focus on the latter, though this is located within the wider youth justice agenda. ASB was presented as a national issue, and one that reflected concern about the state of the country, and the moral decline evident within society. While other sections of the population can engage in anti-social behaviour, it has been largely associated with the behaviour of young people, not least in terms of the preoccupations of the media, which influence both public and political perceptions of social issues. As is noted below:

> Youthful misbehaviour came to be regarded as symbolizing all that is wrong with adult society: family failure, inadequate parenting, and all these perceptions influenced policy proposals and legislative changes throughout the twentieth century. (Brown, 2005: 104)

These worries about young people, their families and broader society have continued to dominate at the start of the 21st century under both the New Labour and Coalition governments. It is also a matter of public concern, with a lot of media coverage given to the area, though Hodgkinson and Tilley (2011) suggest it is more likely to affect the quality of life for the most disadvantaged in society.

The definition of anti-social behaviour is vague, subject to interpretation, and, in particular, depends on the perception of those affected by negative behaviours that could then be labelled anti-social. Anti-social Behaviour Orders (ASBOs) were introduced in England and Wales in the

Crime and Disorder Act (CDA) 1998. Anti-social behaviour was defined as 'acting in a manner that caused, or was likely to cause harassment, alarm or distress to one or more persons not of the same household (as the defendant)' (Hodgkinson and Tilley, 2011: 289). ASBOs were civil orders that could be imposed on those aged 10 or over by the police or local authority. Breach of an order becomes a criminal offence and can lead to incarceration (Goldson and Muncie, 2006). Other sanctions that can be applied to young offenders and their families included Child Curfew Orders and Parenting Orders (POs). The Act abolished the principle of *doli incapax*, meaning that 10–13-year-olds could be held responsible for their actions. The Youth Justice Board (YJB) and Youth Offending Teams (YOTs) were also set up. The Anti-Social Behaviour Act 2003 was a further development in this area of policy, extending the powers of the police and local authorities. The legislation relating to ASBOs was significant as it extended the remit of the criminal justice system by including behaviour that was not necessarily criminal (Goldson and Muncie, 2006). Figures show that 70 per cent of 10–17-year-olds breach their ASBO (Ministry of Justice, 2011). Concern has been expressed by the number of young people in prison in this country, and putting young people into prison or secure environments can result in bullying, self-harm and suicide attempts (Goldson and Muncie, 2006).

In the past, youth crime had been dealt with differently in Scotland, via The Children's Hearing system which was established in 1971. This reflected an approach based on prioritizing the needs of young people (McAra, 2006). However, the Crime and Disorder Act Scotland (CDAS) 1998 introduced ASBOs, and the Antisocial Behaviour Act Scotland 2004 built on this. Parenting Orders were also introduced. Whereas the hearing system focused on the child's welfare which had to be 'the paramount consideration' (Tisdall, 2006: 105), the use of ASBOs is more about punishing young people and making them responsible for their behaviour. In the UK, the New Labour agenda on behaviour, on community, and on making people responsible for their actions was important in shifting the emphasis within the youth justice system. This punitive trend in youth justice systems is also evident in other countries (Muncie, 2009). The introduction of ASBOs means that the behaviour of young people as individuals and within groups has come under the spotlight, and that the regulation and control of the behaviour of children and young people, and their parents, has been legitimized.

Dispersal orders were introduced in England and Wales, and Scotland, allowing the police to move groups of two or more people from a specified area (Hodgkinson and Tilley, 2011). Young people can be asked to move on if they are seen to present a threat to others – even if they have not actually done anything criminal (Tisdall, 2006). This elevates the concepts of place and community as somewhere that should be protected, by removing problem groups. At the same time, 'this sets boundaries around communities, including some and excluding others' (Shaw, 2010: 102), with a lack of reflection on what this actually means to those young people affected. The concepts of place and community, and inclusion and exclusion, are particularly relevant to the discussion on the 2011 riots that ends the chapter.

One of the consequences of public debates about ASB and young people has been to conceptualize them as 'other', and to give the impression that all young people are a risk to the rest of society. They are seen not only as an *actual* risk, but also as a *potential* risk to individuals and to communities, particularly when they gather together in groups. Unfortunately, this negative image of youth is often applied more widely to all young people. Overall, legislation has facilitated the regulation and control of young people, and public spaces (Tisdall, 2006; Garrett, 2007). In addition, the behaviour of some families and of parents becomes problematic, with Parenting Orders and Family Intervention Projects a means for exercising surveillance over such families.

Despite the fact that ASBOs were central to New Labour policy, Hodgkinson and Tilley (2011) show that there was a decline in the use of ASBOs between 2005 and 2009. ASBOs can be effective and work for some. They can make individuals or their families behave differently, but they do not necessarily work for everyone (Hodgkinson and Tilley, 2011). Successful interventions may mean using a range of strategies with young people and their families, and within communities. However, these authors also note that there is a lack of evidence on what actually works in terms of reducing ASB.

The diversity of young people and ASBOs

Young people tend to be treated as an homogeneous group when ASB is discussed, but their experiences vary. Those involved in ASB can have associated problems, such as drug and alcohol use, and may suffer from learning difficulties (Fyson and Yates, 2011) or mental health issues (Nixon et al., 2007, cited in Hodgkinson and Tilley, 2011). This is in addition to risk factors often associated with criminal behaviour and ASB, such as growing up in poverty and disadvantage, coming from problem families, having an offender in the family, poor educational achievement and behavioural problems (Farrington, 1996, cited in Archard, 2007). Race/ethnicity is another factor to consider, and here there is a need for further research. An article by Prior (2009) considers responses to ASB-related matters in three areas in England with ethnically diverse populations, looking at 'settled' minority communities, young people from those communities and 'new' immigrant communities (2009: 133). There was variation in inter-generational tensions within communities, with a longer history of this within the African-Caribbean community. As young South Asian people turned away from traditional cultural norms, this also led to tensions. The author goes on to state that:

> Just as the advent of ASB powers has been widely viewed as providing an additional means of disciplining disadvantaged and disengaged White youth ... so those powers have been co-opted as a means of disciplining the disadvantaged and disengaged youth of ethnic minority communities. And, importantly, the purpose of this is not just to punish perpetrators or to protect the wider public, it is to alter attitudes and behaviours in order to steer young people on to a path toward a more constructive life: 'how to change behaviour via ASBOs'. (Prior, 2009: 139)

According to this study, new immigrant communities – from Somalia, other African and Eastern European countries, coming to Britain as refugees or economic migrants – are subject to complaints about their behaviour and this comes 'as much from settled ethnic minority residents as well as White residents' (Prior, 2009: 140). New groups with different norms and behaviour conflict with the expectations of the already settled but 'diverse populations' (Prior, 2009: 140). This author suggests ASB policy in practice changes and responsibilizes 'attitudes and behaviour' and 'disciplines the members of "new immigrant communities"' (Prior, 2009: 141).

Conservative/Liberal Democrat Coalition policies

The ASB policies of New Labour have been subject to a lot of criticism, most notably around the infringement of the rights of children and young people (Goldson and Muncie, 2006; Muncie, 2009). On the other hand, there is some evidence that they work for some people (Hodgkinson and Tilley, 2011; Prior, 2009). There is a need for more evidence about what works to provide a platform for designing and delivering effective policies. However, in February 2011, the Coalition government set out their review of anti-social behaviour measures, which involved a critique of the New Labour approach, and set out their plans for reform in *More Effective Responses to Anti-Social Behaviour* (Home Office, 2011).

Anti-social Behaviour Orders were seen as too costly and not working effectively, and a range of alternative proposals was set out. These included: The Criminal Behaviour Order; The Crime Prevention Injunction; The Community Protection Order; The Direction Power; Informal tools and out-of-court disposals; and The Community Trigger. The intention is to repeal the ASBO and other court orders for individuals and introduce a Criminal Behaviour Order that can be attached to a criminal injunction and a Crime Prevention Injunction to stop ASB quickly. This effectively makes ASB a criminal matter from the outset, which has the potential to heighten some of the concerns already expressed about the rights of children and young people, and their welfare. Dispersal powers become 'direction' powers, and there is an emphasis on rehabilitation and restoration. The Community Trigger, which was subject to media debate in 2012, means that victims and communities have a right to 'require agencies' to deal with ASB.

Political ideology and anti-social behaviour

The debate over anti-social behaviour can be related to New Labour communitarian philosophy, wherein values and norms are shared across society and within communities (Etzioni, 1997). People who behave in a way that flouts these values and norms of behaviour can be labelled anti-social. This implies that people within communities and society self-regulate their behaviour to fit in, and that this is something that is done willingly (Heron and Dwyer, 1999). Where people do not do this, then the law can step in to enforce these shared ideas about what is acceptable. Hodgkinson and Tilley (2011) note a potential continuity of ideas between New Labour and the Coalition government, and in particular an association between communitarian values and David Cameron's idea of 'the Big Society' (Cabinet Office, 2010). The latter seems to reflect a continuation of New Labour concerns with 'community engagement, community problem-solving and community mobilization' (Hodgkinson and Tilley, 2011: 296), as can be seen, for example, in the use of community triggers. The challenges are whether or not ASB can be dealt with by engaging communities – who are most likely to get involved – and, at a time of widespread cuts in public expenditure, how this would be financed. Issues of place, community and young people came to the fore in the riots of 2011 which are discussed below.

The 2011 riots and young people

In August 2011, there was an outbreak of rioting in the UK. This began in London after the shooting of Mark Duggan in Tottenham by the police on 4 August 2011. A peaceful protest by his family and supporters on 6 August descended into violence, which then spread to nearby areas. By Sunday 7 August, the riots had spread to 12 areas within London, and by Monday 8 August had spread nationally, with 60 areas experiencing rioting (Riots Committee and Victims Panel [RCVP], 2012). The riots were subject to widespread media coverage by 24-hour news channels and other media. From the outset, there was concern about the response of the police and the speed at which the rioting spread throughout the country, though not all major cities were involved. There was a lot of debate about the causes of the riots, and potential solutions for dealing with the problem. In terms of dealing with the after-effects, the judicial system set up a 'fast-track' process for dealing with offenders, and the punishment for crimes was often tough, due to the connection to rioting. Subsequent to the rioting, a number of pieces of research were undertaken. Some of the findings of two of these are explored in this final part of the chapter.

The riots lasted five days, leading to hundreds of people losing their homes and businesses and five people dying. It is estimated that 13,000–15,000 people were involved, and out of those arrested nine out of ten were known to the police (RCVP, 2012). Figures from the Ministry of Justice released on 23 February 2012 show that 2,710 people had appeared before the courts by midday on 11 February of that year. More than 5,000 crimes were committed during the riots. The majority of those that came before the courts were male with a previous conviction and 84 had multiple previous offences. Three-quarters were aged 24 or under (RCVP, 2012: 17).

Reading the Riots by The Guardian and LSE (2011) is based on research in London, Birmingham, Manchester, Salford, Nottingham and Liverpool. This involved interviewing 270 individuals directly involved in the riots, four fifths of whom were male and one fifth female. Out of these, 30 per cent were juveniles, and over 49 per cent were aged 18–25, reflecting the age categories of young people already discussed in this chapter. Respondents were asked to identify their own ethnicity and the figures were as follows: 5% Asian; 26% white; 47% black; 17% mixed or other. The riots were not seen to be about race, but the findings indicate a number of other factors that were important. These include: anger towards the police; the extensive use of BlackBerry Messenger to share information and plan in advance; the involvement of students and unemployed people; opportunism by many; and the significance of poverty. Other issues were also cited, including student fees, cuts to youth services, the stopping of EMA, and social and economic injustice, as well as the shooting in London. Interestingly, this study found that the involvement of gangs in the riots was over-stated in the media.

According to this research, and the work by the RCVP – both based on official records – there is a link between deprivation and the rioting. Out of 1,000 court records, 59 per cent were from the most deprived 20 per cent of areas in the UK (The *Guardian* and LSE, 2011). Rioting did not occur in all deprived areas, but just under half of the areas where rioting occurred were in the top 25 per cent most deprived areas in England (RCVP, 2012). Associated with poverty are other factors such as special educational needs, persistent absence from school, permanent exclusion from school, claiming free school meals and low educational achievement at GSCE level. Research undertaken in Manchester also found that a third of looters in Manchester and Salford came from the poorest districts (cited in RCVP, 2012). The MP for Tottenham, David Lammy in *Out of the Ashes* (2011), stated that there was a variety of long-term causes leading to the riots. These included: poor education; ineffective parental guidance; poor role models; father absence; ill-discipline; unemployment; and a variety of social and developmental problems.

The death of Mark Duggan provided a 'spark' for the riot, and the slow response of the police left the way open for extensive rioting in Tottenham (RCVP, 2012). Loss of confidence in the police is believed to have led to people testing their reactions in other areas, with trouble mostly beginning in retail areas, with large groups of people. The police seemed to have lost control and people felt they would be able 'to get away with' what they did. However, there seems to be no single reason for people's involvement, and some crime was opportunist. The *Guardian* and LSE research (2011) notes poor relationships between communities and the police, with many rioters known to the police. However, the majority of people did not riot. The RCVP (2012: 25) report suggests this was because they felt they had a stake in society and an awareness of shared values.

The RCVP (2012) study focused on six key themes aimed at improving the situation in communities. These include a focus on improving parenting, building personal resilience in young people, and encouraging young people – including NEETs – to have hopes and dreams. Other areas include looking at the influence of commercial brands, rehabilitating persistent offenders, and improving relationships between the police and communities. This report makes the link between factors associated with poverty, disadvantage, social exclusion, special educational needs, poor parenting, truancy and previous offending, and the way that these can lead to poor life outcomes for young people. Not all young people growing up in disadvantage will become rioters or anti-social or involved in crime, but the risks are high for those experiencing a wide range of disadvantage. The danger is that unless sufficient investment is made in the most deprived areas of the country, many young people will grow up feeling marginalized, and similar problems could occur again.

Summary/Conclusions

- Young people in the NEETs category are less likely to be able to make the transition to independent adulthood and could continue to experience poverty and disadvantage throughout their lives.
- Policies on anti-social behaviour illustrate how negative perceptions of youth and the concept of risk underpin this area, and that it continues to be a significant area of concern in the 21st century.
- The riots in the UK in 2011 highlight the problem of the marginalization of many young people, and a number of risk factors for involvement in a range of anti-social and criminal behaviours.
- Research on the riots shows links across the material covered in this and the previous chapter, and also points the way to building a future where young people can develop aspirations and feel socially included in society.
- Young people are not an homogeneous group and the emphasis on 'youth' with masculine overtones ignores the experiences of young women. In addition, more information is needed on ethnicity, and on other social factors, such as disability, which impact on young people's lives.

Questions

1 What are the connections between not being in education, employment and training and youth poverty, and what are the consequences for young people?
2 What evidence is there to suggest that policies on anti-social behaviour have been effective?
3 How can young people be active, responsible citizens and exercise their right to participate fully in society when they cannot find paid work?
4 What do the research findings on the riots of 2011 indicate about the involvement of young people?

Recommended reading

Bradley, H. and van Hoof, J. (2005) *Young People in Europe: Labour Markets and Citizenship*. Bristol: The Policy Press.

Furlong, A. and Cartmel, F. (2007) *Young People and Social Change*. Maidenhead: Open University Press.

Hodgkinson, S. and Tilley, N. (2011) 'Tackling anti-social behaviour: lessons from New Labour for the Coalition government', *Criminology and Criminal Justice*, 11(4): 283–305.

Shaw, S. (2010) *Parents, Children, Young People and the State*. Maidenhead: Open University Press/ McGraw Hill Education.

Relevant websites

For information on policies related to employment, see the Department of Work and Pensions – www.dwp.gov.uk/

For information on anti-social behaviour and youth justice, see the Home Office – www.homeoffice. gov.uk/crime/ – and NACRO – www.nacro.org.uk/

References

Archard, D. (2007) 'Children's rights and juvenile justice', in M. Hill, A Lockyer and F. Stone (eds) *Youth Justice and Child Protection*. London: Jessica Kingsley.

Biehal, N. (2007) 'Reuniting children with their families: reconsidering the evidence on timing, contact and outcomes', *British Journal of Social Work*, 37: 807–823.

Bradley, H. and van Hoof, J. (2005) 'Fractured transitions: the changing context of young people's labour market situations in Europe', in *Young People in Europe: Labour Markets and Citizenship*. Bristol: The Policy Press.

Broadhurst, K., Grover, C. and Jamieson, J. (2009) *Critical Perspectives on Safeguarding Children*. Chichester: Wiley Blackwell.

Brown, S. (2005) *Understanding Youth and Crime: Listening to Youth?* Maidenhead: Open University Press.

Cabinet Office (2010) *Minister calls for a radical shift in the relationship between citizens and the state*. Available at: www.cabinetoffice.gov.uk/news_releases/2010/ (accessed 21 June 2006).

Cabinet Office (2012) *Radical new approach to defuse 'ticking time bomb' of NEETs*. Available at: www.dpm.cabinetoffice.gov.uk/new/radical-new-approach-defuse-ticking-time (accessed 18 July 2012).

Cohen, S. (1972) *Folk Devils and Moral Panics*. London: Paladin.

Department for Education and Skills (DfES) (2003) *Every Child Matters*. London: The Stationery Office.

Department for Work and Pensions (DWP) (2011) *25 November: £1 billion package to tackle youth unemployment*. Available at: www.dwp.gov.uk/newsroom/press-releases/2011/nov-2011/dwp132-11.shtml (accessed 18 July 2012).

Etzioni, A. (1997) *The New Golden Rule*. London: Profile Books.

France, A. (2008) 'From being to becoming: the importance of tackling youth poverty in transitions to adulthood', *Social Policy and Society*, 7(4): 495–505.

Furlong, A. and Cartmel, F. (2007) *Young People and Social Change*. Maidenhead: Open University Press.

Fyson, R. and Yates, J. (2011) 'Anti-social behaviour orders and young people with learning disabilities', *Critical Social Policy*, 31: 102.

Garrett, P.M. (2007) 'Making "anti-social behaviour": a fragment on the evolution of "ASBO politics"', *British Journal of Social work*, 37: 839–856.

Gladwin, M. and Collins, J. (2008) 'Anxiety and risks', in J. Collins and P. Foley (eds) *Promoting Children's Wellbeing: Policy and Practice*. Bristol: The Policy Press.

Goldson, B. and Muncie, J. (2006) *Youth Crime and Justice*. London: Sage.

Heron, E. and Dwyer, P. (1999) 'Doing the right thing: Labour's attempt to forge a new welfare deal between the individual and the state', *Social Policy and Administration*, 33(1): 91–104.

HM Government (2010) *State of the Nation Report: Poverty, Worklessness and Welfare Dependency in the UK*. Available at: www.cabinetoffice.gov.uk/media/ (accessed 21 June 2010).

Hodgkinson, S. and Tilley, N. (2011) 'Tackling anti-social behaviour: lessons from New Labour for the Coalition government', *Criminology and Criminal Justice*, 11(4): 283–305.

Home Office (2011) *More Effective Responses to Anti-Social Behaviour*. London: Home Office. Available at: www.homeoffice.gov.uk/publications/consultations/cons-2010-antisocial-behaviour/ (accessed 18 July 2012).

Hopkins, P. E. (2010) *Young People, Place and Identity*. London: Routledge.

Iacovou, M. and Aassve, A. (2007) *Youth Poverty in Europe*. York: Joseph Rowntree Foundation. Available at: www.jrf.org.uk (accessed 26 July 2012).

Inside Government (2010) *Looking for a NEET Solution: Tackling the Problem of those 'Not in Education, Employment or Training' (NEET)*. Available at: www.insidegovernment.co.uk/children/neets-employment (accessed 18 July 2012).

James, A. and James, A. (2008) *Childhood Studies*. London: Sage.

Kehily, M.J. (2007) *Understanding Youth: Perspectives, Identities and Practices*. London: Sage, in association with the Open University.

Lammy, D. (2011) *Out of the Ashes*. London: Guardian Books.

Lewis, J. (2006) *Children, Changing Families and Welfare States*. Cheltenham: Edward Elgar.

Lister, R. (2005) 'Investing in the citizen-workers of the future', in H. Hendrick (ed.) *Child Welfare and Social Policy: The Essential Reader.* Bristol: The Policy Press.

McAra, L. (2006) 'Welfare in crisis? Key developments in Scottish youth justice', in B. Goldson and J. Muncie (eds) *Comparative Youth Justice*. London: Sage.

Mendola, D., Busetta, A. and Aassve, A. (2009) 'What keeps young adults in permanent poverty? A comparative analysis using EHCP', *Social Science Research*, 38(4): 840–937.

Ministry of Justice (2011) *Anti-Social Behaviour Order Statistics: England and Wales 2009*. London: Ministry of Justice.

Muncie, J. (2009) *Youth and Crime*. London: Sage.

Nayak, A. and Kehily, M. (2008) *Gender, Youth and Culture: Young Masculinities and Femininities*. Basingstoke: Palgrave Macmillan.

ONS (2012) *Labour Market Statistics*, April 2012: 'Young People in the Labour Market'. Available at: www.ons.gov.uk/ons/rel/lms/labour-market-statistics/april-2012/statistical-bulletin.html#tab-Young-people-in-the-labour-market (accessed 25 April 2012).

Pearson, G. (1983) *Hooligan: A History of Respectable Fears*. Basingstoke: Macmillan.

Prior, D. (2009) 'Disciplining the multicultural community: ethnic diversity and the governance of anti-social behaviour', *Social Policy & Society*, 9(1): 133–143.

Riots Communities and Victims Panel (RCVP) (2012) *After the Riots: The Final Report of the Riots Communities and Victims Panel.* Available at: http://riotspanel.independent.gov.uk/wp-content/uploads/2012/03/Riots-Panel-Final-Report.pdf (accessed 12 July 2012).

Robb, M.R. (2007) 'Gender', in M.J. Kehily (ed.) *Understanding Youth: Perspectives, Identities and Practices.* London: Sage.

Roche, J., Tucker, S., Thomson, R. and Flynn, R. (2004) *Youth in Society* (2nd edn). London: Sage, in association with the Open University.

Sharland, E. (2006) 'Young people, risk taking and risk making: some thoughts for social work', *British Journal of Social Work*, 36: 247–265.

Shaw, S. (2010) *Parents, Children, Young People and the State.* Maidenhead: Open University Press/McGraw Hill Education.

Smith, C., Stainton Rogers, W. and Tucker, S. (2007) 'Risk', in M. Robb (ed.) *Youth in Context: Frameworks, Settings and Encounters.* London: Sage, in association with the Open University.

The Guardian and London School of Economics (LSE) (2011) *Reading the Riots.* Available at: www.guardian.co.uk/uk/interactive/2011/dec/14/reading-the-riots-investigating-england-s-summer-of-disorder-full-report (accessed 18 July 2012).

Tisdall, E. (2006) 'Antisocial behaviour legislation meets children's services: challenging perspectives on children, parents and the state', *Critical Social Policy*, 26(1): 101–120.

United Nations (UN) (1989) *United Nations Convention on the Rights of the Child* (UNCRC). Geneva: United Nations.

8

Older People

Rita Haworth

Overview

- Since the 19th century, there has been a significant rise in the number of older people in society.
- 'Old age' is a contested concept but for the purpose of this chapter 'older people' will be defined as those aged 60 years or over.
- Older people are the greatest consumers of welfare services. Three areas – housing, health and social care and pensions – will be highlighted to show how successive governments' policies have attempted to meet the needs of older people.
- Political ideologies and their impact on policy formulation and outcomes for older people will be discussed.
- Government approaches to the sustainability of services for older people will be considered.
- This chapter provides an introduction to understanding policy development in the given areas and their outcomes in practice in relation to older people.

Introduction

Demographic changes throughout the 20th century have led to the global phenomenon of population ageing, though each society has experienced this at a different rate. Old age is a social construct but for the purpose of definition, the World Health Organization (WHO) defines old age chronologically starting at 60 or 65 years, roughly equivalent to retirement age in most developing countries (WHO, 2010). In the UK however, the retirement age is currently being raised to 66 years for both men and women (Chapmen, 2010). In Europe, a decline in fertility and an increase in life expectancy have been key factors in the perception of old age as problematic. A declining birth rate coupled with a growing ageing population has facilitated a rising demand for welfare services by older people. At the end of 2008, a demographic milestone was passed when the number of pensioners in the UK outnumbered that of children (Nursing and Midwifery Council, 2009). Put simply, it has been argued that future spending on welfare services would be unable to keep pace with the demands of an escalating older population (Hicks and Allen, 1999). In the UK, between 1901 and 1991, the population overall increased by 51 per cent. In 1901, life expectancy was 45.5 years for men and 49 years for women (Hicks and Allen, 1999). Women on average live longer than men, however by the 21st century the age gap at death has somewhat decreased. Statistics suggest life expectancy from the age of 65 years in the UK is now 17.8 years for men and 20.4 years for women (Office for National Statistics, 2010). Glasby (2007) predicted that in the UK the number of people aged 80 and over will reach 7 million by 2051, whilse Murray (2011) forecast over half a million centenarians by 2066.

From the start of the 20th century and until the 1960s, old age was based on a medical model in which 'old age' was constructed as a diseased, inactive 'stage of life' and perceived very much as an individual problem. Key themes in both ageing research and policy were disengagement, decline and adjustment. Though these ideas now have little currency with social scientists who view the medical model as derogatory to older people, the medical model remains central to the contemporary discourse of old age used by the media, the general public and, to a more limited extent, policy makers (Phillipson and Baars, 2007). The 1970s saw the emergence of the political economy perspective on later life which focuses on the social construction of old age and structured dependency (Walker, 1993). Around the same time, the idea that ageing populations constituted a threat to economies across the western world began to take hold and these changes were reflected in governmental attitudes and policy towards older people. This chapter will focus on three key areas of UK welfare policy – housing, health and social care and pensions – to offer outlines of the ways in which policies in these areas have developed since the Second World War.

Housing, older people and social policy

Following the Second World War, the UK government promised 'a separate house for every family that wants one' (Hicks and Allen, 1999: 12). Over four million local authority houses were built in the post-war period to replace bombed homes and housing stock no longer deemed acceptable. Rows of terraced housing in urban areas – many with outside toilets – were demolished and residents were moved to more modern social housing in the suburbs. This surge of house building reached a peak in 1968 (Hicks and Allen, 1999). The housing needs of families were given priority and older people living in homes with several bedrooms were encouraged to move to smaller accommodation, releasing larger houses for families. Older people living in homes of a size considered appropriate were encouraged to stay and maintain the property (Hicks and Allen, 1999).

Prior to the Second World War most homes were rented, but financial growth in the UK in the immediate post-war years meant that home ownership increased. An attempt by the government to reverse this trend in the late 1950s was unsuccessful as tax advantages for home owners in conjunction with a rise in the number of building societies offering long-term mortgages meant that home owner-ship became a viable option for the majority and not just the few in the UK population (Hicks and Allen, 1999). Owner occupation by 2008 accounted for 69.8 per cent of tenure across all households and among younger retired people was almost 80 per cent (BBC, 2008). However, holding housing equity is not always positive in later life when income is likely to be low, thus making maintenance an issue. Throughout the 1980s and 1990s, a series of Housing Acts by the New Right Conservative government brought about major changes in home ownership. For example, the Housing Act 1980 gave certain groups the right to buy their council houses, but many older people past retirement age could not secure a mortgage, trapping them in social housing (Hicks and Allen, 1999).

A small percentage of older people have always required long- or short-term residential care and even today many spend their final days in hospital or residential/nursing homes (Nursing and Midwifery Council, 2009). However, Townsend's (1962) critique of institutions for the care of older people led to the perceived best alternative – sheltered housing – being placed high on the policy agenda. Until the 1980s, there was major investment in social housing by local authorities which was replaced in the 1990s by the growth of privately owned sheltered housing. Initially, each development had a warden on site but this changed as high-tech alarm systems became avail-able. During the same period, the move from public to private sector funding was reflected in funding for residential care, due to new funding structures outlined in the NHS and Community Care Act 1990. This still remains largely the case today and the size of residential/nursing homes has increased over time and ownership has become more concentrated. However, two things have remained constant: only 1 per cent of individuals between the ages of 65 and 74 years live in insti-tutional settings and the majority of older people state a preference for continuing to live in their own homes. This widespread desire, alongside the realization by policy makers that remaining at home is both cost-effective and enhances quality of life for many older people, has led to the con-cept of 'ageing in place' taking centre-stage during recent years (Balchin and Rhoden, 2002). The New Labour government paper *Quality and Choice for Older Peoples' Housing* (DH, 2001b) outlined two major objectives:

> To ensure that older people are able to maintain their independence in a home that is appro-priate for their needs.

> To enable older people to make informed choices about where they live and the services that are available to support their decisions.

[and further noted:]

> There is certainly empirical evidence of mental and physical benefits associated with con-tinuing to live in one's own home in later life, however, most housing in the UK has barriers which make this difficult. (Department of the Environment, 2001: 8)

The New Labour government housing strategy published in 2008 aimed to change this by ensuring that by 2011 all newly built public housing would adhere to lifetime home standards, and private builders were also being encouraged to ensure that new builds were older-person-friendly by 2013, though this would not be mandatory. It was assumed that these measures would enable the majority of older people to remain in their own homes while at the same time reducing the cost of health and social care. The funding for local authority Disabled Facilities Grants to assist with adaptations to dwellings for older and disabled people also increased from £146 to £166 million (Direct.Gov.uk, undated). This was to increase again by 2011 and funding was to be made available to provide housing help and advice to all older people as required.

As yet, there has been no policy statement from the current Coalition government relating to older people's housing needs though the assumption is that the key themes of diversity and extra care schemes as outlined in the New Labour government's 2009 paper *Building a Society for all Ages* will be supported. However, one of the problems which the Coalition government faces is to reconcile the needs of an ageing society with cuts in public expenditure aimed at dealing with the economic crisis. This, in turn, will impact on housing policy as by 2020 80–90 per cent of older people are expected to be living in the community while current funding streams will decrease or disappear (Brown and Yates, 2010).

Older people and health and social care

Although an ageing population is often viewed as problematic, it can also be seen as a success of the welfare state. Services that were unaffordable to many prior to 1946 became accessible following the setting up of the welfare state. Universality of services including the NHS enabled better health and social care, leading to greater longevity of life. The issue of paying for services in particular for an ever-increasing older population remains central to policy planning and debate (Alcock, 2008). By the turn of the 21st century, the average age of death had risen to 85 years and is forecast to rise to 90 years by 2015 (Tallis, 2005). Since the establishment of the NHS in 1948, life expectancy from birth increased by almost 10 years in the first 50 years of the NHS. Prior to the NHS, 40 per cent of people died before pension age (Tallis, 2005). Consequently, this rise in the proportion of older people living longer has been viewed as a 'social problem that politicians from both the left and right have grappled to deal with from the mid-20th century to the present day' (Alcock, 2008: 50). From the political left throughout the 1940s to the mid-1970s, older people were viewed as 'impotent victims' of mandatory retirement and seen as the deserving poor for whom collective welfare provisions, for example, social security benefits, social services and health care, should be favourably provided (Arber and Ginn, 1994a).

From the mid-1970s, Britain was witnessing an economic crisis, inflation soared, unemployment stood at almost 3 million and the country was in the grip of mass industrial strikes. Such economic pressure coupled with the growing demand for services by older people led to increased resource restraints (Tanner, 2010). By the late 1970s, people began to lose faith in the Labour government and in 1979 a Conservative government, influenced by neoliberal ideas, was elected with a large majority; a result that signalled the beginning of 18 years of Conservative government in the UK. Successive Conservative administrations rejected the mix of Social Democratic and 'Middle Way' Conservative policies that had characterized the approach of their predecessors in the post-Second World War period. They argued that over-generous welfare provisions had created a breeding ground for a culture of welfare dependency (Walker, 1993). Throughout the 1980s, New Right rhetoric concerning older people began to emerge in phases such as 'the growing burden of dependency' and 'the growing pension's time bomb' (Arber and Ginn, 1994a). As opposed to the compassionate approach, an era of 'conflictual' ageism had arrived. Older people as service users were no longer to be treated with the 'compassion' of the past (Arber and Ginn, 1994a). Influenced by New Right ideology, which emphasized individualism and self-sufficiency, the main aim of policy relating to this was to reduce the role of the state in the management and financing of welfare for older people (Arber and Ginn, 1994a).

In 1986, the government asked the Audit Commission to review Community Care; the report *Making a Reality of Community Care* (1986) identified increased spending on residential care for adults as a growing concern (Tanner, 2010). The subsequent Griffiths report, *Community Care: An Agenda for Action* (1988), suggested that social service departments should take the lead role in assessing needs, planning and coordinating services, including those provided by the private and voluntary sector. The proposal intended to remove the incentive for institutional care by transferring funding from the social security budget to local social service providers and to impose an assessment 'gateway' for those who needed access to state-funded care (Tanner, 2010). In response to the Griffiths report, the government published a White Paper, *Community Care: The Next Decade and Beyond* (1989), which stated that:

> People who enter homes under the new funding structure and who need public financial support will no longer have their care costs met by social security. They will receive assistance on the same basis as that which they could obtain in their own homes. The financial incentive towards residential care under the present rules will therefore be eliminated. (DH, 1989: 7)

Such sentiments were echoed in the NHS and Community Care Act 1990 which stimulated a mixed economy of welfare, a system whereby care is provided by a range of agencies including the state, private and voluntary sectors and the family. The Community Care Act 1990 shifted the state from being providers of care to enablers and purchasers, with social services departments becoming enablers of care rather than main providers, purchasing services from the private and voluntary sectors (Tanner, 2010). A major incentive of the 1990 NHS Act was to promote more domiciliary services to enable older people to remain in their own homes (DH, 1990). In addition to tightening financial provision for funding residential care for older people, there was also a preference for care by the family. However, despite the introduction of a 'mixed economy of care', demand for health and social care services for older people continued to rise (Glasby, 2007).

Similar objectives and themes informed the policy of the incoming New Labour government elected in 1997. In the main, the New Labour government accepted the role of the market, and the necessity of a purchaser provider split in meeting health and social care needs. Simultaneously, however, New Labour placed greater emphasis on managerial control and regulation as a way of controlling policy and practice outcomes (Tanner, 2010). New Labour's adult social care policy did however 'shift from primary concerns with the organization, delivery and efficiency of services that drove the previous new right policy objective to a greater emphasis on enhancing service user control and choice over their own care' (Tanner, 2010: 29). In 1997, the government commissioned a review of long-term care and the Royal Commission report *Respect to Old Age*, published in 1999, recommended free nursing and personal care for older people to be paid for from taxation (Denney, 2008). However, the government ruled out the recommendations of the report on grounds of cost. Nursing care provided by qualified staff would be free and paid for from taxation, while personal care would be means-tested, with those with means paying for personal care. In Scotland (see Chapter 11 on devolution), the Scottish Executive agreed that both nursing care and personal care would be provided for free (Bochel and Bochel, 2005).

The National Service Framework for Older People (DH, 2001a) set out a 10-year reform programme to ensure a higher quality of service provision for older people (Glasby, 2007). Nevertheless, despite the National Service Framework, criticisms of older people's services continued. Reports by the Commission for Social Care Inspection and the Health Care Commission suggested that large numbers of older people received poor hospital care, and more recently it has been suggested that this is in part due to ageism (Age Concern, 2007). The publication of the White Papers *Our Health: Our Care Our Say* (DH, 2006) and *Putting People First* (DH, 2007) fostered a transformation of adult social care (Tanner, 2010), and signalled New Labour's intention to ensure 'people have maximum choice, control and power over services received' (DH, 2007: 2). Within this policy shift, the personalization agenda was born, with the extension of direct payments and the introduction of individual budgets where monies are directly paid into service users' bank accounts, giving them more control over purchasing care services that best suit individual needs. Although in principle direct payments and individual budgets have been viewed as a positive directive, Glendinning's (2008) research on the modernization of adult social care raises concerns about the adequacy of effective information and support mechanisms for assisting older people to make the best decisions about commissioning care (Newman et al., 2008).

By 2009, Britain was facing economic recession and in May 2010 the Conservatives and Liberal Democrats formed the first UK coalition government since 1945. With Britain in the grip of recession, rising unemployment and the public purse being used to prop up the failing banking system, the deficit in public finances reached unprecedented levels. The Coalition was quick to act on reducing the deficit and following a comprehensive Spending Review, published in October 2010 (HM Treasury, 2010), the government announced that spending cuts of £80 billion a year over the next three years would be necessary, £18 billion of which would be saved by a reduction in welfare spending (Brewer and Brown, 2011). Following the Spending Review (HM Treasury, 2010), the government pledged protection for adult social services by providing £1 billion by 2014/15 and an additional £1 billion to be provided by the NHS through joint working with local authorities. However, as Walker points out, 'this un-ring-fenced "protection" relies on money being transferred to adult social services from the NHS which itself is facing the tightest financial constraints for 30 years' (Walker, 2011: 23). This, coupled with a central government reduction in local government funding of 26 per cent between 2011 and 2015, is unlikely to lead to favourable outcomes for older people's services. As Walker notes, 'in relation to older people and social care cuts look likely to be severe' (2011: 23).

In 2010, the government commissioned an independent committee to review the funding of care and support in England. The resulting report *Fairer Care Funding* (DH, 2011) proposed that those who receive free care should continue to do so and those with means (including home owners who have previously had to sell property to fund residential care) should pay a limited maximum cost for care over a lifetime of £35,000 after which individuals should be eligible for full support. The report also stated that the threshold above which people would become liable for their full care costs should be increased from £23,250 to £100,000 (Dilnot, 2011). Given the lukewarm response by the government to the Dilnot Report and the current economic climate, the Joseph Rowntree Foundation suggests it is unlikely we will see any immediate improvement in services for older people (JRF, 2011).

NHS services for older people have also come under increased scrutiny. The Independent Regulator for Health and Social Care for England, the Care Quality Commission (CQC) undertook a survey of older people's hospital care throughout 2011. The survey was conducted following a wave of media reports alleging the poor standard of hospital care for older people. The CQC made spot checks on 100 hospitals. All of the first 12 hospitals surveyed showed they were failing to meet essential standards for dignity and nutrition for older in-patients (CQC, 2011). Therefore, although free at the point of delivery, the standards and adequacy of health services for older people remain a concern. When over 60 per cent of all NHS admissions are people aged over 65, good NHS care is imperative for older people. The Equalities Act 2012 aims to outlaw age discrimination and in theory should be a positive step (Mitchell, 2011). However, in light of the most revolutionary shake-up of the NHS in the form of the 2012 Health and Social Care Act (DH, 2012) that will disband health trusts and put GP consortiums at the helm of commissioning services, it is unlikely that services for older people will initially be given precedence, as issues of organization, structure and procedure may initially take priority (Joseph Rowntree Foundation, 2011).

Developments in medicine, medical technology and a rise in living standards have all contributed to people living longer. With an ongoing economic recession and a rising population of older people across the western world, it is unlikely that older people will, at least for the foreseeable future, be top of the agenda for welfare spending. Following the Coalition government's 2010 Spending Review (HM Treasury, 2010), English local authorities and the NHS will lose over a quarter of their budgets (Yeates et al., 2011). Cuts in support for services for older people, especially those with moderate needs, remain likely. Alongside this, an increase in charges for those who are able to pay for services is forecast (JRF, 2011).

Pensions, social policy and older people

It is generally accepted that the UK's ability to maintain incomes for individuals post-retirement is in crisis. Pemberton (2006) maintains that while the increasing number of older people has played a part in this, it is also due to the complexity and ineffectiveness of the current pension scheme and the way it has developed from the start of the 20th century. The Pensions Commission Report (Pensions Policy Institute, 2011) concluded that major reform of the system was essential, but in order to bring about such a change Pemberton argues that an understanding of historical context is required. In 1908, a non-contributory, stringently means-tested pension scheme was introduced for those over 70 years of age. It was fixed at less than subsistence level to encourage saving while in work and to ensure family support post-retirement. Looking at life expectancy at this time, it is clear that many people would be dead before they reached pensionable age. A minor change was made in 1925 when a contributory element was added but other than this, pension policy remained the same until the Beveridge Committee report of 1942 attempted to unify the previous two schemes (Pemberton, 2006).

Following the establishment of the post-war welfare state in 1945, a state-run, universal, contributory national insurance pension, based on the findings of the Beveridge Committee, was introduced but, unfortunately, not all its aims could be met. Whereas Beveridge had envisaged a 20-year transition period to full pension rights, the incoming Labour government felt that this delay was impractical. Full pensions were therefore paid at once to those individuals of pensionable age who had contributed since 1925 and after 10 years for those who had joined the scheme at a later date. Thus, current contributions paid for current pensions, that is, the scheme was established on a 'pay as you go' system. In addition, the level of contribution was set at a flat rate which the lowest paid employee could afford, which meant that pensions could not be paid at a level which eliminated the need for supplementary payments. The constraint this placed on the system continued to be a problem until 1960 (Pemberton, 2006).

As early as the 1950s, it became apparent that old age pensions would be a burden on the Exchequer so only small increases were allowed which meant that in real terms pensions fell below the lowest scale of benefits paid by the national assistance board (Summerskills, 1950). The demand for a pension that reflected the cost of living and average earnings led to employers offering top-up occupational pension schemes and by 1960 these played a major role in pension provision, though the majority of employees still remained dependent on the inadequate state pension (Pemberton, 2006). A gap developed between those reliant on the state pension and those who also received a pension from their employer via occupational schemes. From 1974, the Labour government closed the gap by introducing the State Earnings Related Pension Scheme (SERPS) in which every worker was entitled to the basic state pension and most workers would also be eligible for SERPS income retirement provision based on their earnings (Whitehouse, 1998). The Conservative governments during the Thatcher years from 1979 linked increases in pensions to prices, thus lowering the real value of the state pension. In line with the expansion of a free market economy, individuals were encouraged to purchase private pensions to ensure financial security in old age. Incentives to providers resulted in many people being sold pensions which did not deliver on their promises and public confidence in pension systems more generally decreased. The 1985 Green Paper *Reform of Social Security* engendered opposition from the Labour party, the unions and perhaps more surprisingly the Treasury, and the government eventually backed down and reduced the value of SERPS provision rather than eliminating it altogether (Whitehouse, 1998). The subsequent Social Security Act 1986 however further undermined SERPS, proposing a preference for more private pensions.

On coming to power in 1997, the New Labour government proclaimed it was to make radical changes to the pension system. In 2002, the Pensions Commission was established by the government and produced three reports in 2004, 2005 and 2006. All three strongly recommended deferment of the retirement age, encouraging individuals to purchase private pension schemes and an increase in national insurance contributions. The reality was a policy preference for more of the same, privately funded pension plans for the majority with those on the lowest incomes reliant on the state pension. Reform of pensions has been and still is the subject of ongoing discussion. Arguably, successive recent governments have made minor changes, often based on the desire for quick political gain, but these have simply increased the complexity of the system without bringing about the major reorganization which is required (Price, 2007).

Pension policy was an early priority of the Coalition government on assuming power in 2010 and some of its first actions were to phase out the default retirement age and increase the minimum retirement age to 66 years from 2016 for men and 2020 for women. In addition, Coalition plans include a simplification of pension rules: 'Reform of the pensions for public sector employees is also planned and to this end an Independent Commission has been set up to ascertain the long term affordability of public sector pensions' (Hutton, 2011: 56).

In the past, proposed governmental overhauls of the pensions system in Britain have resulted in little more than cosmetic change and increased complexity; however, the economic downturn may ensure that the Coalition government is forced to create real reform. It is likely that, in the future, the majority of people in the UK will have to work to an older age and make increased contributions to their pensions for reduced returns.

Summary/Conclusions

- Demographic changes throughout the 20th century have led to the global phenomenon of population ageing.
- It is predicted that in the UK the number of people aged 80 years or older will reach seven million by 2051 (Glasby, 2007).
- No one can predict how housing, health, social care and pensions for older people will be met in policy terms in the future as governments, political ideologies and economies change.
- The economic downturn of the early 21st century and austerity measures being considered by UK policy makers will most likely lead to reductions in government spending on housing, health and social care and pension initiatives for older people.

- If these welfare services for older people are to be sustained and improved, government funding needs to be adequate and ring-fenced.
- Resourcing older people's services may in future be taken one step further with compulsory insurance schemes or death taxes for care in later life being introduced.

Questions

1 What are the major changes that have taken place since the 1950s regarding the housing needs of older people?
2 What part has demography played in the growing demand for older people's health and social care services since the post-Second World War welfare state was set up?
3 How have successive government policies changed the provision of health and social care services for older people?
4 What policy developments have led to the complexity of the present pensions system in the UK?

Recommended reading

The first three texts listed provide an historical overview of housing, health, social care and pension policy as discussed within this chapter. The fourth text offers an analytical overview of possible trends for the above areas post-2010.

Bond, J., Peace, S., Dittman-Kohli, F. and Westerhof, G. (2007) *Ageing in Society: European Perspectives on Gerontology* (3rd edn). London: Sage.

Pemberton, H. (2006) *Politics and Pensions in Post War Britain*. Available at: www.historyandpolicy. org/papers/policy-paper-41.html

Tanner, D. (2010) *Managing the Ageing Experience: Learning from Older People*. Bristol: The Policy Press.

Yeates, N., Haux, T., Jawad, R. and Kilkey, M. (2011) *In Defense of Welfare: The Impacts of the Spending Review*. Available at: www.social-policy.org.uk/downloads/idow.pdf

Relevant websites

For housing policy, see the Department for Communities and Local Government – www.communities.gov.uk/housing

For health policy, see the Department of Health – www.dh.gov.uk

For social care, see the Social Care Institute for Excellence – www.scie.org.uk

For pensions policy, see the Department for Work and Pensions – www.dwp.gov.uk

References

Age Concern (2007) *Age of Equality? Outlawing Age Discrimination Beyond the Workplace*. London: Age Concern.

Alcock, P. (2008) *Social Policy in Britain* (4th edn). Basingstoke: Palgrave Macmillan.

Arber, S. and Ginn, J. (1994a) *Gender and Later Life: A Sociological Analysis of Resources and Constants*. London: Sage.

Arber, S. and Ginn, J. (1994b) 'Women and ageing in review', *Clinical Gerontology*, 4(4): 93–102.

Audit Commission (1986) *Making Reality of Community Care*. London: HMSO.

Balchin, P. and Rhoden, M. (2002) *Housing Policy: An Introduction* (4th edn). London: Routledge.

BBC News (2008) Home ownership dips to decade low. Available at: www.bbc.co.uk/1/hi/business/72492.st

Bochel, H. and Bochel, C. (2005) *Social Policy: Issues and Developments*. Harlow: Pearson.

Brewer, M. and Brown, J.B. (2011) *Cuts to Welfare Spending*. Available at: www.social-policy.uk/downloads/idow.pdf (accessed 9 August 2012).

Brown, T. and Yeates, N. (2010) 'Choice, empowerment and personalisation', in J. Richardson (ed.) *From Recession to Renewal*. Bristol: The Policy Press.

Care Quality Commission (CQC) (2011) *Hospital Standards for the Elderly*. Available at: http://nhsuk/news/2011/05may/pages/cqc-elderly-hospitalstandards.aspx (accessed 6 June 2012).

Chapmen, J. (2010) 'Government speed up plans to raise retirement age', *Daily Mail*, 19 July, p. 10.

Denney, D. (2008) 'Risk and the Blair legacy', in M. Powell (ed.) *Modernising the Welfare State: The Blair Legacy*. Bristol: The Policy Press, pp. 143–159.

Department for Employment (DfE) (1986) *Social Security Act*. London: HMSO.

Department of the Environment (DoTE) (2001) *Quality of Choice for Older Peoples' Housing: A Strategic Framework*. London: HMSO.

Department of Health (DH) (1989) *Caring for People: Community Care in the Next Decade and Beyond*. London: HMSO.

Department of Health (DH) (1990) *The Health and Community Care Act*. London: HMSO.

Department of Health (DH) (2001a) *The National Service Framework for Older People*. London: HMSO.

Department of Health (DH) (2001b) *Quality and Choice for Older People's Housing: A Strategic Framework*. London: HMSO.

Department of Health (DH) (2006) *Our Health, Our Care, Our Say: A New Direction for Community Care Services*, CM 6737. London: DH.

Department of Health (DH) (2007) *Putting People First: A Shared Vision and Commitment to the Transformation of Adult Social Care*. London: HMSO.

Department of Health (DH) (2011) *Fairer Care Funding*. London: HMSO.

Department of Health (DH) (2012) *Health and Social Care Act*. London: HMSO.

Dilnot, A. (2011) *Commission on Funding of Care and Support*. Available at: www.dilnotcommision.dh.gov.uk/2011/07/04 commissioning-report/ (accessed 12 July 2011).

Direct.Gov.uk (undated) *Disabled People*. Available at: www.direct.gov.uk/en/disabledpeople/H (accessed 11 July 2012).

Glasby, J. (2007) *Understanding Health Policy and Social Care*. Bristol: The Policy Press.

Glendinning, C. (2008) 'Increasing choice and control for older and disabled people: a critical review of new developments in England', *Social Policy and Administration*, 42(5): 451–469.

Griffiths, R. (1988) *Community Care: An Agenda for Action* (The Griffiths Report). London: HMSO.

Hicks, J. and Allen, G. (1999) *A Century of Change: Trends in UK Statistics Since 1900*. Research paper 99/111. London: House of Commons Library.

HM Treasury (2010) *Spending Review*, cm 7942. London: The Stationery Office.

Hutton, W. (March 2011) *Independent Public Service Pensions Commission: Final Report*. London: HM Treasury.

Joseph Rowntree Foundation (JRF) (2011) *White Paper within Nine Months of the Dilnot Report have been Dashed*. Available at: www.jrf.org.uk/media-centre/Joseph-Rowntree-foundation-urges.Coalition.Action now (accessed 12 December 2011).

Mitchell, M. (2011) 'Poor treatment of older people in the NHS: an attitude problem', guardian.co.uk, 15 February.

Murray, J. (2011) 'Live to 100? Only if I am still able to flirt like Denis Healey!', *The Mail on Sunday*, 7 August, p. 31.

Newman, J., Glendinning, C. and Hughes, M. (2008) 'Beyond modernisation? Social care and the transformation of welfare governance', *Journal of Social Policy*, 37(4): 531–557.

Nursing and Midwifery Council (2009) *Guidance for the Care of Older People*. Available at: www.nmc-uk.org/documents/guidance/Gu (accessed 6 August 2012).

Office for National Statistics (ONS) (2010) *Life Expectancies*. Available at: www.statisticsgov.uk/hub/office-for-nationalstatistics/index.html (accessed 12 July 2012)

Pemberton, H. (2006) *Politics and Pensions in Post War Britain*. Available at: www.historyandpolicy.org/papers/policy-paper-41.html (accessed 10 October 2011).

Pensions Policy Institute (2011) *What Could the Coalition Government Mean for Pensions Policy?* Briefing note 56. Available at: www.pensionspolicy.or-uk/defa (accessed 13 July 2012).

Phillipson, C. and Baars, J. (2007) 'Social theory and social ageing', in S. Bond and F. Pearce (eds) *Ageing in Society: European Perspectives on Gerontology*. London: Sage, pp. 68–84.

Price, D. (2007) 'Closing the gender gap in retirement income: what difference will recent UK pension reforms make?', *Journal of Social Policy*, 36(12): 561–583.

Summerskills, E. (1950) 'National assistance scales (increase)', *Hansard*, 3 May (474): cc.1803–68.

Tallis, J. (2005) 'Living longer healthier lives', *The Times*, 22 October.

Tanner, T. (2010) *Managing the Ageing Experience: Learning from Older People*. Bristol: The Policy Press.

Townsend, P. (1962) *The Last Refuge: A Survey of Residential Institutions and Homes for the Aged in England and Wales*. London: Routledge and Kegan Paul.

Walker, A. (1993) 'Community care policy: from consensus to conflict', in J. Bornet (ed.) *Community Care: A Reader*. London: Macmillan, pp. 196–220.

Walker, A. (2011) 'Older people', in N. Yeates (ed.) *In Defense of Welfare: The Impact of the Spending Review*, Social Policy Association, pp. 21–23. Available at: www.social-policy.org.uk/downloads/idow.pdf (accessed 23 November 2011).

Whitehouse, E. (1998) *Pension Reform in Britain: World Bank Social Protection*. Discussion paper no. 9810. Available at: www.pensionspolicyinstitute.org.uk (accessed 9 July 2012).

World Health Organization (WHO) (2010) *Health Statistics and Health Information System (HSI)*. Available at: www.who.int/healthinfo/survey/ageing (accessed 11 July 2012).

Yeates, N., Haux, T., Jawad, R. and Kilkey, M. (2011) 'The impacts of the spending review', in N. Yeates (ed.) *In Defense of Welfare: The Impact of the Spending Review*, Social Policy Association. Available at: www.social-policy.org.uk/downloads/idow.pdf (accessed 11 December 2011).

9

Death and the End of Life

Karen Kinghorn

Overview

- Autonomy and self-determination have altered attitudes to death and dying and brought about change to end of life care.
- The social status and culture of an individual throughout life is reflected in the way his/her death is perceived and practices concerned with dying.
- The hospice movement introduced the concept of palliative care.
- The *End of Life Care Strategy* introduced by New Labour (2008) aimed to provide access to high quality care and autonomy for all those approaching the end of life.
- Preferred priorities of care/advance care planning enable individuals to state their wishes with regard to care and preferred location of death.
- Assisted suicide is still a contested subject within the UK.
- The GP consortia, introduced by the Coalition government, has the objectives of monitoring and evaluating local services which will inevitably be affected by the economic situation. This may mean that the aim of the *End of Life Care Strategy* to eradicate inequality at the end of life is not achieved.

Introduction

The influence of medicine, and debates around euthanasia and assisted suicide in the media, have raised the profile of death in the UK. Attitudes to death and dying now encompass the concepts of choice and autonomy to achieve a good death. Holloway (2007: 100) describes cross-cultural features of a 'good death' as being able to anticipate and prepare for death, retaining control over the place of death, who will be present and having time to say goodbye, dignity and privacy in the final stages, symptom control that includes pain relief, having access to information, expertise (possibly in the form of hospice care), emotional and spiritual support, respecting the wishes of the dying through advance directives and, more recently, being able to die rather than pointlessly extending life. Strategies to enhance end of life care in the UK have adopted a palliative care approach. This method supports the holistic care of dying patients to manage pain and other symptoms with provision for psychological, social and spiritual care with the aim of achieving the best quality of life for patients and families (WHO, 2002). As a result, the strategies and interventions discussed in this chapter are altering the way death is accommodated and perceived. This chapter examines the connections between the causes and patterns of death, government priorities for end of life care policy, services which include advance care planning, and the current debate on assisted dying.

Death and dying

In 1900, most people died from acute infectious illnesses in childhood or early adulthood and death mainly took place in people's own homes. The Office for National Statistics (2012b) reported that in 2009 there were approximately 500,000 registered deaths in the UK. Almost two thirds were aged 75 or over and, of these, 58 per cent died in hospital following a period of chronic ill health. The fastest growing population group are those aged over 85 and advances in pharmacology and medical procedures are producing a prolonged old age, which may be characterized for many by an increasing incidence of frailty, illness and disease towards the end of their lives (Gomes and Higginson, 2008). The leading cause of death in the age group 35–64 years is dominated by chronic diseases which include coronary heart disease, breast and lung cancer (ONS, 2012c). Between the ages of 5 and 34 years, the major causes of death are accident or suicide with twice as many deaths for males than females. Infant deaths (children between the ages of 1 and 4 years) account for around 500 deaths per year and are associated with congenital anomalies. Neonatal deaths (birth to 28 days) accounted for approximately 4,500 deaths per year in 2009, attributable to premature birth and congenital anomalies (ONS, 2012a).

Advances in medicine have increased the number of children surviving life-limiting and life-threatening conditions into adulthood and currently there are 40,000 children (in England alone) requiring care services (NEoLCIN, 2012). Palliative care for children is different, due to the variety of childhood conditions and lengths of illness. Children with life-limiting conditions can require holistic care that takes into account educational, medical and social requirements as they continue to develop. Care services for children are organized differently as paediatricians tend to work alongside palliative care services (Warrick et al., 2011). At whatever age death occurs, it is likely that in the weeks prior to death more use will be made of health services than at any other time throughout the lifespan. Public awareness and media coverage of death, alongside access to advice, support and guidance, have directed the need and expectation of a good death for those of all ages (NEoLCIN, 2012). The debate around end of life care has become increasingly important for a number of reasons. First, people with serious illnesses and congenital conditions are living longer; second, the number of people living with dementia and requiring care is increasing; and third, family care has become fragmented due to changing work patterns and the lack of available carers in the family (Watts, 2012).

Recent large-scale surveys about end of life care show that most people would prefer high quality care at home if they felt that this did not place too great a burden on their family and other carers (Gott et al., 2004; Luptak, 2006; Twomey et al., 2007). The majority of people did not want to die alone or in hospital and yet the latter is the reality for most people (Hockey, 1990). As death becomes imminent, many older people are admitted to hospital, though this is often unnecessary. Consequently, they die in high-tech surroundings and not in the more homely environment which many would prefer (Gott et al., 2007). This occurs despite autonomy often being cited as a key ingredient of a 'good death'. Inequalities among older people also impact on their death, and the social status of an individual during their lifetime is reflected in both the way in which their death is perceived and in the practices concerned with dying, for example choice about where to die and control over end of life care may be easier for wealthy individuals (Twomey et al., 2007). A hospital or residential care bed can be the only option for those who cannot afford to pay for the support required to remain in their own homes at the end of life. Luptak (2006) found that over 50 per cent of older people who said they never wished to be a in a nursing home died in one. In the last year of life, many older people move several times. A potential solution is the preparation of an advance care plan, discussed later in the chapter.

Palliative care is often associated with the hospice movement and care for cancer patients. Cicely Saunders pioneered the idea of a broader concept of palliative care, founding St Christopher's Hospice in South London in 1967 (Reith and Payne, 2009) This development was the beginning of a worldwide movement to improve the philosophy and services behind end of life care. A holistic multidisciplinary approach is provided that respects death as a natural process supporting an active life and enhancing quality of life until death (Reith and Payne, 2009). The purpose is to alleviate pain and other distressing symptoms while offering support to patients and their families during illness and in bereavement (Healthcare Commission, 2007). Older people are less likely to be moved to hospice or palliative care services because policies tend to focus on particular terminal conditions. Ageism may play some part in this claim, as it is difficult to make predictions about an end of life trajectory for older people and they are often assumed to have no specific palliative care needs (Luptak, 2006). Analysis of NHS patient complaints carried out between 2004 and 2006 showed that over half were concerns about end of life care, particularly with the lack of information staff provided to both patients and their families (Healthcare Commission, 2007). Since the majority of those dying in acute settings are older people, Gomes and Higginson (2008) concluded that a significant number of older people were receiving poor care at the end of life. Quality care services at the end of life were the objectives for national policy development.

Policy developments in end of life care

The UK leads the world on policy relating to end of life care and 'quality of death' issues (EIU, 2010). The themes adopted were built on existing practice from the hospice sector and the Department of Health's End of Life Care Programme (2004–2007). A whole-system approach leads to pathways which include the Gold Standards Framework (GSF: DH, 2005b), Liverpool Care Pathway for the Dying Patient (LCP) and Preferred Priorities of Care (PPC). These are plans or templates for the organization and management of multi-professional services. The methods were previously utilized in manufacturing to standardize processes and contain costs. Transferring the practice to end of life care, national policies attempt to standardize services, quality and coordination, and measure outcomes while aiming to provide choice for patients (Watts, 2012). The National Institute for Clinical Excellence recommends three approaches to end of life care. The National Gold Standards Framework (DH, 2005b) is designed to identify a terminally ill patient to services upon diagnosis and plan for an impending death. The Liverpool Care Pathway (LCP) is a system to improve communication and coordination between services in the last few days of life. During 2012, the LCP was criticized in the media, with concerns expressed that it had been used inappropriately and without consent by patients and/or their families (NHS Choices, 2012). At the time of writing it remains in place with the support of organizations and agencies involved in palliative care (see Association for Palliative Medicine, 2012). Preferred priorities of care is the mechanism by which the patient's requests are recorded. Palliative care for children is recognized separately in *Better Care: Better Lives* (DH, 2008). The devolved governments have followed suit with their own management of end of life care in Scotland and Wales (2008) and Northern Ireland (2010), contributing to a raised profile of planning care for all with life-limiting conditions. The *End of Life Care Strategy* (2008) sets out key areas to develop a care pathway approach for commissioning services and the delivery of integrated care.

The *End of Life Care Strategy* (2008)

The *End of Life Care Strategy* (2008) is designed to build capacity to include home-based care and lessen the divisions between specialist palliative and end of life care, promoting integrated services for all adults across England and Wales (Reith and Payne, 2009). Care at the end of life integrates health and social care services. The organization of social care, unlike health, has developed in a piecemeal fashion and is the responsibility of social services departments. Personal social services provided by local authorities are situated in a unique arena for funding and service delivery because there is a strict eligibility criteria to target resources at crisis cases (Holloway, 2007). Initially, the strategy paper *Building on the Best: Choice, Responsiveness and Equity in the NHS* (DH, 2003), published by New Labour, aimed to increase choice by developing more responsive services. One of the six priorities was end of life care. However, it was the White Paper *Our Health, Our Care, Our Say* (DH, 2006) that offered a significant commitment to end of life care by pledging funding, improved service coordination and the national implementation of specific pathways. As a result,

The End of Life Care Strategy (DH, 2008: 10) 'focuses on high quality care irrespective of age, gender, ethnicity, religious belief, sexual orientation, diagnosis, or socio-economic status', with consumerism and choice driving the commissioning and delivery of services. The strategy has since been adapted to suit various settings while maintaining common features (Henry, 2011).

Initially, a medical prediction that someone has months or days to live is required; this will activate the pathway delivery of services. Estimating a prognosis is not an exact science and is more likely to occur at a review appointment rather than in a time of crisis (Coombs and Long, 2008). Originally designed for primary care settings in 2000, the Gold Standards Framework (GSF) recognizes that once clinicians are able to identify terminally ill and dying patients, the process moves forward to examine care needs, symptoms and the wishes of the patient. The GSF encourages inter-professional teams to collaborate and provides tools such as the 'surprise question' (would they be surprised if the patient died within a number of time periods?). This would prompt professionals to code patients based on life expectancy (Thomas, 2010: 62). The sensitive conversations required between doctors, health and social care professionals, patients and families are the main issue. Ethical problems arise over when it is acceptable or appropriate to discuss end of life issues, as time-pressured clinical encounters make it easy to set aside discussions around death and dying (Byock, 2004; Leadbeater and Garber, 2010; Woods, 2007).

The strategy outlines six crucial steps that include discussion with the patient and family to determine preferences, assessment and care planning (preferred priorities of care/advance care planning), coordination of care and the delivery of services through to bereavement counselling after death for family members. Throughout the process, access to information, support for carers and spiritual care are also addressed (Addicott and Ross, 2010). There are mechanisms to support people at particular stages, such as regular reviews of support plans and the availability of rapid response teams. Coordination is a key theme across the boundaries of service delivery and at service level. Making palliative care available across all disease trajectories and age ranges adds layers of complication. It is difficult to determine whether an older person is living with or dying from a specific condition, and those with some illnesses are less likely to have the intermediary stage between living and dying recognized (Sutton and Coast, 2012). Conditions such as dementia, heart failure and HIV/AIDS do not follow predictable patterns that allow for accurate planning. Support for people with learning difficulties is variable. Challenges include a lack of easy access to information, late diagnosis due to difficulty in assessing pain and other symptoms, breaking bad news and inadequate facilities in residential care homes to cope with a terminal illness (Tuffrey-Wijne, 2010). Despite the problem of finding the services that fit every variable, there is a convincing argument under unpredictable circumstances for giving patient views priority by utilizing a preferred priorities of care/advance care planning pathway (Woods, 2007).

Close interdisciplinary collaboration is required to avoid fragmented and disconnected services for people choosing to die in a residential setting. Combining services requires the integration of commissioning across the whole spectrum of welfare in the UK, from benefits to health and social care, through to public, private, voluntary and informal provision. Often, a plethora of disconnected services from an increasing array of professionals are presented as patients are devolved into categories such as child/adult/older person and cancer/mental health/heart disease (Holloway, 2007).

This untidy progression takes many routes before end of life care can be implemented. To alleviate the problem in a community setting, there is a Single Assessment Process (SAP) aimed at providing a holistic, multi-disciplinary response intended to operate within established care management. A trigger is required from a medical professional to indicate that an individual has entered the last stages of life (normally a general practitioner). This system has been transferred from local authority social services to Primary Care (Leadbeater and Garber, 2010). The way information is shared and disseminated between services is not always reliable. There is a need for a continuous supportive relationship between welfare provision and the family. Omega (2009) suggests a single point of contact should be available to assist in finding the best mix of services and support available. However, only around 30 per cent of those requiring coordination have a key worker. The National End of Life Care Intelligence Network (NEoLCIN) (2012) reports a poor awareness of the services available, especially for families of children with a terminal illness, and a lack of coordination during the delivery of palliative care.

The policy and process ends with the Liverpool Care Pathway which focuses on the last days of life in non-specialist settings and is designed to improve comfort measures, communication and coordination of care. The assessment continues the person-centred plan, guiding care professionals to initiate symptom control and anticipatory prescribing and to know when to discontinue treatments, with psychological and spiritual support for the patient and family (Holloway, 2007). Judging the shift in health specifically to when the patient has days or hours to live is difficult. While the benefits of the system are evident, unfortunately slow progress has been made in implementing the necessary services. Potential problems include: a lack of availability of nursing and personal care services (which may not be available out of normal working hours), and some GP practices not being proficient at identifying or coordinating the services required for people to die in their own homes (Omega, 2009). Out of hours services vary by time, type and geographical location with urban areas having more provision than rural areas (Macmillan, 2010). One of the main concerns for families and carers is access to pain relief out of normal working hours. These concerns are shared by care homes.

The *End of Life Care Strategy* (2008) in nursing homes is necessary to improve end of life care for older people in this site of care. The adaptation takes the form of the Gold Standards Framework in the Care Homes Programme which aims to provide choice for patients/residents and minimize inappropriate admission to hospital. Yet crisis dying (admissions to hospital via the emergency route) is still a reality due to the lack of resources (Audit Commission, 2011). Funding was a matter of concern for The Royal Commission on Long Term Care (2008) as Primary Health Care Trust resources are unavailable to nursing homes. Pathways may be adopted but this does not mean they are funded, as the cost of participating in some of the GSF programmes inhibits some care homes from taking part (Hughes-Hallett et al., 2011). Nursing homes rely on networks and personal links within the community for support with care – notably pain relief, access to training and the goodwill of GPs. To develop their capability as chronic disease management centres in order to deliver end of life care, nursing homes have to be brought into the wider system that facilitates health and social care – especially in the arenas of funding and collaboration between statutory and private/voluntary sectors (Seymour et al., 2011).

Policy documents discuss end of life care within a short time frame and in a residential setting. This is clear in the tools utilized that require a diagnosis of impending death, usually within six months for the Gold Standards Framework but reduced to days in the Liverpool Care Pathway. These mechanisms do not easily transfer to the care of certain conditions as complex symptoms may cause hospital admission even with a good local service infrastructure in place (Froggatt, 2005; Watts, 2012). Good coordination via health and social care is vital to enable the delivery of a complex array of services, especially for those people wishing to die at home. Unfortunately, priority given by social services departments to crisis cases indicates that accessing resources is complicated, therefore the effective use of the prescribed tools may not provide for patient choice and needs if funding is scarce (Froggatt, 2005; Holloway, 2007; Leadbeater and Garber, 2010). There is conflict between 'bureaucratic, clinical and political agendas', making holistic practice, choice, quality and equity unrealistic targets alongside budget-driven constraints, nevertheless the pathways have been actively implemented (Watts, 2012: 25).

The *End of Life Care Strategy* (2008) attemps to deliver a good death focusing on physical care and comfort in the dying stage. The concept of a good death is complex and personal and subject to diverse cultural meaning (Watts, 2012). Different cultures and religious beliefs can accentuate the divisions between patient, family and service providers. Death may be a universal event but the process is required to incorporate a multi-cultural population. The *End of Life Care Strategy* (2008) acknowledges that inequalities exist in access to services, but the lack of specific guidance to meet the needs of some patient groups is notably absent. Jones (2005: 443) argues against a generic approach, stating that the hospice movement method of 'facilitating mental and spiritual preparation for death' for every individual is more appropriate.

Recent political and policy changes by the Coalition government include the development of GP consortia to take over commissioning primary and acute care services (Health and Social Care Act 2012). A review of End of Life Care is due in 2013 with a commitment to a 'per patient tariff' that applies to clinical needs (DH, 2011: 14). This type of funding will follow the patient, and will be available to pay for palliative care in all settings (Hughes-Hallett et al., 2011). There is a risk that in the current economic climate the focus will be on scaling down costs rather than redesigning to fit consumer needs. Reforming current patterns of care to reduce unnecessary hospital admissions at the end of life would ensure the best use of financial resources while ensuring quality provision (Addicott and Ross, 2010). Although the *End of Life Care Strategy* recognizes inequalities in health and family resources that may affect the capacity to cope, there is no obligation for the new GP consortia to promote integrated services or reduce inequalities. However, preferred priorities of care/advance care planning has the potential to overcome some barriers by focusing on patient requirements.

Preferred priorities of care/advance care planning

An advance care plan, sometimes referred to as a living will, is a 'statement of wishes and preferences' that indicate an individual's written or verbal request for the type of care and treatment they would like when incapacitated and unable to make those requests directly (Leadbeater and Garber, 2010). The wording of an Advance Decision is explicit:

> Should I be unable to communicate, please note that I have signed, in the presence of two witnesses the following Declaration: if the time comes when I can no longer take part in decisions for my own future, let this Declaration stand as the testament to my wishes; if there is no reasonable prospect of my recovery from physical illness or impairment expected to cause me severe distress or to render me incapable of rational existence, I request that I be allowed to die and not be kept alive by artificial means and that I receive whatever quantity of drugs may be required to keep me free from pain or distress even if the moment of death is hastened. (Odone, 2010: 50)

These requests can be around medical care, for example the desire not to be resuscitated, and non-medical issues such as where a patient would like to die. An advance decision, if legitimate, ensures that preferences are taken into account at a time when physical and/or mental capacity is diminished (Henry and Seymour, 2007; Royal College of Nursing, 2011). Advanced planning is available to adults aged over 18. Occasionally, palliative care plans for babies are a requirement as a communication aid between hospital, community teams, the GP and the family (Warrick et al., 2011). Parents generally have the right to consent to treatment for their child. Advance care planning made by the parent on behalf of a child is legally binding and open to negotiation depending on the child's progress. More recently, a life-limited female, aged 13 years, supported by relatives, won the right to refuse treatment via the court system. Hannah Jones, aged 13, was required to plead her case when her local hospital began High Court proceedings to temporarily remove her from her parents' custody in order to continue treatment (Verkaik, 2008).

Lhussier et al. (2007) describe advance care planning as enabling, as it provides a clear authority to stop some treatments. The greatest issue around the notion of choice is the assumption made that everyone is able to accept the prospect of death, is willing to discuss an impending demise, and is prepared to plan for the event (Sutton and Coast, 2012). The practice of advance planning may also complicate decision making because it involves the emotional and intimate circle of people around the dying person. Relatives may be unaware of a plan, be unwilling to adhere to the wishes of a loved one, and will try to sustain life at any cost (Perkins, 2007). Research from the USA found that frail older people particularly did not want to consider planning for death, even though geriatricians found that the document aided the decision-making process. Terminally ill people tend to concentrate on living the remainder of their life and are more likely to document financial and funeral arrangements than a care plan (Sutton and Coast, 2012). The lack of knowledge around end of life care planning in the public and professional arenas obstructs conversations that organize personal wishes because sensitive timing is unique to each person. The ethnicity and religious views of the patient, family and health professionals may exhort considerable influence, for example Jewish and Muslim law states that withholding or withdrawing treatment is an act of omission and against their teaching (Warrick et al., 2011).

The General Medical Council has warned doctors that there are serious repercussions if a living will/advance decision is ignored (Bell, 2010). Specific decisions to refuse food, water, support systems and resuscitation can only be disregarded when there is evidence that the patient has changed their mind, which can and does happen (Sutton and Coast, 2012). Advance decisions cannot authorize anything illegal, instruct doctors to provide specific treatments if not clinically appropriate, or predict a crisis (Perkins, 2007; Odone, 2010). The benefits include empowerment of patients and planning for the services required at end of life, but implementation during an emergency is a major obstacle. Currently, the emergency services are not usually privy to documents of this type and family members can nullify advance care plans in their attempt to keep their loved one alive (Perkins, 2007). Advance care plans are becoming more popular in the mental health sector, but are still quite rare. The practice is likely to become more widespread as the provisions of The Mental Capacity Act (DH, 2005a) and end of life choices become more familiar to both professionals and the public (Morgan, 2008). There is slight variation between countries, nevertheless these documents are legally recognized across the UK (Royal College of Nursing, 2011). Choice is the key characteristic of the end of life pathways and the gateway for patients is preferred priorities of care/advance care planning, but current debate has extended this to include the right to choose when to die.

Assisted dying: an alternative approach?

Media coverage has highlighted choices made by some individuals actively seeking to end their own life. Challenges to the law, alongside the social and moral issues of assisted dying/suicide, are being debated in public forums as an alternative to living, some commentators argue, a pointlessly extended life (Mappes et al., 2012). UK Law has explicit boundaries between causing someone to die, assisting a suicide or withdrawing/withholding life sustaining treatment. The term assisted suicide is when an individual is provided with the assistance and means by another person to take their own life/commit suicide. Euthanasia is the direct action of a medical practitioner to end a person's life. Both terms come under the umbrella of assisted dying (Royal College of Nursing, 2011).

Media coverage of high-profile court cases has generated public sympathy, as a number of these have highlighted prosecutorial discretion and sought to clarify the law and/or legalize assisted suicide. Actions have included the right to be euthanized 'lawfully' by a health professional instigated by a locked-in syndrome sufferer, and a student suffering from severe anorexia and wanting to die but being kept alive by a ruling stating that she should be force-fed (Holehouse, 2012; Marsden, 2012). Diane Pretty (suffering from Motor Neurone Disease) was the first to challenge Article 8(1) of the Human Rights Act 1998, drawing on the right to respect for private and family life, home and correspondence. The case of *Pretty vs. UK 2002* made clear that immunities for future assistance of suicide would not be granted. Suicide tourism has become a grey area due to the uncertainty of whether a person commits an offence by helping someone to die in a country where assisted suicide is legal (Hambly, 2010). Dignitas in Switzerland is the only clinic that currently accepts non-Swiss citizens and as yet no one accompanying an individual to die has been prosecuted (Odone, 2010).

Debbie Purdy sought clarity on the legal position of someone who assists an individual to travel abroad for an assisted death. Her final appeal in the House of Lords resulted in a landmark judgment that stated in future the balance between supporting quality of life as opposed to the sanctity of life (recognized under Article 2 of the Human Rights Act 1998) will be judged on the individual merit of each case (Odone, 2010). The implications for policy are wide as the value of self-determination seems to extend to the time and manner of an individual's death, difficulties in regulation and the possibility of invalid consent (Mappes et al., 2012). The Coroners and Justice Act 2009 focuses on the motive of the 'perpetrator/assistor', rather than on the 'victim's' circumstances, when deciding which cases should be prosecuted. Therefore, there is a separation between malicious intent and compassionate assistance (Hambly, 2010). Although the criteria for prosecution have been made clearer, the law has not changed. The guidelines set by the Director of Public Prosecutions state that each case should be studied on its facts and no individual is immune from prosecution if deemed appropriate. Nevertheless, the policy does not appear to uphold Parliament's anti-euthanasia approach (Bennion, 2009).

Debates concerned with assisted suicide remain contentious because they bring into sharp focus differing opinions on the quality and value of life with often conflicting and strongly held views on an individual's right to choose to die and the sanctity of life. There is a complex array of inter-related factors that impede autonomous decision making, including: quality of life, availability of care services, the perception of being a burden, and religious and moral views (Sutton and Coast, 2012). The two main arguments are: the duty of medical practitioners to reduce pain and distress at the end of life (beneficence), and the right of an individual to decide when their own life is no longer worth living (autonomy) (BMA, 1998).

Right-to-die campaigners want the choice, for adults who can make the decision of their own free will, of an assisted death within strict legal safeguards (Hough, 2011). In some cases, medical intervention sustains life rather than restoring health. Under these conditions, the General Medical Council states that there is no obligation to provide treatment that is futile, and clinicians are supported when treatment is withdrawn or withheld (Warrick et al., 2011). This is translated into a complicated debate on assisting suicide and who will provide and/or administer the fatal medication (Sutton and Coast, 2012). Legally, patients can refuse life-sustaining treatment but patients with a debilitating condition complain that they either have the choice of committing suicide when they are able, which may result in a premature death, or face the consequences of leaving it too late and being unable to accomplish the act themselves (Byock, 2004).

Pro-life supporters examine the issue from a vulnerable individual's perspective, which may or may not include a religious view. Data available from other countries supporting assisted dying (the Netherlands and the USA) have shown stable numbers of deaths of elderly people, minors and people with a physical disability or mental illness, questioning the claim that the risks associated with legalizing the practice will affect vulnerable groups (Quill, 2007). Comparative information from Australia (a country with prohibitive laws) shows higher rates of non-voluntary euthanasia than in Holland – which allows the practice (BMA, 2009). Health professionals are still, on the whole, reluctant to play a role in assisted dying. Byock (2004) states that intentionally causing death falls outside the range of acceptable interaction, that the practice would alter the concept of medicine. Strong feelings are aroused on this topic on both sides of the debate; politicians and policy makers are not eager or willing to change the law at present but it is unlikely to be the end of the assisted dying debate.

Summary/Conclusions

- Achieving a good death has become a political and social priority which is influenced by scientific advances and debates around assisted dying.
- Strategies to enhance care for people who are dying invite people to plan for their death and promote the use of end of life care pathways.
- The *End of Life Care Strategy* (2008) offers a number of choices to the patient but the availability and coordination of services may hamper the delivery.
- The system could accommodate a diverse range of conditions requiring end of life care. However, not everyone can or wants to plan for death.
- The debate on assisted dying is ongoing. Acceptance of the practice will depend upon media coverage of high-profile cases and public attitude around the issue of autonomy and beneficence.

Questions

1 Why has the debate around end of life care become important?
2 What are the issues when applying the pathways to nursing home care?
3 What are the advantages and disadvantages of advance care planning?
4 What are the arguments for and against assisted suicide?

Recommended reading

DeSpelder, L.A. and Strickland, A.L. (2011) *The Last Dance* (9th edn). New York: McGraw-Hill.
Holloway, M. (2007) *Negotiating Death in Contemporary Health and Social Care*. Bristol: The Policy Press.
Reith, M. and Payne, M. (2009) *Social Work in End-of-life and Palliative Care*. Bristol: The Policy Press.
Woods, S. (2007) *Death's Dominion: Ethics at the End of Life*. Maidenhead: Open University Press.

Relevant websites

End of Life Care for Adults – www.endoflifecareforadults.nhs.uk – is an NHS site designed to support health and social care staff.

Help the Hospices – www.helpthehospices.org.uk – provides information and support to families and professionals.

An annotated list of websites for end of life researchers and policy makers, written by Kip Jones – www2.warwick.ac.uk/fac/med/research/csri/ethnicityhealth/research/end_of_life/end_of_life_web.pdf

References

Addicott, R. and Ross, S. (2010) *Implementing the End of Life Care Strategy: Lessons for Good Practice*. London: The King's Fund.

Association for Palliative Medicine (2012) *Consensus Statement: Liverpool Care Pathway for the Dying Patient (LCP)*. Available at: www.apmonline.org/documents/134927304880177.pdf (accessed 21 November 2012).

Audit Commission (2011) *Joining up Health and Social Care*. London: Audit Commission. Available at: www.auditcommission.gov.uk/SiteCollectionDocuments/Downloads/vfmhscinterface.pdf (accessed 18 July 2012).

Bell, D. (2010) 'GMC guidance on end of life care', *British Medical Journal*, 340: C321.

Bennion, F. (2009) 'Assisted suicide: a constitutional change', *Criminal Law & Justice*, 173: 519–523.

BMA (1998) Euthanasia and physician assisted suicide – do the moral arguments differ? A discussion paper from the BMA's Medical Ethics Department, April. Available at: www.bma.org.uk/images/Euthanasia%20%26%20PVS%20%20ARM%20discussion%20paper_tcm41-146697.pdf (accessed 9 June 2012).

BMA (2009) Assisted dying: a summary of the BMA's position. Available at: www.bma.org.uk/ethics/end_life_issues/Assisdyingsum.jsp (accessed 8 June 2012).

Byock, I. (2004) *The Ethics of Loving Care: Palliative Care, Like Pediatrics, Understands that Patients Should Always Be Seen as Capable of Growth*. Health Progress, July–August. Available at: www.dyingwell.org/downloads/lovingcarehp0704.pdf (accessed 9 June 2012).

Coombs, M. and Long, T. (2008) 'Managing a good death in critical care: can health policy help?', *Nursing in Critical Care*, 13(4): 208–214.

Department of Health (DH) (2003) *Building on the Best: Choice, Responsiveness and Equity in the NHS*. London: HMSO. Available at: www.dh.gov.uk/en/Publicationsandstatistics/Publications/PublicationsPolicyAndGuidance/DH_4075, 29, 2 (accessed 29 November 2007).

Department of Health (DH) (2005a) *The Mental Capacity Act 2005*. London: HMSO. Available at: www.legislation.gov.uk/ukpga/2005/9/contents/enacted (accessed 25 July 2011).

Department of Health (DH) (2005b) *Gold Standards Framework: A Programme for Community Palliative Care*. London: HMSO. Available at: wwwgoldstandardsframework.nhs.uk (accessed 8 March 2007).

Department of Health (DH) (2006) *Our Health, Our Care, Our Say*. London: HMSO. Available at: www.dh.gov.uk/prod_consum_dh/idcplg?IdcService=SS_GET_PAGE&siteId=en&ssTargetNodeId=566&ssDocName=DH_41, 27357 (accessed 29 November 2007).

Department of Health (2008) *End of Life Care Strategy: Promoting High Quality of Care for all Adults at the End of Life*. London: HMSO. Available at: www.dh.gov.uk/en/Publicationsandstatistics/Publications/PublicationsPolicyAndGuidance/DH_086277 (accessed 25 July 2011).

Department of Health (DH) (2011) *End of Life Care Strategy: Third Annual Report*. London, HMSO. Available at: www.dh.gov.uk/prod_consum_dh/groups/dh_digitalassets/documents/digitalasset/dh_130570.pdf (accessed 18 July 2012).

Economist Intelligence Unit (EIU) (2010) *The Quality of Death: Ranking End-of-life Care across the World*. A report commissioned by the Lien Foundation. Available at: www.eiu.com/sponsor/lienfoundation/qualityofdeath (accessed 28 July 2011).

Froggatt, K. (2005) 'Choice over care at end of life: implications of the End of Life Care initiative for older people in care homes', *Journal of Research in Nursing*, 10: 189. Available at: http://jrn.sagepub.com/content/10/2/189 (accessed 28 July 2011).

Gomes, B. and Higginson, I. (2008) 'Where people die (1974–2030): past trends, future projections and implications for care', *Palliative Medicine*, 22(1): 33–41.

Gott, M., Barnes, S., Payne, S., Parker, C., Seamark, D., Gariballa, S. and Small, N. (2007) 'Patient views of social service provision for older people with advanced heart failure', *Health and Social Care in the Community*, 15(4): 333–342.

Gott, M., Seymour, J.E., Bellamy, G., Clark, D. and Ahmedzai, S. (2004) 'Older people's views about home as a place of care at the end of life', *Palliative Medicine*, 18(5): 460–467.

Hambly, S. (2010) 'The choice to give up living: compassionate assistance and the Suicide Act', *Diffusion*, 3(2). Available at: http://atp.uclan.ac.uk/buddypress/diffusion/?p=79 (accessed 18 July 2012).

Healthcare Commission (2007) *State of Healthcare 2007: Improvements and Challenges in Services in England and Wales*. London: HMSO. Available at: www.official documents.gov.uk/document/hc0708/hc00/0097/0097.pdf (accessed 21 June 2012).

Henry, C. (2011) 'National End of Life Care Programme: progress and future directions', *International Journal of Palliative Nursing*, 17(3).

Henry, C. and Seymour, J. (2007) *Advance Care Planning: A Guide for Health and Social Care Staff*. London: Department of Health. Available at: www.nhs.uk/eolc/files/F2023_EoLC_ACP_guide_for staff_Aug2008.pdf (accessed 12 September 2011).

Hockey, J. (1990) *Experiences of Death: An Anthropological Account*. Edinburgh: Edinburgh University Press.

Holehouse, M. (2012) 'Tony Nicklinson right-to-die case: legal action can go ahead', *The Telegraph*, 12 March.

Holloway, M. (2007) *Negotiating Death in Contemporary Health and Social Care*. Bristol: The Policy Press.

Hough, A. (2011) 'Sir Terry Pratchet defends BBC assisted suicide film amid backlash', *Daily Telegraph*, 14 June 2011. Available at: www.telegraph.co.uk/health/healthnews/8574080/Sir-Terry-Pratchett-defends-BBC-assisted-suicide-film-amid-backlash.html (accessed 18 June 2011).

Hughes-Hallett, T., Craft, A., Davies, C., Mackay, I. and Nielsson, T. (2011) *Funding the Right Care and Support for Everyone Creating a Fair and Transparent Funding System: The Final Report of the Palliative Care Funding Review, July 2011.* Available at: http://palliativecarefunding.org.uk/wp-content/uploads/2011/07/PCFRStakeholderReport.pdf (accessed 3 July 2012).

Jones, K. (2005) 'Diversities in approach to end-of-life: a view from Britain of the qualitative literature', *Journal of Research in Nursing*, 10(4): 431–454. Available at: http://jrn.sagepub.com/content/10/4/431.full.pdf+html/ (accessed 30 July 2011).

Leadbeater, C. and Garber, J. (2010) *Dying for Change.* London: Demos. Available at: www.demos.co.uk/publications/dyingforchange (accessed 12 September 2011).

Lhussier, M., Carr, S. and Wilcoxson, J. (2007) 'The evaluation of an end of life integrated care pathway', *International Journal of Palliative Nursing*, 13(2): 74–81.

Luptak (2006) 'End of life preferences for older adults and family members who care for them', *Journal of Social Work in End-Of-Life and Palliative Care*, 2(6): 23–24.

Macmillan (2010) *Always There? The Impact of the End of Life Care Strategy on 24/7 Community Nursing in England.* Available at: www.macmillan.org.uk/Documents/GetInvolved/Campaigns/Endoflife/AlwaysThere.pdf (accessed 9 June 2012).

Mappes, T., Zembaty, A. Jane, S. and DeGrazia, D. (2012) *Social Ethics, Morality and Social Policy.* New York: McGraw-Hill.

Marsden, S. (2012) 'Woman who wants to die must be force-fed', *The Telegraph*, 15 June.

Morgan, J. (2008) 'End-of-life care in UK critical care units: a literature review', *Nursing in Critical Care*, 13(3): 152–161.

National End of Life Care Intelligence Network (NEoLCIN) (2012) *What do We Know Now that we Didn't Know a Year Ago? New Intelligence on End of Life Care in England.* Available at: www.endoflifecareintelligence.org.uk/resources/publications/what_we_know_now.aspx (accessed 13 June 2012).

NHS Choices (2012) *What is the Liverpool Care Pathway? Behind the Headlines.* Available at: www.nhs.uk/news/2012/11November/Pages/What-is-the-Liverpool-Care-Pathway.aspx (accessed 21 November 2012).

Odone, C. (2010) *Assisted Suicide: How the Chattering Classes Have Got it Wrong.* Surrey: Centre for Policy Studies.

Office for National Statistics (ONS) (2012a) *Child Mortality Statistics Metadata, April 2012.* London: ONS. Available at: www.ons.gov.uk/ons/taxonomy/index.html?nscl=Mortality+Rates (accessed 18 June 2012).

Office for National Statistics (ONS) (2012b) *Death Registrations Summary Tables, England and Wales, 2011* (provisional). London: ONS. Available at: www.ons.gov.uk/ons/rel/vsob1/death-reg-sum-tables/2011--provisional-/index.html (accessed 18 July 2012).

Office for National Statistics (ONS) (2012c) *Leading Causes of Death in England and Wales 2009.* London: ONS. Available at: www.ons.gov.uk/ons/rel/subnational-health1/leading-causes-of-death/2009/leading-causes-of-death-in-england-and-wales---2009.html (accessed 18 July 2012).

Omega (2009) *National Snapshot*. Shrewsbury: National Association of End of Life Care. Available at: www.omega.uk.net/admin/uploads/file/National%20snapshot%20of%20end%20of%20life%20care%20-%20key%20findings.pdf (accessed 9 June 2012).

Perkins, H.S. (2007) 'Controlling death: the false promise of advance directives', *Annals of Internal Medicine*, 147: 51–57. Available at: www.annals.org/content/147/1/51 (accessed 28 July 2011).

Quill, T. (2007) 'Vulnerable groups are not at higher risk of physician assisted death', *British Medical Journal*, 335: 625–626.

Reith, M. and Payne, M. (2009) *Social Work in End-of-life and Palliative Care*. Bristol: The Policy Press.

Royal College of Nursing (2011) *When Someone Asks for Your Assistance to Die*. London: The Royal College of Nursing.

Seymour, J.E., Kumar, A. and Froggatt, K. (2011) 'Do nursing homes for older people have the support they need to provide end of life care? A mixed methods enquiry in England', *Palliative Medicine*, 25: 125. Available at: http://pmj.sagepub.com/content/25/2/125 (accessed 31 January 2011).

Sutton, E. and Coast, J. (2012) 'Choice is a small word with a huge meaning: autonomy and decision making at the end of life', *Policy & Politics*, 40(2): 211–226.

Thomas, K. (2010) 'The Gold Standards Framework: The GSF Prognostic Indicator Guidance End of Life Care', *Royal College of General Practitioners*, 4(1): 62–64. Available at: www.goldstandardsframework.org.uk/Resources/Gold%20Standards%20Framework/PDF%20Documents/PrognosticIndicatorGuidancePaper.pdf (accessed 10 January 2012).

Tuffrey-Wijne, I. (2010) *Living with Learning Disabilities, Dying with Cancer: Thirteen Personal Stories*. London: Jessica Kingsley.

Twomey, F., McDowell, D. and Corcoran, G. (2007) 'End of life care for older patients dying in an acute general hospital: can we do better?', *Age and Ageing*, 36(4): 462–464.

Verkaik, R. (2008) 'Girl 13, wins right to refuse heart transplant', *The Independent*, 11 November. Available at: www.independent.co.uk/life-style/health-and-families/health-news/girl-13-wins-right-to-refuse-heart-transplant-1009569.html (accessed 14 June 2012).

Warrick, C., Perera, L., Murdoch, E. and Nicholl, R.M. (2011) 'Guidance for withdrawal and withholding of intensive care as part of neonatal end-of-life care', *British Medical Bulletin*, 98: 99–113. Available at: http://bmb.oxfordjournals.org/content/98/1/99.short (accessed 13 June 2012).

Watts, T. (2012) 'End-of-life care pathways as tools to promote and support a good death: a critical commentary', *European Journal of Cancer Care*, 21: 20–30. Available at: http://onlinelibrary.wiley.com/doi/10.1111/j.1365-2354.2011.01301.x/pdf (accessed 9 June 2012).

Woods, S. (2007) *Death's Dominion: Ethics at the End of Life*. Maidenhead: Open University Press.

World Health Organization (WHO) (2002) *Definition of Palliative Care*. Geneva: WHO. Available at: www.who.int/cancer/palliative/definition/en/ (accessed 18 July 2012).

PART 3

Comparative and Supranational Dimensions of Policy

10

Devolution in the UK

Karen Kinghorn

Overview

- Devolution involves the transfer of legislative powers from a central governing body to subsidiary institutions.
- A series of Acts introduced by New Labour governments from the late 1990s onward established devolved administrations in Scotland, Wales, and Northern Ireland.
- The powers and internal structures of the elected bodies of Scotland, Wales and Northern Ireland are diverse and evolving.
- The Barnett Formula and the 'West Lothian Question' have become more contentious issues since the onset of devolution in the UK.
- This type of devolution allows for the convergence and divergence of policy in a number of areas and is dependent on the political climate.
- Devolution has implications for the welfare services that are available to citizens in different parts of the UK. An overview of the different arrangements that now exist in respect of personal care for older people in England, Scotland, Wales and Northern Ireland illustrates the impact that devolution may have on welfare services.

Introduction

The UK consists of England, Wales, Scotland and Northern Ireland. In 1999, the way the UK is governed was changed by the establishment of devolved administrations in Scotland, Wales and Northern Ireland. New Labour decentralized government and transferred some functions of administration from the UK government to three separately elected bodies. A new Scottish Parliament was granted legislative powers in designated areas, Northern Ireland gained an elected Assembly with power-sharing agreements with the UK government, and in Wales an elected Assembly was established with lesser legislative power as changes to primary legislation had to be approved by Westminster (Deacon, 2010). Devolution is the transfer of power from a central governing body to a subsidiary. Within the UK, devolution is described as asymmetrical because there are fundamental differences in the arrangements for each of the devolved administrations of Scotland, Wales and Northern Ireland. This is a structure that shifts power and policy making by altering the Administration (the ability to govern a particular country), Executive (enabling decisions to be made within the country) and Legislative (the ability to make laws for the country) bodies (Leek et al., 2003; Deacon, 2010).

This chapter examines how power is devolved in the UK and explains the structure of devolved nations. Against this background, the chapter summarizes the main similarities and differences between the devolved administrations. The discussion will take into account the main arguments around funding and the anomaly of the 'West Lothian Question'. It is problematic to analyse policy without taking into consideration the historical context of each territory and the different governance arrangements prior to devolution in 1999 (Birrell, 2009). Prior to devolution, central government in the UK was organized horizontally by function within Whitehall departments in charge of Health, Work and Pensions, etc. In the last quarter of the 20th century, a vertical dimension was added in the form of territorial areas. The Scottish Office (1885) and Welsh Office (1964) were joined by a Northern Ireland Office in 1972, all with different responsibilities and powers. Pre-devolution, as part of the administration in Whitehall, these offices were responsible to Parliament through a Member of Parliament (MP) (Mitchell, 2002). Post-devolution, their functions were transferred to the new devolved administrations.

Following the Scotland Act 1998, the Government of Wales Act 1998 and the Northern Ireland Act 1998, the range of devolved policy matters has become similar across all three countries and includes local government, education and training, health and social services and also housing and planning matters. Communication between Westminster and devolved administrations takes place under a Memorandum of Understanding (MoU); this is a collection of agreements setting out the relationship between the devolved administrations in Scotland, Wales and Northern Ireland and the UK government to ensure an effective working relationship (Birrell, 2009). The Joint Ministerial Committee (JMC) is one of a number of formal mechanisms that exchanges information on EU matters and policy development between the UK and devolved governments. Concordats (working agreements) apply broad consistent arrangements across UK government departments and their counterparts in the devolved countries (MoU, 2010). The Memorandum of Understanding and the concordats are not legally binding. Differences exist within the voting systems used to elect members of the different parliaments in operation post-devolution (Keating, 2009). The UK Parliament operates a first-past-the-post election system; in contrast, seats within the three devolved administrations are elected by systems that include proportional representation. The use of proportional representation appears to have altered the composition of the devolved administrations with younger people and women more likely to be elected. For example, in the National Assembly of Wales 2003 election, 50 per cent of the elected members were women – a first for any legislative body (Leek et al., 2003). The structure, composition and power of each country are different due to the level of enthusiasm for devolution (Drakeford, 2005).

The devolved governments of the UK

Before outlining the current arrangement of the various devolved administrations, it is important to highlight the continuing significance and role of the UK government. A New Labour government coordinated the legislation which brought about the devolved administrations. Importantly, this legislation makes the UK Parliament sovereign in all matters and the devolved governments constitutionally subordinate (Laffin et al., 2007). The Acts of Devolution (Scotland Act 1998, the Government of Wales Act 1998 and the Northern Ireland Act 1998) can be repealed by the UK central government and power returned to Westminster. Within these Acts, there are clauses that allow the UK Parliament to legislate in all areas if required, but in practice it will only do so with the consent of devolved administrations (Mitchell, 2002). For example in the past, the Northern Ireland Assembly has been suspended on occasion, due to the breakdown in peace negotiations, and its powers have been returned to Westminster. The key powers that are retained by Westminster include constitutional matters (including the Crown), foreign policy, defence, European Union relations, economic policy and taxation (with variance for Scotland), overseas trade, employment legislation, social security, and broadcasting (Leek et al., 2003; Knox and Carmichael, 2010). The UK government also controls access to funding for welfare services which creates some tensions with the devolved governments (Mitchell, 2002).

Scotland

The Scotland Acts 1998 and 2012 have provided Scotland's Parliament with considerably more power than the other devolved nations (Mooney et al., 2006). Able to pass primary and secondary legislation in most domestic policy areas, Members of the Scottish Parliament are also able to set income tax rates and from 2016 the Scottish government will be able to increase its borrowing power to £5 billion. Elections are held every four years to create a Scottish Parliament of 129 members comprising 72 constituency MPs and 56 regional Members of the Scottish Parliament (MSPs). Each Scottish voter casts two votes in a general election. The initial vote is cast, on a first-past-the-post basis, to elect a constituency MP who can sit both at Westminster (the UK Parliament) and in the Scottish Parliament in Edinburgh. The elector's second vote is cast using a form of proportional representation (i.e. the additional member system) to elect Members of the Scottish Parliament known as regional members. The system used for the second vote is designed to ensure that the make-up of the Scottish Parliament proportionally reflects the level of support for each political party at the ballot box (Trench, 2007). The major political parties are the Scottish National Party (SNP), winning the majority of seats in 2011 (69 in total) and forming the Scottish government, the Labour Party (37), the Conservative Party (15) and the Liberal Democrats (5).

Wales

The Government for Wales Act 1998 conferred an Assembly of 40 constituency and 20 regional representatives (elected in the same manner as Scotland) – initially as a single body combining representative and executive functions. The Assembly's power was limited to executive matters. However, legislative power was acquired with the Government of Wales Act 2006, either directly by an Act of Parliament (via Westminster) or as a Legislative Competence Order which required approval at Westminster before the Assembly could legislate (Greer and Trench, 2008). A referendum on further law-making powers for the Assembly (2011) approved an order to make laws under broad headings covering the delivery of services, including: education and training; fire and rescue services; health services; highways and transport; housing; local government; social welfare; planning (except major energy infrastructure); water supplies; agriculture; fisheries; forestry; culture including the Welsh language and ancient monuments; economic development; and the environment (Wales Office, 2012). The formal process to transfer these legislative powers is under way (Gallagher, 2012).

The blurred lines between UK government and Welsh Assembly policy making have been divisive because communication and liaison between the two governments has been an issue (Drakeford, 2005). This is because unlike Scotland and Northern Ireland, the legal and administration systems in Wales had been absorbed into the English system. The powers granted were restricted with a heavy dependence on the UK government before the system was rendered impractical in 2011. The Government of Wales Act 2006 was a compromise but also a time-consuming method of having powers transferred, piece by piece, from the UK Parliament to the Welsh Assembly (Gallagher, 2012). The referendum in 2011 granted Wales their own legislative power, and autonomy in devolved matters.

Northern Ireland

The signing of the Good Friday Agreement in 1998 signalled an end to the widespread, prolonged and bitter conflict between the nationalist (favouring a union with the Irish Republic) and unionist (favouring remaining part of the UK) communities, and paved the way for the devolution of some powers to the Northern Ireland Assembly (Bochel et al., 2009). The first elections to the Assembly were held in 1998 utilizing a single transferable vote system, a form of proportional representation which involved voting for individual candidates in order of preference, chosen to reflect the power sharing philosophy that was central to the wider peace process. The Northern Ireland Assembly consists of 108 members and returns 18 members to the UK government. The First Minister and Deputy First Minister appointments are linked, due to the power sharing in the Executive between two parties considered to be on the more extreme edges of Unionism and Republicanism – the Democratic Unionist Party (DUP) and Sinn Fein – each therefore with the power of a potential veto to block changes (Schwartz, 2010).

At a fully functioning level, the Northern Ireland Assembly holds legislative and executive authority in the devolved areas set out in the Northern Ireland Act 1998: these include local government, education and training, health and social services, and housing and planning (Leek et al., 2003). Westminster legislates in 'excepted' subjects where issues are to remain in the UK, or in 'reserved' subjects which could be transferred by Order in future with the agreement of all parties (Leek et al., 2003). Some of the 'reserved' matters include criminal law, policing and prisons, and can be transferred eventually under the Good Friday Agreement 1998 (Gallagher, 2012). Although Northern Ireland had an established infrastructure for governance, it was 2007 before the DUP and Sinn Fein formed a working coalition, due to initial concerns about the legitimacy of the government and matters of social justice arising from the prolonged period of conflict that preceded the Good Friday Agreement.

Devolution and the dilemma of funding

Although political power was restructured by devolution, pre-existing anomalies in the funding mechanisms remain unresolved and provide different amounts of financial resources to Scotland, Wales and Northern Ireland (Bell, 2010). Funding for the devolved nations of the UK is integrated within the wider UK public expenditure system and derived from the Assigned Budget or Block Grant (known as Departmental Expenditure Limit [DEL]), the Nonassigned Budget (also DEL) and spending within an Annually Managed Expenditure (AME). AME relates to programmes that require up-to-date information and have to be reviewed twice a year, for example pensions for public sector workers. The DEL is the total budget for devolved administrations to finance flexible public services according to their chosen policies. It is financed directly from the UK government from centrally collected taxes, referred to as a 'block grant' and determined by the Barnett Formula (Scotland Office, 2009). Scotland also has the ability to vary the rate of income tax to raise funds. The block grant is a budget provided via the UK government for the services that the Scottish Parliament, and Welsh and Northern Ireland Assemblies are responsible for, based on historic levels of public spending (Heald and McLeod, 2002; Greer and Trench, 2010a). This part of the funding is determined by the Barnett Formula. Originally, the formula was based on the percentage of population in each country: 85 per cent in England, 10 per cent in Scotland and 5 per cent in Wales (Heald and McLeod, 2002). This mechanism is designed to apply a proportional increase or decrease in funding based on the fluctuations of a comparable English spending programme (Leek et al., 2003; HPERU, 2010). Currently, the formula identifies the population proportions for 2011–14 as 10.3 per cent for Scotland, 5.79 per cent for Wales and 3.45 per cent for Northern Ireland. It takes into account the sparse population in rural areas and the need to recognize that spending levels are different. Substantial discretion is enjoyed by the devolved governments when deciding spending priorities within the block funding they receive from the UK government (Laffin et al., 2007).

The Barnett Formula does not therefore take into consideration any kind of needs assessment across the devolved nations, and the current view is that Scotland is overfunded and Wales is underfunded (Greer and Trench, 2010b). Wales has consistently requested a system based on need to take into account areas of deprivation (House of Lords Liaison Committee, 2008). Need is a contentious term, based on the perception of what public services should be available in different areas. Whether needs are adequately met by the public services provided depends on the point of view of those making the judgement. A needs-based system would have to take into account unit cost (for example, cost per school child) across a range of public services with differing participation rates (Heald and Mcleod, 2002). The Barnett Formula was never designed to take devolution into account and there are currently no indications that it will be revised despite the anomalies that exist (HM Treasury, 2010a). Scotland's increasing prosperity has led to a situation where spending per capita on public services has increased considerably in relation to the same services in England (Heald and McLeod, 2002; Justice Committee, 2009). This type of funding system means that policy decisions in one location lead to unintended outcomes in the other countries. For example, when the UK government decided to make free prescriptions available to cancer patients in England, this created a rise in the financial support for Scotland and Wales where prescriptions are already freely available (Justice Committee, 2009).

The block grants in Scotland, Wales and Northern Ireland account for approximately half of the resources provided in each country. The remainder is provided by the UK government, usually for reserved matters. The devolved governments can allocate funding as they see fit but are constrained by the spending priorities in England (Greer and Trench, 2010a). The formula is applied to 'comparable programmes' across the territories, such as Health, but there are debates around the precise 'fit' of programmes. The Department of Health has a history of under-spending, causing the Treasury to reduce its allocation by £3 billion. These reductions were consequently passed on to the devolved governments and Scotland 'lost' £300 million in health funding. This example demonstrates how the Barnett Formula can be an instrument for reducing as well as increasing public funding (Greer and Trench, 2010b). One of the benefits of the formula is that budgets remain static and predictable. However, the Barnett Formula is an example of non-statutory policy and the devolved governments remain very much dependent upon the goodwill of the UK government to provide funding.

Debates concerned the fairness of the Barnett Formula (Jones and Norton, 2010), and financial autonomy may yet break relations between the central UK and devolved governments. The block grants awarded to the devolved nations three decades ago were calculated on the premise 'that all three were on balance places of greater need' (Jones et al., 2001: 281), and today public spending in Scotland, Northern Ireland and Wales per capita is significantly higher than in England due to the grants awarded to boost economic development and reduce social disadvantage. Although there have been various attempts to narrow this spending gap, the average per capita spending for England remains the lowest at £8,559, compared to Scotland at £10,083, Wales at £9,597 and Northern Ireland at £10,662 (HM Treasury, 2010b). Such discrepancies have proved to be unpopular with some in England, with some commentators asking why relatively disadvantaged regions such as the North East of England attract lower levels of per capita spending than certain more affluent areas of Scotland (Birrell, 2009).

Funding matters remain a point of contention in the relationship between the devolved and UK governments. For example, the administrations in Scotland, Wales and Northern Ireland claimed that the regeneration of London's East End for the 2012 Olympics should fall into the category of comparable funding with the appropriate budgetary increases given to them (Gallagher, 2012). Given the Scottish National Party's ambition for financial autonomy and/or independence, the Welsh Assembly's campaign for a block grant based on need, and the ongoing fiscal crisis which has led to unprecedented cuts in the funding available to English public authorities as well as the devolved administrations, questions about the levels and equity of funding are likely to remain contentious.

The West Lothian Question

The West Lothian Question, first pondered by UK MP Tam Dalyell in the 1970s, is a further prime example of debates about equity that can arise with devolution. He pointed out that devolution can create perverse situations dependent upon the institutional arrangements that exist. To explain, in simple terms, it needs to be remembered that MPs in the UK Parliament are elected from Scottish, Welsh and Northern Ireland constituencies alongside their English colleagues. As members of the UK Parliament, MPs from the devolved nations are therefore able to debate and vote on matters that will affect English constituencies (McLean, 2005). Two relatively recent and controversial examples where this has mattered are the introduction, by the UK New Labour government, of university tuition fees and foundation hospitals in England. In both cases, the New Labour government faced opposition from their own MPs in Westminster. Nonetheless, the votes of Scottish and Welsh members of the UK Parliament ensured the legislation was passed, even though many of the same MPs had supported the devolved Scottish government and Welsh Assembly in opposing the proposed changes (Greer and Trench, 2008). Essentially, Scottish and Welsh MPs were effective in inflicting unpopular policy measures on England but English members of the UK Parliament do not enjoy similar powers to vote or influence policy in the devolved administrations. Subsequently, there have been suggestions that Scottish and Welsh members of the UK Parliament should be banned from voting on English matters.

However, this may cause other contrary debates around the West Lothian Question, and the Barnett Formula has brought up the matter of fairness in England and a sense that the 'other' national groups' request for independence is unreasonable. The argument becomes about 'them and us' and assumes the devolved governments are seen to be in a more privileged position (Skey, 2012). This perspective overlooks any unequal relations between the different governments and presents the view that devolved governments face quite different social problems that require country-specific solutions (Smith et al., 2009). If we take the example of caring for people in the community, the preferences and welfare services that have evolved are based upon political ideology because people in all four nations will have the same or similar needs. The reality, as shown in the brief discussion of personal social care below, is that the various constituent nations of the UK often face similar social issues but that there is a degree of variance in their policy response, dependent upon different political environments and working cultures (Birrell, 2007; Smith and Hellowell, 2012).

Social care in the UK following devolution: differing responses to a common issue

Social care is a system of support for people with long-term conditions which is operated by the NHS, local authorities and the benefit system (Bell, 2010). Services are provided for a number of groups such as terminally ill people, those living with long-term chronic conditions, people with disabilities and older people who are frail and vulnerable. Social care has been developed from different pieces of legislation over the last 60 years to provide essential assistance, support and protection to people in their own homes or community settings such as a nursing home (Means et al., 2008; Bell, 2010; Glasby, 2012).

Under the National Assistance Act 1948, the role of local authorities is defined and provides the right to set charges for personal care services. Broadly, the principles have been the same across all four countries and therefore personal care is means-tested and based on the client's ability to pay (Birrell, 2007). England, Scotland and Wales have been attempting to integrate health and social care services in the community as a cheaper alternative to hospital or forms of institutionalized care (Means et al., 2008). Different approaches have been adopted across the four nations: England prefers formal partnerships between agencies, Scotland favours a uniform approach with joint resources and working, while in Wales local authorities work with local Health Boards to formulate health and social care strategies. Northern Ireland is the only country with clear integrated health and social care teams for community settings (Birrell, 2007).

A defining policy for the Scottish government was the introduction of free personal social care for those over the age of 65 in 2002 (Birrrell, 2009; Keating, 2009). This policy expanded the idea of a universal welfare state free at the point of delivery causing controversy and considerable debate elsewhere in the UK where only nursing care is provided free of charge (Birrell, 2007). This change in policy had certain implications as previously Attendance Allowance was paid by the Department of Work and Pensions (DWP) to anyone in the UK over the age of 65 to assist with personal care. When Scotland decided to provide free personal care (with the Scottish government compensating Scottish local authorities for the consequent lack of chargeable income), a rule stating that personal care cannot be paid for twice came into play. Therefore, Attendance Allowance has been withdrawn from clients in Scottish care homes who were receiving free personal care, a saving of over £200 million for the DWP. Individuals living in Scotland who may have been means-tested for care in their own home continue to benefit from the allowance, providing another funding anomaly. The significant feature is that Scotland's government pays all of the allowances (in care homes) and in England the Department of Health, local authorities and the DWP share the costs (Bell, 2010). Apart from in Scotland, where personal care is provided free of charge, individuals living in Wales, Northern Ireland and England are subject to a means test to determine whether they have to pay in full or in part for the social care services provided.

Initially, within the limits of their budget and devolved powers, the Welsh Assembly attempted to follow the Scottish approach but a scarcity of available resources led to an abandonment of the aim to provide free personal care (Keating, 2009). Also, as the Welsh Assembly did not have the legislative power to prevent local authorities charging for services, Welsh policy makers switched their focus in order to increase the threshold at which charges are made to clients, thus allowing individuals to keep a larger proportion of their income after means tests are applied. The Welsh Assembly also increased grants to local authorities to reduce charges for those receiving personal care in their own homes (Bell, 2010).

Northern Ireland has an established practice of combined Health and Social Care Trusts without political input. There is uniformity in assessment, provision and charging mechanisms as the Trusts manage multi-professional teams (Heenan and Birrell, 2009). In practice, funding and provision for social care are heavily weighted in favour of publically funded residential care homes as the independent or private sector is under-developed (Birrell, 2007; Bell, 2010). Considering that current reforms in the other constituent nations (England, Scotland and Wales) aim to integrate health and social care services to a greater extent than at present, it is surprising that the method of combining these sectors has not been copied (Heenan and Birrell, 2009).

In England, consumer choice is the underpinning rationale for a system that favours self-directed personal care variously facilitated by the Independent Living Fund, Direct Payments and, more recently, personal and individual budgets. These are forms of payment transfer providing a specific amount of funding (determined following assessment by social workers) so that the client themselves can organize and pay for their own personal care (Bell, 2010). Knowing the amount of resources available allows a certain amount of freedom for individuals to decide how their personal care services should be provided. This may include private and publicly provided services, support from the independent and/or informal sectors or any combination of these. Support to operate the schemes is normally limited to social services, Centres for Independent Living (CIL) and family and friends. However, this consumer-orientated approach to the provision of social care in England may be under threat from the current economic crisis as funding cuts to CILs and personal budgets roll out in the future (Glasby, 2012). Nonetheless, in England the role of the private sector in providing personal care continues to expand (Bell, 2010).

The relationship between the UK government and the devolved administrations is likely to change in the future given ongoing political and fiscal developments. Calls from the Scottish government to move towards independence and the devolved governments' desire for more power and clarity around funding mechanisms may add further strains (Mooney and Williams, 2006). The current financial climate will also have an effect on budgetary debates as unprecedented reductions in public expenditure are already in place across the UK, including in England (Grimshaw and Rubery, 2012).

Although there are expectations in the UK that all nations will provide the same entitlements and rights for each citizen (HPERU, 2010), the introduction of free personal care in Scotland has created the perception in some quarters that certain UK citizens living in particular nations get more for their taxes (Carvel, 2006). A consideration of differences in approach to the funding and provision of personal care now ongoing across the constituent parts of the UK highlights how devolution can impact on welfare policy. Scotland and Wales have positioned their social care policies within a social democratic tradition, reflecting perhaps their traditional support for the Labour Party in the past (Keating, 2009). This is somewhat at odds with the preferred policies of New

Labour and more latterly the UK Coalition government. Client control over care packages in the devolved nations is limited and Peckham et al. (2012) argue that distinctive approaches to practice across the UK suggest that local authorities in Scotland, Wales and Northern Ireland are far less likely to widen the choice of services, or adopt a consumerist approach.

Summary/Conclusions

- Devolution has introduced a new dimension to politics and policy making within the UK.
- As devolution is relatively new in the UK, the relationship between the UK government and the newly established devolved governments is evolving.
- Ongoing fiscal pressures and demands from the devolved governments for more powers may trigger further change in the future.
- Issues of equity related to the mechanisms by which the UK government calculates and provides block grants to the devolved administrations and the 'West Lothian Question' remain, at present, unresolved.
- As the brief discussion of personal social care has shown, devolution has resulted in differing approaches to the funding and provision of certain welfare services across the UK.

Questions

1 What are the main arguments for and against the Barnett Formula?
2 Outline and explain the 'West Lothian Question'.
3 Outline and discuss the differing approaches to the provision of personal social care in England, Scotland, Wales and Northern Ireland.
4 To what extent should personal care services be funded and provided in an identical way across the UK?

Recommended reading

Birrell, D. (2009) *The Impact of Devolution on Social Policy*. Bristol: The Policy Press. Social policy students will find that this text offers an accessible and valuable account of the impact of devolution on social policy from a number of perspectives.

Deacon, R. (2010) 'Devolution', in B. Jones and P. Norton (eds) *Politics UK* (7th edn). Harlow: Pearson Education, pp. 225–245. This provides a history of devolution in the UK.

Greer, S.L. (ed.) (2009) *Devolution and Social Citizenship in the UK*. Bristol: The Policy Press. This book considers the impact of devolution on citizenship.

Relevant websites

Individual government websites provide details of policies and links to current debates:

The Welsh Assembly – www.wales.gov.uk

The Scottish Government – www.scotland.gov.uk

The Northern Ireland Assembly – www.northernireland.gov.uk

The Houses of Parliament – www.parliament.uk

Alan Trench, an academic from the University of Edinburgh and the Constitution Unit at The University College London, provides up-to-date information and links about devolution in his blog – http://devolutionmatters.wordpress.com/

References

Bell, D. (2010) *The Impact of Devolution on Long Term Care Provision in the UK*. York: Joseph Rowntree Foundation. Available at: www.jrf.org.uk/sites/files/jrf/impact-of-devolution-long-term-care.pdf (accessed 31 May 2012).

Birrell, D. (2007) *Devolution and Social Care: Are there Four Systems of Social Care in the United Kingdom?* Paper presented at the Social Policy Association Conference, University of Birmingham, July. Available at: www.sochealth.co.uk/news/birrell.htm (accessed 14 May 2012).

Birrell, D. (2009) *The Impact of Devolution on Social Policy*. Bristol: The Policy Press

Bochel, H., Bochel, C., Page, R. and Sykes, R. (eds) (2009) *Social Policy Themes, Issues and Debates* (2nd edn). Harlow: Pearson Education.

Carvel, J. (2006) 'Scotland's free personal care for elderly praised', *The Guardian*, 1 February. Available at: www.guardian.co.uk/society/2006/feb/01/longtermcare.uknews1 (accessed 21 August 2012).

Deacon, R. (2010) 'Devolution', in B. Jones and P. Norton (eds) *Politics UK* (7th edn). Harlow: Pearson Education, pp. 225–245.

Drakeford, M. (2005) 'Wales and a third term of New Labour: devolution and the development of difference', *Critical Social Policy*, 25(4): 497–506.

Gallagher, J. (2012) 'Intergovernmental relations in the UK: co-operation, competition and constitutional change', *British Journal of Politics and International Relations*, 14: 198–213. Available at: http://onlinelibrary.wiley.com/doi/10.1111/j.1467-856X.2011.00485.x/full (accessed 31 May 2012).

Glasby, J. (2012) *Understanding Health and Social Care* (2nd edn). Bristol: The Policy Press.

Greer, S.L. and Trench, A. (2008) *Health and Intergovernmental Relations in the Devolved United Kingdom*. London: The Nuffield Trust. Available at: www.nuffieldtrust.org.uk/sites/files/

nuffield/publication/health-and-intergovernmental-relations-in-the-devolved-united-kingdom-jul08-web-final.pdf (accessed 10 July 2012).

Greer, S.L. and Trench, A. (2010a) *Health and Intergovernmental Relations in the Devolved United Kingdom.* London: The Nuffield Trust.

Greer, S.L. and Trench, A. (2010b) 'Intergovernmental relations and health in Great Britain after devolution', *Policy and Politics*, 38(4): 509–529.

Grimshaw, D. and Rubery, J. (2012) 'The end of the UK's liberal collectivist social model? The implications of the coalition government's policy during the austerity crisis', *Cambridge Journal of Economics*, 36: 105–126.

Heald, D. and McLeod, A. (2002) 'Public expenditure', *Constitutional Law: The Laws of Scotland – Stair Memorial Encyclopaedia*. Edinburgh: Butterworths, paras 530, 532–536.

Health Policy and Economic Research Unit (HPERU) (2010) *Devolution: A Map of Divergence*. London: British Medical Association.

Heenan, D. and Birrell, D. (2009) 'Organisational integration in health and social care: some reflections on the Northern Ireland experience', *Journal of Integrated Care*, 17(5): 3–12.

HM Treasury (2010a) *Funding the Scottish Parliament, National Assembly for Wales, and Northern Ireland Assembly: Statement of Funding Policy*. London: The Stationery Office. Available at: http://cdn.hm-treasury.gov.uk/sr2010_fundingpolicy.pdf (accessed 6 March 2012).

HM Treasury (2010b) *Public Expenditure by Country, Region and Function*. London: The Stationery Office. Available at: www.hmtreasury.gov.uk/d/pera_2010_chapter9.pdf (accessed 29 January 2012).

House of Lords Liaison Committee (2008) *First Report of Session 2007–08*, HL Paper 33. London: The Stationery Office. Available at: www.publications.parliament.uk/pa/ld200708/ldselect/ldliaisn/33/33.pdf (accessed 15 January 2008).

Jones, B. and Norton, P. (2010) *Politics UK* (7th edn). Harlow: Pearson Education.

Jones, B., Kavanagh, D., Moran, M. and Norton, P. (2001) *Politics UK* (4th edn). London: Pearson Education.

Justice Committee (2009) *Justice Committee Devolution: A Decade On – Fifth Report of Session 2008–09*. Volume 1. HC529. London: The Stationery Office. Available at: www.publications.parliament.uk/pa/cm200809/cmselect/cmjust/529/529i.pdf (accessed 5 February 2012).

Keating, M. (2009) 'Social citizenship, devolution and policy divergence', in S.L. Greer (ed.) *Devolution and Social Citizenship in the UK*. Bristol: The Policy Press.

Knox, C. and Carmichael, P. (2010) 'Devolution in Northern Ireland', *Public Money & Management*, 30(2): 79–80.

Laffin, M., Shaw, E. and Taylor, G. (2007) 'The new sub-national politics of the British Labour party', *Party Politics*, 13(1): 88–108.

Leek, M., Sear, C. and Gay, O. (2003) *An Introduction to Devolution in the UK*. Research paper 03/84. London: House of Commons Library. Available at: www.parliament.uk/documents/commons/lib/research/rp2003/rp03-084.pdf (accessed 28 November 2011).

McLean, I. (2005) *Barnett and the West Lothian Question: No Nearer to Solutions than When the Devolution Programme Started*. Paper presented at ESRC Devolution Conference, London,

December. Available at: www.nuff.ox.ac.uk/politics/papers/2005/BarnettandtheWestLothian Question.pdf (accessed 26 November 2011).

Means, R., Richards, S. and Smith, R. (2008) *Community Care*. Basingstoke: Palgrave Macmillan.

Memorandum of Understanding (MoU) (2010) *Memorandum of Understanding and Supplementary Agreements.* London: HMSO. Available at: www.ofmdfmni.gov.uk/memorandum_ of_understanding_and_concordate_on_co-ordination_of_eu_issues_-_march_2010.pdf (accessed 14 May 2012).

Mitchell, J. (2002) 'England and the centre', *Regional Studies*, 36(7): 757–765.

Mooney, G. and Williams, C. (2006) 'Forging new "ways of life"? Social policy and nation building in devolved Scotland and Wales', *Critical Social Policy*, 26: 608.

Mooney, G., Scott, G. and Williams, C. (2006) 'Introduction: rethinking social policy through devolution', *Critical Social Policy*, 26: 483.

Peckham, S., Mays, N., Hughes, D., Sanderson, M., Allen, P., Prior, L., et al. (2012) 'Devolution and patient choice: policy rhetoric versus experience in practice', *Social Policy & Administration*, 46(2): 199–218.

Schwartz, A. (2010) 'How unfair is cross-community consent? Voting power in the Northern Ireland Assembly', *Northern Ireland Legal Quarterly*, 61(4): 349–362.

Scotland Office (2009) *The Scottish Budget since Devolution*. Available at: www.scotlandoffice. gov.uk/scotlandoffice/files/The%20Scottish%20Budget%20since%20Devolution.pdf (accessed 16 September 2012).

Skey, M. (2012) '"Sod them, I'm English": the changing status of the "majority" English in post-devolution Britain', *Ethnicities*, 12: 106.

Smith, K. and Hellowell, M. (2012) 'Beyond rhetorical differences: a cohesive account of post-devolution developments in UK health policy', *Social Policy & Administration*, 46(2): 178–198.

Smith, K.E., Hunter, D.J., Blackman, T., Elliott, E., Greene, A., Harrington, B.E., et al. (2009) 'Divergence or convergence? Health inequalities and policy in a devolved Britain', *Critical Social Policy*, 29: 216. Available at: http://csp.sagepub.com/content/29/2/216 (accessed 2 June 2012).

Trench, A. (2007) *Devolution and Power in the United Kingdom*. Manchester: Manchester University Press.

Wales Office (2012) *Devolution Guidance Notes 17*. London: The Stationery Office. Available at: http://update.cabinetoffice.gov.uk/resource-library/devolution-guidance-notes (accessed 12 May 2012).

11

Comparative Welfare

Sandra Shaw

Overview

- Comparative study of welfare systems and social policies has become increasingly important in social policy.
- One way of facilitating comparative study is to organize countries into categories or clusters, associated with particular ways of organizing and delivering welfare – welfare regimes.
- Esping-Andersen (1990, 1996) identified three main welfare regimes: Conservative/Corporatist, Liberal, and Social Democratic/Scandinavian.
- The work of this author, and his model of welfare regimes, have been critiqued on a number of grounds, and this has led to suggestions for the modification and expansion of the model.
- Social, political and economic changes will continue to impact on the classification and study of welfare regimes.

Introduction

Comparing welfare systems and interventions across and between societies has become increasingly important in the subject of social policy (Cousins, 2005). Comparative social policy can include studies that look at a particular country, or make comparisons between one or more countries. It includes looking at policies at the systems level, that is how the welfare state or welfare system (or one aspect of it) is funded, organized and delivered, or it can focus on the enactment and consequences of policies for individuals and communities. Comparative work can be based on statistical analysis – both collecting factual information, and comparing data sets across countries. This is not without problems, as statistics that are collected can vary between countries (May, 2012). There is a trend towards collating and compiling statistics at the international level which are more readily comparable, for example the Organization for Economic Cooperation and Development (OECD) databases provide information for Member States on topics such as health care and families. Comparative work can also be qualitative and focus much more on people's experiences of welfare provisions – both as users and as workers within a welfare system. An important aspect of comparative study is the generation of knowledge that can be shared by policy makers and national governments. This raises the possibility of policy transfer. By finding out what policies are in place in one country, the potential exists for another country to take a policy or an aspect of a policy, and transfer it to their country. As countries vary according to historical, cultural, economic, social and political context, it will not always be possible to simply transfer a policy, and Alcock and Craig (2009) use the term 'policy translation' to refer to the way that a policy may have to be adapted to fit the context in another country. The concepts of policy transfer and policy translation imply that national governments and policy makers are looking for good examples of policies to import, but comparative research can also highlight policies that are not successful or have inherent problems. It is worth pointing out, however, that it is not always the case that governments base their policies on research. Policies can be devised and implemented very quickly, and policy ideas or initiatives can be 'borrowed' without a solid research or evidence base for their effectiveness.

One way to further the analysis of welfare systems has been the development of models or typologies of welfare states or systems. Not all countries have a clearly defined welfare state as in the UK or in Scandinavian countries, but it is possible to think about systems of welfare instead, and the classification of welfare states/systems is an important part of comparative study. One influential example of this has been the work of Esping-Andersen (1990, 1996), who classified groups of countries in the developed world into three main welfare regimes. His work has subsequently been critiqued on a number of grounds, and suggestions for modifying and expanding on the model have been made. This chapter provides a basic outline of Esping-Andersen's typology of welfare regimes and then moves on to look at some of the critiques that have developed. Debate and discussion around this area are ongoing and will continue to develop as the social, political and economic context changes, and the drive to respond to such changes will put pressure on welfare systems, whether they are embryonic or well established.

Welfare regimes

The word 'regime' implies some way of organizing or running something. Here, we are considering ways of organizing and delivering welfare. This attempt to classify or categorize welfare regimes is described by Esping-Andersen (1990) as a generalized description or an approximation of the way that welfare provision has developed. Those countries within a particular category will have some commonality, but there will also be differences related to historical, political, social and cultural factors (including religion). There may be some movement towards convergence, that is similar patterns in providing welfare, but there will also be divergence related to specific differences within countries. But overall, it is the similarities that lead to particular countries being grouped together, and this approach can be useful in comparative analysis in understanding how welfare delivery is shaped and in making cross-national comparisons (Cousins, 2005).

While other authors have written about the ways that welfare is organized (see for example, Titmuss, 1974), the focus here is on the work of Esping-Andersen as his ideas have proven very influential. Other authors have analysed and criticized his model, identifying omissions and making suggestions for a further expansion of the model. It is through this process of debate, discussion and critique that ideas develop within academic subjects. A summary of Esping-Andersen's classification of welfare regimes is presented, followed by an outline of some critiques of his model.

Esping-Andersen's work focused on welfare systems in the developed western world. To classify countries, he used national data on public expenditure on employment sickness and pensions, and looked at the social and political history of welfare development. This approach leads to concentrating on paid employment and ignoring other unpaid work, for example, care work done within and by families. He examined key features of welfare states and the extent of decommodifcation and levels of stratification. These two criteria were used to classify countries, leading to the identification of three broad clusters or types of welfare regimes (Alcock and Craig, 2009: 17–18). *Stratification* refers to the structuring of access to welfare by social class, and *decommodification* refers to the way that welfare was provided, regardless of the fluctuations of the economy. Decommodification refers to 'the extent to which individuals and families can maintain a normal and socially acceptable standard of living regardless of their market performance' (Esping-Andersen, 1987: 86). Commodification signifies the way that workers are reliant on selling their labour in the paid labour market. Labour became extensively commodified during the industrial revolution as workers became entirely dependent upon the market for their survival (Bambra, 2005: 201), though Lewis (2000) notes that Esping-Andersen's concept of decommodification was based on male workers. However, during the 20th century, the introduction of social rights and access to social welfare brought about a change in the pure commodity status of labour. The welfare state provided services and a basic standard of living as a right of citizenship, meaning that the market was less essential for survival (Esping-Andersen, 1990: 22). What is crucial is the degree to which individuals are protected from dependence on the labour market provided by welfare state cash benefits and services. When related to health care, for example, decommodification refers to the extent to which an individual's access to health care is dependent upon their market position and the extent to which a country's provision of health is independent from the market (Bambra, 2005). In a country like the UK, where the NHS provides free health care at the point of access (though there are prescription charges), no one has to be in paid employment to be entitled to health care.

Having briefly considered the basis for his analysis of welfare systems, Esping-Andersen's (1990, 1996) model of welfare regimes is summarized below. He argues that within a cluster there will be similar features with regard to welfare provision and social and political circumstances, and significant variations between the three clusters. The model could also be used to predict how different regimes would respond to new economic and political challenges. The three main clusters or categories that he identified are: Conservative Corporatist, Liberal or Neo-Liberal, and Social Democratic or Scandinavian, which are outlined below (adapted from Pringle, 1993), and are also shown in Table 11.1 which follows.

For countries within the **Conservative Corporatist** grouping, the state is important, but not usually in a direct fashion. Financial welfare provision relies more on the principle of social insurance, whereby people pay something in to get something back. High employment levels are necessary in order to secure sufficient funding for welfare benefits. The principle of subsidiarity implies that individuals and families should look after themselves first, only turning to the state as a last resort. This can often perpetuate existing class, gender and status differentiation – for example, traditional gender divisions can be reinforced if it is seen that care for older or disabled relatives should be provided within the family. This approach is evident in countries where religion (and particularly the Catholic Church) has been influential, where there has been a more authoritarian approach to government, and the political left has been weaker. Due to the influence of religion in such societies, there will be a strong commitment to traditional family forms and values. Countries identified as having a welfare system reflecting this type of approach include Austria, France, Germany and Italy, with Germany often cited as the prime example.

Liberal welfare systems depend upon market-based social insurance, and have relatively low state benefits for the residual poor, which are means-tested. Universal benefits are not favoured, and there is stigma associated with benefits, which are also seen as providing a disincentive to work. Private forms of welfare provision are encouraged to provide people with more than the bare minimum. Social inequality is not seen as problematic, and regimes like this tend to lead to high levels of stratification (inequality). The USA, the UK and New Zealand are examples of the liberal welfare regime, with the USA the most extreme. To a lesser extent, Canada and Australia could also fit within this type.

Social Democratic welfare regimes have welfare states founded on the core principles of universalism, social solidarity and equality across classes. The welfare state is highly developed, with benefits provided mainly by the state, and high levels of taxation fund the provision of welfare. Rewards tend to be high for all citizens, reflecting the principles of social solidarity and equality. This model depends more than either of the others on full employment in order to fund the system via taxation, and also limit what is paid out in benefits. Many responsibilities of the 'traditional family' are fulfilled by the state, for example, childcare, and this means that individuals, particularly women, have more access to the paid labour market, resulting in a higher degree of gender equality. Scandinavian countries best exemplify this kind of welfare system.

TABLE 11.1   Esping-Andersen's characteristics of welfare regimes

	Sweden	Germany	USA
Regime	Social Democratic	Corporatist	Liberal
Political base	Broad-based compromise	Employer/worker coalition	Free market
Service type	Universal	Occupational	Residual
Public expenditure	High level	High level	Low level
Labour market	High employment/high wage	Low employment/high wage	High employment/low wage

Source: Alcock and Craig (2009: 18)

Criticisms of the model

A number of critiques of Esping-Andersen's model have developed. The first criticism centres on the range of material which a full comparative analysis of welfare systems demands. There are major areas of social welfare that are not readily quantifiable, for example, the provision of personal/social care, yet they ought to be integral to comparative analysis. Concentrating on the welfare state and welfare systems also fails to consider the full impact of tax measures which can be an alternative way of providing welfare (Titmuss, 1974). For example, tax allowances and tax credits, such as working tax credits in the UK, are additional ways of providing support to individuals and families. The framework that Esping-Andersen used is based on a very narrow set of quantifiable welfare data, such as social security and pensions expenditure. In addition, when looking at welfare regimes, not all welfare is provided by states/governments. Titmuss's social division of welfare thesis includes private and occupational welfare, as well as state welfare. The latter is not reflected within the welfare regimes model, but continues to be significant in many countries. Furthermore, private agencies and/or actors are involved in managing and distributing public benefits and services and public/private partnerships are also important in delivering welfare services. The mixed economy of welfare is important in many countries, and includes state, voluntary sector and the private sector (Lewis, 2000), and the role of the family should not be overlooked.

How well do countries fit the model?

It is also questionable whether looking at the level of the country provides the whole picture. The USA and Canada, both placed with the liberal regime cluster, are examples of federal systems. This leads to policy decentralization, with some powers devolved to the level of the state. While the 'Canadian welfare state is more decentralized' (Béland, 2010: 61), in the USA states play a key role in policy areas such as health care and unemployment insurance. The relationships between central and federal government are complex and will vary between countries, but this work is important for highlighting how grouping countries together will obscure some significant differences in the way welfare is organized and delivered. Another example is the way in which the process of devolution in the UK has given more power to the three nations with devolved administrations – Scotland, Wales and Northern Ireland – with the Scottish Parliament having the most power, and reflecting a different political approach from that of the central UK government (see Kinghorn's chapter in this book). This situation did not exist when Esping-Andersen's original work was published, but it does represent a further challenge to the idea of focusing on the country level, and for the study of social policy.

There is ongoing debate around the grouping of countries within regimes. Leisering (2009: 163) questions whether Germany – often seen as the exemplar of the Conservative Corporatist regime – does in fact fit that label. It is a consensus democracy, with a coordinated market economy. According to Esping-Andersen's model, Germany is a conservative welfare regime, with a medium degree of decommodification, with welfare organized around traditional values. However, Leisering qualifies this and states: 'First the German welfare state is more egalitarian and universalist than it looks ... Second, politically, the German regime is "centrist" rather than conservative' (Leisering, 2009: 164). There is a wide range of social insurance coverage, and the health system is strongly egalitarian. (Germany is also a federal system with *länder* [local states] responsible for some welfare policies.) With regard to Australia and New Zealand, Castles and Mitchell (cited in Pierson, 2006) argue that these systems differ from the Liberal regime referred to in Esping-Andersen's model.

Southern European/Mediterranean countries

An early critique of the welfare regimes model was based on the omission of Southern European/ Mediterranean countries (Greece, Spain and Portugal) with Ferrara (1996) suggesting that there is a southern welfare state regime. These countries are sometimes referred to as 'Latin Rim'/'rudimentary' welfare states (Leibfried, 1993, cited in Pierson, 2006). These include Spain, Portugal, Greece, and possibly Italy and France. These have been countries with less-developed welfare systems that are more reliant on support from the family and the Catholic Church.

Central and Eastern Europe

Countries in Central and Eastern Europe were not included in Esping-Andersen's original analysis, and were part of the former Soviet Union (Cousins, 2005). Since the gaining of independence, there has been interest around developments in these countries, particularly with regard to whether there would be a continuation of Socialist welfare provision, or if new ways of delivering welfare are being developed. All of the countries referred to here have been through a period of extensive political and economic change, including change in political regime, massive privatization and high inflation. Aspalter et al. (2009) examine welfare developments in Poland, Hungary, the Czech Republic and Slovenia. They identify a strong emphasis on a social insurance approach to welfare, and attributes of neoliberalism as in Western European countries. They also refer to these four countries as being part of the Christian Democratic tradition of welfare provision in Continental Europe (before the Soviet Union was formed). When considering the Baltic states of Estonia, Latvia and Lithuania – all part of the Soviet Union and gaining independence in the early 1990s – Aidukaite (2006) notes that all three countries were replacing the old system with a social insurance model, related to contributions made when in paid employment. In the Soviet era, pensions were financed by the state and no social insurance contributions were collected. Elements of different approaches to welfare provision exist. Hacker (2009) suggests that in Central and Eastern Europe there may be a hybridization process in effect, that is a mixing of policy approaches, rather than a clustering as in Esping-Andersen's model. Estonia, Latvia and Lithuania managed to stabilize their economies, but still have social problems and are dealing with issues like an ageing population and poverty (Aidukaite, 2006). Another factor to bear in mind is that these countries are now members of the European Union, which raises questions about whether there will be a convergence of welfare approaches within the EU, and if an EU social model can be identified, as discussed in Chapter 12.

East Asian countries

A further type of welfare regime may be necessary to account for East Asian countries (Jones, 1993, cited in Béland, 2010). Hill (2012b: 441) defines East Asian nations as on the western side of the Pacific Ocean, with the north-eastern Asian nations attracting the most attention. These include China, Japan and South Korea, while other countries in the area have received less attention. In China, the tradition of Confucianism is important, with the family having a key role in welfare. In addition, subsequent to the Communist revolution, the political philosophy of Maoism has prioritized the work unit, which can provide for all citizens (Hill, 2012b). A complex set of social policies has developed with differences between urban and rural areas, and currently it is difficult to be certain about the direction of China's social policies. Japan is seen as being a conservative nation in Esping-Andersen's model, but he has acknowledged it is a 'marginal' case between the conservative and liberal clusters (Hill, 2012b: 44). Important points to consider are whether or not regime theory can be applied to developing welfare systems, and to what extent it is possible to predict what shape these new emerging welfare systems will take. Gough and Wood (2004: 400) write that the regime approach is not as applicable to the 'less-developed, the developing and the transitional societies of the South and the East, namely most of the countries in Africa, Asia and Latin America'. They also identify 'informal security regimes' and 'insecurity regimes'. In informal regimes, people rely on the family to support them, and the state is not clearly differentiated from other systems of power, such as caste, ethnicity and kinship group. Insecurity regimes involve high levels of insecurity for inhabitants living in countries that are unstable politically, with governments weakened by corruption and weak politicians. To add to the complexity of debates around welfare regimes and comparative analysis, Jawad (2012) raises questions about social policy in Middle Eastern societies. This author challenges the assumption that there is no welfare provision in this area, but it varies considerably. Emerging issues include moving beyond the use of oil reserves to support the development of social services, and political instability. The recent 'Arab Spring' has led to significant political changes in the Middle East, for example in Libya and Egypt, and these new governments will shape social policies and welfare provision. In Moslem countries, it is also important to note the influence of religion.

Race/Ethnicity

Béland also notes how race/ethnicity has been a major factor in the development of American social policy, which is not included in the welfare regimes model. The USA has a long history of immigration, and of slavery, and as in Australia and New Zealand the impact of colonization on the indigenous population has to be considered. Poole (2000) has also noted the importance of both race and gender in understanding change and welfare developments in the former Soviet bloc. Hill (2012a: 435) argues that the use of the term 'Anglo-Saxon', sometimes used to refer to liberal market systems, is 'pseudo-racial' as it obscures the fact that these societies are multi-ethnic, though he notes that there will be shared cultural influences within these countries. The potential for the expansion of the model to other regions of the world also highlights the issues of race and ethnicity, and gender, how these interconnect, and the extent to which the development of welfare systems alleviates or perpetuates existing inequalities.

Gender and welfare regimes

A strong strand of criticism has developed around gender. While Esping-Andersen (1990) acknowledged the need to look at the interconnections between the state, the market and the family, his analysis was 'built around questions of class inequality rather than gender difference, market obligation in employment rather than care obligation in families' (Pascall, 2012: 18). A feminist analysis of welfare systems highlights how unpaid work provided by women is significant in terms of supporting systems, and of supporting economies, and the gendered connections between 'paid work, unpaid work and welfare' (Lewis, 2000: 38). It is difficult to quantify the costs of such unpaid work, which of course takes place outside of the paid labour market, and Esping-Andersen's focus was on labour market participation. Any analysis which focuses on the sphere of public welfare, and excludes private provision within the family, ignores the contribution of the domestic economy, in sustaining and reproducing public welfare relationships. Modern welfare regimes, though varying in degree, have been based around the male-breadwinner model with women as carers (outside of the labour market), and women's entitlement to benefits has been via men (Lewis, 2000). Women also play an absolutely central role in the formal welfare services of all European countries, that is, as workers – teachers, social workers, nurses, doctors, and so on. The concept of decommodification should be used to analyse services that enable labour market participation. Unpaid labour in the home which is often done by women also facilitates men's labour market participation. An analysis of the status of women inside and outside of the home is an important aspect of welfare systems that is not included in Esping-Andersen's original work. These critiques of his model or typology are a key aspect of feminist critiques of welfare systems and of social policy more generally. Gender should be a critical element of thinking about welfare systems and social policies. However, while gender and unpaid work is neglected in the model, it has helped to show how welfare states work, and why some are more effective than others (Pascall, 2012: 19). Thus, the social democratic welfare states in Scandinavian (also referred to as Nordic) countries have been more effective in supporting families and women, and facilitating gender equality. However, Ellingsaeter and Leira (2006) point out that family changes including labour market participation have often come before welfare reform. In liberal, market-oriented welfare regimes such as that of the UK, progress towards full gender equality has been slower. In *The Incomplete Revolution*, Esping-Andersen (2009) focused on women's role, seeing changes in the family, in women's labour market participation as a 'revolution'. However, complete equality has not been achieved, and social divisions remain. He sees benefits in completing this revolution and achieving gender parity, and argues that social welfare and social policies need to support this. This work provides a contribution to the wider literature on changing gender roles and work–life balance (Lewis, 2009; Pascall, 2012). There also need to be 'incentives to draw men towards a more feminine life course, with caring responsibilities' (Pascall, 2012: 22).

Where next?

This chapter has introduced students to the work of Esping Andersen, who has been influential in shaping debate and discussion around the development of welfare systems. It is still referred to in the literature, and is relevant as a starting point to understanding welfare provision. Critiques have been developed, and further contribute to our understanding of welfare systems today. This is not a static area and as countries develop new welfare systems, for example, Eastern European countries and Asian countries, it allows for comparisons to be made with earlier examples. Other developments to be incorporated into the debate around this area include the potential for the development of an EU social policy, and developments in global social policy. The current global economic recession has meant significant reductions in public sector spending in the UK, but also more significant cuts in other European countries including Italy and Greece, and it is impacting on other countries around the world. This is an additional factor currently re-shaping welfare provision in countries and regions around the world, meaning that the analysis of welfare regimes will continue to evolve.

Summary/Conclusions

- The comparison of welfare and social policies between countries continues to evolve.
- Esping-Andersen's model of welfare regimes was written at a time when theorizing on welfare states and systems was still at an early stage, and his work has been influential in stimulating debate and discussion in this area.
- A number of critiques have developed including those that look at which countries are included and how these are clustered.
- Interest has grown in classifying or theorizing developments in welfare provision in other regions, including Central and Eastern Europe and Eastern Asia.
- Critique based on gender has been significant as it highlights the omission of important aspects of the way care has been provided outside of formal welfare systems, and the centrality of gender to welfare provision.
- Both the European and global context are also important in determining current and future directions in welfare provision.
- This chapter has provided an overview of Esping-Andersen's ideas and subsequent challenges to this, and it is evident that as economies and societies develop, debate and discussion of the model will continue.

Questions

1 Why is comparative social policy important?
2 What are the main characteristics of Esping-Andersen's classification of welfare regimes?
3 What are the main features of the feminist critique?
4 What other critiques have developed and why are they important?

Recommended reading

Alcock, P. and Craig, G. (2009) *International Social Policy Welfare Regimes in the Developed World* (2nd edn). Basingstoke: Palgrave Macmillan.

Alcock, P., May, M. and Wright, S. (eds) (2012) *The Student's Companion to Social Policy*. Chichester: Wiley-Blackwell.

Relevant websites

The websites recommended in Chapter 13 on global social policy will also be relevant here.

References

Aidukaite, J. (2006) 'The formation of social insurance institutions of the Baltic States in the post-socialist era', *Journal of European Social Policy*, 16: 259.

Alcock, P. and Craig, G. (2009) *International Social Policy Welfare Regimes in the Developed World* (2nd edn). Basingstoke: Palgrave Macmillan.

Aspalter, C., Jinsoo, K. and Sojeung, P. (2009) 'Analysing the welfare state in Poland, the Czech Republic, Hungary and Slovenia: an ideal-type perspective ', *Social Policy and Administration*, 43(2): 170–185.

Bambra, C. (2005) 'Cash versus services: "worlds of welfare" and the decommodification of cash benefits and health care services', *Journal of Social Policy*, 34(2): 196–213.

Béland, D. (2010) *What is Social Policy? Understanding the Welfare State*. Cambridge: Polity Press.

Cousins, M. (2005) *European Welfare States: Comparative Perspectives*. London: Sage.

Ellingsaeter, A. L. and Leira, A. (2006) *Politicising Parenthood in Scandinavia*. Bristol: Policy Press.

Esping-Andersen, G. (1987) 'Citizenship and socialism: solidarity in the welfare state', in G. Esping-Andersen and L. Rainwater (eds) *Stagnation and Renewal in Social Policy: the Rise and Fall of Policy Regimes*. London: Sharpe.

Esping-Andersen, G. (1990) *The Three Worlds of Welfare Capitalism*. Cambridge: Polity Press.

Esping-Andersen, G. (1996) *Welfare States in Transition National Adaptations in Global Economies*. London: Sage.

Esping-Andersen, G. (2009) *The Incomplete Revolution: Adapting to Women's New Roles*. Cambridge: Polity Press.

Ferrara, M. (1996) 'The "southern model" of welfare in Southern Europe', *Journal of European Social Policy*, 6(1): 17–37.

Gough, I. and Wood, G. (2004) *Insecurity and Welfare Regimes in Asia, Africa and Latin America: Social Policy in Development Contexts*. Cambridge: Cambridge University Press.

Hacker, B. (2009) 'Hybridization instead of clustering: transformation processes of welfare policies in Central and Eastern Europe', *Social Policy and Administration*, 43(2): 152–169.

Hill, M. (2012a) 'Social policy in liberal market societies', in P. Alcock, M. May and S. Wright (eds) *The Student's Companion to Social Policy*. Chichester: Wiley-Blackwell.

Hill, M. (2012b) 'Social policy in East Asian societies', in P. Alcock, M. May and S. Wright (eds) *The Student's Companion to Social Policy*. Chichester: Wiley-Blackwell.

Jawad, R. (2012) ' Social policy in Middle Eastern societies', in P. Alcock, M. May and S. Wright (eds) *The Student's Companion to Social Policy*. Chichester: Wiley-Blackwell.

Leisering, L. (2009) 'Germany: a centrist welfare state at the crossroads', in P. Alcock, and G. Craig (eds) *International Social Policy Welfare Regimes in the Developed World* (2nd edition). Basingstoke: Palgrave Macmillan.

Lewis, J. (2000) 'Gender and welfare regimes', in G. Lewis, S. Gewirtz and J. Clarke (eds) *Rethinking Social Policy*. London: Sage.

Lewis, J. (2009) *Work–Family Balance, Gender and Policy*. Cheltenham: Edward Elgar.

May, M. (2012) 'Comparative analysis', in P. Alcock, M. May and S. Wright (eds) *The Student's Companion to Social Policy*. Chichester: Wiley-Blackwell.

Pascall, G. (2012) *Gender Inequality in the Welfare State?* Bristol: The Policy Press.

Pierson, C. (2006) *Beyond the Welfare State: The New Political Economy of Welfare* (3rd edn). Cambridge: Polity.

Poole, L. (2000) 'New approaches to comparative social policy: the changing face of Central and Eastern European welfare', in G. Lewis, S. Gewirtz and J. Clarke (eds) *Rethinking Social Policy*. London: Sage.

Titmuss, R. (1974) *Social Policy*. London: Allen and Unwin.

12

The European Union and Social Policy

Paul Copeland

Overview

- The European Union contains nearly all of the countries of the European continent and is the most advanced form of regional integration within the global economy.
- The European integration process has predominantly been concerned with market integration.
- EU legislation within social policy mainly concerns the protection of workers.
- The EU has developed a coordinating role within a broader social policy that utilizes flexible agreements between the Member States.
- Fundamental obstacles remain towards the creation of a more substantive EU social policy.
- This chapter provides an introductory overview of the process of European integration and the EU's competence within social policy, and analyses whether it is possible to talk of a European social model.

Introduction

Originally founded in 1957 with six Member States, the European Union (EU) includes nearly all of the European continent and affects both directly and indirectly the majority of domestic policy within its Members. The institutional and political configuration of the EU is both complex and multifaceted and for the vast majority who read this volume, both this, and the EU's sphere of influence on the policies of its Member States, may be unfamiliar terrains. The aim of this chapter is to provide an overview of the historical development of the EU, its key political institutions and policy competences, and, in particular, the EU's competence within the area of social policy.

Before proceeding, it is worth noting that the EU's competence within social policy is rather weak. There is no transnational European welfare state that either complements or supersedes the social policies of its Member States. The EU has developed additional powers to regulate and coordinate social policy rather than the redistributive policies found at the national level. This chapter argues that the process of European integration is a predominantly market-making process in which integration within social policy has more often than not resulted from concerns to prevent a distortion of competition within the EU economy. In this respect, the vast majority of EU directives (legislation) relate to the protection of workers and not the broader concerns of EU citizens. When attempts to establish a more comprehensive EU social policy have been made, they have predominantly featured legally non-binding agreements that had a limited impact and have failed to produce any formal legal expansion of EU social policy. Central to these punctuated moments of activity are moments in which the EU's political constellations have been favourable to progress within EU social policy (i.e. a majority of centre-left), but, as the chapter explains, there are rather specific characteristics to the EU integration process that limit progress beyond this situation.

This chapter is divided into four sections. The first section provides a brief historical overview of the development of the EU and its main decision-making institutions. This is intended to provide the novice reader with the necessary background to understand both the process of European integration and the EU's institutions. The second section analyses the development of the EU's social policy and outlines its main policy competences. It argues that EU integration predominantly concerns the rights of workers rather than citizens and explains the reasons for this particular trait. The third section discusses the extent to which a European social model can be identified. It draws on the existing literature within this debate to argue it to be a concept that waxes and wanes along with the EU's centre-left political configuration. Finally, the chapter concludes with a discussion concerning the likelihood of a more expansive EU social policy developing in the future.

The historical development of the European Union

The EU is the most advanced form of regional cooperation/integration within the global economy. Founded in 1957, the Union is based on the four principles of the free movement of goods, services, people and capital, and its legal mandate is set out in the Treaty. In its current form, the EU is comprised of 27 Member States, a Single European Market (SEM), a European Monetary Union (EMU) with a single currency known as the Eurozone (for those Member States who have opted to join), and internal borderless travel between Member States known as the Schengen Area (again for those who have joined). Both the SEM and EMU, alongside agricultural policy, competition policy and international trade agreements, are policy areas in which Member States have pooled sovereignty for the EU to have exclusive legal competence. Policy areas such as economic growth, energy, the environment, employment, transport, food and fisheries currently have a shared competence between the EU and its Member States, while policy areas such as education and training, social policy and health policy are almost exclusively the remit of the Member States (Hix, 2005; El-Agraa, 2007; Nugent, 2010; Wallace et al., 2010). As a result of these varying levels of integration across the different policy areas, the EU is often referred to as being characterized by differentiated levels of integration in which neither a fully-fledged federal European state exists, nor do its Members enjoy complete autonomy over their domestic policy.

Four main institutions govern the EU: the European Commission, the European Council, the European Court of Justice (ECJ), and the European Parliament. The European Commission is comprised of one Commissioner from each of the 27 Member States and is headed by the Commission President. The Commission is charged with the responsibility of proposing measures that are likely to advance the development of the EU (Article 17 of the Treaty of the European Union). Where legislation is envisaged, this power is exclusive to the Commission (with the exception of justice and home affairs and foreign policy) and it is also delegated rule-making powers (Nugent, 2010: 122–137). The Council is comprised of the heads of government from the Member States and its principal responsibility is to take policy and legislative decisions. Under the ordinary legislative procedure (which applies to the majority of EU policy making), the Council is required to take into consideration the position of the European Parliament when reaching an agreement. Comprised of some 754 members from across the EU, the European Parliament is the EU's only directly elected institution. In terms of initiating legislation, the Parliament is a relatively weak institution (and the weakest of all EU institutions). Although in theory it is possible for the Parliament to request the Commission to submit an appropriate proposal on which it considers that a Union act is required for the purpose of implementing the Treaty, in reality this rarely happens. Not only has the Commission been slow to act on such requests (Judge and Earnshaw, 2008: 195–196), but such requests require an absolute majority vote in the Parliament which is difficult to obtain (Nugent, 2010: 180). Finally, the ECJ is tasked with interpreting EU law and ensuring its equal application across all EU Member States.

This current EU institutional and political configuration has taken over half a century to develop. Cooperation between the six founding Member States (Belgium, France, Germany, Italy, Luxembourg and the Netherlands) was formed against the backdrop of the Second World War to ensure that economic and political cooperation on the Continent would promote peace and stability. This culminated in 1957 with the six states signing what is now referred to as the Treaty of Rome (Nugent, 2010: 3–26). The general principles of the Treaty of Rome such as the four freedoms, a Common Market, and the prohibition of anti-competitive practices, remain the central underpinning principles of the EU, despite numerous revisions expanding its competences and modifying the decision-making process. In conjunction with an expanding role and function, the EU has also been open to including other countries on the Continent (Nugent, 2010: 27–50). 1973 witnessed the first round of enlargement by expanding membership to Denmark, Ireland and the UK; this was followed by Greece, Spain and Portugal during the 1980s; Austria, Finland and Sweden in 1995; the Baltic States, Central Eastern Europe, Cyprus and Malta in 2004; and Bulgaria and Romania in 2007. Future rounds of enlargement to include the Balkans and Turkey are also expected.

Why has the EU expanded beyond its seemingly simple initial aims and objectives? Schmidt (2002) argues that European integration is in fact a regional response to the forces of globalization (see Chapter 14 for further discussion). European integration has acted as a conduit for global neoliberal forces and as a shield against them, opening up Member States to international competition in the capital and product markets and simultaneously protecting them through EMU and the SEM. As European governments attempted to respond to the economic crisis of the 1970s, it became increasingly apparent that unilateral action was reaching its limit. A more coordinated attempt to respond to the new global order of neoliberalism gained support across the then Member States, resulting in the first major revision of the Treaty and a reinvigoration of the integration project with the signing of the Single European Act (SEA) in 1986. In fact, the current institutional and political configuration of the EU owes much to developments since 1986, as the EU has attempted to integrate and push for higher rates of growth and improved competitiveness relative to its main competitors outside of the continent. So while the original aim of European integration was to create peace and prosperity on the Continent, the limited cooperation and integration that had taken place prior to the 1980s proved itself to be a useful backdrop in which to respond to the new neoliberal global order.

With this in mind, it should be noted that the process of European integration has been a predominantly market-making process (Leibfried, 2010; Young, 2010). The aim of the SEA was to 'complete' the SEM in goods and remove any remaining barriers to free trade by 1992, as well as give the EU institutions more powers. The success of the SEA created a spillover effect to other (mainly service sector) policy areas such as telecommunications, air transport and financial services (Armstrong and Bulmer, 1998). A further effect was the signing of the Treaty of the European Union 1992 (TEU) which set out the procedures and timetable for moving towards, and the completion of, an Economic and Monetary Union (EMU) (Hodson, 2010).

Further revisions were agreed under the 1997 Treaty of Amsterdam. The main purpose of Amsterdam was to reform the EU institutions in the run-up to the 2004 enlargement and, importantly, to add a new title on employment. This gave the EU a specific mandate to promote high levels of employment within its Member States. But Amsterdam and subsequent Treaty revisions since (Nice in 2001 and Lisbon in 2008) have been more modest in comparison to the SEA and Maastricht (Nugent, 2010: 53–67). Rather than expanding the EU's competences, they have been more concerned with reforming the EU's decision-making processes and other procedural matters. More recently, the European integration project has been thrown into turmoil as the financial crisis has spilled over into a fully-fledged Eurozone crisis. It is clear that current events will dominate the political landscape for years to come and the direction in which the European integration project will proceed is an open question.

The development of EU social policy

The construction of EU social policy has predominantly developed as a by-product of the functioning of the SEM and has mainly concerned a prevention of the distortion of competition and the free movement of workers (not citizens). This has often led to claims that EU social policy is predominantly based on establishing 'social rights' (Leibfried, 2010; Keune, 2012). Where attempts have been made to create a broader EU social policy, they have taken the form of non-binding agreements, as opposed to the traditional hard law which is more commonly associated with the rights of workers and more generally the SEM. Before proceeding to outline the historical development of EU social policy, it is worth briefly considering why progress towards EU social policy has been so limited.

Stone Sweet and Sandholtz (1998) argue that the process of European integration is influenced and generated by cross-border flows from business. As companies seek to expand their market share across the region, they encounter barriers to trade, such as tariffs and quotas, along with less obvious restrictions such as different legal and technical standards for certain goods. In turn, business actors exert pressure on governments at both the national and EU level to create a harmonization of policy that can reduce costs. Over time, such a process may generate spillover effects into other policy areas. As the business community is the main driver and beneficiary of European integration and is significantly more transnational than actors surrounding social policy, EU policy outcomes tend to be more favourable to business. EU welfare states are very specific to the territory in which they operate and unlike companies, they do not operate in other Member States and thereby encounter transaction costs that generate political pressure for their removal/harmonization.

Typologies of welfare state literature also point to a second factor behind the limited progress within EU social policy (Esping-Andersen, 1990; Cousins, 2005). There are vast differences between EU welfare states that make agreement towards a broader EU social policy difficult, even when there is substantial political will at EU level. Europe is a mixture of Continental, Mediterranean, Scandinavian, Eastern European and Liberal welfare states with very different aims, objectives and policy outcomes (Esping-Andersen, 1990; Ferrera, 1996, 2005; Huber and Stephens, 2001; Feldmann, 2006, 2007; Keune, 2006; and see also Chapter 12 of this volume). Such differences are embedded at the national level, making transnational agreements for integration and harmonization difficult. The extensive Scandinavian model of welfare typified by Sweden with its universal benefit system and extensive public services (such as childcare facilities) producing low levels of inequality, stands as a polar opposite to the liberal model typified by the UK, with its means-tested benefit system and a much lower level of public services producing relatively higher levels of inequality. Even if governments can agree that a particular aspect of social policy should be addressed at the transnational level, agreeing on how this should be done is often fraught with difficulties.

From the signing of the Treaty of Rome (1957) until the Single European Act (1986), there was little progress in the area of social policy. The Treaty of Rome set up a 'modest, cautious and narrowly focused social policy' in which only 12 of the 248 articles in the Treaty related to social policy (Hantrais, 2000: 2–3). The Commission was given the responsibility of promoting close cooperation between Member States in matters relating to training, employment, labour law and working conditions, social security and collective bargaining, but without specifying the form such cooperation should take. Directives were also allowed in order to eliminate laws and practices that were considered to be distorting competition, and, importantly, to secure the free movement of workers between Member States. Provision was also made for gender equality in pay, as well as to prevent discrimination on the grounds of nationality. Finally, the Structural Funds were established (one of the few redistributive EU policies) to provide financial assistance to areas affected by deindustrialization and high levels of unemployment.

Despite progress in the areas of health and safety and social security rights for workers, the political momentum during the 1970s amounted to very little output for EU social policy. The signing of the SEA in 1986 signified a new impetus for both the European integration process and EU social policy. The then French President, François Mitterrand, put forward the idea of an *espace social* that was taken up by the then President of the Commission Jacques Delors (Wendon, 1998: 59; Martin and Ross, 1999: 323–324). Delors aimed to develop a social dimension as a means of strengthening economic cohesion and to counter-balance the EU's market-making project. The limited EU budget meant that the only way for the Commission to expand its scope was through the regulation of industry and labour. In 1989 the governments of the Member States, with the exception of the British, adopted the Community Charter of Fundamental Social Rights of Workers, heralded as the social dimension of the SEA (Hantrais, 2000: 8). The objective was to create a level playing field between Member States in the area of social policy (in a similar manner to the SEM), but disagreement remained as to whether the leveling should be one of an increase or decrease in standards. As such, the Community Charter did not have the force of law and decisions concerning its implementation were left to the Member States. The rights were set out under 12 headings, including freedom of movement, working conditions and social protection.[1] Despite this, the Charter was instrumental in the launching of initiatives in employment and industrial relations policy which produced a number of directives during the 1990s concerning: pregnancy and maternity leave; working time; posting of workers; the 1994 European Works Council Directive; and directives based on framework agreements between EU social partners on parental leave, part-time work and fixed-term work.

Both the Commission and a group of Member States (led by the Mediterranean countries) aimed to give the Charter full legal recognition in the Treaty, but continued opposition by the UK relegated such a provision to a 'Chapter' annexed to the Maastricht Treaty (Hantrais, 2000: 11; Vaughan-Whitehead, 2003: 13). The Chapter declared 30 general principles to guide EU social policy, including the promotion of employment, proper social protection, dialogue between management and labour, combating poverty and social exclusion. The 11 Member States that signed the Chapter were permitted to integrate in social policy without it affecting the UK. These attempts to broaden the EU's remit within social policy never quite matched the vision of an *espace social*. Furthermore, broader changes to the EU's Treaty at Maastricht in 1992 were to essentially limit the EU's remit in EU social policy (as well as its policy competences more generally). The principle of subsidiarity was intended to regulate the exercise of EU powers and determine whether the EU could take action or not in areas of shared competence. The principle is based on the idea that decisions must be taken as closely as possible to the citizen and the EU should not undertake action unless Union action is more effective. The subsidiarity principle has proved itself to be a powerful weapon for governments who have aimed to limit encroaching EU intervention, including opposition towards EU social policy.

1997 witnessed a change in the British government's attitude following the election of a New Labour administration. Britain opted into the Social Chapter, allowing it to be incorporated into the Treaty changes agreed at Amsterdam. The end of the 20th century also signified a period of great optimism for a more expansive role for the EU in social policy. The majority of governments from the Member States were centre-left and the EU was suffering from high levels of unemployment. Inspired by Scandinavian experiences of welfare and employment policy, governments agreed to add a new title on employment to the Treaty (Rhodes, 2010: 283–306; Velluti, 2010: 81–121). This gave the EU a specific mandate to promote high levels of employment, but increasing reluctance to cede more powers to the EU institutions, combined with the diversity of welfare states, resulted in the EU playing a coordinating role in the policy area. The European Employment Strategy (EES) would therefore utilize an experimental decentralized mode of governance based on commonly agreed EU-level targets (e.g. an EU-wide employment rate of 70 per cent) to be achieved via annual reporting by the Member States, the sharing of 'best practice' and peer review (Trubek and Mosher, 2003; Ashiagbor, 2004; Velluti, 2010).

Towards the end of the 20th century, European leaders were becoming increasingly concerned with the region's declining competitiveness relative to its main competitors. The result was the launching of the EU's Lisbon Strategy in 2000 which aimed to make the EU: 'the most competitive and dynamic knowledge-based economy in the world capable of sustainable economic growth with more and better jobs and greater social cohesion' by 2010 (European Commission, 2000: 2). This was to be achieved via completing the SEM (in the area of services), favourable macro-economic policies, micro-economic reforms, increases in employment, and, importantly, the modernization and future preservation of EU welfare states. In this respect, social policy was conceived to be just as important for economic growth as economic policies per se. The Lisbon Strategy represented the EU's first broad and genuine consensus to balance economic growth with social cohesion. Guidelines and/or targets were set for a wide range of policy areas from research and innovation, to education, pensions and social exclusion and at-risk-of-poverty. These were to be achieved by 'soft governance' procedures similar to the EES that became known as the Open Method of Coordination (OMC).

The optimism that surrounded the launching of the Lisbon Strategy for a more substantive EU social policy proved to be short-lived (James, 2012: 20). Against a damning critique of a lack of progress within the Member States (known as the Kok Report, 2004), the Strategy was re-launched by a centre-right Council and Commission in 2005 under the banner of 'a strategy for growth and jobs'. Lisbon II, as it became known, put growth and jobs at the centre of the Strategy and relegated social policy to an 'add-on' status. In other words, progress within EU social policy was to become dependent upon developments within the macro economy, as opposed to it being a more equal and independent objective in 2000.

In 2009/2010, the European Commission reviewed the Lisbon Strategy and concluded that progress had been slow (European Commission, 2010). In fact, the Lisbon Strategy was something of a failure in which only limited progress towards the guidelines and targets was actually achieved. Furthermore, in terms of this impact we are normally referring to changes in national ways of thinking (cognitive shifts) within political actors about policy problems and their solutions, as opposed to concrete policy outcomes and EU convergence. Within areas such as pensions, health care and social exclusion, activity had generated very little in terms of policy convergence other than agreements on definitions and indicators (Copeland and Papadimitriou, 2012). A central problem for the Lisbon Strategy (and EU social policy) was that although centre-left governments dominated the EU institutions during its launch, the 'soft' governance processes chosen to achieve its aims and objectives were not only weak, but also proved themselves to be easily sidelined and undermined when the EU's political constellations shifted to the centre-right.

The signing of the Lisbon Treaty in 2009 mainly expanded the EU's competences in energy, tourism and climate change. In the areas of employment and social policy, Article 3 (Treaty on European Union) commits the EU to achieving full employment and social progress, and the combating of social exclusion and discrimination. Despite this, the EU's legal remit within social policy remains narrow. Against this backdrop, the successor to the Lisbon Strategy, known as Europe 2020, launched in 2010, contains near identical social policy aims to that of Lisbon II. Europe 2020 contains the explicit aim to lift at least 20 million people out of poverty by 2020. Given that such a target continues to utilize the OMC as established during Lisbon, combined with the financial crisis in the EU, it is highly unlikely that Europe 2020 will produce anything substantial for the development of a broader EU social policy.

Is there a European social model?

As a market-making process, European integration favours the liberalization and deregulation of markets to stimulate growth and jobs. When the EU has intervened within the social policies of its Member States, it has predominantly been concerned with the prevention of distorting competition within the SEM. Attempts to create a more encompassing EU social policy have resulted in voluntary agreements with limited impact on Member States. National governments therefore maintain a high degree of autonomy within their social policies. Is it then possible to speak of a European social model (ESM) that can be identified at the transnational level in a similar way to the SEM?

The answer to this question is one of the most contested aspects of the European integration process (Leibfried and Pierson, 1995; Adnett, 2001; Tidow, 2003; Wincott, 2003; Ferrera, 2005). A problem with the debate is that the European Commission has been reluctant to provide an official definition of the ESM, yet it has continually made reference to its existence in its various documents. To add further confusion, the Commission has, on occasion, made reference to the European social model and the European social models: the two are clearly different. The ESM refers to the EU social policy that exists at EU level and is implemented at the Member State level, while European social models are the various models of welfare state in the Member States that underpin and implement EU social policy.

In their 2005 work, Jepsen and Serrano Pascual highlight no less than four definitions of the ESM within the current academic literature, highlighting the difficulties posed by using the term. First, the ESM can be defined as an entity (common institutions, values or forms of regulation) that has specific aims or focuses on the capacity for political regulation of the market economy. Second, it can be defined whereby specific models of the welfare state are identified with the aim of the EU moving towards a particular type (such as the Scandinavian model). Third, there are those who see the social model as a 'European project' under which the European welfare states are, after all, committed to a certain basic level of welfare provision that distinguishes them from more strictly liberal models such as that of the USA (which includes the argument that the UK is not a strict liberal welfare state). Finally, Jepsen and Serrano Pascual (2005) add their own definition in which they argue that the existence of an ESM is utilized within European discourse as an instrument for optimizing the adjustment of social protection systems to market forces.

While these different definitions are indicative of the debate surrounding the topic, an inventory of the actual components of EU social policy serves to provide a more concrete answer to the question in mind. Ter Haar and Copeland (2010) provide an analysis of the various hard law, soft law and normative components of the European social model. The hard law found in the Treaties and EU Directives concerns health and safety legislation, equal opportunity and anti-discrimination legislation, free movement of workers, as well as social partner recognition and the Structural Funds. Soft law, associated with the Lisbon Strategy and Europe 2020, concerns poverty and social exclusion, the European Employment Strategy, education and training, pensions, social protection systems, adequate health care provision and the reconciliation of work and family life. Finally, the normative component compares the EU with the USA and argues for a belief at the EU level that economic growth should be combined with social cohesion. Crucially, Ter Haar's and Copeland's (2010) definition is that unlike the SEM, which is predominantly comprised of hard law and backed by the European Court of Justice, the ESM is particularly vulnerable to shifts in political configurations at both EU and Member State level.

The particular problem then with identifying an ESM is that its very existence depends on the political constellations at the various levels of EU governance at any one moment in time. Between 1997 and 2005, the European Council was dominated by social democratic governments, the Parliament by the centre-left, and a Commission that was sympathetic to the forging of an EU social policy. The result was considerable activity and enthusiasm at the EU level in terms of placing new policy areas onto the agenda and experimental attempts to coordinate and engage Member State activity. This was a period of great optimism within the EU in which average growth levels were relatively high and a significant amount of political energy was put into forging a genuine ESM. However, this particular momentum soon disappeared from 2005 onwards, as the EU's political configuration shifted to the centre-right. A result was that with the exception of employment, the other social OMCs (social exclusion, pensions and health care) were relegated to a third order of priority within the political hierarchy (Tholoniat, 2010) and governments only engaged in a light-touch way. Furthermore, even though employment remained high on the list of EU priorities post-2005, it succumbed to changes in the political climate as a much greater emphasis was put on job creation per se, as opposed to the pre-2005 discourse of 'more and better [quality] jobs' (Velluti, 2012). Increasing the number of individuals in work, regardless of whether such jobs are low paid with potentially poor employment conditions, is very different from increasing employment and ensuring that jobs provide employees with sufficient pay, working conditions and training opportunities.

At the transnational level, the ESM is therefore a project that waxes and wanes over time. Unlike the SEM, which remains a constant feature of the EU regardless of the transnational political configurations, the ESM requires a majority of centre-left governments to be in office to fully exploit the EU's soft law components in the social policy field, although they are unable to generate agreements beyond the flexible OMC to create legislation. During more centre-right dominated periods, such as the current phase of European integration, governments take a narrower interpretation of EU social policy and predominantly focus on the rights of workers.

Towards a more expansive EU social policy

The creation of a more substantive EU social policy to protect citizens and not just workers rests on a double jeopardy. First, despite the presence of transnational social actors within the European political arena (such as the European Anti-Poverty Network), their influence remains limited in comparison to that exerted by business groups. Only a small fraction of the estimated 2,500 interest groups in Brussels represent social policy issues. There is no genuine European demos or EU society capable of organizing itself across borders to exert political pressure for a more substantive social policy. Furthermore, in comparison to the USA, EU intra-migration remains small and is unlikely to increase in the short term given the language barriers for citizens to such a process (Boswell, 2005).

The second jeopardy is that despite the pressures of the last 30 years exerted by globalization (and European integration) to retrench welfare/social policy, EU welfare states remain hugely diverse. While there has been some limited convergence of social policies, the EU has simultaneously expanded to include the former state-socialist countries of Eastern Europe whose welfare states are not only different, but whose levels of wealth and social problems also differ from those of the pre-2004 group of EU members (Vaughan-Whitehead, 2003). Therefore, forging concrete agreements for EU citizens in the area of social policy between a large number of very diverse Member States remains as problematic today as it did between 12 Member States during the Delors era.

But there is some hope for a more substantive EU social policy and it would be inaccurate to conclude that all future developments are likely to amount to very little beyond protecting workers. While the political effort required for such developments would be huge, it is not insurmountable. The recent financial and Eurozone crises have initiated a lively debate at both national and EU levels of governance concerning the virtues of the neoliberal orthodoxy of the last three decades. While this is unlikely to represent a paradigm shift away from such policies in the near future, it could provide the political foundation from which national governments, via the EU, construct policies to appease such criticism and thereby establish social rights to protect all citizens. Europe is facing its worst crisis since the Second World War and how the process of European integration will develop over the next decade remains unclear. Furthermore, since 2005 the European Parliament has positioned itself as a defender of EU citizens and has continuously called for 'an EU for all citizens'. As the only directly elected EU institution, MEPs are continuously asking to be returned to the Parliament by their electorate. In doing so, regardless of their political inclinations, the majority of MEPs have been attempting to create stronger links with their electorates and want to be seen to be doing something for citizens. Furthermore, although the European Parliament remains the weakest of the EU institutions and it is continuously striving to increase its position and influence relative to the Commission and the Council, the area of social policy is considered to be one in which the Parliament can gain some influence. Should EU citizens be the beneficiaries of such parliamentary activity, this would not necessarily be such a bad thing.

Summary/Conclusions

- The EU legislation that exists within the social policy field almost exclusively concerns the protection of workers, as opposed to all citizens.
- This has mainly developed as a spillover effect from the Single European Market over concerns that differences in employment standards distort competition and could give some Member States a competitive advantage over others.
- When Member States have attempted to forge ahead with a more substantive EU social policy (e.g. to fight poverty and social exclusion), the result has been flexible, legally non-binding agreements. Such agreements stem from periods of centre-left political domination across the Union.
- Difficulties in forming a transnational group of social policy actors capable of exerting political pressure at EU and national levels, combined with significant variations in welfare policy within the Member States, are identified as key reasons behind these developments.
- Whether a European social model exists depends very much on political constellations in the Union. Centre-left majorities tend to exploit legally non-binding agreements to generate a more encompassing EU social policy, while centre-right governments narrowly interpret EU social policy to protect workers.
- While challenges towards a more concrete EU social policy for all citizens are large, they are not insurmountable. There is some evidence of political activity that suggests future EU developments could be favourable to a more encompassing EU social policy.

Questions

1 What areas of social policy does the EU cover?
2 Why has the development of EU social policy been so limited?
3 Does a European social model exist?
4 How could current obstacles to the development of a broader EU social policy be overcome?

Recommended reading

Copeland, P. and Daly, M. (2012) 'Varieties of poverty reduction: inserting the poverty and social exclusion target into Europe 2020', *Journal of European Social Policy*, 22(3): 273–287. This provides an overview of the difficulties in agreeing EU social policy.

Copeland, P. and Papadimitriou, D. (eds) (2012) *Evaluating the EU's Lisbon Strategy*. Basingstoke: Palgrave Macmillan. This text provides more general developments within the EU integration process and EU social policy since 2000, especially the chapters by Daly, Tinios and de Ruijter and Hervey.

General introductions to EU social policy can be found in the following two texts:

Hantrais (2007) *Social Policy and the European Union* (3rd edn). Basingstoke: Palgrave Macmillan.

Leibfried, S. (2010) 'Social policy: left to the markets and the judges', in H. Wallace, W. Wallace and M. Pollack (eds) *Policy Making in the European Union*. Oxford: Oxford University Press.

Relevant websites

The Directorate-General for Employment, Social Affairs and Inclusion in the European Commission provides an excellent overview of both past and present activities of the EU in social policy – http://ec.europa.eu/social/home.jsp.

See also the websites of the European Trade Union Confederation – www.etuc.org/ – and the European Anti-Poverty Network – www.eapn.eu/

Note

1   Under this Charter, the Community is obliged to provide for the fundamental social rights of workers under the following headings: freedom of movement; employment and remuneration; improvement of living and working conditions; social protection; freedom of association and collective bargaining; vocational training; equal treatment for men and women; information and consultation and participation for workers; health protection and safety at the workplace; protection of children and adolescents; elderly persons; disabled persons.

References

Adnett, N. (2001) 'Modernizing the European social model: developing the guidelines', *Journal of Common Market Studies*, 39(2): 353–364.

Armstrong, K. and Bulmer, S. (1998) *The Governance of the Single European Market*. Manchester: Manchester University Press.

Ashiagbor, D. (2004) *The European Employment Strategy: Labour Market Regulation and New Governance*. Oxford: Oxford University Press.

Boswell, C. (2005) *Migration in Europe*. Hamburg: Global Commission on International Migration, Hamburg Institute of International Economics.

Copeland, P. and Daly, M. (2012) 'Varieties of poverty reduction: inserting the poverty and social exclusion target into Europe 2020', *Journal of European Social Policy*, 22(3): 273–287.

Copeland, P. and Papadimitriou, D. (eds) (2012) *Evaluating the EU's Lisbon Strategy*. Basingstoke: Palgrave Macmillan.

Cousins, M. (2005) *European Welfare States: Comparative Perspectives*. London: Sage.

El-Agraa, A.M. (ed.) (2007) *The European Union: Economics and Policies*. Cambridge: Cambridge University Press.

Esping-Andersen, G. (1990) *Three Words of Welfare Capitalism*. Cambridge: Polity.

European Commission (2000) 'The Lisbon European Council: An Agenda of Economic and Social Renewal for Europe', Contribution of the European Commission to the Special European Council in Lisbon, DOC/00/7, Brussels, 28 February.

European Commission (2010) 'Lisbon Strategy Evaluation Document', Commission Working Document, SEC (2010) 114 Final, 2 February.

Feldmann, M. (2006) 'Emerging varieties of capitalism in transition countries: industrial relations and wage bargaining in Estonia and Slovenia', *Comparative Political Studies*, 39: 829–854.

Feldmann, M. (2007) 'The origins of varieties of capitalism: lessons from post-socialist transition in Estonia and Slovenia', in B. Hancké, M. Rhodes and M. Thatcher (eds) *Beyond Varieties of Capitalism*. Oxford: Oxford University Press.

Ferrera, M. (1996) 'Is there a southern model of welfare?', *Journal of European Social Policy*, 6(1): 17–37.

Ferrera, M. (2005) *The Boundaries of Welfare: European Integration and the New Spatial Politics of Social Protection*. Oxford: Oxford University Press.

Hantrais (2000) *Social Policy and the European Union* (2nd edn). Basingstoke: Palgrave Macmillan.

Hantrais (2007) *Social Policy and the European Union* (3rd edn). Basingstoke: Palgrave Macmillan.

Hix, S. (2005) *The Political System of the European Union*. Basingstoke: Palgrave Macmillan.

Hodson, D. (2010) 'Economic and monetary policy: an experiment in new modes of EU policy-making', in H. Wallace, M. Pollack and A. Young (eds) *Policy-Making in the European Union*. Oxford: Oxford University Press.

Huber, E. and Stephens, J. (2001) 'Welfare states and production regimes in the era of retrenchment', in P. Pierson (ed.) *The New Politics of the Welfare State*. Oxford: Oxford University Press.

James, S. (2012) 'The origins and evolution of the Lisbon Agenda', in P. Copeland and D. Papadimitriou (eds) *Evaluating the EU's Lisbon Strategy*. Basingstoke: Palgrave Macmillan.

Jepsen, M. and Serrano Pascual, A. (2005) 'The European social model: an exercise in deconstruction', *Journal of European Social Policy*, 15(3): 231–245.

Judge, D. and Earnshaw, D. (2008) *The European Parliament* (2nd edn). Basingstoke: Palgrave Macmillan.

Keune, M. (2006) 'The European social model and enlargement', in M. Jepsen and A. Serrano Pasual (eds) *Unwrapping the European Social Model*. Bristol: Polity Press.

Keune, M. (2012) 'The social dimension of European integration', in L. Burroni, M. Keune and G. Meardi (eds) *Economy and Society in Europe: A Relationship in Crisis*. Cheltenham: Edward Elgar, pp. 19–39.

Kok, W. (2004) *Facing the Challenge: The Lisbon Strategy for Growth and Employment*. Report from the High Level Group chaired by Wim Kok, November. Available at: http://ec.europa.eu/research/evaluations/pdf/archive/fp6-evidence-base/evaluation_studies_and_reports/evaluation_studies_and_reports_2004/the_lisbon_strategy_for_growth_and_employment__report_from_the_high_level_group.pdf -(accessed 14 August 2012).

Leibfried, S. (2010) 'Social policy: left to the markets and the judges', in H. Wallace, W. Wallace and M. Pollack (eds) *Policy Making in the European Union*. Oxford: Oxford University Press.

Leibfried, S. and Pierson, P. (1995) *European Social Policy between Fragmentation and Integration*. Washington, DC: Brookings Institute.

Martin, A. and Ross, G. (1999) 'In the line of fire: the Europeanisation of labour representation', in A. Martin and G. Ross (eds) *The Brave New World of European Labour: European Trade Unions and the Millennium*. Oxford: Berghahn Books.

Nugent, N. (2010) *The Government and Politics of the European Union* (7th edn). Basingstoke: Palgrave Macmillan.

Rhodes, M. (2010) 'Employment policy: between efficacy and experimentation', in H. Wallace, M. Pollack and A. Young (eds) *Policy-Making in the European Union*. Oxford: Oxford University Press.

Schmidt, V. (2002) *The Futures of European Capitalism*. Oxford: Oxford University Press

Stone Sweet, S. and Sandholtz, W. (1998) 'Integration, supranational governance, and the institutionalisation of the European polity', in S. Stone-Sweet and W. Sandholtz (eds) *European Integration and Supranational Governance*. Oxford: Oxford University Press.

Ter Haar, B.P. and Copeland, P. (2010) 'What are the future prospects for the European social model? An analysis of EU equal opportunities and employment policy', *European Law Journal*, 16(3): 273–291.

Tholoniat, L. (2010) 'The career of the open method of coordination: lessons from a "soft" EU instrument', *West European Politics*, 33(1): 93–117.

Tidow, S. (2003) 'The emergence of European employment policy as a transnational political arena', in H. Overbeek (ed.) *The Political Economy of European Employment: European Integration and the Transnationalisation of the (Un)employment question*. London: Routledge.

Trubek, D.M. and Mosher, J.S. (2003) 'New governance, employment policy, and the European social model', in J. Zeitlin and D.M. Trubek (eds) *Governing Work and Welfare in a New Economy: European and American Experiments*. Oxford: Oxford University Press.

Vaughan-Whitehead, D. (2003) *EU Enlargement Versus Social Europe? The Uncertain Future of the European Social Model*. New York: Edward Elgar.

Velluti, S. (2010) *New Governance and the European Employment Strategy*. London: Routledge.

Velluti, S. (2012) 'Employment and the Lisbon Strategy', in P. Copeland and D. Papadimitriou (eds) *Evaluating the EU's Lisbon Strategy*. Basingstoke: Palgrave Macmillan.

Wallace, H., Pollack, M. and Young, A. (eds) (2010) *Policy-Making in the European Union*. Oxford: Oxford University Press.

Wendon, B. (1998) 'The Commission and European social policy', in R. Sykes and P. Alcock (eds) *Developments in European Social Policy: Convergence and Diversity*. Bristol: The Policy Press.

Wincott, D. (2003) 'The idea of the European Social Model: limits and paradoxes of Europeanization', in K. Featherstone and C. Radaelli (eds) *The Politics of Europeanization*. Oxford: Oxford University Press.

Young, A. (2010) 'The Single Market: deregulation, reregulation, and integration', in H. Wallace, M. Pollack and A. Young (eds) *Policy-Making in the European Union*. Oxford: Oxford University Press.

13

Global Social Policy: Globalized Health Policy

Sandra Shaw

Overview

- Globalization is a process that has been occurring over a long period of time, but which has intensified in the 20th century, and is associated with the development of a global capitalist economy.
- Globalization is seen as having positive and negative consequences, with a potential for creating and deepening inequalities.
- Global social policy opens up new opportunities for developing social policies that transcend national boundaries and new areas of study for social policy students.
- Global governance refers to the way that influence on policy making can be diverse, including a range of 'actors' such as non-governmental organizations (NGOs), inter-national governmental organizations (IGOs), governments, multinational corporations (MNCs), voluntary sector organizations and pressure groups.
- Health policy provides a good example of the complexity of global social policy that highlights a range of global issues and the evolving responses to them.

Introduction

Studying social policy today entails looking outside of the national state, and developing an awareness of what is happening in this broader global context, and how this impacts on social policy. Yeates argues that global social policy:

has broadened and invigorated the study of social policy itself and has undergone substantial developments itself, bringing in a new range of concerns and a new set of theoretical, conceptual and methodological approaches to understanding social policy and welfare provision. (2008a: 14–15)

This chapter starts by providing a brief discussion of globalization, before moving on to consider global governance – the way that social policies are influenced at the global level. The chapter focuses on health policy as it provides an interesting illustration of how a range of different actors can exert influence on health policy at the global level, and the role of some of these organizations, including the World Health Organization (WHO), is outlined. A key aspect of global health policy has been prevention of the spread of infectious diseases. However, the chapter also recognizes that the global health agenda is complex, continuously evolving and extends across all areas of life which impact on the health and well-being of individuals, nations, regions and the world.

Globalization

The idea of globalization is very powerful, and Clarke (2000) suggests that it forms a discourse – a dominant set of knowledge and ideas – about how globalization has developed. It is associated with liberal market ideas about the global economy and the development of a capitalist economic system (George and Wilding, 2002), and can come to be seen as the only way that the world can be organized (Clarke, 2000). Globalization is seen as a process that has taken place over centuries, with a number of authors identifying different periods of globalization (see, for example, George and Wilding, 2002; Held and McGrew, 2007). The process of globalization intensified during the 20th and 21st centuries and this intensification and the speeding up of the process of globalization have taken place across a number of areas (George and Wilding, 2002; Yeates, 2008a). One of the key debates around globalization has been whether or not it has, or will, erode the power of the nation state. Mishra (1999) argued that the role of the nation state would decline, with a consequent undermining of the welfare state. Pierson (2000), while recognizing the pressures on the welfare state, thought that it would continue in most countries. Today, nation-states and national governments still have a significant role to play in global governance, and in providing funding to transnational organizations (McCoy et al., 2011; Schrecker, 2012).

The development of new technologies, such as computers and telephones, is one of the driving forces behind globalization (George and Wilding, 2002). These technologies create a global network, resulting in a sense of 'interconnectedness' as we can see what is happening in other parts of the world and communicate with others around the globe (Cockerham and Cockerham, 2010). Knowledge and information can be accessed and shared, and cultural values and ideas exchanged or turned into commodities that can be bought and sold around the world in areas such as film, music, fashion and the food industry. This creates the perception of a universalization of culture and identity (de Benoist, 1996, cited in George and Wilding, 2002). At the same time, the local and the particular have also become important in terms of identity and culture – the 'global experience' will be mediated by the national and the local (McGrew, 1992). It also means that we are more aware of a range of social, economic and environmental problems, such as poverty and inequality, armed conflict, global warming and natural disasters. Globalization has opened up opportunities for the development of new international social networks, for example around the environment (see Chapter 14). The development of new modes of transport over the last 200 years (e.g. air travel) has meant that it is easier for people to move around the world – in greater numbers, more quickly and at a lower cost than in the past, bringing both benefits and pressures, for example, international migration, for national governments (George and Wilding, 2002). At the same time, our increasing awareness of the global context and the impact of international migration opens up questions of 'cosmopolitan citizenship, social equity and justice on a global scale' (Yeates, 2008b: 246), including the importance of global human rights (George and Wilding, 2009; Dwyer, 2010).

Perhaps the most significant negative effect of globalization is the abject poverty experienced by many in poorer areas of the world and the risk of creating new inequalities, or worsening existing inequalities (Clarke, 2000). Yeates (2008c) examines 'wealth', 'income' and 'poverty' in the world context, providing an overview of income distribution across the world. Different measures result in different findings, but it is clear that wealth is concentrated in the top 10 per cent, and there is a huge gap between the richest and the poorest in the world (Yeates, 2008c). In addition, global inequality has increased (Milanovic, 2005, cited in Béland, 2010). While wealth is distributed unequally around the world, it is also distributed unequally within countries and regions. Some of the poorest people in the world live in what are seen as rich countries, while conversely some of the richest people in the world live in 'poor' countries (Yeates, 2008c), and globalization can have a differential impact within countries, worsening existing inequalities (Alston, 2007). Poverty impacts on all aspects of a person's life, including their health status and length of life, with children and women particularly vulnerable. Wealth is linked to power and in extreme cases those with power such as dictators and the military have the ability to control access to national resources, and to wealth, meaning that even where a country has the means of generating income for all, the distribution of this income is tightly controlled (Bertram, 2008). This illustrates that while the global context is important, so too is the particular historical, cultural and political context within countries.

Recognizing the adverse effects of globalization and the development of the global capitalist economy has figured prominently in analyses of the process of globalization (George and Wilding, 2002; Held and McGrew, 2007). Other factors are also significant, including war and conflict, as well as natural phenomena such as drought and earthquakes. However, it is the way that these events, whether human or natural, are shaped and mediated that will determine who will be most adversely affected.

Global governance

As globalization has progressed, transnational organizations have developed, which can be comprised of representatives of national governments, but stand outside of the traditional process of policy making within countries, though policy making may reflect the interests of dominant powers (Held and McGrew, 2007). Examples of these include the European Union (EU) (see the discussion in Chapter 12), the United Nations (UN) and the World Health Organization (WHO) (see Deacon, 2008). The making of social policies is increasingly complex. Yeates (2008a: 16) refers to an 'extended welfare mix' within countries where social welfare can be provided by the state, the market, the voluntary sector, the community and households, with each of these areas reflected at the global level.

Governance promotes cooperation by 'providing structure and regulation', which is 'more informal and diffuse and includes actors other than national governments' (Cockerham and Cockerham, 2010: 18) whereas government is more formal, legalistic and hierarchical. Where cooperative arrangements are established, there is not the same degree of regulation and enforcement as with a national government, and there is no world government, meaning that global governance is diffuse and complex (Deacon, 2008; Hill, 2011). Held and McGrew (2007: 151) refer to global governance as a '*multilayered*, *multisectoral* and *multiactor* system in which institutions and politics matter a great deal to the determination of global policy outcomes, that is, to who gets what, when and why'.

Examples of inter-governmental organizations (IGOs) include the United Nations (UN), the World Trade Organization (WTO), the World Bank (WB), the International Monetary Fund (IMF) and the World Health Organization (WHO). They are part of global governance and provide 'rules and mechanisms that states have to follow in resolving international policy disputes' (Cockerham and Cockerham, 2010: 19). 'Global advocacy coalitions', 'transnational knowledge networks' and 'global public–private partnerships' (Deacon, 2008: 27) can also be added to the list of those involved in policy making at the global level. Non-governmental organizations (NGOs) include voluntary organizations focusing on particular issues, and having a similar role to pressure groups within nations. The Red Cross, Greenpeace, Amnesty International and Oxfam are examples of well-known and influential NGOs. Philanthropic organizations such as the Bill and Melinda Gates Foundation can be important in the context of global welfare provision and international development (Farnsworth, 2008). Multinational Companies (MNCs) promote business at the international level, with the aim of making profits. Foreign capital can provide a source of income for nations, and so economic and social policies may be shaped to favour MNCs. There are also what can be referred to as 'epistemic communities', which includes groups of experts, research institutions, private industry and academia. These may be seen as less politically biased, and can exert influence on policy making, for example in the area of health care, due to their expertise (Koivusalo and Ollila, 2008). The power of nation-states is still important, both in terms of funding and influencing the global policy agenda, though some states have more power than others. The G8 member states (France, the USA, the UK, Germany, Italy, Japan, Canada and Russia) have a prominent role across a broad range of policy areas relating to energy and the environment, food and nutrition and global health issues (G8, 2012).

Global health policy

The concepts of welfare, health and well-being have always been a central concern for the subject of social policy and for those who make policies (see Chapters 1 and 6). Chen et al. (1996: 9, cited in Frenk et al., 2011) suggest that we are in a time of global 'health interdependence', mirroring the interdependence of the global economy. This reflects the permeability of national borders, and the capacity for people to move around the world, opening up the potential for the spread of disease and infection, and the way that the exploitation of the natural world in one country or region can have a wider environmental impact. At the same time, this global interdependence opens up opportunities for sharing information, knowledge and good practice (Frenk et al., 2011). The World Health Organization (WHO) defines health as 'a state of complete, physical, mental, and social well-being, and not merely the absence of disease or injury' (Cockerham and Cockerham, 2010). The remit of global health policy has expanded considerably, and global health governance has become increasingly complex, and continues to evolve, as new challenges emerge. Some of the main organizations involved are outlined below.

The World Health Organization (WHO)

The World Health Organization was created in 1948. The primary decision-making body is the World Health Assembly (WHA), which has three delegates from each member state; all are experts on health and each state has one vote. The WHA has the authority to adopt regulations binding on all members states, unless a particular state objects within a designated period of time (Cockerham and Cockerham, 2010: 123). The WHO also has an executive board of 32 representatives which enacts the WHA's decisions and policies. International Health Regulations (IHR) provide international legal rules on the spread of infectious diseases (Koivusalo and Ollila, 2008), the objective being to facilitate cooperation between states to control the spread of infectious diseases. In its early years, the WHO was closely aligned with the interests of the USA and its allies and an early priority was the elimination of malaria. The Soviet Union opted out between 1949 and 1956, returning later when the agenda shifted from the elimination of malaria to the elimination of smallpox, which was then also backed by the USA and proved to be a successful campaign (Brown and Cueto, 2011).

At the Alma Ata conference in Kazahkstan in 1981, a proposal for a primary health care strategy was endorsed by the WHA (see Yeates and Holden, 2009), with the aim of achieving the objective of 'Health for All by the year 2000' (Brown and Cueto, 2011: 21). Health was and continues to be seen as a *fundamental* human right (Koivusalo and Ollila, 2008), reflecting the way the issue of human rights has become central to debates around global policy (Dwyer, 2010). The Alma Ata conference stimulated debate and discussion on health care, and the concept of 'health for all' is still important, as is the emphasis on primary health care, though the ideal of an equitable distribution of health, and health care provision still remains unrealized.

While Brown and Cueto (2011) note that the WHO struggled from the 1980s to the late 1990s due to competition from other IGOs, further developments led to an enhancement of the WHO's role internationally. For example, the Framework Convention on Tobacco Control in 2003 is a treaty containing a comprehensive ban on the advertising of tobacco products, on content and packaging, and labelling (WHO, 2012a), and non-communicable disease including smoking-related disease and obesity are priorities for the WHO in terms of global health. The IHR were revised in the 1990s with a new set of rules approved in 2005, and put into effect in 2007. This expanded the scope of diseases covered by regulations. The 2005 IHR defines disease as 'an illness or medical condition, irrespective of origin or source, which presents or could present significant harm to humans' (IHR, 2005, cited in Cockerham and Cockerham, 2010: 126). States should notify the WHO of all events constituting a public health emergency of international concern. The WHO continues to play a key leadership role despite the participation of other organizations, and, despite inadequacies in terms of funding, still has power 'on account of its moral and expert authority' (Cockerham and Cockerham, 2010: 127). Members of the WHA are health experts, and the secretariat also includes medical doctors, health specialists and epidemiologists. However, as global health governance has developed and become increasingly pluralistic (Kickbush and Berger, 2011), the WHO has had to develop and respond, becoming more of a coordinating organization focusing on global partnerships and funding and on specific targets, while also seeking to retain an authoritative role (Brown and Cueto, 2011). Alongside increasingly complex global governance, the funding of global health is also complicated (McCoy et al., 2009).

The World Bank (WB) and the IMF

The WB and the IMF have become important actors in global health governance (Koivusalo and Ollila, 2008; Cockerham and Cockerham, 2010; Brown and Cueto, 2011; WB, 2012). Both were established around the same time as the UN and the WHO. The WB has been criticized for having a negative impact on social policy, and it is suggested that it serves the interests of the Global North (Deacon, 2008). However, over time its social policies have become more progressive. The WB has funding resources – from private capital markets and from Member States (Brown and Cueto, 2011). It provides interest-bearing loans to states to assist with development projects, for example in education and health care, that would not be supported by private banks. In the 1950s and 1960s, the WB was mainly interested in funding large infrastructure projects in poor countries, such as dams and bridges to promote economic development and quality of life. The focus changed in the 1970s to a basic needs approach, with an emphasis on family planning, education and health (Cockerham and Cockerham, 2010). The World Bank Development Report 1993 was devoted to health (Brown and Cueto, 2011), and there has been a continuing emphasis on research and development, with the Policy Research Department spending $1 million annually on health, nutrition and population studies (Cockerham and Cockerham, 2010). The WB has also adopted more collaborative relationships with the WHO. While a recent participant in the arena of global health policy, it makes a significant contribution and is the largest external funder of health care (Ruger, 2005, cited in Cockerham and Cockerham, 2010).

The IMF does not play as prominent a role as the WB but is still relevant. While the IMF is directed at finance, with its original function to lend money to states to meet fluctuations in currency exchange rates, its purpose has changed. The IMF receives funds from Member States, and like the WB can attach conditions to loans. IMF programmes can have important indirect (sometimes negative) effects on health, and need to be more flexible to allow for greater public spending as circumstances change (Deacon, 2008; Koivusalo and Ollila, 2008; Cockerham and Cockerham, 2010). Other organizations which have a role to play include the World Trade Organization (WTO) and the Organization for Economic Cooperation and Development (OECD), which collect comparative data on the health systems of Member States. The United Nations (UN) also has a key role in terms of broader issues related to health and well-being and the UN Millennium Development Goals are referred to later in the chapter.

Multinational Companies (MNCs)

MNCS are profit-making organizations and are seen as having the potential to create harm including 'physical harm', 'financial/economic harm' and 'emotional and psychological harm' (Farnsworth, 2008: 81) – for example, environmental damage, poor wages or the negative effects of poor working environments. There has been pressure for the development of an agenda around 'corporate social responsibility' (CSR) and many corporations have 'corporate codes of conduct' (Farnsworth, 2008: 85). The UN's Global Compact is self-regulatory and voluntary, and the OECD has drawn up guidelines for MNCs. A cynical analysis of CSR is that it can create a positive image for consumers and open up new 'ethical' markets, which is to their advantage in a global economy (Sklair and Miller, 2010). At times, there can be a convergence of interest between business and the development of social policies, with the latter linked to the development of economic policies – for example, in the European Union the development of a social policy agenda has been linked to economic imperatives.

MNCs also include pharmaceutical companies (McCoy et al., 2009), which undertake research, produce drugs, own the intellectual property rights to these and are competing in a global health economy. These MNCs influence a number of areas, including where research is focused, which drugs are developed, the pricing of drugs and international legislation on the intellectual rights to drugs that are developed. The WHO has a role in ensuring that medicines are developed to meet global public health needs and to 'improve equitable access to medicines' for those in the developing world (Pang, 2011: 295). The GAVI Alliance (2012) is working to ensure that all children receive equitable access to vaccines. The price of drugs developed by pharmaceutical companies can be prohibitively high for poorer countries. Generic (un-branded) drugs are cheaper but cannot be developed until intellectual property rights have ended (Cockerham and Cockerham, 2010). An example of an alternative approach to the research and development of drugs is OneWorldHealth 2000, which is the first non-profit pharmaceutical company founded in the USA. It is significant in terms of its research and development potential, with a commitment to discover, develop and deliver safe, effective and affordable treatment for diseases in the developing world (OneWorldHealth, 2012).

Non-Governmental Organizations (NGOs)

The Bill and Melinda Gates Foundation was established in 1994 and is an example of a philanthropic organization with programmes relating to global development and global advocacy, with a focus on health problems that get too little attention and funding (Bill and Melinda Gates Foundation, 2012). The Foundation invests in research and development, provides grants and supports work across a range of areas, including the prevention of ethnic and diarrhoeal disease, HIV/AIDs, malaria, tuberculosis and other infectious diseases. It is notable for the amount of funding it provides that 'takes private, philanthropic funding to new and unprecedented heights' (McCoy et al., 2009: 410). Its wider global development programmes look at issues related to poverty and development. The Foundation is increasingly significant in terms of its influence and access to significant amounts of funding for health and development programmes.

Other philanthropic organizations have a longer history. The Red Cross was established in 1863 in Geneva. At the national level, it can substitute for government in poor states, providing health services, for example in sub-Saharan Africa. In Tanzania, hospitals that are administered by NGOs account for 43 per cent of all medical services (Cockerham and Cockerham, 2010: 145). Where there is political conflict within countries or regions, organizations like the Red Cross and Medecin Sans Frontiers also play an important role in providing aid to those affected.

The global health agenda: infectious diseases

The control of communicable infectious diseases has been a central aspect of the WHO agenda for some time. Infectious diseases can be spread around the world much more quickly today. Collaborative, international action is taken to try and ensure that disease is identified and contained as early as possible and that effective vaccines are developed and circulated rapidly (Cockerham and Cockerham, 2010). In 1918 Spanish Flu took 40 million lives worldwide and 1 million died in 1968 from Hong Kong Flu. At the end of the 20th century, new diseases emerged. These included HIV/AIDs (see below) and SARS (severe acute respiratory syndrome), bovine spongiform encephalopathy (mad cow disease), the Ebola virus and different variants of the influenza virus. As well as concern about the spread of disease, there has also been a rise in concerns about the possibility of bio-terrorism, and health policy also becomes security policy (UN, 2004; Koivusalo and Ollila, 2008; Cockerham and Cockerham, 2010). Health risks are not only a global problem, they also affect individual countries due to the trans-border risks associated with globalization, including the transmission of disease, population migration, people and drug trafficking (Collin and Lee, 2003).

HIV/AIDS

HIV/AIDs first emerged in Africa, spreading around the world at the end of the 20th century, and a cure has yet to be found. The acquired immune deficiency syndrome known as AIDS destroys an individual's immunity against infection, leaving them vulnerable to a range of illnesses and viruses. AIDS is a virus – the human immunodeficiency virus (HIV). This is transmitted via sexual intercourse, intravenous drug use and blood transfusion, or passed to newborns by infected mothers, and health intervention programmes focus on these areas (Sharma and Atri, 2010). The virus can remain in the body for a long time without triggering the disease; AIDs carriers can therefore infect others unknowingly. The first international conference on AIDs held in Atlanta in 1985 was co-sponsored by the WHO, which continues to play a significant role in tackling the disease (Brown and Cueto, 2011). There are differences in patterns of transmission, and who is most likely to be affected by this. The major route of transmission in Africa and Asia is heterosexual activity, whereas in Europe, HIV/AIDS is most frequent in major cities among homosexual and bisexual men, and IV drug users (Cockerham and Cockerham, 2010). In 2011, there were around 34.2 million people living with HIV, which has claimed more than 24 million lives over the past three decades, and over 60 per cent of people living with AIDs are in sub-Saharan Africa (WHO, 2012b). The cost of infection is potentially catastrophic not only in terms of the welfare of infected individuals and their families, but also in terms of the economy and development potential of Sub-Saharan Africa (George and Wilding, 2002), where population growth and life expectancy are falling (Cockerham and Cockerham, 2010: 54). AIDS now affects more women in Africa than men, which is related to tradition and culture and women's lack of power within sexual relationships, with infidelity and the non-use of condoms putting them at risk (Bandali, 2011). Poverty and disadvantage mean women are highly dependent on their partners, or may be pushed into prostitution due to a lack of employment opportunities. It is important to challenge traditional norms and values, while also providing women with opportunities to become financially independent (Bandali, 2011). Health is a gendered issue and the vulnerability of women is recognized across a range of areas (Glass et al., 2011).

The Global Fund was established in 2002 and provides grants to fight AIDs, tuberculosis and malaria. It is a public–private partnership, receiving funding from governments, the private sector, social enterprises, foundations and individuals (The Global Fund, 2012), providing an example of the plurality of organizations involved in tackling disease. To date, 78 per cent of its funds have been supplied by the G8 (G8, 2012). The WHO is a co-sponsor of the Joint United Nations Programme on AIDs (UNAIDS) and in 2011, the WHO member states adopted a new Global Health Sector Strategy on HIV/AIDS for 2011–2015.

While dealing with the spread of infectious disease is important, illness that is related to lifestyle choices is also significant. Tobacco-related death and disease (Collin and Lee, 2003) cause serious illness, and obesity carries health risks (Shaw, 2010). Tackling both these areas is a global priority, and they are referred to as non-communicable diseases or 'pandemics', indicating how serious they are in terms of the health of the world's population. However, these areas present a significant challenge for global health governance due to the considerable influence of the tobacco and food industries.

A broader agenda

It is not possible to consider health in isolation from other factors that will impact upon an individual's health opportunities and outcomes, including the socio-economic determinants of health (Beaglehole and Bonita, 2008). There is a link between poverty and health, with those in poorer countries or regions experiencing poorer health (this also applies within countries). The majority of risk factors in developing countries are poverty-related, such as lack of access to safe water and being underweight, whereas in developed countries they are lifestyle-related, for example obesity and tobacco use (Pang, 2011). The Millennium Development Goals (MDGs) were set out in 2002, involving a range of partner organizations such as the WHO and the WB. The eight goals for 2015 include: eradicating poverty and hunger; achieving universal primary education; promoting gender equality; reducing child mortality; improving maternal health; combating HIV/AIDs, malaria and other diseases; ensuring environmental sustainability; and developing a global partnership for development (United Nations Development Programme [UNDP], 2012a). Health is both an explicit and implicit priority within these goals. They reflect a commitment to 'measurable development accomplishments' (Schrecker, 2012: 566). There has been progress towards meeting them, though fully achieving all of these by 2015 will be a challenge, and regional reports show that progress varies (UNDP, 2012b). The Health Eight (H8) is an informal group of health-related organizations including representatives from the WHO, GAVI, The Global Fund, UNAIDs, the UN Population Fund (UNFPA), UNICEF, the WB, and the Bill and Melinda Gates Foundation, aiming to stimulate urgency over achieving the MDG goals (see UNAIDS, 2011). Extreme poverty of less than US$1 a day has decreased in developing countries, but 'much of this reduction can be attributed to the rising income of China alone' (Cockerham and Cockerham, 2010: 36) and in sub-Saharan Africa extreme poverty has increased substantially. Pang (2011) notes that 1 billion people still live on less than one US dollar a day.

The health and well-being of children and young people is also a global priority (Shaw, 2010). UNICEF is an organization that provides information and support for children and young people across a range of areas, for example, protecting children who work from exploitation and from 'hazardous' work, and protecting children in areas where there is armed conflict, as well as focusing on their human rights (UNICEF, 2008). The WHO has global strategies relating to child health problems, including: child and adolescent mental health, and diet, physical activity and obesity, with the latter seen as 'one of the most serious public health challenges of the 21st century' (WHO, 2012c, d, e).

Dealing with environmental hazards is crucial, as shown by the list below:

- Each year, at least three million children under the age of 5 die due to environment-related disease.
- Acute respiratory infections annually kill an estimated two million children under the age of 5. As much as 60 per cent of acute respiratory infections worldwide are related to environmental conditions.
- Diarrhoeal diseases claim the lives of nearly two million children every year; 80–90 per cent of these diarrhoea cases are related to environmental conditions, in, particularly, contaminated water and inadequate sanitation.
- Nearly one million children under the age of 5 died of malaria in 1998. Upto 90 per cent of malaria cases are attributed to environmental factors. (WHO, 2012f)

Global environmental changes will impact on this (Beaglehole and Bonita, 2008) with the poorest children in the world the most seriously affected (Hanna et al., 2011). Global warming has health implications (Schrecker, 2012), allowing new viruses and temperature-related illnesses to develop, as well as food and water shortages due to environmental change. Extreme weather events such as floods, hurricanes and droughts have been associated with global warming and lead to a loss of sanitary facilities and clean water, creating conditions that are favourable for the spread of infectious disease such as malaria (Hanna et al., 2011). Better management of international health disasters, such as tsunamis and earthquakes, could help prevent loss of life, and some of the health problems that follow on from such disasters. The content of this final part of the chapter indicates how the global health agenda has expanded, and as new challenges and crises confront the world, it will continue to do so.

Summary/Conclusions

- Globalization impacts on a wide range of areas, including health and social welfare, the economy, culture and the environment.
- The idea of a global social policy is important in terms of ameliorating some of the disadvantage that exists in the world, and is linked to concepts such as human rights, citizenship and social justice.
- Globalized health policy provides an important example of how social policies can be enacted at the international level, and illustrates how global governance is enacted by a range of different organizations, agencies and governments.
- The primary focus of global health policy has been around disease management and control, with the notion of 'health for all' and equal human rights important ideologically, but still to be achieved. However, the global health agenda has broadened and is constantly evolving.

Questions

1 What are the consequences of globalization?
2 What is meant by 'governance', and who is involved in global health governance?
3 What are key areas of concern for the WHO and other global health policy organizations?
4 What are the connections between poverty, inequality and health?

Recommended reading

Cockerham, G.B. and Cockerham, W. (2010) *Health and Globalization*. Cambridge: Polity.

Parker, R. and Sommer, M. (eds) (2011) *Routledge Handbook in Global Public Health*. Abingdon: Routledge.

Yeates, N. (2008) *Understanding Global Social Policy*. Bristol: The Policy Press.

Yeates, N. and Holden, C. (eds) (2009) *The Global Social Policy Reader*. Bristol: The Policy Press.

Relevant websites

A number of sites are recommended here, and often provide links to other useful websites.

The Bill and Melinda Gates Foundation (2012) at www.gatesfoundation.org./ provides comprehensive information on projects relating to international development and health.

The UNDP (2012) Human Development Reports is an interactive site, located at http://hdr.undp.org/en/ where information on development, poverty and health issues at country and regional levels can be accessed. The Global Policy Forum at www.globalpolicy.org/home.html is an informative and educational site providing information across a range of areas.

The World Health Organization (WHO) has a central role to play in regard to the global health agenda, and information can be accessed at www.who.int/en/. The United Nations deals with a broader range of issues relating to poverty, inequality and health and can be located at www.un.org/en/.

References

Alston, M. (2007) 'Globalisation, rural restructuring and health service delivery in Australia: policy failure and the role of social work?', *Health and Social Care in the Community*, 15(3): 195–202.

Bandali, S. (2011) 'Norms and practices within marriage which shape gender roles, HIV/AIDs risk and risk reduction strategies in Cabo Delgado, Mozambique', *AIDS Care*, 23 September: 1171–1176.

Beaglehole, R. and Bonita, R. (2008) 'Global public health: a scorecard in *The Lancet*', 372, 6 December. Available at: www.thelancet.com (accessed 19 September 2012).

Béland, D. (2010) *What is Social Policy? Understanding the Welfare State*. Cambridge: Polity.

Bertram, C. (2008) 'Globalisation, social justice and the politics of aid', in C. Graig, T. Burchardt and D. Gordon (eds) *Social Justice and Public Policy*. Bristol: The Policy Press.

Bill and Melinda Gates Foundation (2012) *Topics Overview*. Available at: www.gatesfoundation.org/topics/Pages/topics-overview.aspx (accessed 19 September, 2012).

Brown, T.M. and Cueto, M. (2011) 'The World Health Organization and the world of global health', in R. Parker and M. Sommer (eds) *Routledge Handbook in Global Public Health*. Abingdon: Routledge.

Clarke, J. (2000) 'A world of difference? Globalization and the study of social policy', in G. Lewis, S. Gewirtz and J. Clarke (eds) *Rethinking Social Policy*. London: Sage.

Cockerham, G.B. and Cockerham, W. (2010) *Health and Globalization*. Cambridge: Polity Press.

Collin, J. and Lee, K. (2003) *Globalisation and Transborder Health Risk in the UK: Case Studies in Tobacco Control and Population Mobility*. London: The Nuffield Trust.

Deacon, (2008) 'Global and regional social governance', in N. Yeates (ed.) *Understanding Global Social Policy*. Bristol: The Policy Press.

Dwyer, P. (2010) *Understanding Social Citizenship: Themes and Perspectives for Policy and Practice*. Bristol: The Policy Press.

Farnsworth, K. (2008) 'Business and social policy formation', in N. Yeates (ed.) *Understanding Global Social Policy*. Bristol: The Policy Press.

Frenk, J., Gomez-Dantes, O. and Chacon, F. (2011) 'Global health in transition', in R. Parker and M. Sommer (eds) *Routledge Handbook in Global Public Health*. Abingdon: Routledge.

G8 (2012) *Summit*. Camp David Accountability Report. Available at: www.who.int/workforcealliance/media/news/2012/CampDavidG8AccountabilityReport_2012.pdf (accessed 19 September 2012).

GAVI Alliance (2012) *GAVI's Mission: Saving Children's Lives and Protecting People's Health by Increasing Access to Immunisation in Poor Countries*. Available at: www.gavialliance.org/about/mission/ (accessed 19 September 2012).

George, V. and Wilding, P. (2002) *Globalization and Human Welfare*. Basingstoke: Palgrave.

George, V. and Wilding, P. (2009) 'Globalization and human welfare: why is there a need for a global social policy?', in N. Yeates and C. Holden (eds) *The Global Social Policy Reader*. Bristol: Policy Press.

Glass, N., Campbell, J., Njie-Carr, V. and Thompson, T. (2011) 'Ending violence against women: essential to global health and human rights', in R. Parker and M. Sommer (eds) *Routledge Handbook in Global Public Health*. Abingdon: Routledge.

Hanna, E., McMichael, A.J. and Butler, C.D. (2011) 'Climate change and global public health: impacts, research and actions', in R. Parker and M. Sommer (eds) *Routledge Handbook in Global Public Health*. Abingdon: Routledge.

Held, D. and McGrew, A. (2007) *Globalization/Anti-Globalization: Beyond The Great Divide*. Cambridge: Polity.

Hill, P.S. (2011) 'Understanding global health governance as a complex adaptive system', *Global Public Health* 6(6), Sept.: 593–605.

Kickbush, I. and Berger, C. (2011) 'Global health diplomacy', in R. Parker and M. Sommer (eds) *Routledge Handbook in Global Public Health*. Abingdon: Routledge.

Koivusalo, M. and Ollila, E. (2008) 'Global health policy', in N. Yeates (ed.) *Understanding Global Social Policy*. Bristol: The Policy Press.

McCoy, D., Chand, S. and Sridhar, D. (2009) 'Global health funding: how much, where it comes from and where it goes', *Health Policy and Planning*, 24(6): 407–417.

McGrew, A. (1992) 'A global society?', in S. Hall, D. Held and T. McGrew (eds) *Modernity and its Futures*. Cambridge: Polity Press in association with The Open University.

Mishra, R. (1999) *Globalization and the Welfare State*. Edward Elgar: Cheltenham.

OneWorldHealth (2012) www.oneworldhealth.org/aboutus (accessed 29 August 2012).

Pang, T. (2011) 'Developing medicines in line with global public health needs: the role of the World Health Organization', *Cambridge Quarterly of Healthcare Ethics*, 20: 290–297.

Pierson, P. (2000) *The New Politics of the Welfare State*. Oxford: Oxford University Press.

Schrecker, T. (2012) 'Multiple crises and global health: new and necessary frontiers of health politics', *Global Public Health*, 7(6): 557–573.

Sharma, M. and Atri, A. (2010) *Essentials of International Health*. London: Jones and Bartlett.

Shaw, S. (2010) *Parents, Children, Young People and the State*. Maidenhead: Open University Press/McGraw Hill Education.

Sklair, L. and Miller, D. (2010) 'Capitalist globalization, corporate social responsibility and social policy', *Critical Social Policy*, 30(4): 472–495.

The Global Fund to Fight AIDS, Tuberculosis and Malaria (2012) *10 Years of Impact*. Available at: www.theglobalfund.org/en/ (accessed 29 August 2012).

UNAIDS (2011) *Health 8 Group Meet to Discuss Maximizing Health Outcomes with Available Resources and Getting 'More Health for the Money'*, 23 February. Available at: www.unaids.org/en/resources/presscentre/featurestories/2011/february/20110223bh8 (accessed 19 September 2012).

UNICEF (2008) *Progress for Children: A World Fit for Children*. Statistical Review No. 6, December 2007. Available at: www.childinfo.org/files/worldfit_progress_for_children.pdf (accessed 19 September 2012).

United Nations (UN) (2004) *A More Secure World: Our Shared Responsibility. Report of the Secretary-General's High-level Panel on Threats, Challenges and Change – Executive Summary*. Available at: www.un.org/secureworld/brochure.pdf (accessed 19 September 2012).

United Nations Development Programme (UNDP) (2012a) *Eight Goals for 2015*. Available at: www.undp.org/content/undp/en/home/mdgoverview/html (accessed 4 September 2012).

United Nations Development Programme (UNDP) (2012b) *MDG Progress Reports*. Available at: www.undp.org/content/undp/en/home/librarypage/mdg/mdg-reports/ (accessed 4 September 2012).

World Bank (WB) (2012) *Human Development and Public Services*. Available at: http://econ.worldbank.org/external/default/main?menuPK=477927&pagePK=64168176&piPK=64168140&theSitePK=477916

World Health Organization (WHO) (2012a) *About the WHO Framework Convention on Tobacco Control*. Available at: www.who.int/fctc/about/en/index.html (accessed 4 September 2012).

World Health Organization (WHO) (2012b) *HIV/AIDS Fact Sheet No. 360*, July. Available at: www.who.int/mediacentre/factshets/fs360/en/index.html (accessed 4 September 2012).

World Health Organization (WHO) (2012c) *Consultation on the 'Zero Draft' of the Global Mental Health Action Plan 2013–2020*. Available at: www.who.int/mental_health/en/ (accessed 19 September 2012).

World Health Organization (WHO) (2012d) *Child and Adolescent Mental Health*. Available at: www.who.int/mental_health/prevention/childado/en/ (accessed 19 September 2012).

World Health Organization (WHO) (2012e) *Childhood Overweight and Obesity*. Available at: www.who.int/dietphysicalactivity/childhood/en/ (accessed 19 September 2012).

World Health Organization (WHO) (2012f) *Global Plan of Action for Children's Health and the Environment*. Available at: www.who.int/ceh/en/ (accessed 19 September 2012).

Yeates, N. (2008a) 'The idea of global social policy', in N. Yeates (ed.) *Understanding Global Social Policy*. Bristol: The Policy Press.

Yeates, N. (2008b) 'Global migration policy', in N. Yeates (ed.) *Understanding Global Social Policy*. Bristol: The Policy Press.

Yeates, N. (2008c) 'Global inequality, poverty and wealth', in T. Ridge and S. Wright (eds) *Understanding Inequality, Poverty and Wealth*. Bristol: The Policy Press.

Yeates, N. and Holden, C. (eds) (2009) *The Global Social Policy Reader*. Bristol: The Policy Press.

14

Social Policy and the Environment

Anya Ahmed

Overview

- Climate change poses a number of environmental challenges to contemporary welfare states.
- Climate change and debates about sustainability of resources have shaped policy debates.
- There are relationships between the 'new' challenges posed by climate change and 'traditional' social policy concerns.
- Until relatively recently, environmental concerns have not been a concern of 'traditional' social policy.
- There are a number of key 'green' documents and policies which are relevant to social policy.
- There is significant debate on whether social justice and environmental justice are ultimately incompatible.

Introduction

The overarching aim of this chapter is to consider whether social policy and environmental policy have compatible or conflicting objectives. The chapter is divided into four parts. The first part includes a discussion of the key environmental challenges confronting contemporary welfare states and examines how climate change and concerns about the 'sustainability' of resources and pollution have shaped policy debates. Part two explores the relationship between the 'new' challenges posed by climate change and 'traditional' social policy concerns, and examines how and why environmental issues have previously not been a primary concern for social policy. In part three, an overview of some of the relevant landmark 'green' documents and policies relevant to social policy is provided, along with an assessment of their implications for political priorities and welfare debates. Part three also considers the role of environmental social movements, highlighting that the pressure for policy change can be 'bottom-up' as well as 'top-down'. Finally, in part four, the question of whether social justice and environmental justice are ultimately at odds is considered. This discussion is placed within the context of rethinking the current neoliberal market model of welfare and considering how a new 'green social policy agenda' can be incorporated.

New challenges for social policy: climate change in context

Concerns with the environment began in the 1980s when the hole in the ozone layer and global warming were highlighted. However, it was not until the 1990s that the focus shifted to climate change (Cahill, 2012). Climate change is a contested term and refers to the main contemporary global environmental challenge (Dominelli, 2012) and is caused by a build-up of carbon dioxide (CO_2) and other polluting gases in the earth's atmosphere. These gases remain in the atmosphere for many years and trap heat by effectively forming a 'greenhouse' around the earth. 'Greenhouse gases' (GHG) are released into the atmosphere through the burning of fossil fuels – coal, oil and gas – and also by deforestation (IPCC, 2007; Dominelli, 2012).

Most climate change models predict a rise in global temperatures of between 2 and 5°C by 2060 which represents the difference between the temperature now and at the time of the last ice age (Gough, 2008). The earth is warming faster than it has for centuries with 11 of the 12 years from 1995 to 2006 being the warmest on record since 1850, and it is estimated that human activity is responsible for 95 per cent of GHG emissions (IPPC, 2007). As little as a 2°C increase in temperature is regarded as dangerous and an increase of above 4°C is likely to seriously affect global food production (Fitzpatrick, 2011a). Environmental pressure groups like Friends of the Earth argue that the impetus to reduce GHG emissions and, therefore, reduce climate change is strong. Climate change encompasses more than global warming and increased temperature: it also describes drought and increased rainfall and extremes in weather (Hodgson and Phillips, 2011). However, although climate change is perceived as the biggest potential threat to global stability, there are others (IPPC, 2007). The depletion of natural resources, for example fossil fuels, water, wood and minerals, also poses a threat since some of these resources are irreplaceable. The level of pollution caused by landfill and dumping waste into the world's oceans creates further problems. Drought and flooding can also lead to water stress, which includes both water shortages and unsustainable increases in demand (IPCC, 2007).

Anthropogenic climate change can be understood as global warming caused by human behaviour. In other words, the earth is becoming hotter – and there are associated changes in weather – through what we as a species are doing. Industry, power stations, waste disposal, home and domestic use, fossil fuel excavation, agriculture and transport all increase GHG and contribute to raising the earth's temperature (Hodgson and Phillips, 2011). Possible future effects of anthropogenic climate change include: the ice caps melting, leading to increased sea levels and temperature; floods; droughts; heat waves; extreme and unpredictable weather; and ocean acidity causing damage to marine species and the outright extinction of some species (Hodgson and Phillips, 2011). The potential ecological damage posed by the extinction of animal and plant species is as yet unknown. It is likely that disease and drought will mainly affect the poorest in developing countries in terms of their health and environmental damage (Dominelli, 2012; Fitzpatrick, 2011a). For example, current projections predict that in Africa, by 2020, between 75 and 250 million people will be exposed to increased water stress due to climate change (IPCC, 2007).

However, it is not only poorer countries that are expected to experience the effects of climate change. There are also potential consequences for the industrialized world in terms of social well-being, 'social risks' and social policies (Dominelli, 2012). Gough (2008) frames these in terms of direct and indirect risks. Direct risks to Europe include rising sea levels in coastal regions and water shortages and forest fires in Mediterranean regions, which could also lead to crop failures. Indirect risks include possible rises in migration from developing countries most affected by climate change (Dominelli, 2012) and a damaged infrastructure which will also have impacts on tourism and the European economy (Hodgson and Phillips, 2011). Environmentalists and scientists also predict that there is a risk of extreme weather, which could mean hotter summers causing serious droughts combined with heavy rainfall in wetter winters leading to severe flooding (IPPC, 2007).

Since these increases in global warming are in the main caused by human activity rather than natural causes, many environmentalists and scientists now widely believe that there is some urgency for us to change our behaviour and consumption habits to halt the rise in the present and reduce it for the future (IPPC, 2007; Hodgson and Phillips, 2011). Redressing the imbalances caused by climate change is often framed within the remit of 'sustainability', or managing how we use the world's resources and reducing the level of polluting emissions. Environmental pressure groups like Friends of the Earth point out that historically rich industrialized countries are responsible for three quarters of emissions, despite representing only 15 per cent of the world's population. They also argue that these countries have a legal and moral duty to take the lead to address climate change and to support ecological growth in developing countries as well as to compensate them for harmful impacts (Friends of the Earth, 2012). There is a link, then, between sustainability, social justice and social policy, and Gough (2008) frames this in terms of: 'New concerns with social justice and social policy are raised by the pressures (moral and practical) to drastically curb carbon emissions' (pp. 325–326). These issues will be developed more fully later in the chapter.

There are two related approaches to managing environmental damage caused by climate change and these can be understood as mitigation and adaptation policies (Gough, 2008). Mitigation policies include reducing greenhouse gas emissions (GHG), through reducing energy use and increasing efficiency, whereas adaptation policies involve relocation from areas at risk of flooding, and adopting water conservation schemes and disease prevention initiatives. The implications of both adaptation and mitigation polices are huge: on the one hand, climate change adaptation policies will need careful planning and budgeting since there could be conflicting priorities, for example should sea defences be built or flood plains cleared? On the other hand, adopting climate change mitigation policies will mean the introduction of carbon budgets or targets (Annetts et al., 2009; Gough, 2008) which have social justice implications. This will be discussed in the last part of this chapter.

Environmental pressure groups like Friends of the Earth advocate switching to renewable forms of energy – that is, forms of energy that will not be depleted – since they are safe, in plentiful supply and will not cause climate change. Nuclear power is expensive (and has been highly subsidized at the expense of renewable energy options), dangerous and produces difficult-to-dispose-of toxic waste. Renewable or natural energy includes solar power, hydroelectric power and biomass fuels. The production of renewable – or sustainable – energy involves burning natural materials to create gas energy (Friends of the Earth, 2012). However, writing in *The Guardian* (3 July 2012), the environmentalist George Monbiot argues that new evidence has emerged which indicates that oil supplies are not yet depleted and that new technologies like biofuels and petrol made from coal are actually more damaging to the environment than drilling for oil. Along with James Lovelock, a renowned scientist, his position on wind and nuclear power differs from that of Friends of the Earth – they both argue that carbon emissions and the environmental risks from nuclear energy are low and that wind power is inefficient and unsightly.

Having outlined the key environmental challenges confronting contemporary welfare states, the discussion now shifts to explore the relationship between the 'new' challenges posed by climate change and 'traditional' social policy concerns, and why environmental issues have previously not been a primary concern for social policy.

Social policy and the environment: past and present concerns

Although the debate on social policy and the environment originated in the early 1990s, it is only recently that these issues have become part of the mainstream (see Gough et al., 2008). Historically, social policy has neglected the environment and environmental studies have not taken full account of social policy (Fitzpatrick, 1998). Social policy needs to be understood within the context of industrialized systems, and the implementation of social policies is premised on the existence of capitalism and continued economic growth. Economic growth itself is also based on certain assumptions, for example, continued carbon emissions from production, manufacturing and consumption (Fitzpatrick, 2011a). Traditionally therefore, although resource use and allocation have been integral to social policy agendas across the ideological spectrum (see Chapter 3), welfare policies have previously failed to consider environmental concerns. The current challenge for social policy and environment policy then, is to balance the imperative for continuous economic growth with environmental concerns (Hannigan, 2011).

In this very important sense, climate change has significant implications for traditional notions of welfare and social policy interventions. This significance is twofold: first, in terms of academic research; and second, in terms of welfare interventions and welfare states. Gough (2008) emphasizes the strong links between climate change and the traditional remit of social policy. Drawing on Esping-Andersen (1999), he highlights that the established role of social policy has been to publicly manage risks to society. Climate change presents new uncertain risks to society and creates a new agenda. Consequently, Gough (2008) in arguing that 'social policy is the public management of social risks' (2008: 326) questions whether the risks posed by climate change are any different from risks addressed by traditional social policies. The basis of this argument is that both social and environmental policies are responses to problems generated by industrialization and increased urbanization, and that both bodies of policy attempt to tackle issues that cannot be dealt with by the market or uncoordinated voluntary action. Finally, both social policy and environmental policy deal with resource allocation and equity; in other words, who gets what and what is fair.

Fitzpatrick (2011a) also highlights a number of points to consider in terms of the congruities between environmental and social policy. Congruities include the fact that ultimately both social and environmental problems need global solutions and a global coordination of 'local organizations' to fulfil the green agenda. Additionally, like sustainability, citizenship and responsibility also have temporal, that is, past, present and future considerations as well as global dimensions. This means that they affect future generations and people in other countries. Finally, environmental well-being and social well-being cannot be accurately measured by GDP alone, since quality of life – and social well-being – amount to more than this crude measure. In other words, social welfare cannot be reduced to just economic well-being or consumerism (Barry and Doherty, 2001). Other factors – for example, social, physical and psychological well-being – need to be taken into account (Annetts et al., 2009). Further, Barry and Doherty (2001: 602) point out that 'the increase in inequality in the UK over the last 20 years can be interpreted as evidence of this relationship between economic growth and socio-economic inequality – as the economy has grown (as measured by conventional GDP/GNP accounting), so has inequality'. Gough (2008) also highlights a number of inconsistencies between environmental and social policies. For example, the effects of industrialization are tangible, that is, they are experienced and felt by people in the present. However, the effects of climate change are not yet fully felt, instead avoiding risks has a future dimension. Fitzpatrick (2011a) adds to this debate, outlining further incongruities between social and environment policy. For example, the adoption of green technologies could impact on communities dependent on employment in manufacturing, since this would involve reductions in emissions through mass production.

'Green' landmarks: towards a sustainable future?

This section provides an overview of some of the landmark 'green' documents and policies relevant to social policy and assesses their implications for mainstream political priorities and social policy debates. It also considers the role of environmental social movements, highlighting that pressure for policy change can be 'bottom-up' as well as 'top-down'.

The Brundtland Report *Our Common Future*, published in 1987, can be understood as the first key landmark 'green' document, which introduced the concept of 'sustainable development'. As discussed above, sustainable development can be understood as meeting the needs of the human population while also taking account of – and care of – the environment, both in the present and future. In 1988, the United Nations established the Intergovernmental Panel on Climate Change (IPCC). The IPCC is a globally accepted authority on climate change, undertaking research and producing reports on the risks posed by climate change. In addition, green social movement activists have highlighted scientific evidence which points to the negative environmental side-effects of industrialism and capitalism – these include campaigning pressure groups like Friends of the Earth and Greenpeace and also conservation groups such as the Royal Society for the Protection of Birds (RSPB) (Annetts et al., 2009). The influence of such 'bottom-up' pressure groups is discussed further below. The Brundtland Report was later endorsed by political leaders at the UN Conference on Environment and Development (UNCED), known as the Rio Summit of 1992. The Rio Summit focused on the central role of planning in securing sustainable development for the future (Catney and Doyle, 2011a), and an outcome of the Rio Summit was the signing of the 'Agenda 21' agreement. The signing of Agenda 21 was voluntary and had a global, national and local focus. It effectively comprised a plan of action to control and manage the impact of human behaviour on the environment by reducing carbon emissions and controlling consumption patterns.

At the Earth Summit in 1992, all UN nations agreed that industrialized countries – those who were instrumental in causing climate change – should take the lead in addressing it. The Kyoto Protocol is an international agreement on tackling climate change and committed developed nations to reducing GHG by 5.2 per cent below 1990 levels with the first phase to end in 2012 (Friends of the Earth, 2012). It became law in 2005, although there is still reluctance to sign up to this from many countries and significantly none are on track to meet their target. The USA in particular is a significant obstacle since it refused to sign (Fitzpatrick, 2011a) and has declined to endorse the outcomes of the Copenhagen talks in 2009 which were meant to build on the Protocol. In line with the 2007 EU agenda to cut greenhouse gas emissions and to produce a fifth of its energy via renewable sources by 2020, the UK government passed the Climate Change Act in 2008. This committed to an 80 per cent reduction in GHG by 2050 and a 26 per cent reduction in CO_2 by 2018–22. However, the intermediate target of a 20 per cent reduction in GHG by 2010 has not been met (Fitzpatrick, 2011a).

Although environmentalists broadly agree on an agenda which critiques continued economic growth and advocates changing the human relationship with nature to make it more sustainable (Annetts et al., 2009), there are many variations in green thought. Cahill (2012) makes the distinction between dark greens and light greens, while Dryzek (2008) conceptualizes these as radical and reformist approaches. 'Dark greens' place a central focus on nature and the planet and have more radical solutions to achieving sustainability. 'Dark green' approaches advocate a structural transformation of industrialized countries to bring consumption habits to levels similar to those in poorer countries. 'Light green' approaches seek to work within and reform capitalist systems and are usually described as 'Environmental (or Ecological) Modernism' (EM) (Cahill, 2012), which, in the years since the Rio Summit, is a reconfigured version of 'sustainable development'. EM is a term encapsulating attempts to resolve the tensions between economic growth and protecting the environment (Catney and Doyle, 2011a). Simply put, EM argues that governments, corporations and civil society need to take more responsibility for protecting the global environment, mainly through the use of new technologies (EM has become a central priority across the political spectrum and for social policy debates and can take a variety of forms). These range from weak EM, which involves low levels of reform to established systems and economic models, to strong EM which incorporates a realignment of state structures which encourage participation (bottom-up) and promotes a more environmentally orientated form of capitalism and economic growth. Although EM has been influential in the UK, it has only been adopted in a very weak form by both left and right political parties (Catney and Doyle, 2011a; Cahill, 2012). It is clear therefore that there is a 'top-down' impetus to addressing climate change; 'bottom-up' pressures for policy change will now be addressed.

The 'Green Movement', then, is largely associated with a variety of groups whose primary concern is to protect the environment. Barry and Doherty (2001) identify three types of green social movement groups: green political parties, for example the Green Party in the UK, which gained its first elected MP in May 2010; more radical environmental movement organizations (EMOs), including pressure groups like Friends of the Earth as discussed above; and direct action groups, for example Earth First!, a radical element of the green movement, the Anti-Roads Protest Movement and Camp for Climate Action. The Anti-Roads Protest Movement developed across the UK from the mid-1990s as a reaction against the government's road and motorway building programme. There were approximately 300 individual protests initiated across the UK, for example at Twyford Down in response to the M3 bypass, in Newbury against the A34 bypass and against the M77 extension at Glasgow (Annetts et al., 2009). Environmental pressure groups like Camp for Climate Action (CCA) evolved from anarchist roots and take a radical approach to climate change and frame this in terms of both environmental and social priorities (Schlembach, 2011). With the ultimate goal of sustainable living, CCA advocate direct action and confrontation against the root causes of climate change which they perceive as a combination of economic growth and consumerism. CCA actively campaign against climate change and capitalism. This group has a history of action including camping outside power stations, coal mines and airports.

Reconciling social justice with environmental justice?

In this final part of the chapter, the question of whether social justice and environmental justice are ultimately at odds is considered within the context of rethinking the current neoliberal market model of welfare and considering how a new 'green social policy agenda' can be incorporated. As indicated in the first part of this chapter, the welfare state (and social policy) needs to be understood within the context of capitalist systems and liberal democracies. However, 'a welfare state which depends upon growth, and which largely fuels demands for more, is helping to exhaust the very resources on which it depends' (Fitzpatrick, 1998: 10). It is clear, then, that there are a number of key considerations to address when attempting to reconcile environmental and social justice. These can be framed within the remit of balancing potential tensions; first, between industrialized countries and rural developing countries; second, in achieving equity within countries; and third, in balancing the human rights of present and future generations (IPCC, 2007; Fitzpatrick, 2011a; Dominelli, 2012). There is some overlap between each of these priorities since it is difficult to separate temporal and global dimensions and domestic considerations. These issues will be discussed in this final part of the chapter.

Catney and Doyle (2011b) refer to the 'post-political' to describe how wealthy industrialized countries dominate current debates on the environment and how rural developing countries have been neglected. It could be said that industrialized and rural developing countries have conflicting priorities in reconciling environmental and welfare concerns and this will be a theme running through the final section of this chapter. For rural developing countries, green welfare goals are more focused on the basic – and present – needs for survival, for example shelter, water supplies and food sources. The concerns of these countries are very rooted in the here and now; concerns for future generations are by necessity secondary since those people actually living on the planet are experiencing shortages of the most basic forms of safety, security and sustenance. Therefore, the intersection between environmental and welfare concerns in both industrialized and industrializing countries has significant divergences (Catney and Doyle, 2011b).

For industrialized countries – as discussed above – social justice priorities centre on ecological modernization and sustainable development. However, for rural industrializing countries, and in spite of agreement at the Rio Earth Summit in 1992, the historical legacy of disadvantage has not being addressed. In this sense, the social justice implications and priorities inevitably differ between industrialized and non-industrialized countries. Further, although there is a convergence in emphasis from both the developed and developing worlds on the well-being of 'citizens', there is a temporal divergence in that the concerns for developing countries are very much in the here and now and not based on what might happen in the future. On the one hand, wealthy industrialized countries have historically benefited from economic growth and unregulated emission generation and their priority is concern about the future. On the other hand, countries that are currently industrializing have not enjoyed the same benefits of economic growth and the most pressing priority for them is to deal with the difficulties of the present. Catney and Doyle (2011b) convincingly argue that the debate about a green state with welfare aspirations must be built on an understanding of what it is to be green across the globe and not just from the perspective of the developed world. This raises important ethical questions in terms of social justice. There are difficulties in considering the moral standing and human rights of future generations, and this needs to be reconciled with social justice for current generations who are geographically distant in industrializing countries (Carter, 2011).

As discussed earlier, it is generally accepted by researchers that CO_2 emissions need to be cut to reduce the risks of climate change. However, climate change mitigation policies have potentially regressive effects. Because regressive taxes are applied uniformly, they therefore take a larger percentage from low-income people than from high-income people. This means that poorer households face higher costs in proportion to their income, whereas progressive taxes take a larger percentage of income from high earners. Discussions of equity are central to social justice concerns and could potentially act as a barrier to such policies being introduced or the area of emission, for example energy costs or transport (Buchs et al., 2011). Debates about how such burdens should be distributed are in the early stages and ongoing but some writers now recognize that: 'climate change policy will have an immediate impact on social policy through various channels, in particular redistribution effects' (Buchs et al., 2011: 285).

Drawing from Helm (2005) and the OECD (1994), Buchs et al. (2011) distinguish between different kinds of mitigation policies: regulation, taxes or charges and subsidies and trading schemes. Regulation is legally binding and stipulates levels of CO_2 emissions, energy use and efficiency. Alternatively, economic instruments include a carbon taxes cap and trade schemes which set a price on energy consumption and GHG emissions. They offer (financial) incentives to use alternative production methods and for individuals to reduce their 'carbon footprint' through lifestyle changes. There would also be taxes for furthering environmental damage through exceeding agreed levels of consumption and emissions. Cap and trade mitigation policies fix the amount of emissions by establishing a 'cap' which denotes the maximum amount of pollution allowed.

The consensus among a number of researchers is that since regressivity is inherent in taxes on consumption, it is likely taxing schemes will disproportionately affect poorer households (Buchs et al., 2011). In other words, low-income households spend proportionally more of their income on home energy than richer households. Buchs et al. (2011) argue that it is possible to implement schemes to redistribute income but that these must be designed progressively. For example, in the Netherlands there is a tax-free electricity allowance and in Portugal a progressive water system. Also, regressivity does not seem to affect transport in the same manner since fewer low-income households fly or have cars. However, among motorists motoring taxes are again regressive (Buchs et al., 2011). It is possible that climate change policy could exacerbate existing social inequalities. Therefore, in terms of social justice, consideration needs to be given to how the adverse effects of taxing carbon emissions could be mitigated (Markandya and Ortiz, 2008). Gough (2008) argues that eventually climate change policies could displace social policies but reiterates the synergies of both in understanding this. The move towards individual carbon budgets has implications for redistribution and equity, so strong social policies to redress inequalities will be needed. Markandya and Ortiz (2008) predict that carbon taxing without redistribution will be mildly regressive and that three key areas need to be considered: first, how much tax will be redistributed; second, how it will affect the rates of other tax; third, how fuel poverty will be accounted for.

Mitigation and adaptation polices need to be placed within the context of social policy in terms of interventions and as academic study. Issues of fairness, equity, social well-being and justice need to be evident in policy outcomes, which means that costs and burdens need to be redistributed between different social groups (Gough, 2008). In particular, distributive consequences need careful research within housing. In the UK, for example, 30 per cent of the poorest quintile of households use more energy than the national average due to living in fuel-inefficient homes. Urban design and housing policy have further significance, particularly for countries like the UK which has inefficient housing. There are potential benefits in both policy and environmental terms since improvements to housing quality also reduce CO_2 emissions (Gough, 2008). The location of any new developments is now considered to be the most important ecological feature since the presence of an existing infrastructure and established transport links causes least disruption to the environment (Wheeler, 2011). However, energy efficiency is also crucial and the regulations governing new construction emphasize increased energy efficiency. For housing development and design, the goal is to create 'carbon-neutral' dwellings. These 'carbon-neutral' buildings are well-insulated (from heat and cold) and actually generate their own power. In the UK, all new buildings must be carbon-neutral by 2016. All building components can be 'greened' through recycling or using materials with lower carbon emissions (Wheeler, 2011). For example, 'The Salford House' was designed in 1976 for Salford City Council in a joint project with the University of Salford. Its passive design and high thermal capacity showed huge energy savings. A new study of the house was launched in 2010 to explore its long-term energy performance. It was found that this 'passivhaus' consumed approximately 25 per cent of the energy consumed by general needs housing. This means that the Salford house will be one of the few existing dwellings to meet the zero carbon target by 2016 (Brown et al., 2011).

Although transport is important for the economy, society and globalization, it too must be understood within a context of dangerous carbon emissions (Cahill, 2011). Sustainable growth needs to be within the earth's capacity which involves a careful use of resources which means thinking about the longer term, although, as indicated above, there is disagreement among environmentalists on how this could be best achieved. Groups like Friends of the Earth argue that this presents us with an opportunity to rethink our attitude towards employment and national insurance contributions, which could involve recognizing that contributions other than paid work should count in terms of benefit payments. There is also the potential for new jobs in the 'green' industries, for example renewable energy (Friends of the Earth, 2012). And, finally, 'the task for a Green social policy is not only to consider how social welfare may be made compatible with a sustainable society, but to speculate as to how social policies can themselves effect sustainability' (Fitzpatrick, 1998: 22), and 'climate change policy could be interpreted as an aspect of social policy, as both benefit the relatively poor' (Dryzek, 2008: 335).

Schlembach (2011) argues that 'questions of climate change and social justice are inseparable' (2011: 194). Dryzek (2008) believes that industrialized countries with strongly embedded welfare states are in the best position to implement climate change polices and deal with the challenges they present. This is because economic and environmental objectives are seen as inseparable and inextricably linked. This leads Dryzek to conclude that 'the relationship between environmental policy effort and social policy effort does not have to be conflictual'

(2008: 334–335). Countries like the UK and the USA are not in such a strong position and they have poorer records on environmental protection. However, it is too early to draw conclusions at this stage. Climate change policy is now an integral part of EU environmental policy. However, for climate change policies to be adopted and successfully implemented by Member State governments within, it is important that EU citizens understand and support environmental concerns since individual behaviour and lifestyle choices are significant (Gerhards and Lengfeld, 2008). Climate change policy and environmental modernism would need to be strongly embedded and given high priority within the welfare systems of Member States. Traditional social policy will still have a role to play, although in a manner that is consistent with environmental and climate change policy (Fitzpatrick, 2011b). As Barry and Doherty (2001: 604) state: 'A more sustainable society is likely to mean one in which available resources are invested in public services and institutions (education, welfare, health, transport), rather than increases in personal disposable income'.

Summary/Conclusions

- Climate change caused by human activity represents one of the most significant threats to global welfare and environmentalists call for changes in production and consumption.
- Social policies are as a result of, and embedded in, capitalist systems and economic growth.
- There is a need to rethink economic growth in terms of future sustainability.
- Pressure for environmental change can be 'top-down' via international and government policy and legislation and also 'bottom-up' from environmental groups.
- Environmental and social policies potentially have compatible and conflicting objectives.
- Market economies with strongly embedded welfare states are in the best position to implement climate change policies.

Questions

1 Which model of sustainability do you most identify with and why?
2 Which of the tensions in balancing environmental and global policy (global/local; within nations; balancing the rights of present and future citizens) do you think is the most difficult to reconcile and why?
3 Do you think that environment and social policies are ultimately at odds and if so why?
4 Why do you think that those industrialized countries with strongly established and embedded welfare provision are best placed to implement climate change policies?

Recommended reading

Fitzpatrick, T. (ed.) (2001) *Understanding the Environment and Social Policy*. Bristol: The Policy Press. This book provides a comprehensive introduction to the debates around the environment and social policy.

Gough, I., Meadowcroft, J., Dryzek, J., Gerhards, J., Lengfield, H., Markandya, A. and Ortiz, R. (2008) 'JESP symposium: climate change and social policy', *Journal of European Social Policy*, 18: 325. This journal article brings together the different perspectives of key writers on the environment and social policy.

Relevant websites

Friends of the Earth International is an international network of environmental campaigning organizations across the world – www.foei.org; www.foe.co.uk

The Intergovernmental Panel on Climate Change (IPCC) is a globally recognized authority on climate change – www.ipcc.ch/

George Monbiot is an environmental and political activist who regularly writes a column in *The Guardian* – www.monbiot.com

The United Nations Department of Economic and Social Affairs Division for Sustainable Development promotes global sustainable development – www.un.org

References

Annetts, J., Law, A., McNeish, W. and Mooney, G. (2009) *Understanding Social Movements*. Bristol: The Policy Press and the Social Policy Association.

Barry, J. and Doherty, B. (2001) 'The Greens and social policy: movements, politics and practice?', *Social Policy and Administration*, 35(5): 587–607.

Brown, P., Burke, M.E., Morris, G. and Webster, P.J. (2011) *The Salford Low-Energy House: Learning from our Past*. Salford: University of Salford.

Buchs, M., Bardsley, N. and Duwe, A. (2011) 'Who bears the brunt? Distributional effects of climate change mitigation policies', *Critical Social Policy*, 31(2): 285–307.

Cahill, M. (2011) 'Transport', in T. Fitzpatrick (ed.) *Understanding the Environment and Social Policy*. Bristol: The Policy Press.

Cahill, M. (2012) 'Green perspectives', in P. Alcock, M. May and S. Wright (eds) *The Student's Companion to Social Policy* (4th edn). Chichester: Wiley-Blackwell.

Carter, A. (2011) 'Environmental ethics', in T. Fitzpatrick (ed.) *Understanding the Environment and Social Policy*. Bristol: The Policy Press.

Catney, P. and Doyle, T. (2011a) 'The welfare of now and the green (post) politics of the future', *Critical Social Policy*, 31(2): 174–193.

Catney, P. and Doyle, T. (2011b) 'Challenges to the state', in T. Fitzpatrick (ed.) *Understanding the Environment and Social Policy*. Bristol: The Policy Press.

Dominelli, L. (2012) *Green Social Work: From Environmental Crises to Environmental Justice*. Cambridge: Polity.

Dryzek, J.S. (2008) 'The ecological crisis of the welfare state', in I. Gough, J. Meadowcroft, J. Dryzek, J. Gerhards, H. Lengfield, A. Markandya and R. Ortiz (eds) 'JESP symposium: climate change and social policy', *Journal of European Social Policy*, 18: 325.

Dean, H. (2006) *Social Policy*. Cambridge: Polity.

Esping-Andersen, G. (1990) *The Three Worlds of Welfare Capitalism*. Cambridge: Polity.

Esping-Andersen, G. (1999) *The Social Foundations of Postindustrial Economies*. Oxford: Oxford University Press.

Fitzpatrick, T. (1998) 'The implications of ecological thought for social welfare', *Critical Social Policy*, 18(1): 5–26.

Fitzpatrick, T. (2011a) 'Introduction', in *Understanding the Environment and Social Policy*. Bristol: The Policy Press.

Fitzpatrick, T. (2011b) 'Environmental justice: philosophies and practices', in *Understanding the Environment and Social Policy*. Bristol: The Policy Press.

Friends of the Earth (2010) Briefing: Climate Change – the facts. Available at: www.foe.co.uk (accessed 21 November 2012).

Gerhards, J. and Lengfeld, H. (2008) 'The growing remit of the EU in climate change policy and citizens' support across the Union', in I. Gough, J. Meadowcroft, J. Dryzek, J. Gerhards, H. Lengfield, A. Markandya and R. Ortiz (eds) 'JESP symposium: climate change and social policy', *Journal of European Social Policy*, 18: 325.

Gough, I. (2008) 'Introduction', in I. Gough, J. Meadowcroft, J. Dryzek, J. Gerhards, H. Lengfield, A. Markandya and R. Ortiz (eds) 'JESP symposium: climate change and social policy', *Journal of European Social Policy*, 18: 325.

Gough, I., Meadowcroft, J., Dryzek, J., Gerhards, J., Lengfield, H., Markandya, A. and Ortiz, R. (2008) 'JESP symposium: climate change and social policy', *Journal of European Social Policy*, 18: 325.

Hannigan, J. (2011) 'Social challenges: causes, explanations and solutions', in T. Fitzpatrick (ed.) *Understanding the Environment and Social Policy*. Bristol: The Policy Press.

Hodgson, S.M. and Phillips, D. (2011) 'The environmental challenge', in T. Fitzpatrick (ed.) *Understanding the Environment and Social Policy*. Bristol: The Policy Press.

IPCC (2007) *IPCC Fourth Assessment Report (AR4): Climate Change – Contribution of Working Groups I, II and III to the Fourth Assessment Report of the Intergovernmental Panel on Climate Change* (R.K. Pachauri and A. Reisinger, eds). Geneva: IPCC.

Markandya, A. and Ortiz, R. A. (2008) 'A note on the distributional effects of carbon taxes in the EU', in I. Gough, J. Meadowcroft, J. Dryzek, J. Gerhards, H. Lengfield, A. Markandya and R. Ortiz (eds) 'JESP symposium: climate change and social policy', *Journal of European Social Policy*, 18: 325.

Schlembach, R. (2011) 'How do radical climate movements negotiate their environmental and their social agendas? A study of debates within the Camp for Climate Action (UK)', *Critical Social Policy*, 31(2): 194–215.

Wheeler, S.M. (2011) 'Planning and the urban environment', in T. Fitzpatrick (ed.) *Understanding the Environment and Social Policy*. Bristol: The Policy Press.

Index